Portia Da Costa is one of the most internationally renowned authors of erotica.

She is the author of over fifteen *Black Lace* novels, as well as being a contributing author to a number of short story collections.

Also by Portia Da Costa

The Accidental Bride

PORTIA DA COSTA

BLACK
LACE

1 3 5 7 9 10 8 6 4 2

First published in 2013 by Black Lace, an imprint of Ebury Publishing
A Random House Group Company

Copyright © Portia Da Costa 2013

Portia Da Costa has asserted her right to be identified as the author of this
Work in accordance with the Copyright, Designs and Patents Act 1988

The Random House Group Limited Reg. No. 954009

Addresses for companies within the Random House Group can be found at:
www.randomhouse.co.uk

A CIP catalogue record for this book is
available from the British Library

The Random House Group Limited supports the Forest Stewardship
Council® (FSC®), the leading international forest-certification organisation.
Our books carrying the FSC label are printed on FSC®-certified paper. FSC is
the only forest-certification scheme supported by the leading environmental
organisations, including Greenpeace. Our paper procurement policy
can be found at: www.randomhouse.co.uk/environment

Printed and bound by CPI Group (UK) Ltd, Croydon, CR0 4YY

ISBN 9780352347626

To buy books by your favourite authors and register for offers visit:
www.randomhouse.co.uk
www.blacklace.co.uk

*Dedicated to 'himself' for services to international
cat rescue and general heroism*

From Call Girl to Mistress to . . .

Previously, in THE ACCIDENTAL CALL GIRL and
THE ACCIDENTAL MISTRESS

When Lizzie Aitchison first met John Smith in the Lawns
Bar of the Waverley Grange Hotel he mistakenly thought
she was an escort in search of a client. The chemistry
between them was dynamite from the outset, and Lizzie
couldn't resist the allure of John's fallen angel face and the
way his lean body looked in a sharp business suit. In a daring
leap, she decided to play along with his misapprehension,
and become 'Bettie', the high-class call girl, if only for one
night.

John was captivated too. Shaken out of a state of gathering
ennui, he experienced an unstoppable urge to possess this
beautiful young woman whose combination of a distinctive
vintage style and a bold yet strangely vulnerable personality
was the ultimate call to his senses.

They embarked on an intense, kinky affair, initially for
just the duration of John's stay in the area on business,
but the two quickly became a couple, both realising they

wanted more than a temporary relationship. But each had issues to overcome, and a troubled history. John's need to control and Lizzie's feisty independence were a volatile mix, both in the bedroom and out of it, stirred to flash-point by John's insistence that they live together.

But when a dark shadow from John's past falls over their happiness, Lizzie realises that she has a dangerous rival...

Now read on...

1

In the Garden

The garden was mysterious after dark. The air heavy with the scents of pine, lemon and night-blooming flowers. Lizzie had never visited this part of France before, and had never stayed in a villa. Everything was new to her, latent with promise, thrilling to the senses.

Where was he, this man of hers whom she lived with? He was as mysterious in his own way as the garden and its ambiance, yet closer to her, and more intimate with her, than any human being who'd ever lived.

The path amongst the trees was uneven and not lit, although she could see a lantern ahead. Glad of her flat sandals, she picked her way along it, nervous. He'd promised her a treat, but knowing the perversity of her lover's imagination sometimes, well, that could mean just about anything. Something to long for, or something to fear. Well, a little.

The night breeze was warm and balmy, riffling through the branches and making the leaves dance, but she shivered in her thin, loose-fitting cotton dress. It wasn't her usual style, and she wasn't wearing underwear, but that was what he'd suggested – specified – so she'd complied. It was like being more than naked, lightly clad like this, and somehow the spirit of the garden was mischievous, and had searching hands and probing fingers that sometimes brushed against her body beneath her thin dress. She would have paused on the path, to touch herself, but she knew he was waiting for her ahead, her beautiful man.

Speeding up, she strode down the path. So what if she tripped; she just had to be with him. And there was nobody to see her tumble except the flitting night insects, and whatever scary snakes or frogs lurked in the undergrowth. Another reason to get a move on and reach him!

Ahead, now, the lamp flickered. Yellow light that seemed to dance. Intrigued, she hurried on, and after a moment, emerged into a little clearing. What was it about them and clearings, in woods? It'd brought the very devil out in them in the past, and she sincerely hoped it would do the same tonight.

It'd certainly created a demon out of her lover. She scudded to a halt, breath knocked out of her by the sight of him, so magnificent.

The glorious man she lived with was sitting at a long, rustic table set in front of a little summerhouse-like structure. Like a Lord of Darkness or the monarch of the night, he lounged in a high-backed wooden seat that fit his lithe body like a throne. It was turned to one side, and he'd stretched out his long legs before him; his pose was relaxed. Despite her awe of him, she had to bite her lower lip to stop herself grinning at the sight of his strong, gorgeous thighs, and his knees, and his calves.

He was wearing black denim jeans and low black canvas boots. Not exactly the leather trousers and riding boots she'd once described to him from one of her mad fantasies, not long after they'd met. But a good approximation, all the same. The giggles threatened as she imagined him really wearing 'leather strides', as he'd call them. He'd look fabulous in leather, of course, but it was such a 1980s rock god dominant-master-type cliché.

'What's so funny?' he said as she drew near, then halted at respectful distance.

Ack, he'd seen it. Seen her fighting not to laugh. She was for it now. His brilliant blue eyes were dazzlingly fierce behind the black silk domino mask he wore. Another 'prop' straight out of her fantasy, pure drama, and all the more so against the gold of his curling blond hair.

'You may speak,' he said, his voice soft and husky, and musical with an amusement that matched her own.

This was going to be fun, even if it would hurt a bit too. There was a broad strip of black leather draped across the table, in the pool of light created by the old-fashioned oil lantern. Beside it lay a thinner, much more dainty strip, this one with a buckle. Alongside these sat a small, carved wooden box and a black silk mask much like the one he was wearing.

'Nothing is funny, master,' she said, eyes lowered, even though it gouged her not to be able to look at him, at his dear, handsome face. 'I'm just a little bit nervous, master. Sometimes I laugh when I'm on edge...'

'On edge, are we?' Stirring in his seat, he reached for the big strip of leather and toyed with it for a moment, as if demonstrating to her how fearsome it was. When he let it drop, he laid his long, elegant hand across his chest, as if he were demonstrating, or exhibiting that to her too. He was naked from the waist up, and his smooth skin gleamed lightly gold, having already caught a little bit of a tan from their sojourn here. The soft peppering of his sandy body hair made her fingers tingle, wanting to touch it, to tug it, or perhaps to fondle and pinch his nipples in the way he liked so much, and which sometimes made him growl and throw her on her back to ravish her.

'Well, I certainly am. I don't know about you.'

Uh oh! She'd done it again. As she always did. Acknowledging herself as possibly the world's most useless submissive, she stared down at her sandal-clad toes again, trying to get back into her role. The way he hissed slightly, through his teeth, told her of his amusement, and his fond despair of her ever getting it right.

You wouldn't want me to, even if I could, though, would you?

He liked her the way she was, lack of discipline and adherence to the niceties notwithstanding.

'That'll cost you, slave.'

I thought it might.

She didn't speak, though. She was getting to the stage now where it was difficult. It was hard to frame words, and stay in a role, when you were being turned inside out by rampaging lust. He was the most gorgeous man on the face of the earth to her, and possibly might be to the majority of other women who set their lucky eyes on him. It was still hard to believe he was hers, this gilded god, or as near as dammit. He'd chosen to be with her. She had no way of knowing whether that choice would last for ever, but now was not the moment to debate the unknowable future.

All she did know was that he was honouring her fantasy. This wasn't the dungeon she'd told him about, all those weeks ago, on the phone. But like the jeans, it was near enough.

'Move a little closer.'

She shuffled forward across the brushed flagstones, still fighting the irresistible temptation to just ogle him. Closer, she could smell another delicious odour in the night-blend. His distinctive cologne: spicy, fresh, yet fruity. A bit like him. Nearer, if she were allowed to look, she'd see the distinctiveness of his beauty too. His elegant, sculpted face, his sensuous mouth, and the faint lines around his eyes, just visible behind the mask, the weathering that made him far more handsome than a younger man would have been. He had the bearing of a mature man, and an aristocrat. Which was just exactly what he was, even though he was wont to dismiss the latter as meaningless.

Attempting to stand statue-still, she shook, overcome anew by him as she always was.

'Don't be afraid, slave.' There was a smile in his voice, familiar to her, and beloved. 'I won't hurt you.' He paused again, and the faint creak of old wood told her that he was adjusting his position in the throne-like chair. Was he aroused? Oh, silly question…Was the sky above the trees midnight blue? 'Well, I won't hurt you any more than you want me to.'

She drew in a deep breath, conscious of the way it made her breasts lift beneath the thin dress. The pale fabric was barely more than voile, and he'd be able to see her nipples straight through it. He could probably see the dark hair of her pussy too, and he'd most likely planned it that way. Putting a girl with jet black hair in a flimsy, light-coloured dress…

'You look very pretty in that frock, sweetheart. But I'd

like to see your tits and your cunt now, so let's have you naked, shall we?'

Oh, she loved it when he was crude like this. In their everyday dealings, his manners were perfect, and his language sophisticated. Which made it all the more of a turn-on when he got down and dirty. But he'd slipped there. Forgotten himself for a moment. She'd been 'sweetheart' not 'slave'. Still, nobody was perfect, not even him.

'Well then? Strip off. Enough with the daydreaming.'

Dipping down, she crossed her arms, grasped the frock's hem and pulled it up and off over her head in one movement. It was loose, with no fastenings, so really easy to get off when her handsome lover required her to be naked. She'd been wearing quite a few similar dresses during the days they'd been here. He wasn't the only one who wanted to fuck at a moment's notice.

'It isn't day,' she said, flinging the garment away with a flourish. The light frock seemed to float, even though there was barely a breeze, and ended up draped across a bush.

'And enough with the answering back too.' His voice was amiable, amused. He never shouted or got harsh and stroppy in these situations. His dominance and self-possession didn't depend on posturing.

They'd only been together a relatively short time, and yet in that little while he'd seen all of her, and somehow, seen her more intensely than any other man had. He had some kind of 'sight', a beautifully focused way of looking that revealed not only the intimacies of her flesh, but her heart's secrets too, and her soul. The way he looked now was like that: perceptive, penetrating, like a laser. Idiotically, she tried to cover herself, a hand over her pubis, and an arm across her breasts.

'What on earth do you think you're doing?' He laughed softly, his smile like the sun rising in the dark of night.

'Um…sorry.' She dropped her arms to her sides, and tried to stand proudly, without meeting his eyes. Slaves were supposed to be modest and humble – fat chance of that.

'Better. Now come here.' Lifting her eyes again, as she knew he probably expected her to, she caught his elegant, beckoning gesture. His shapely hands were as gorgeous as the rest of him, and they settled on his black-clad thighs as he made space for her between them.

In slow, even steps, she approached. Right up to him, her bare legs just an inch or so from his clothed ones. Without speaking, he nodded to the mask, and the leather collar, lying on the gnarled wood of the old table, beside the box. Curious, and a little fearful of what the casket might contain, she lifted the mask and fastened it around her upper face, framing her eyes. It created a weird shadow round the edge of her vision, and vaguely reminded her of another mask, a far more elaborate and costly one, that she'd once worn to attend a risqué party with him. Tying the black ribbon at the back of her head, she managed to get it right, first time. She'd been practising in the mirror, imagining how the great Bettie Page might have looked, in one of her fetish films.

'Good,' he said, reaching out and touching her cheek, just below the mask, the contact feather-light in a way other contacts, coming soon, would not be. 'Now kneel.'

She sank to her knees, trying not to shake, but it was hard to avoid. The smell of him, and the sight of him, were like the yummy, rambunctiously rustic local wine they'd been drinking. Wildly and intensely intoxicating. Heady. His skin gleamed like satin this close up, and beneath the soft, weathered denim of his trousers lay a huge bulge.

'Uh oh, naughty, naughty. None of that until later.' In an efficient gesture, he swept up the thick, black curtain of her hair. 'Hold it out of the way,' he instructed, and when she did so, he fastened the little leather collar neatly around her throat. Then, hooking a finger into it, he tugged, drawing her face towards his denim-covered erection, and just holding her there. She could feel the raw heat of him, through the fabric, against her cheek.

'You'd like some of that, wouldn't you?'

She nodded, rubbing her face against the object in question. Rubbing more enthusiastically than he probably wanted her to, but not caring. In a bold, pre-emptive strike, she kissed it through the dark cloth. She'd pressed her face to his crotch like this on the first night they'd ever met, in a quaint, old-fashioned hotel room, in another country.

'I'll fuck you, slave, but you've got to earn it.' He tweaked on the collar. 'You know that, don't you? You'll have to indulge my nasty foibles and predilections. Let me spank that perfectly beautiful, perfectly creamy bottom of yours until it's pink.'

She kissed his crotch again.

'I take it that's a "Yes, I concur" then?'

She nodded.

He slid his fingers beneath her chin, compelling her to look up at him, her mate – and despite everything – her equal in his matching black mask. 'You haven't forgotten our safe word, have you?'

'It's "chintz". But you won't hear it.'

'Is that so?' His smile was like Lucifer's, beautiful yet infinitely dangerous.

'Yes!'

'Well then…Let's see, shall we?' He touched her hair, her cheek, her mouth, rubbing his thumb over her lower lip. 'Up you get!'

As she started to rise, he slipped a hand beneath her elbow to help her. Even at his most magisterial, his manners were faultless, ingrained in him by his background and his natural humanity. These were the qualities that made her happy to submit to him. To her, he was worthy of her awe, as no other man ever would be.

Guiding her with his touch, he positioned her across the table. The old wooden surface was firm against her crotch, and the urge to massage herself against it was powerful. Her pussy ached. For touch, and for him, but there was a road to travel yet, and it was one that promised to be hard. But still she could barely control her excitement, and she savoured the feel of the polished wood against her mound, her belly and her breasts. Cradling her head on her folded arms, she attempted to harness the biofeedback techniques he'd started to teach her. But it was hopeless. She was a turbulent mass of fear, anticipation and raw lust.

'I think we should make this a bit more interesting, don't you?' His hand was cool as it smoothed over her back and her buttocks, testing her resilience. Each fingertip was distinct, especially when he dipped two into the cleft between her buttocks, coasting teasingly over her anus, but not lingering. What was he planning? There was something in that wooden box, she was sure of it. Something that would go somewhere, but she wasn't quite sure exactly where. It could be something for her mouth, her pussy…or her arse. A long shiver swept through her.

'Are you cold? Would you like a blanket?'

She shook her head. 'No, master. I'm fine. Quite comfortable.'

He laughed. 'Really? Well, we'd better change that, hadn't we?' His voice was merry, and she could imagine his blue eyes twinkling behind the mask. She wanted to twist round and look at him, but she had to stay still and compliant, no wriggling and no looking. Focusing on the sight of moonlight filtering through the green darkness of the shrubs and trees, she reached for a calm place.

It was tough, though, when she heard him open the box, and she couldn't see what it was that he took out.

All she could hear was tiny, deft little movements, so quiet they were indecipherable. It was only when something very cold and slick made contact with the entrance of her vagina that she knew, or at least could guess, what was coming.

He was applying lube. Lots of it, even though she barely needed it. She was pretty sure she was already making a wet spot on the table edge, she was so slippery. He pushed plenty in, though, compelling it into her with two unyielding fingers. More, then more. She was scared she'd squelch in a most uncouth way.

'Steady.' His free hand on the small of her back, he applied more, then, before she could prepare herself, he reached for something and pressed it against her, cold, smooth and hard.

An egg. A tempered glass egg. Quite a big one. Despite her resolve to stay quiet, to best him with silence, she moaned as he pushed the devilish thing into her. Its unyielding bulk taxed her as it went in, nudging around inside, pushing against the muscular channel as he pressed it higher. When it settled against her womb, it felt gigantic inside her, jostling the root of her clitoris from within as she breathed. She could feel the tickle of a fine silk cord, too, trailing from her entrance.

You devil. You know how this gets to me. You know I'm already almost coming, before you've even got started!

She didn't have to speak it. She knew he'd heard her.

'I bet you'd really like to touch yourself, wouldn't you?' he said, striding around behind her, clearly admiring the way she was arranged, her thighs parted and the little cord dangling. Was it white? Or black? Or some other colour?

'Yes…Yes, master. I do want to touch myself.' Defiantly, she churned her hips, then yelped out loud at the wicked sensations of the rolling egg inside her. Her clit felt enormous, as if it were bulging out from between her pussy lips, pushed by the obstruction inside her body.

'Be still, wicked girl. Be still.' He reached beneath her, just stroking her entrance, then giving the tiniest tug on the cord.

Breathing hard, she fought not to whine. God, if she was like this now, how on earth would she feel like when he really went to work?

'Would you like me to make you come? It might make the ordeal easier if your body is filled with pleasure endorphins.'

'No! That's no true test…master. And I'm an old-fashioned girl. I'm used to earning my rewards. I enjoy them more that way.'

It was nonsense. She was dying to come. But it seemed a better way to play the game.

He leaned over the table at her side, and she could feel his mouth close to her ear, and his breathing ruffling strands of her hair. 'I adore you. You know that, don't you?'

said her lover, not her master, his voice softer, gentler, more emotional.

She didn't answer. She didn't have to. He knew she adored him right back.

Then, he straightened again, and passed his hands over her buttocks and thighs, in a slow, almost insulting glide. He was testing her muscle tone, assessing her susceptibility, and that made her hornier than ever. His arrogance made her want to touch herself all the more.

'Very well, then. Let's proceed.' As he spoke, he lifted the wide strip of leather – the slapper – and trailed it over her bottom slowly and tauntingly. It was supple, yet substantial, and she feared it. He'd spanked her with his hands, and with rulers and switches, and even with a table tennis bat, when they'd been fooling about, back at home. But he'd never punished her with actual leather before, apart from the sole of his slipper once, ad hoc, and then only a couple of strokes. She had a feeling this would be far more momentous. Far more painful.

She didn't know why she wanted it. But she did.

'Be ready, dear slave.' He let the leather rest horizontally across her bottom as if he were sighting the first blow, measuring exactly where he wanted it to fall, and then he lifted it up.

Holding her breath, she willed him: *Do it! Do it!*

And he did.

There was a whoosh through the air, and then the impact. For a moment she couldn't even quantify the sensations. Had it hurt? She couldn't tell. She could only mewl out, like an animal, but she didn't know whether it was from leather on flesh, or the way the egg bounced inside her, rocking against sensitive nerve ends and stimulating her clit from within. Was she coming? Perhaps…But just as pleasure bloomed, a flaming wall of red agony slammed into the muscles of her backside, the sensation delayed by warped time and perception.

Not sure whether she was in heaven or hell, and suspecting it was both, she rocked and squirmed against the wood, hands clutching her buttocks as if that might assuage the fire. Her clit throbbed in time to the pulsation of heat in her buttocks.

God, yes, she was coming! Her vagina clenched, rocking the egg more, making things worse…better…worse…Fuck alone knew!

'No, no, you know better than that.' He dropped the leather for a moment, and prised her hands away from her bum. 'Hold on to the table.' Gently, he drew her hands forward, and reaching out, she obeyed him, grasping the far edge.

He didn't speak again, but the leather spoke for him, flashing down again, hitting her like a chunk of the very wood she was lying against. So hard. So merciless. Pummelling. Pounding. He whole rear was in flames after one, or was it two blows? She'd lost the ability to count. Holding the table as if it were the last spar of a wrecked ship that had gone down, she hurled her pelvis to and fro, grinding her crotch against its resistance, still not sure if she was climaxing even while she burned. Her bottom felt as if it had been savaged, yet, wildly, she lifted it. Enticing him. *Give me more*, her sizzling, walloped flesh seemed to be saying. *Do your worst, you demon, fuck you, I can take it!*

How long had he been spanking her? Part of her mind suggested hours, a thousand long hours, but the one last little bit of her consciousness that was still able to record such things told her he'd laid on only five blows and it had taken less than a minute.

'Oh my darling...' His voice cracked and she heard the leather slapper fall on the stone flags, somewhere at their feet. He flung his body over hers, his thighs and the fly of his trousers cruel against the agony in her buttocks. He slid his hands along her arms, lacing his fingers with hers at the edge of the table, circling his hips, stirring her pain, yet pressing her against the table's edge to give delicious pressure to her clit, working it, massaging it. She cried out, high and clear, her soaring voice nothing to do with the torture in her bum, and everything to do with a fresh orgasm that melted beauty in her loins, circling and knotting around the obstruction of the egg. He completed it by reaching beneath her to stroke between her legs.

'Oh God...Oh hell...' She surged again, writhing beneath him, arching and pushing against him. She didn't need the table edge now; he was doing the work, rubbing her clit with his fingers, working it with a rough, tender magic.

'I love you,' he gasped, and she broke apart into a million happy pieces. How she'd wanted to hear those words, even when she'd told herself that they didn't matter, and it was actions that mattered more, and loving deeds. He still didn't speak them randomly, spilling them meaninglessly at every opportunity. When her lover said 'I love you' it was always with momentum, always fresh and as precious as the first time.

'I love you,' she answered, rubbing her painful bottom against his groin, actions complementing words again. 'I want you,' she added, barely any breath to get it out as her body gathered, ready to shine again.

'Here? Now?' he asked, as if she were offering to grant him a magnificent privilege. He was still her master, but she was his mistress now, his equal. They were matched creatures, sex deities of the night.

'Hell yes!' she cried, widening her stance to invite him in. 'Bloody well have me! But you'd better get that fucking egg out of me first. You're a big man, lover, there isn't room for both of you!'

He laughed; the sound was pure happiness. Levering himself away from her, he reached down and plucked at the string. At another time, he might have withdrawn the egg slowly, teasingly, but the need that flashed between them was too great to dally. She growled like a she-wolf as it popped from her body, creating another fleeting orgasm. His fingers had plied her clit, all the while.

The egg rattled and rolled across the flags when it landed, forgotten for the moment.

The sound of his smooth-running zip was like heaven to her ears, as was the barely audible rustle and tear, the condom being unwrapped. The feel of his cock, hot and large, was the perfect pressure against her entrance, the longed for thing. She wiggled and he pushed in, sure and deep, barely noticing the way the teeth of the zip pushed against her burning bottom as he thrust and thrust, ploughing into her, his curse words of happiness almost like lighted sigils flying out into the perfumed air amongst the trees.

'Yes! Oh John, my darling John! Yes! Yes! Yes!' she cried, dishing her back, still gripping the table for purchase as she pushed her punished flesh against him, her hips working in a reciprocating action. She barely needed his touch, but still he bestowed it, caressing her even as he growled and blasphemed and flung his body at her.

'Oh Lizzie,' he answered, his own voice strange with pleasure, broken with joy. His hips hammered, hammered, hammered in the old familiar strokes, and deep where the egg had rocked, his hot seed pulsed and spurted inside latex.

As they collapsed against the table, she came again.

It didn't feel too bad. Not really. Not at all.

Craning around to look over her shoulder into the mirror, Lizzie hiked her nightdress up with one hand and gave her pink bottom cheek a tentative prod with the other. It wasn't even sore enough to make her yelp, but she did suck in her breath rather sharply.

You clever devil. It's just enough to make me know I've been seen to, but not so fierce that it'd ever put me off wanting it again. I knew a little bit about BDSM before we started, but I didn't know people could do what you do. I never knew a man could have such crafty skills, Mr Smith.

Her bottom actually looked quite pretty in a bizarre sort of way. The crown of each cheek had a ragged patch of rosy pink spreading across it, like the map of some obscure independent principality, and she could see faint, finer lines within the redness, which marked out the point of impact of the leather. She knew a lot of people would be horrified by the sight of her marked arse, but to her, the splodges were badges of honour, marks of regard, hard won, but richly rewarded.

He'd been like a wild beast across that flipping table, though, and she was sure she still had splinters in her belly to prove it. Pulling up the long, peach satin nightdress at the front too, she hooked the slithery material in a bunch at her hip, and ran her fingertips over her abdomen. No splinters. Well, none she could detect. She pinched the flesh there. No, no extra inches as yet. They were both eating like horses, here at the villa. The Provençal food was so sumptuous and fresh, with loads of tomatoes and olives and delicious fish. But she supposed the enormous amount of sex they were having, coupled with plenty of healthy walks, and even a few jaunts out on bicycles, was offsetting the billions of calories they were consuming.

'Well, that's the most beautiful view in the entire south of France, and I'll fight any man who says otherwise.'

Lizzie spun round at the sound of his voice. His dear, familiar, low, thrilling voice. John was standing in the open doorway, leaning on the jamb, admiring her. He had that twinkle-eyed predatory look in his eyes, and his lips were curved in a possessive masculine smile. When she prepared to loosen her grip on her nightdress, and let it fall over her belly and legs, he said, 'Uh oh, leave it as it is,' almost before her brain had sent the message to her hand.

He strode towards her, and took up his station right behind her, peering into the mirror.

'Turn,' he instructed, and when she did, he ran his hand down the outer slope of her hip and thigh, thumb just skirting the rosy pink patch he'd created. 'That looks very pretty.' His thumb slid across the punished acreage, testing, assessing, making Lizzie wriggle with a mix of discomfort and renewed desire.

She couldn't believe that she wanted sex all the time. But she did. Being on holiday with John made her libido go ballistic.

'I'm not sure it feels pretty. It feels a bit sore to me.' She rocked against him, still clutching at her skirt, rubbing against his hip. He was wearing midnight-blue pyjama bottoms, and nothing else, and the cotton was very light.

Swaying closer, she pressed against the inevitable bulge. She wasn't the only person this trip was turning into a horn-dog.

'Not too sore, I hope,' he said, pressing his face into her hair. In the mirror, his tanned skin looked startling against the black. They'd both caught the sun in the two weeks they'd been here, and although Lizzie would have said it was impossible for John to look more handsome than he normally did, somehow, with a sun-kissed glow, he was managing to. Her own tan was very light, because her skin was fair, and she burned if she wasn't careful. John was scrupulous, though, keeping a watch on her, and commanding her to get into the shade after a strictly monitored amount of sun. Sometimes, she felt like defying him, just for the sake of it, because he was so prone to act like a boss, but it thrilled her too, his benign domination. She knew he had her welfare at heart, but being a man so used to giving orders, calling the shots, in all things, was second nature to him.

'No…Not really. Just, well, making itself known. Leather makes more of an impact than hands, or plastic rulers, or even switches.'

He frowned in the mirror, his eyes full of concern.

'So it does,' he said quietly. 'You will always tell me, won't you, if I get a bit too enthusiastic for you? You're a rare and cherished treasure to me, you know that, and I can't bear the thought that I might push you too far.'

As they sometimes – in fact quite often – did, the imps of curiosity and jealousy came out to dance. It was daft to be envious of women he'd had and played with before her, but she couldn't help herself.

'Don't worry. If I don't like anything, I'll holler "chintz". But I trust you, John, and I know you've had plenty of practice to perfect your techniques. With plenty of lucky women getting the benefit…I know there have been parties and whatnot. Like the one at the mansion. Lots of gorgeous women there to spank, I guess.'

He slid his arm around her, and as she reciprocated, her nightdress slithered down, the sleek fabric gliding over her punished flesh like a breath. The nightgown was one of quite a few he'd bought her, part of a great haul of gorgeous lingerie. But John was thoughtful. He didn't just buy her things that he liked. Yes, she now owned a lot of delicate, slinky items like this one, but he also bought plenty of the kind of thing she'd have chosen for herself: funky pyjama bottoms in stripes and wild patterns, simple T-shirts and vests, white and coloured. She'd chosen the peach silk number tonight because the delicate fabric was kind to a punished rear.

John turned her in his arms, and looked down at her, his blue eyes clear as the noon day sky here. Honest.

'Yes, there have been women. You know that, love. I've never denied it.'

'I do…I suppose I'm just jealous.' Why lie? 'Women are like that about the ex-girlfriends of the men they love.'

He slid his hand against her cheek, gently cradling, and then pressed his lips to hers in a soft, intense kiss. As she'd noted in the garden, he still didn't come out and say the 'L' word all that often, but he kissed in a way that was just as telling.

'I wouldn't call most of them that. They were more like liaisons than girlfriends.' He kissed her forehead now, his breath ruffling her black fringe. 'In fact, I've never had a girlfriend quite like you before. Never one who's actually been a girl.'

A word, a name, clanged in her brain. Clara!

What was she, then, Mr Smith? She must have been a girlfriend, once. You must have been around the same age. You still are around the same age.

But she didn't mention the 'C' word. It was as rarely heard as the 'L' word. It felt bitchy to remind John of the woman who'd hurt him so much, twice over. Lizzie knew, though, that he knew she was thinking about the woman she considered her rival.

'Don't start the age thing again,' she said instead, side-tracking him with another issue, that wasn't an issue, really, more of a running joke between them.

'I can't help myself. I'm twenty-two years older than you, love.'

'Look, granddad, you're forty-six, that's all. If you were ninety-six, we might have a problem, but you're not, so just be told, will you?'

John grinned. 'Stroppy madam!'

'Bossy tyrant!'

'Shrew!'

'Despot!'

Laughing, he held her face between his two hands, and kissed her again. Hard, this time, tongue pushing in. It was a bossy kiss, a possession of her mouth, but boy, how she liked it.

She was gasping when he freed her mouth, smiling at him, feeling a tenderness in her lips that was a pale echo of the simmering glow in her buttocks.

'But seriously, Lizzie, you're going to have to accept that from time to time, the age difference between us will bother me. And make me feel guilty.'

'I don't know why.'

'Just humour me.' He tidied her fringe, where he'd ruffled it.

'I will. But you're going to have to accept that living the deluxe life, to which you're so accustomed, is going to make me uneasy sometimes too. I'm just an ordinary girl, and sometimes it all gets a bit too rarefied for me and I feel panicky. Travelling first class…private villas…buying honking great mansion houses just so we can live together. It's all very rich for my blood, you know?'

John's brow crumpled. Ah, storm clouds. And not about Dalethwaite Manor either, she guessed.

'And let's not start that again either!' His voice was fierce, not threatening, but not far from it. 'You fucking well aren't an ordinary girl, Lizzie! Didn't I just tell you a moment ago that you're rare and precious to me? And I'm lucky to be with you. Do you hear me?'

'Yes…OK…Truce. I'm a fabulous goddess. I'll try to remember that.'

'Remember it because it's the truth,' said John, smiling again. He looped his hands at the small of her back, carefully avoiding the sore areas in her buttocks. 'Now, can we please find a way to make love without hurting that gorgeous bottom of yours?'

Oh yes! Oh yes!

'Don't worry too much. You are a clever man, Mr Smith, and it really doesn't hurt that much.' She gave him a slow, sultry look from beneath her lashes. 'And even if it did, I can stand a twinge or two if you can cope with the moaning.'

'I love the moaning,' said John roundly, tightening his grip and drawing her inexorably against his erection. 'Especially if it's mine!'

Lizzie kissed the side of his neck as she moved in close. 'I love it when you moan. What can I do to make it happen?' She reached down and cupped his hard flesh. 'Suck you? Squeeze you? Ride you? Your wish is my command, boss man.'

John embraced her, hands roving, fingers not so careful of her soreness now. Not that she cared.

'You're a she-devil, woman. Temptation incarnate. You know how greedy I am. You've made me want all of those…and more!' He kissed her passionately, violently, gripping her bottom, and making her moan and wriggle.

Massaging her pelvis against his cock, Lizzie kissed back. The spanked places on her bottom were fizzing, intoxicating her blood like pink Champagne. She wanted him. Wanted him now.

Laughing, John hauled her across to the bed, and then sat down on the edge, tugging at the cord of his pyjamas and freeing his cock. It bounced up, eager and hard, ready for her.

Lizzie made as if to kneel and give him head, but he drew her towards his pelvis. 'Kneel and straddle me, darling. I need to be in you again. I want to make you come, and see your lovely face as you do.'

Sizing up the situation, Lizzie climbed onto the bed, John shuffling back a little and helping her into position. Her thighs at either side of him, she poised herself as he held his cock, allowing her to view the beautiful length of it as he reached for the ever handy condom.

For a moment, she stood apart from the intimacy of their tableau, wondering if a time would ever come when they no longer used condoms. The wonder of being skin to skin with him was something she'd been thinking about and fantasising about, but there never seemed to be the right moment to raise the issue. And whenever she'd hinted, she'd got the distinct impression that John made a conscious point of not taking that hint. For some reason…Could it be that it was simply a closeness too far for him?

And yet, the way John's eyes flared as his cock nudged her pussy almost made her wonder if the notion was crossing his mind at this very moment. He held her by the waist, supporting her in a sure hold, their intimate flesh touching yet not touching, his and hers, yin and yang, but still separated. She almost spoke, but then held back. Why spoil everything by getting into complications right now?

'You're so beautiful…so beautiful…' he whispered, hips lifting, not pushing right in yet, but breaching her entrance, stretching her. His hands were strong; he was supporting her weight, making it easy for her, even though she wouldn't have minded at all if it wasn't easy and her thighs were screaming from the tension of holding herself aloft. 'I don't know what I've done to deserve you, you wonderful woman, you.'

She wanted to say she was the lucky one. The 'ordinary girl' who'd won the heart of an extraordinary man. He was everything she'd ever dreamed of. Kind, intelligent, sophisticated, funny. As handsome as sin, and a lover nonpareil. All that would have been an embarrassment of wonderfulness; but the whipped Chantilly cream on the top of the dessert of it all was that he was also fabulously wealthy, a man of enormous means who could put resources at her disposal and help her achieve goals and dreams.

'Don't tease me, you beast,' she said, laughing. 'That big beautiful cock of yours…Don't be mean. Let me have it all!'

'Then have it, my sex goddess, have it.' His smile was like the sun, glorious, teasing, loving, wonderful.

And his cock, as he pulled her down onto him, was unequivocal.

He filled her body, her heart, her soul, her life, and when she was settled, he sought her clit and stroked it. Lovingly.

Coming, she praised his name and howled, 'I love you!'

Later, she changed her nightgown for an old one of hers, one of the few she possessed, and John gently massaged a bit of his super-secret muscle balm – formulated by a posh London apothecary – into her bottom to soothe it. He'd told her it was for his tricky knee, although she'd yet to see any evidence of said trickiness. His knees were as magnificent as the rest of him, in her opinion. But the balm was good stuff, nevertheless, and actually did reduce the soreness. She'd probably be able to lie on her back now, but she decided not to chance it, and snuggled onto her front, turning her head on the pillow to watch John.

He was sitting up, leaning against a mound of pillows of his own, flicking through something or other on his iPad. Probably financial reports; he was a terrible workaholic. And working, reading emails, checking weather reports or just about goddamn anything all staved off facing the issue of whether he was going to attempt to sleep beside her tonight.

I wish you'd tell me what it is. I know most things now ... even about that bitch Clara ... but the sleep thing, well, you're keeping me waiting on that one.

Only once or twice in their relatively brief relationship had John ever managed to sleep in the same room as her, never mind the same bed. He claimed he couldn't fall asleep in another person's presence, but, as yet, hadn't fully explained why that was.

Was it something to do with the car crash he'd been in,

all those years ago? He'd fallen asleep as the passenger in the car, believing that Clara, his lover of the time, was fit to drive home from a party. She'd told him she hadn't been drinking, and he'd accepted that as the truth, but hadn't thought to ask her whether she'd taken any drugs.

I bet you think if you'd stayed awake, you could've snatched the wheel at the last moment, don't you?

Perhaps that was the root of it? His psyche kept him awake and on his guard, lest some disaster should occur, like the one that had led Clara to pile their car into another, killing a woman and seriously injuring her daughter. The fact that the injured daughter, Rose, had long since forgiven John for his involvement, and had even become a good friend of his, made no difference. *He* couldn't forgive himself.

Lizzie studied John from beneath her eyelashes, adoring the elegance of his profile, and the way he adorably nibbled at his lower lip when he was concentrating. There was probably nothing he could have done if he'd been awake that night, and he couldn't be blamed for believing the word of the woman he'd loved. Lizzie wondered if, now, he would believe her in the same situation. Or had Clara bolloxed up his complete trust in her sex for ever? Perhaps that was why he was still holding back and, in this one thing, would not confide in her?

'Go to sleep, Lizzie. It's late, and you've had a busy night.' Turning to her, he winked and flicked a glance at her rump beneath the pale flower-sprigged cotton that had replaced the peach satin too beautiful to spoil with sticky balm.

She gave him a 'what about you' look.

'Don't worry about me. I've a few more things I want to

keep tabs on, but I will try soon. Promise. If you're already sleeping, it might be easier for me to nod off, you know.' He reached out and flicked a few strands of her hair that had fallen across her chin out of the way. Then he kissed her, softly, gently. 'If I know you're lying there waiting for me to fall asleep, it'll only make it more difficult.'

'Sorry, boss.' She was feeling tired, actually. There was nothing like being spanked, then shagged, twice, to make you drowsy.

'You've nothing to be sorry for, love. It's me that's the freak.'

'You're not a freak,' she protested, loving he way he smoothed her hair, as if she were their little cat Alice, who was at home at Dalethwaite Manor, being cared for by the efficient and irreplaceable Thursgoods. Alice purred like a high-powered motorboat when she was stroked, and Lizzie felt like doing the same.

'Go to sleep, sweetheart,' he urged again, and almost as if her subconscious was more obedient than her conscious mind, she felt herself slipping.

Even if he didn't sleep himself, his beloved presence at her side helped her to let go and bid adieu to the waking world.

'John...' she breathed, and then she was gone.

2

Dark Knight of the Soul

Lizzie shot up in bed, awake in a flash, and gasped. Somehow she'd ended on her back, and shooting straight up into a sitting position induced a twinge in her bum, a little echo of the spanking that had eluded the apothecary balm and even John's best efforts to pull his strokes.

What had woken her so abruptly? She looked around the room. No John. Despite her resolve to be sensible, her heart ached that he wasn't there, fast asleep beside her. A bit of breeze had come up, and the long voile curtains at the window leading to the balcony were flapping slightly. Maybe that was what had reached into her sleep?

But no, that wasn't it. As if on a time delay, a dream came back to her, strange and unsettling. John had been falling down and away from her into a void, a bit like lost and frozen Jack in the film *Titanic*. And it was all the more troubling because there seemed to be some kind of monster or perhaps luring siren down there in the deep, pulling him, dragging him down.

Bloody fucking Clara! I don't need to be Sigmund Freud to work that one out.

Now Lizzie was the one who couldn't sleep. She didn't need to go down that road, lying awake in the dark, speculating, and yes, despite her better instincts, hating this unknown woman who'd been the love of John's life before she was. And maybe still was, subconsciously, regardless of his conscious protestations that she, Lizzie, was The One.

She rubbed her arms, chilled by the air.

These Provençal nights could sometimes be a bit on the cool side, especially in the early hours. It'd been mild and pleasant when they'd been playing down in the grove, around midnight, but now in the deep, dark night of the soul, it was very cold. Lizzie pushed her feet into her Indian silk slippers as she stood, and dragged the cosy embroidered comforter off the bed, to wrap it around her shoulders.

Where was John? Asleep in his own room? Down in the sitting room, working on his laptop? Or somewhere else?

On instinct she padded to the open doors to the balcony, stepped out soundlessly, and peered out.

A lone figure was sitting at the table on the patio, on the long bench that flanked it. The table reminded her of the one down in the grove. The two had probably been bought as a pair.

John's skin gleamed in the moonlight. Not with the golden, exotic glow it'd reflected from the oil lantern before, but a cooler, more silvery light now. A more troubled light. It seemed that he too was enduring his own dark night of the soul.

Quietly, but still knowing he'd know she was coming, Lizzie crept down the wrought-iron steps that led from their bedroom balcony to the patio below, and joined him. He didn't turn until she was right beside him, and sliding onto the bench. His face had a stark, uneasy quality to it that cut her to the quick on his behalf.

She didn't speak, but draped the voluminous comforter around his shoulders. It was plenty big enough for two.

'Thanks, sweetheart. It's a bit chilly, isn't it?' His smile lightened the mood a little, yet it seemed world weary. The warmth of his shoulder against hers was welcoming, though.

'It certainly is. Which begs the question why you're sitting out here in just your pyjama bottoms, freezing your nuts off?'

John laughed. 'Don't worry, my nuts are fine. How's your bottom? This bench isn't exactly upholstered.' He pressed a kiss to the side of her cheek.

Goodness, she hadn't noticed. She'd plonked down on the hard wood and barely felt anything. Which just showed what the magic of John's beauty in the moonlight could do.

'It's much better now. Barely a twinge.' She shuffled closer, feeling his skin warm in contact with hers. 'What's in there?' She nodded at the cup he was cradling.

Wordlessly, John offered it to her, and she brought it to her lips. Ooh, coffee. When she took a sip she almost reeled back. Good grief it was strong. Delicious, but ferociously potent.

'Jesus, John, swigging this stuff isn't going to help you sleep. With or without me in the room.' Even so, she took another mouthful herself, needing to be braced up, if she was going to ask the thorny questions she'd so far avoided.

When she passed the cup back to him, he stared into it, then put it aside, reaching for her hand.

'I suppose I'm punishing myself. If I can't sleep with you, I don't deserve to sleep at all. Hence the caffeine.'

'That's just stupid.'

He raised his hand to his lips, and kissed it in a vague, almost abstract way. 'It is, isn't it? I'm an idiot.'

'Not an idiot,' she said fiercely, gripping the hand that held hers, twisting it a little, and kissing it in return. 'Just someone with…stuff on his mind, that's all.' She rubbed her cheek against the back of his hand, loving the silk of his skin.

'Yes.'

The single word hung in the air, heavy with all the other words, the ones he didn't, perhaps couldn't, say. Should she force the issue? Ask the questions she normally resisted? She hated being a nag, hated pushing him. It seemed so ungrateful when he was so kind and wonderful, giving her gifts, both material, and of himself, with his mind and heart and body.

'I told you that you should ask things, didn't I?'

He had done, back at Dalethwaite, before she'd moved in. He'd said she could ask him anything, and he'd try to answer. Should she go for it now, in these wee small hours that weren't really like real life, in the light of day?

'Why can't you sleep with anyone else, John?'

There, she'd asked, but not the other great sleep-related question that bugged her.

Did you used to sleep like a baby with Clara, before all the bad stuff happened and changed you for ever? Before you took the fall for her, and went to prison when she should have been the one to go?

'Is it the accident? Or prison? Or something else?'

Despite his words to the contrary, he didn't seem to be able to answer, and while she waited, the night and the garden held its breath.

*

He was a coward, and he knew it. He should just tell her. It would be such a relief, to at least get this one thing clear. The trouble was, he didn't fully understand it himself, despite years and thousands of pounds of therapy. He'd spent so many years not thinking about the reasons he could only sleep alone. It was only loving Lizzie that had compelled him to re-examine this issue.

But she was waiting, waiting. She deserved some kind of explanation. After all, what man in his right mind would avoid sleeping next to this beautiful, compassionate young woman? Even with no sex on the agenda, just being at her side was a thing of wonder. He could want her again in a second, but sharing her blanket and her warmth was enough for the moment. It made him strong.

'It's a bit of both. A muddle really,' he began, impatient with his own prevarication. How long could a man who was supposed to be astute and grown up go on being a craven and adolescent idiot? 'Not clear cut.' He sighed, and tweaked the blanket tighter around them. 'People always think that X leads to Y, in a simple cause and effect, but I've never found anything in life to be like that. If you've got X, Y and Z, you might get nothing, or the answer to the Universe.'

'That's forty-two,' she said, rubbing her face against his shoulder.

'Quite possibly.' He smiled, recognising the reference to *The Hitchhiker's Guide to the Galaxy*. 'But in my case, it's been a mix of the car accident, prison, maybe even a bit of natural insomnia. All jumbled together. All meaning I can't relax and let my guard right down properly. Something inside me's afraid to sleep…even with you.'

'So, what happened, then?' she asked in a low, steady

voice. Not a bossy voice, but one he couldn't deny, or resist. 'I sort of get the car smash element, I think.' She turned to him, her eyes gleaming in the low light. 'You feel that if you had stayed awake as Clara drove, you could have averted what happened. I get that. It makes sense. Your subconscious keeps on telling you that you have to stay awake and "protect" the other person, somehow? Is that it?'

He'd been through all this with various therapists. She'd pinpointed it easily, though. 'Yes, that's part of it.' In some ways, the easiest part; in some ways, not.

'But the rest? Can you talk about it? It's OK if you can't, but maybe it'll help if you share?'

Why not? Why not share? It didn't make him a bad person, what'd happened. He supposed it was the old atavistic male desire to be heroic in the eyes of his mate. But the story of him being someone's prison bitch didn't have much, if anything, in the way of heroic qualities.

Oh God...

He drew in a deep breath and, as he exhaled, a slender hand closed around his arm, reassuring, urging.

'Prison isn't easy for anybody. It's not supposed to be. But when you're a particularly young-looking twenty-four-year-old ex-public-school boy with an über-posh accent and blond curly hair and you're thrown into a closed society of hard, embittered men, some of whom are used to using violence to get exactly what they want...well, it's no birthday party, I can tell you.'

'But you don't have an über-posh accent.'

He laughed again, some of the reluctance and anxiety loosened by her simple words, and the feel of her warm fingertips against his skin. 'I did then, sweetheart, I'm afraid. Awfully cut glass, and upper crust, don't you know?' he said, dredging deep and recreating the 'county' tones that had been so natural to him during the course of his younger life.

She laughed and kissed his shoulder. 'Ooh, you were a snobby git, then.'

'I'm afraid so, love.' He paused, gathered himself and went on, 'I was terrified for my life,' he admitted, feeling the dread again after all these years, like a dowsing in the cold of the North Sea. 'The moment I walked in I suspected I'd be a target, and I was.' Was he shaking? He didn't think so, but she held on tighter to him as if he was. 'But in a way, I got lucky…sort of. I was put in a cell with an older man, Jack. He was a tough, hard-living, and huge. Tattooed. The Full Monty. He could see right through me from the start, and he knew my fear.'

He had to stop. Reaching for the coffee, he took a sip, grimacing because it was cold. 'He laid things out for me. Yes, I would be seen as "a prime piece of arse", and certain prisoners would pursue me and just take what they wanted. Didn't matter if I was fit and could box a bit, and defend myself well enough under normal circumstances. Inside, I didn't stand a chance.'

'Oh, John,' she said softly, rubbing her cheek against his shoulder again. 'It must have been a nightmare. I can't begin to imagine what it must have been like.' She held him harder, almost hurting him, and smothered his upper arm with kisses.

The way she held him gave him strength, just as in the oddest of ways Jack had given him strength all those years ago. It was weird to think of the man by name again; he'd tried to expunge as much as he could of that time from his conscious memory, even if his subconscious seemed to dwell on it constantly, against his will.

'Jack offered me a deal. He could take care of himself. Nobody messed with him. And he offered to take care of me too, and not let anyone mess with me…in return for certain favours. The nature of which I'm sure you can deduce, my sweet.'

'What did you do?'

She already knew. She'd be imagining what he was remembering. Night after night, lying awake, wide awake, wondering if tonight would be the night Jack demanded 'payment', for the protection service he'd so effectively rendered.

'The most logical thing. The least worst thing. It was either that or be gang raped, or repeatedly beaten up, or worse.'

'Oh God, it must have been awful.'

'In some ways it was, even though I'd been with a man before. There was Benjamin at public school, and I'd experimented with a couple of others, at Uni.' He stared into the garden, unable to show his face to her now. The most awful thing had been that he'd actually enjoyed it some of the time, and hated himself for that. The lying awake had always involved a narrow strand of forbidden anticipation, all wound in with the fear and self-loathing and hope that nothing would happen. 'Thankfully, Jack didn't make too many demands. Far fewer than I expected. I think he hated himself for wanting me too, but that didn't stop the wanting. He was just as screwed up as anyone in there, and more so than a lot of them. But mercifully for me, I was the one he'd developed a crush on at first sight.'

'So, you lay awake every night, wondering and waiting if this Jack was going to want sex.'

Not a question. An observation of a logical outcome. She was so wise.

'Yes, and the lying awake, listening to his breathing, and his every movement. That was far, far worse than anything he did to me, or wanted me to do to him.' His eyes prickled suddenly. Tears, possibly, but also the memory of that terrible gritty sensation beneath the eyelids, from being unable to close them, and relax, even though he'd tried and tried to. 'He was quite gentle, in fact, and strangely fastidious. But still, I couldn't sleep, wondering if he'd want me, and wondering if tonight would be the night when things got more brutal.'

'Did they ever get more brutal?' Was she appalled? Repulsed? Was it wishful thinking that led him to believe not?

'No, thankfully. Never. I probably had rougher sex when I was fooling about with Benjamin.' He dragged in a breath. Why did the air suddenly feel so thick and hard to breathe? 'It was mostly oral. Jack didn't care for fucking all that much. I don't think he even considered he might be gay or bi.'

A gentle hand snaked out, cupped his jaw and compelled him to turn his face to her. Her eyes were clear, concerned yet non-judgemental. He blinked, awed by her. She only wanted to understand, and to know him.

'And did this relationship go on all the time you were in prison?' she asked.

'No, only for about six months. I was transferred then. The old man had relented from some of his fury and disappointment in me by then, and I think he must have pulled some strings. I ended up in a really cushy open prison for the rest of my sentence. We all had our own individual cells there, though they called them "rooms", just to make us feel better.' He remembered the relief…hell, the sleep! And yet, paradoxically, he'd missed the presence of Jack, this man he'd almost expunged from his conscious memory, even though it seemed he might never erase the psychological result of being with him. 'I slept again, properly. In fact, I slept better in cushy prison than at any other time in my life. And I was able to eat…I put back on all the weight I'd lost, which was two stones in six months, and got buffed and healthy again, and did a hell of a lot of reading, and thinking about my future. I had an HIV test and I was clear, and I thought I was "all better", body and mind. It wasn't until I was released that I even knew I had a problem.' He laughed. Oh the irony, how he'd remembered.

'It was funny, really. I never knew I couldn't sleep with anyone else in the room until I tried, for probably the first time in my life, to do something to please my father.'

Lizzie breathed slowly, evenly. It was important not to let John know how horrified she was. Not at him, but for him, having to endure what he'd been through in prison. Her heart ached for him, the beautiful young man, wracked by fourteen flavours of guilt, confused, his comfortable, privileged world turned upside down. Maybe, in many ways, it'd been the making of him, but it was a harsh path to travel in order to learn a lesson; especially as the inciting incident had not been his fault, whatever he claimed to the contrary.

'For your father? What did you do?' She had an inkling, though. Something he'd once said to her popped into her mind.

'Well, I'd always known he wanted me to go into the army, and join his regiment, so I gave in, when he did a bit more of his famous string-pulling, and I joined up. You can imagine how that worked out, can't you? In "basic", in the training centre barracks…'

Oh God, sharing a sleeping space with not only one man, or person, but dozens.

'But I thought you couldn't leave the army once you were in? You said you were only in, like, a couple of weeks?'

John heaved a sigh. 'That was something of an under-statement, for dramatic effect. I was in a good while longer than that…But from day one, I was pretty much without a wink of sleep at night. Medication didn't work. I nearly killed myself trying to hack it, but I ended up in a state of total nervous collapse…damn near psychotic.' He turned away from her. He was ashamed. She reached out and cupped his jaw again, making him look round.

'Was it medical grounds, then? That you got out on?'

'Partly. That, and a very decent and compassionate CO. I found out later that he'd lost a sister who'd committed suicide after chronic sleep issues, so he was unusually sympathetic to my problem. But the main reason –' he paused, with a sudden wry smile '– was more of my father's goddamned string-pulling.'

'Must be handy to have a dad who can do that. And it shows that whatever you say about him, he cared enough about you to want to get you out again quickly.'

John threw back his head, his blond curls glinting in the moonlight. His laugh was harsh.

'Oh no, sweetheart, he tried to pull strings to ensure that I had to stay in the army, and that I wouldn't be molly-coddled. If my sainted father had got his way, they'd just have had the RSM hit me on the head with a mallet every night to knock me out. But fortunately the commanding officer could already see my side of things, and he also thoroughly resented the high and mighty Marquess of Welbeck continually trying to stick his oar in. So he gave me a very rare Administrative Discharge just to piss my father off.' He turned to her again, and slid his arm around her beneath the blanket. 'And that was pretty much the final straw between the old man and me, only to be compounded when I married Caroline, a woman old enough to be my mother, with whom I'd never have a child. My elder brother George and his wife Rosemary had just discovered they couldn't have any more kids after Helen, so Pa had pinned his dynastic hopes on yours truly, his second son, to produce a male heir, who could eventually be Marquess after George and me. But instead, I just heaped disgrace and bitter disappointment on him, and he washed his hands of me.'

'Oh, you poor thing, what a drama,' said Lizzie, snuggling in closer. 'It makes my little contretemps with my own father seem like a tale of familial sweetness and light.'

'It could all have been a lot worse,' said John, pressing his lips to her temple. 'As I've pointed out before, my chequered history is what led me to being in a certain place at a certain time…and to meeting you at the Waverley.' He rubbed his face against her hair, and his breath soughed against her forehead. 'And that's something I simply can't contemplate ever having missed, believe me, my love.'

'I can't contemplate it either.' She tightened her hold on him, loving the feel of his bare torso against her own naked arms. His tale had been a nightmare, but it had no effect on the impact he had on her. And no effect on the respect she felt for him, either. In fact, it was just the opposite. He'd gone through all that, and still come out a strong, charismatic, sorted man, a humane man, in control of his destiny and that of others.

'So, you don't think I'm a total screw-up, then? Ex-con, failed soldier, subject to all kinds of disastrously poor judgement…and worse. I thought you might be revolted by it all.'

She dug her nails ever so lightly into his flank. 'No, I just think you're an idiot sometimes. What's past is past, John, and you're doing pretty well for yourself now, in just about every department.' She had to make him believe her. 'And if you think because you had sex with a man in prison I'd think any less of you, you're very much mistaken.'

'I adore you, Lizzie,' he whispered, twisting around to face her, cradling her jaw, then kissing her on the lips, slowly, softly and sweetly. His mouth was like velvet, infinitely desirable.

As they broke apart, Lizzie made a decision. An easy one. 'Look, seeing as you can't sleep, and I'm not sleepy either…What say we go back to bed and make love again? Then, tomorrow, we can catch up on zeds when we get home, and I can even nap on the plane, if I need to.' She stole a quick kiss again. 'That way, everyone's a winner!'

'But what about your sore bottom?' He slid a hand down over the bottom in question, squeezing it gently as they made for the iron staircase leading to the bedroom.

'Oh that? I'd forgotten all about that. Another bout of delicious sex will do it a power of good anyway.'

'Well, in that case, let's get up there, shall we?'

Lizzie gave him a sharp look. There'd been a note in his voice, an odd little twist. Great emotion despite the smile on his face. Gratitude?

Grabbing his hand, she tugged him onwards. Actions spoke louder than words, and having him inside her, making love to her, would speak loudest of all, in this case.

This was another first. Another new experience, courtesy of John. Part of the high life that he led, and which she now shared.

Lizzie peered out of the window at the scene passing by below as they flew home. Beneath them was central France, dotted with chateaux, acres of farmland, winding rivers, and vineyards producing heady wine, white and red. Currently she couldn't see any of those, because there was heavy cloud cover today. Under all that white fluff, it was probably a grey miserable morning, and raining. A good day to be heading back to Blighty, where apparently, according to her weather app, it was warm and sunny.

But it didn't matter what it was like outside, because in the passenger compartment of their small, sleek jet, everything was sumptuous, pampered and deluxe. It was the first time she'd travelled in a private plane. On the outbound journey they'd taken a scheduled flight, first class of course, and that had also been a new experience. She'd never even travelled first class on a train, never mind flying.

But travelling by private jet aced everything!

The leather on the armrest was soft and fine, and Lizzie ran her fingertips over it. She grinned, the super-comfortable seat reminding her of John's 'throne' from their grove adventure. Trust him to remember that silly fantasy of hers, and make it real as part of their first holiday together.

'What's wrong?' he enquired from his seat a few feet away. He was working on his laptop at a small pull-out table. 'Getting pangs of conscience over obscene and conspicuous luxury again?' He grinned, teasing her over her 'issue'.

'A bit, I suppose, although it's all very lovely.' She glanced at her coffee cup, remembering the exquisite pattern in the foam that the flight attendant had created for her. She'd been offered Champagne, but somehow, heading home, it seemed a better idea to get out of their holiday wine-drinking habits and back into more sensible consumption. John was already hard at work, alcohol rejected, and coffee at his side too.

He pushed aside the table, the laptop and whatever deal he was currently in the process of brainstorming. 'We could join the Mile High Club, to take your mind off it, if you like?' The twinkle in his eye was suggestive, but she had a feeling he was still just teasing. He would fuck her in the equally luxurious bathroom compartment, if she wanted him to, she knew that. But…the flight attendant would know exactly what they were doing, and John had more savoir-faire and good taste than to embarrass her that way. This wasn't like the sophisticated fetish party he'd taken her to, where everybody wanted everybody else to know they were shagging or spanking or whatever. This was a form of real life, albeit a very luxurious and rarefied one, and in the real world, outside the bedroom John always behaved like a perfect gentleman.

'That's an incredibly sweet offer, Mr Smith, but I'll take the proverbial rain check, if I may?' She grinned back at him. 'Tempting as the offer of your glorious body is, this is the first time I've travelled in a private jet, and I am enjoying it, even if I do think it's unbelievably extravagant.'

'Well, if it's any comfort,' said John, moving his table

back into position, 'if we hadn't decided to travel in it, this jet would have been returning home empty. So at least that's a slightly less onerous carbon footprint.'

Just before their holiday, John had bought a majority share in a private jet hire company, operating out of their local regional airport, and this was their first opportunity to sample the goods. A celebrity author who lived in the area had flown out for a holiday in the south of France, and in the best use of logistics, John had requisitioned the aircraft for his and Lizzie's journey home.

'I suppose so.'

'I know so,' he said, adjusting his laptop back to face him. 'Ah well, back to work if nookie is off the menu.' He was joking, but there was the shadow of a frown across his forehead.

Oh no, he wasn't worrying about that, was he?

'Look, John, what you told me last night, about your experience in prison. It doesn't put me off you, you know. It doesn't make me want you any less than I did before. It's just something that happened to you. It doesn't make you a different man to me. I still think you're the sexiest thing on two legs, and the best fuck a woman could ever have. You know that, don't you?'

'Thank you. You're an angel, Lizzie, a true angel.' The smile was wide now, unsullied by any doubt. 'I did worry…about that…but you proved to me last night that it wasn't an issue. Several times, in fact.'

They'd made long, tender love after his revelation on the terrace, coming together again and again, touching, kissing. At first it had seemed important to Lizzie to allay any fears of his, but very quickly, she'd simply started enjoying John's body and his fabulous technique, just for the sheer joy of it.

She couldn't imagine any man being more of a man than he.

There were still one or two things she wondered about, but somehow, this wasn't the time, or the place, to explore them. When they were back at home, tucked up in the sitting room, relaxing with a cup of tea, and maybe a slice or two of Mrs Thursgood's lemon cake, well, maybe then she'd ask more questions, but not before.

'Well there you are. No problemo. So, get on with sussing out whatever it is you've got in the cross-hairs today.' She nodded at the laptop. 'What is it? Trying to work out how to persuade Elon Musk to sell you a bit of the SpaceX action? Now that you've got yourself some jets, space rockets and satellites are obviously the next desirable items on the agenda.'

He gave her an old-fashioned look. 'Don't laugh, madam. I've got interests in several telecoms companies so I already own part shares in a satellite or two.'

'Why does that not surprise me? You filthy plutocrat, you.'

'But I like what you say about rockets. I'll put them on the to-do list.'

They lapsed into a companionable silence for a while, John perhaps mulling over how he might obtain his rockets for a competitive price, and Lizzie reading the bunch of emails she'd downloaded before they boarded, and reconnecting with life as she now knew it. Which was full, fuller than it had ever been, and consisted of living at Dalethwaite Manor with John, and working with Marie Lanscombe at the New Again Dress Agency, doing alterations and now a little bit of designing too, special projects for one or two of the shop's most long-standing and high-spending clients. She was also doing her utmost still to be the best friend she could to Brent and Shelley, who'd been her house-mates up until a few weeks ago.

She frowned. That was the hard thing. The three of them had been so close, their lives practically interwoven, but now, no matter how assiduously she tried to maintain the integrity of the bond between them, she could feel it faltering.

Perhaps I'm just being arrogant? Perhaps they don't need me as much as I thought they did? Perhaps I'm just too different now…now that I live with a multi-millionaire?

She'd made a point of dropping in at St Patrick's Road a couple of times before she and John had set off for this holiday, but each time, she'd barely had chance for the briefest of chats with her friends. She'd extended a dinner invitation, regaling Brent and Shelley with the glories of Mrs Thursgood's cookery, but in the days prior to her trip to the south of France with John, there had never seemed to be an evening when everybody was free.

Well, I've got a new man, so why shouldn't you two be all swept up in your new men too?

Especially Shelley, who seemed to have found a kinky hunk all of her own, even though Lizzie still wasn't sure whether or not her friend was paying for the privilege. Sholto Kraft was an escort, just had Brent had once been, and as Lizzie had pretended to be, the first night she'd met John. Shelley claimed she was just having fun with a guy she liked, but even though she was seeing her friend less than before, Lizzie could sense there was more to the Shelley/ Sholto relationship than just a bit of BDSM experimenting.

And as for Brent…Happy as she was for him, Lizzie couldn't for the life of her work out quite why her friend was so cagey about the hot new man in his life. Brent hadn't had a boyfriend for a long, long time, not since his serious lover Steve had been killed; but before then, he'd always loved to dish every last fruity detail about his dates and their prowess. This time, though, he was as close-mouthed as a very close-mouthed thing. Lizzie would have been frantic with concern, but for the fact that she'd never seen Brent so happy before. Which was a bit insulting in a way, because he seemed in far better spirits now than he'd ever been when he'd briefly dated her.

I'm going to prise some intel out of both of you when I get home, if it's the last thing I do. You two were both nosy enough when it came to me telling you about John and his peccadilloes.

But today, there wasn't a single email from either of them amongst the downloaded stuff. It was all newsletters from Amazon and suchlike. Lizzie frowned, about to close the program, but then noticed something that she'd missed amongst all the tempting offers for books and clothes and tech toys.

It was an email from Marie, her boss at New Again. It'd probably be some nice chatty updates on the shop and the expansion they'd been discussing. The two women had rapidly become fast friends since Lizzie had started working at the dress agency. She'd sensed that Marie had been marking time with New Again, and that her own arrival had energised the other woman's interest in the business, suggesting new horizons. With someone on hand who could not only do expert alterations quickly, but also make garments from scratch, the shop could be so much more; a prime example was their unexpected plunge into making bridal gowns. Admittedly, it was just one finished dress so far, with two more on the books and several strong enquiries, but it was all very exciting and could end up being a very big thing indeed!

The title of Marie's email – *You won't believe this!* – was a bit ominous, though. Lizzie opened the message.

After the usual salutation, the other woman was ecstatic.

The little shop on the Kissley Magna village green…I think we've got it! I thought it'd been sold, but suddenly it was back on the market again with another agency, to lease. I thought, what the hell, I'd apply for details again…and blow me if they'd dropped the terms way, way down…I can't believe it. It'll cost us next to nothing, really. I kept asking them if they'd made a mistake, but they said no. And the place is just perfect. Barely anything to do, just a bit of fitting out. We'll need some more stock, but I've got my rainy day savings…and maybe if your bloke John would like to invest a bit, we could go into a proper, formal partnership? If you'd like that, of course. I think he should invest in you as a big-time designer, but being selfish, I'd love it if you'd come in with me, you know?

It was a long, rambling email, happiness in every bit and byte. Lizzie smiled, but sighed silently too.

Here we go again, she thought, recognising a familiar pattern in the suddenly available property at a bargain price.

It was a perplexing situation, and she still didn't quite know how to handle it. But she'd have to find a way. Because it would keep happening, and she couldn't keep getting in a state about it, and becoming confused and irritated.

It wasn't Marie's fault. Lizzie's employer and friend was in seventh heaven, relishing the next exciting step for the business that was suddenly right within her grasp. Something Lizzie really wanted for both of them too…

No, it was the way it had been done that was troubling. Unsettling. Because she, Lizzie, knew exactly how it had come about. Exactly. She'd been manoeuvred, again, by the man she loved. Just as she was previously when the house she'd shared with Brent and Shelley at St Patrick's Road had been purchased by a 'mysterious new owner', who'd promptly dropped the rent to a ludicrously minimal level.

Across the cabin, John's head snapped up, and he gave her a long, shrewd look. She'd never known anyone like him, anyone who could pick up on another person's vibes the way he did. She could swear he'd read her mind. Or maybe it was just because he'd simply been waiting for her to discover what he'd done…and to react. She wondered how long this had been in the works.

Crikey, that's fantastic! she typed in a draft email to Marie, ready to send when they landed. *Totally brilliant! Let's talk about it in detail as soon as I get back, but yes, I'd love to be in on this with you, as a partner, if you think I'm up to it. I don't think there'll be any doubt whatsoever about the fact that John will invest, or loan me some money. That's a given. I can't wait!*

There was no use being mulish about this. He did what he did. Even when he'd said he wouldn't do it, the devil. And just as before, there was no point fighting, or spoiling things for other people. After all, his motives were benign, and it was what she wanted too.

But it was another of his pre-emptive strikes and she was going to give him the mother of all bollockings about that; for the way he'd done it rather than what he'd done. He was going to have to learn to consult her about things first, especially big stuff like this.

You say I'm your equal in all things, John. Well, treat me like one. Equals keep other equals in the picture, don't they? They don't leave them to discover what they've done after the fact.

She held John's gaze for a moment, watching him wait for her to say something. Instead, giving him the faintest smile, she returned to her messages.

Chew on that, control freak.

She added another sentence to the email. *This new leasing company ... it wouldn't happen to be called 'Oldacre Holdings' by any chance, would it?*

She'd absolutely no doubt what the answer to that one would be.

3

Back to the New Reality

Dalethwaite Manor felt both strange and familiar to her. This was the new reality of her life. Before they'd gone away, she'd been ill, then there'd been the kerfuffle of moving her stuff – well, most of it – from St Patrick's Road. Then there'd been catching up with Marie at New Again, not to mention a ton of various 'official' things to sort out with respect to living in a new home. John had offered her the services of one of his cadre of personal assistants and secretaries, but Lizzie had insisted on doing as much of it herself as she could.

I love you, but I don't want to depend totally on you. As long as you insist on benignly manipulating my life, beautiful man, I'm going to insist on maintaining at least some semblance of feminine independence.

But arriving home from the airport was like the king and queen arriving at their palace.

Mrs Thursgood was on the steps to greet them. There were flowers everywhere. A new minion of John's, called Martin, swept forward, reeling off a list of phone calls, meetings and critical messages to be dealt with, and requesting instructions. John's principal personal assistant Willis was now his liaison at his London headquarters, with newly promoted Martin his right-hand man up here in the north.

Even Alice the cat was waiting in the hall too, milling around Lizzie's and John's legs, and graciously accepting the stroking and affection of her human underlings, although as a determinedly independent creature herself she'd quickly wandered off again.

Used to just plonking her holiday luggage somewhere or anywhere for the time being, and then unpacking it haphazardly over a period of days or even weeks, Lizzie found the idea of handing it over to someone else slightly alarming. Alarming but also seductively tempting. She hated unpacking with the power of a thousand suns, which was why it usually got left so long.

'Er…OK then, thanks ever so much,' she said as Mrs Thursgood took charge. 'Everything's a bit mixed up. But the…um…worn stuff is on the top.' God, nice as it was to hand off the chore, it was also embarrassing too.

'Don't worry, Miss Aitchison. Leave everything to me. Just relax and rest after your journey. Mary is in helping us today, and she'll bring you some tea. I'm sure you could do with some. It never tastes right abroad. Perhaps you'd like it served in the orangery? It's lovely in there this afternoon.'

Feeling helpless, Lizzie glanced across at John, who was deep in conversation with Martin. He met her look immediately and grinned. He knew this was all odd to her, and he mimed, *Don't worry!*

'Yes, tea in the orangery would be great. I'm dying for a proper English cuppa. It's been lovely on holiday, but you're so right, tea anywhere else but here just doesn't taste as it should.'

John smiled approvingly at Lizzie, as Mrs Thursgood took control of Lizzie's cases, and the very willing Martin, who clearly didn't stand on official roles and ceremony, lent a hand taking the luggage upstairs.

'Come on, sweetheart, let's have that tea. I'm dying for a cup too.' John slid his hand into hers and led her to the orangery.

Lizzie still had vivid memories of their fun in the orangery that first day, when they'd been viewing the house. The sunny room would always be an evocative space for her. But right now, it was just warm and golden and welcoming. She flung herself down on one of the inviting, pale, deeply upholstered sofas and, as John settled beside her, they heard the sound of a cheery voice singing and, miraculously quickly, Mary, one of Mrs Thursgood's several daily helpers, appeared with a laden tea tray.

'Oops, sorry about that,' Mary said with a grin, setting down the tea things on a low table. 'This is such a lovely house. I always feel like singing when I'm here. Did you have a nice holiday, Miss Aitchison, Mr Smith?'

'Brilliant, thanks,' said Lizzie. Yes, it was a lovely house, if a bit daunting. When she really settled in, she could imagine herself singing all the time too. 'But it's lovely to be home, too.'

'Especially for English tea again,' added John, with a smile that clearly had a powerful effect on Mary. 'Thanks for this, Mary. It all looks lovely. I think we can manage for ourselves now, though. We'll ring if we need anything else.'

Mary drifted out, with a dreamy smile on her face. That was what the John Smith wonder-smile seemed to do to most women.

Sinking back into the comfortable upholstery, Lizzie

sighed with appreciation. Suddenly, a wave of tiredness swept over her. She could feel herself decompressing. France had been an amazing, intense sexual marathon in lush, beautiful surroundings, but in spite of all her qualms and misgivings, Dalethwaite did feel like home. It *was* home. Things were new and strange, but for all that, she was right where she should be, and with exactly the man she was meant to be with.

'Tired, love?'

Her eyes snapped open, and she realised she'd almost been on the edge of dozing. John was holding out a cup of tea to her, one with just the right degree of milkiness. He never forgot anything.

'Yes, a bit. Well, a lot. The villa was fab, but…um…we seemed to be having sex almost all the time we weren't sightseeing or swimming in the villa's pool or walking or cycling or whatever. I feel as if I need a holiday here at home to get over our holiday abroad.'

John laughed. 'You know, I feel just the same.' He picked up his cup, sipped, then sighed happily. He was just as much a tea lover as Lizzie. 'Don't get me wrong, I loved every moment of our time together, because you're just like an irresistible drug to me. But I love being back here too, and us just hanging out together.' He winked. 'That is, until I get horny…which won't be long…In fact, the way you're sitting, in those trousers…' He paused and, for a moment, laid a hand lightly on her thigh. 'But seriously, I love it that you're able to think of Dalethwaite as "home". I want you to be happy here. I think we can both be happy here. But I know this life is an adjustment for you, and I'll do anything I can to make you feel comfortable and able to live how you want to.'

Lizzie drank some tea. It was perfect. She hadn't been hungry when she arrived, but all of a sudden, the slices of lemon cake on the tray looked infinitely enticing. Without being asked, John slipped one on a plate for her.

His blue eyes were lambent, and the gracious light of the sunny room made him look more the golden god than ever, with his blond hair and his confident, sparkling smile. But he looked serious too.

'You mean the world to me, Lizzie, and I know that you're the one having to make the biggest changes, just to be with me. But never forget that I appreciate that.' He looked away for a moment, less sure of himself somehow. 'And if you ever want to take a few days out, spend time with your friends again…Well, I understand that. I'd miss you like hell, but I want you to feel that you're free. Free to do what you want. You're not just an "accessory" of mine; you know that, don't you?'

Lizzie swallowed, her eyes a little blurry. For all his faults, for all his compulsion to be in control, and to act first, then ask questions later, his intentions were good and true. Now was not the time to get into a discussion with him over buying new premises for New Again, or to succumb to the ever-present niggling itch to ask him questions. More questions about his past. About prison. About his rift with his family. About his bloody ex, Clara, whom she simply could not make herself think about without animosity, even though Lizzie usually tried to give just about anybody the benefit of the doubt.

She put aside her cup, and leaned in towards him, touching his handsome face, now a little kissed by the sun, and cradling his cheek. When he set his own cup on the table, she plunged in, kissing him hard on the lips. It was complicated to put into words what she felt, but with a kiss, she could say just about anything. He slid his arms around her, responding but letting her lead, for now. She tasted tea and a hint of lemon from the cake as she slipped her tongue into his mouth, exploring.

Pushing him back onto the long, low sofa, she half climbed on top of him, still kissing, and digging her fingers into his golden hair, loving its silkiness and the way it curled in a wild, youthful way. She smothered his face with kisses, and slid a hand down his body, to find him hard, inevitably, risen to her in the space of seconds. For just a heartbeat, she hesitated. What if someone came into the room? Mrs Thursgood, or Mary? But then, she relaxed again. She would have to learn to live with this, and trust that the people who worked for John, and for her, were no fools, and also the very souls of discretion. They knew that their employers needed to be left alone like this, because they were new lovers, and…well…they were likely to get frisky quite a lot, and very often.

This was the new reality, but in this thing at least, it wasn't any different to the old reality. She would often want John, and he would often want her.

Breathless, she pulled a little way away from him, and was rewarded by that smile, that beautiful, evocative 'I want you' smile. The gilded grin that went with the hard knot of his erection, pushing up against her belly.

'What did I tell you?' he said softly, reaching up, digging his hand into her hair as it trailed over him, like an inky curtain. 'And you haven't even had a slice of cake yet.'

'Ooh, that lovely cake,' she said with a sigh. John was infinitely more delicious to her, but Mrs Thursgood's lemon drizzle cake was almost as addictive in a different kind of way. Lizzie straightened up, a knee on either side of his pelvis, and one foot on the floor. Lowering herself across his bulging groin, she reached for her cake, broke off a piece, and nibbled it. 'Glorious,' she purred. The sharp but sweet flavour was divine, and so was the erection pressing against her. She took another bite, and massaged John with her crotch.

'Indeed,' he agreed, his eyes narrowing salaciously. She licked crumbs from her lower lip, and could have sworn his cock kicked against her. 'Have some more.'

As she broke off some more cake and conveyed it to her lips, John reached for the zip of her trousers and whizzed it down. While she was still chewing the divine confection, he crooked his wrist and wiggled his hand inside her trousers and her underwear both, burrowing unerringly between her sex lips. 'Glorious,' he said softly, finding her clit.

She started to ride his hand, but he said, 'Uh oh, concentrate on your cake. Mrs Thursgood would be disappointed to know you weren't fully savouring the results of her hard work.'

'But, John,' she protested, the words devolving into a demi-groan as he rubbed her with his fingers, working her clitoris firmly but with tenderness.

'But nothing,' he replied, steel in his voice.

Rocking against him, squashing his hand between his crotch and her pussy, Lizzie obeyed him, eating a little more cake, trying to concentrate, and to taste it. Her senses were awhirl. It was like a crossed circuit inside her brain; the intersection of two pleasures was making her feel dizzy. Lemon sweetness filled her mouth, while her sex was overtaken by gathering, gouging need, the assembling of pleasure and orgasm. John's fingers were remorseless, taxing her hard with a rough circular action one moment, the next minute rubbing back and forth.

'Oh John,' she gasped, aching for completion, bearing down.

But instead, he said, 'Hup!' and as she lifted, wild with frustration, he twisted his wrist again, reconfiguring his contact with her, and pushed two fingers into her vagina, while squashing his thumb mercilessly against her clit. Then he gripped, not cruelly, but with a wicked assertion, that thumb doing just the trick she was dying for.

Cake forgotten, Lizzie clapped a hand over her mouth, suppressing her cries as orgasm spiralled down through her, finding its ignition point where his hand cupped her crotch. She tossed her head, her hair flying around her as her flesh clamped down on him, pulsing in waves, rippling around his fingers. Still fighting to contain her voice, in this house full of people, she pitched forward, grabbing at the back of his neck with her free hand, and drawing their faces together, first forehead pressed to forehead, then closing, closing.

'Lizzie, Lizzie, Lizzie,' he chanted against her cheek, the scent of lemon beautiful as his breath twined with hers and his lips, settling on hers, stifled her moans.

What on earth had got into him?

John sat in his new office, staring at messages both written and digital that demanded his attention. A man like him could not go off the grid on holiday for two weeks without expecting a mountain of work to come back to.

But all he could think of was Lizzie, and how desire for her had got the better of him, both in the orangery and afterwards. He'd behaved like a randy lad – again – copping a feel on the settee, then sneaking her away into the nearest downstairs cloakroom, to have her hurriedly, bent over the sink.

What the hell is the matter with you, man? The whole idea of moving in together was to have time and space to make love, and to indulge in any kind of erotic play they fancied, in the comfort of a large and beautiful bedroom, a civilised, grown-up setting.

And here he was, grabbing her and rutting at the first opportunity, taking the risk of compromising her in an open part of the house, with staff around. He knew none of them would dream of intruding, and even in an emergency they'd make sure to announce their approach from a way off first. But still…He'd seduced Lizzie without thought for her sensibilities. He'd put her in danger of massive embarrassment. He'd been selfish, as usual, despite his intention not to be, and to put her feelings first, in all instances.

Fat chance of that, though. He was still waiting for the other shoe to fall in respect of the additional premises for New Again, for the bridal shop, if that was still the plan. He should have consulted Lizzie first, he knew that; but the property had cropped up, meeting the right criteria, and he just hadn't stopped to think. He'd tasked Martin with securing it, and then making the offer to Marie Lanscombe. It'd been too good to miss, and he hadn't wanted to interrupt Lizzie's away-from-it-all holiday with 'complications'. The mood at the villa had been too perfect, too hedonistic. He'd been greedy. Again.

Running his tongue over his lips, he imagined he could still taste the lemon cake, and his cock stirred, stiffening in his underwear.

Oh, how she'd been with him, though, risk of discovery or not. She hadn't hesitated. She'd risen to his selfish demands like a beneficent goddess. Hell, really, she'd been the one to initiate it all. Despite the issues that they were exploring – his past, the changes they were both going through, the compromises, and the promise that lay ahead for them – despite all that, nothing could suppress his wild, beautiful, bold and savvy Lizzie. Nothing could put a damper on her sensual spirit, her generosity, her willingness.

They didn't discuss the 'L' word much, and he still wondered whether he knew what the hell it really meant. But Lizzie showed it in everything she said and everything she did. And because she was brave, she wasn't afraid to come out and say it freely either, goddammit.

But would she still feel the same if she knew about all this?

Messages. Ones that were nothing to do with deals and acquisitions and business.

La Condesa Sanchez de la Villareal rang.

La Condesa Sanchez de la Villareal would like you to ring her.

How many of them were there? Six? No, seven? Bland little notes on telephone message stationery headed with 'Dalethwaite Manor'.

He could only assume she'd wheedled the Dalethwaite number out of his mother, or his sister-in-law, from Ma's big address book of everything, that she kept in her morning room at Montcalm. He wondered what other contact information of his had been noted down by his parent; she was proud of the encyclopaedic nature of her 'people bible', and assiduously gathered every possible detail for everyone she knew.

Clara, I told you in New York that I was with someone now. And I told you it was serious. What is it that's so important that you won't leave me alone, all of sudden? And why ring Dalethwaite rather than my mobile? What point are you trying to make?

Licking his lips again, he sought the elusive taste of lemon, and from his memory he drew the sublime sensation of thrusting into Lizzie's beautiful body as she leaned over the washbasin, grinning like a minx at him in the mirror over the sink.

His love was straightforward, not devious, and only she could help him expunge the dark memories. Only she could make him forget the pain of Clara and her emotional manipulations, and memories that still clung to him, even after all these years.

Closing the bathroom door, Lizzie padded through the little vestibule and back into the bedroom. Her bedroom. Would she ever get used to it? So spacious and comfortable. So beautifully furnished, yet somehow also homely. So tidy!

God, that was the weirdest thing of all. Would she ever get used to such neatness and order, a state that miraculously repaired itself thanks to the efforts of a superb household staff?

By the time she'd gone upstairs, all pink-faced and flurried after cavorting with John, her suitcases had been unpacked, her laundry whisked away and everything that needed hanging was hanging up in the wardrobe. All her personal items were symmetrically arranged on her dressing table, and her toiletries were similarly deployed in her bathroom.

A certain locked, leather-bound case sat innocuously on

a shelf in the wardrobe too. Lizzie grinned, wondering if Mrs Thursgood, or Mary, whichever of them had unpacked for her, knew what it contained. As John had pointed out on Lizzie's first night here, there were some things that even the most broad-minded staff shouldn't have to deal with. Specifically, stashes of condoms, sex toys, various leather items...

I wonder what they think is in it, Mr Smith? Surely they must speculate about what we get up to?

Speaking of getting up to things with John...

Where was he? She'd no doubt he'd come to her, even if they weren't going to sleep together. His sleep 'thing' still stood between them, but they'd resolve it sooner or later, especially now she understood it better. She had to believe that.

And she'd have to resolve her own, most private issue too. Her subversive, niggling jealousy over Clara. She'd have to fess up to it, because John would know something was bothering her. He probably already did know, because he always did in his uncanny way.

Over dinner – eaten surprisingly informally off trays in front of the telly in the sitting room – she'd caught him watching her instead of the cop show on the telly. Waiting for her to raise the issue of the new premises for New Again, no doubt, and for a while it had amused her to say nothing at all, just to tease him. She'd met his gaze, and just given him a challenging little smile...and he'd laughed.

They didn't have to speak to play this particular game.

'It's all right. I'm not going to give you a bollocking,' she'd said over the delicious coffee Mrs Thursgood had served them, before she and her husband had retired to their flat for the evening.

'A bollocking? What would that be for?' John's blue eyes sparkled.

'You know.' As Lizzie put aside her cup, he set his aside too, and drew her close to him on the settee. It was an easy, companionable gesture. So natural, and yet, somehow, she felt tension in him. Was it about the new shop? Or something else? She almost got the feeling he might be seeking solace somehow, but about what, she couldn't decide. It might even be pure imagination.

'Yes, I do know. I did it again, didn't I?' His hand smoothed over her shoulder, the touch sweet, not sexual. His fingertips seemed to say, *Yes, I'll want you again soon, and you'll want me, but for the moment, this is good too. This is what I need.*

'But it was too good an opportunity to let slip by,' he went on. 'I couldn't lose it, then kick myself for allowing you and Marie to miss out.'

Lizzie laid her head on his shoulder, loving the simple feel of his strong sure body. She was an individualist, and a feminist, but having a powerful man to look out for her too didn't compromise that.

'It *was* too good to miss,' she said. It was the honest truth. 'I know I've been critical of your pre-emptive strikes in the past, but there's no use getting my knickers in a twist about this one. It's what I want. I'd probably have asked you to help us anyway, so you've saved me the bother.'

John kissed the side of her face, a quick peck. 'You're a wise girl, Lizzie, but nothing you ask for could ever be a bother.'

She turned to him, and gave him a firm look. 'OK, and thank you. It is the most wonderful thing you've done, and I adore you for it. But this still doesn't mean I don't wish to be consulted in future. You're always at pains to impress on me that we're equals, so you must treat me like one.'

John snagged his plush lower lip between his teeth. For a man of forty-six, he could do a marvellous impression of a naughty, shamefaced boy sometimes.

'I will, my love. I will…And you're not just my equal. You're my better. In every way.'

Did he mean it? She had a feeling he did. His heart certainly did, even if sometimes his actions, and his controlling benevolence, made her feel like a pampered doll.

But there was still that adorably guilty look on his face…over something else?

'What?' she demanded. What else had he done? That expression said it all.

'There might be a car.'

Oh John…

'How do you know I can drive?'

'I made a point of finding out. Apparently you're quite a good driver.'

Lizzie shook her head. 'You're hopeless, you know that, don't you? I should go all dominatrix on you for this. Give you a damn good thrashing and all that.' She reached up and caught his earlobe between her fingertips and gave it a warning squeeze. 'But I'm tired from the journey…and everything…so I'll take a rain check on that.' She tried giving him a stern look, but the wicked glint in his eyes, and the way he quirked his sandy eyebrows at her, made that almost impossible.

'You'll like the car. It's nothing too posh or racy…Just an Audi S3. I thought a hatchback would be most useful to you, for transporting sewing projects and whatever to and fro.' He held her gaze. Goodness, he looked genuinely nervous. Troubled…and, perhaps, not about the car. 'But if you want something different. Well, just say the word.'

'An Audi of that ilk sounds pretty posh to me! But seeing as how my Dad has one…a rather old one, I might add, I'll let you off.' She released his ear, and slid her hand to cradle his cheek. He'd shaved recently and his skin felt deliciously smooth. He smelt amazing too, as she leaned in and kissed his lips. 'And I thank you too, John. You're a very thoughtful man. A car to ferry stuff about in will make life so much easier.' She kissed him again. 'You give me so much. Don't ever believe I'm not grateful, even if I do get a bit shirty with you sometimes.'

'I don't mind shirty,' he said, sliding his hand into her hair, cradling her skull and effortlessly taking control of the kiss. His lips met hers again, assertive yet tender, making it a proper kiss, latent with promise. Despite their coming together earlier, the demon imp of desire stirred again.

As the television played on in the background, and the cops argued some ethical point, and then dismissed it, Lizzie and John kissed on, taking pleasure in the simple act, tasting each other, and embracing. It wasn't sex yet, but Lizzie had no doubt it soon would be.

But then the phone rang, and the slight tension Lizzie had sensed in him, and had believed she'd banished, was suddenly back again.

John broke away from her, frowning.

'Shouldn't we answer that? It might be important?' Lizzie asked him, wanting to gnash her teeth and shout, their beautiful moments snatched away by the damned phone. John's frown turned to a glare at the extension in the sitting room, as it trilled on, and then abruptly fell silent, as if whoever was calling was now satisfied that they'd already knackered everything up.

With a sigh, he rose to his feet. 'Actually, there are a couple of calls I really should make before we turn in.' He bent down and kissed her forehead. 'I'll just slip to the office for a few minutes. Why don't you go to bed, and wait for me, and I'll drop by in a little while to tuck you in, and read you a story.'

His smile had been naughty, and the way he'd slid his hand to her breast and briefly cupped it had been even naughtier, but still she'd sensed his unease.

And now, later, here she was, climbing into bed, and wondering, wondering, wondering about those phone calls. It shouldn't be anything to worry about. John had taken all sorts of calls while they'd been on holiday, even though he'd promised he'd keep business to a minimum. And some of those conversations had taken place at odd times of the day and night, because his business interests spanned the globe. Someone who worked for him, or from whom he was buying something, or to whom he was selling something; well, there was always someone that John might speak to at any time, night or day, in respect of the care and feeding of his empire.

So why did these calls feel different?

Don't be idiotic, Lizzie. It surely wasn't Clara. Why would it be?

Yet, as she switched out the main lights and clicked on the television for some dodgy late-night documentaries on Quest, Lizzie had a horrible spooked feeling. Staring blankly at the technological wonders of a high-speed train she'd probably never ride, she mentally flicked through the Google images she'd found of Clara, like shuffling a deck of evil cards. None of the pictures she'd discovered so far had been high res enough to see John's ex crystal-clearly, but they'd certainly been sufficient to show Lizzie that her 'rival' was a beauty. Elegant, refined…bewitching.

John spun his chair. He didn't want to make the call, but he had to. If he didn't, she'd just keep ringing and ringing until one of these days, Lizzie would pick up the phone instead of him.

Not that I don't think you're a match for her, sweetheart. Because you are. A thousand times over. But Clara can be ruthless in the pursuit of what she wants.

And he had a fairly shrewd idea of what his ex-lover wanted from him now. Even though he sincerely hoped he might be mistaken.

Tapping the desk, he considered trying to reach Tom again, as a sage, brotherly sounding board, but when he punched in the number, as was so often recently, his brother's phone went to voicemail.

Was he with the new man again? John hoped so. And he hoped this man, whoever he might be, was treating his brother right. John wasn't the only Wyngarde Smith sibling who'd had a chequered love life, although he doubted that Tom's was anywhere near as disastrous as his own had been. Or had been up until now.

But trying to reach Tom was just staving off the inevitable. John straightened his chair, facing his desk. Facing the unpleasant task like a grown up instead of a recalcitrant boy.

It would be early evening where she was now. He picked up the phone. Entered the number again. Listened to the ring, willing it to go on and on, with no answer. The number was a mobile one, though, and she'd have the phone with her, anticipating this very call.

His luck ran out.

'Clara Sanchez de la Villareal.'

The sound of that soft, familiar voice made him angry. A great start! She knew the Dalethwaite number, and he'd not concealed it. So why play games and answer as if he might just be anybody?

Why? Because she was Clara, and that was her style, and there'd been a time when her provocations had bewitched him.

'Good evening, Clara. It's John.'

'Jonathan, darling, how wonderful to hear from you. How are you? I was so hoping you'd call this evening.'

Her tone was husky, intimate, as if they'd seen each other only yesterday, as if they'd been lovers the night before. John clenched his fist against the desk, digging his nails into his palm. There'd been a time when he'd craved the sound of this voice, ached for it. Long, agonised wakeful nights in his prison cell, listening for the slightest change in another man's breathing, he'd consoled himself with the thought of Clara whispering sweet nothings to him when they were reunited. Her laughter. Her moans when they'd made love. As the months had passed, without a word from her, that voice had faded, but still he'd hoped. And hoped.

'You've been leaving messages for me. What can I do for you, Clara?' He schooled his own voice to easy friendliness. He wouldn't let her get to him. With his free hand, he scrolled through images on his computer, double-clicked one, and brought up a picture of Lizzie on the terrace at their Provençal villa. She was wearing a polka dot bikini and cats-eye sunglasses, the very image of a 1950s film goddess with her glossy black hair tied back with a vintage Pucci scarf she'd treated herself to from New Again.

'Can't an old friend ring you up for a chat, darling? Just to touch base? There's no need to sound so suspicious, Jonathan.' His faux friendly tone clearly hadn't fooled Clara. He could almost see the pout that he'd once thought so adorable, and it irked him. As did her calling him 'Jonathan', as she'd done in the old days. In New York, he'd specifically told her, more than once, that he always went by 'John' now.

'Forgive me, Clara…It's late here…' Of course, she'd know the precise time. 'And I'm just back from a trip and I'm slightly jet-lagged.' He grimaced at the little lie. 'I'm sorry if I sounded a bit curt.'

There was a pause. Clara was the mistress of keeping a man on tenterhooks. 'Business, darling? You work far too hard, Jonathan. It was wonderful to see you in New York, but you did look weary. Surely you have people you can delegate to?'

'No, it was a holiday, actually. A week or so in the south of France, staying at a villa belonging to some friends. It was a welcome break…I have been working hard.' He flipped through to another photo. This one a selfie, on timer, of Lizzie and himself together, in the evening. Not always comfortable in front of the camera, he looked a bit tense, but Lizzie was doing rabbit ears above his head, and despite the situation he now found himself in, he smiled. Happy days…they'd done at least as much laughing as fucking.

'Ah…France…Sounds divine. I wish I'd known. I could have flown over to keep you company. We could have caught up…had some fun.'

So blatant! Her breath-taking gall sideswiped him. Did

she not remember that she'd dumped him? Not once, but twice? It was his turn to pause, flailing around for his biofeedback…but then abandoning it, and focusing hard on Lizzie's happy grin in the image.

'I wasn't alone, Clara. I'm with someone now. I told you in New York, don't you remember?'

Yes, someone who won't dump me just when I need her most. Someone decent, who'll stand by me, unless I behave like a total shit and end up driving her away.

'Oh…I see…I rather thought that was just one of your casual things, John. I didn't realise it was slightly more long-lived.' She still sounded silky, but he could hear the edge, the sound of vexation.

'She isn't a thing. Her name is Lizzie, and I care a great deal for her, Clara. If you must know, we're living together, here at Dalethwaite. And as far as I'm concerned, it's going to be very long-lived, if she'll put up with me.'

Another pause. 'Well, that's wonderful for you, darling. I'm so glad for you. I'm sure she's utterly charming. Is she someone I know? Who are her people?'

John ground his teeth. He could almost imagine Clara knew all about Lizzie, and was deliberately being dismissive.

'She's perfect, Clara…and she doesn't have "people". She has a family, like a normal person does.' Anger surged like molten metal. The urge to fight and defend. 'She's a beautiful, intelligent, funny, accomplished young woman. And she has a job.' He paused himself now. Two could play at those tactics. He smiled, preparing the killer blow, knowing it would be cruel…but unable to stop himself. 'She's twenty-four…and I love her.'

The resulting pause wasn't calculated. He knew he'd hurt the woman at the end of the line, and there was no pleasure in the fact that it was only a small fraction of the pain she'd inflicted on him. It just felt mean.

'She sounds lovely, Jonathan. I'm so happy you've found someone again. You always did have the best taste in women.' She laughed softly. It sounded sincere. Had he misjudged her? 'Have you introduced her to Mother?' Ah, perhaps not. The delicate jibe was there, albeit understated. Clara would never forgive him for marrying her own mother, and never forgive her mother for marrying him. He suspected that was why she'd taken such relish in dumping him the second time, and why perhaps, now, Clara might take some perverse kind of comfort from the notion that him having a much younger girlfriend might be painful to Caroline.

'No, but I hope to soon. Caroline is in London again, something to do with her art foundation. Perhaps I'll invite her and Ralph to dinner.'

For a moment, he thought about the prospect of introducing Lizzie to his ex-wife. Whatever Clara believed, he knew Caroline would adore Lizzie, although the meeting might still be a bit of an ordeal for his beloved. But Lizzie would rise to it, as she always did. Be charming and inimitable, even if she was shaking inside.

'Oh…I miss London so much! Perhaps I'll fly over soon. Maybe for that dinner party? I'd love to meet your Lizzie.' John snapped back to the moment, frowning. What was she up to? 'I envy women who make careers for themselves, and have skills. I…I always wish I'd done more with my education. Made different choices…'

What was she hinting now? The Clara he'd known had always been delightfully archaic, making no bones of the fact that she was anticipating having a husband to provide for her, the richer and more exalted the better. Even when they'd first been together, she'd teased him over that. Playfully threatening to discard him because he was only the second son of a family whose finances were far from rich-list, despite their blue blood. Twenty-twenty hindsight was a wonderful thing, he thought bitterly. She hadn't been teasing. She'd meant it.

And now, he didn't know what to say to her. He tried to imagine the love he'd once felt for her, and it was thin and pale, like mist. On the screen of his laptop was the image of what love could be, what love should be: a vibrant, sassy, warm-hearted sexy princess of a girl. A woman who had a life, not 'people', and who thrived by her own devices and made the best of things in all situations.

Lost in Lizzie's smile, he didn't hate Clara any more. He felt sorry for her, and just hoped that somehow she could find what he had. In New York, the hints had been as loud as the billboards of Times Square that Clara and her latest husband Ernesto weren't happy, and hadn't been for a long time.

'Yes, perhaps it would be nice to meet up some time. I'm sure you'll love Lizzie.' He didn't know how to end the conversation without being unkind, but he sensed he had to do it. He could almost feel Clara scenting for openings, preparing gambits. That was another thing that might as well have been on a billboard. She was interested. After all the bloody nonsense she'd put him through all those years ago, she wanted him back.

'Well, I mustn't keep you from her. It must be late where you are.' Just as she'd always proved herself a mistress of surprises, Clara sounded brisk, bright, no-nonsense. 'It's been wonderful to speak to you again, Jonathan. And I hope we'll meet again soon. And that we can be friends again, after all these years.'

'Perhaps so,' he said cautiously, not wanting to give false hope. 'Now…as you say, it's late. Goodnight, Clara. Take care of yourself.' His finger hovered, ready to close the connection, but somehow, idiotically, it seemed too harsh to do it.

'You too, darling. Goodnight. I'll see you soon.'

Then, crisp and decisive, she'd gone; and John's anger surged. He wasn't sure who he was angry with, probably himself mostly. Even after all these years, even now he'd found Lizzie, somehow Clara still had the power to wrong-foot him. But whether it was with the seductive skills she'd kept sharply honed since they were last together, he didn't know; or perhaps with the vulnerability and fear he'd heard in her voice, that he could swear was genuine, and not a guise.

Putting down the phone, he turned to his laptop, loving the sweet image there, and his spirits lifted, anticipating the even sweeter reality.

Oh, Lizzie, Lizzie, Lizzie…

He stood up. Determined. The living shade of Clara was fast fading.

Tonight…Tonight he was really going to go for it. He was going to do his best to sleep, really sleep with Lizzie.

4

To Sleep, Perchance to Dream

Lizzie snapped awake. She'd been aware of voices in the room, the television droning on, and the sudden silence shocked her out of her puzzled doze. The light from the bedside lamp made her blink, but she smiled. John was sitting on the edge of the bed, looking down at her.

'Wake up, slumbering princess, your handsome young prince is here.' He reached out and smoothed her hair back from where it had fallen across her face. 'Or, should I say, the ugly old woodcutter, or maybe even the big, bad bear.'

Pushing with her elbows, she sat up. 'Nah…the big, bad, handsome prince, I think. Slightly wicked, but in the prime of his life.'

He leaned forward and kissed her, a hand on her shoulder. His grip was quite hard, not painful, but with an intense, almost desperate quality to it, much like the kiss itself.

What is it, John? What is it? She slid her arms around him, feeling the tension in his muscles, so taut beneath his satin skin. He wore just his favourite blue cotton pyjama bottoms, but even though the northern night was far chillier than the Provençal ones, his skin was hot. Hugging him, she lay back, drawing him down with her.

'So, Prince Charming, are you staying a while?' she asked, when they broke apart, gasping.

'Yes, I think I am,' he said, kissing the corner of her mouth, 'And not just because I can't resist your gorgeous body.' The intensity was in his eyes now, dark and vaguely troubled. She wanted to ask again, this time out loud, what it was, what it was… 'I want to sleep with you, Lizzie, and there's no way to know if that's possible without trying properly, is there?' He kissed her again, his hand sliding down her flank.

She wanted to say, *but we tried at the villa and it didn't really happen*, but she just accepted the kiss. Something had happened in the last half hour, something that bothered him, and now wasn't the time to start raising issues. Now was the time just to be here for him, and inwardly shout 'Yippee!' at the thought of having him beside her.

'Makes sense, Princey Boy, and there's plenty of room.' She slid over a bit in the wide bed, making a larger and more enticing space for him. He followed her over, right over, closing the gap up tight until he was lying hard up against her – with the emphasis on hard. Through the cotton of his pyjama bottoms and of hers, his cock was even hotter than the rest of him, and she moved her hips against it as he kissed her again, probing with his tongue. Sliding her hands down his back, she cupped his buttocks, pressing herself closer.

'We don't have to make love, you know,' he purred against her ear as they came up for air again. 'I mean, it's been a long day, and you were tired, and I've already had more than my quota.'

Lizzie chuckled. 'Well, you might be working on the quota system, but I'm not. And neither is this beast.' She darted a hand to his cock and cradled her fingers around it.

John made an appreciative sound, a sort of growl. 'Well, the beast in question is a greedy sod, and pretty much disconnected from the niceties of considerate behaviour...but he doesn't always have to have his own way, you know.'

'I like the beast. His ways are my ways. And it might help you sleep, you know.'

'Well, I thought that too.' John rocked his hips against her. 'That, and a nip of gin. I thought a shag and a little nightcap might help us both nod off.'

Sure enough, there on the bedside table was the familiar green bottle and two cut-crystal glasses. 'Let's try the most natural means first, shall we? And keep the demon drink for our fallback position,' said Lizzie. Gosh, he really was determined. Whatever the something was that had happened, it had shaken him up and steeled his resolve to normalise their sleeping arrangements.

Pushing her speculations aside, and hiding them right at the back of her mind, in the part normally inaccessible when she was having gorgeous sex with John, she redoubled her efforts, with hands and lips, to encourage him.

Not that the beast needed any encouragement at all. He seemed bigger and harder than ever, against her.

'So, what's it to be? Straight sex or "fancy"? Which do you think will help you sleep the best? I'm easy...'

John laughed. 'You, my dear Lizzie, are both easy and complicated.' He paused to kiss her, fierce and hard. 'A complex and sophisticated conundrum...and easy, oh so easy to adore.'

'But which do you want?'

'Straight sex will do very nicely, beautiful girl. I don't want to get hyped up into some weird mental place with role-play. Not tonight.'

A dark shadow taunted her again. Something was bothering him. But she brushed it aside and took another kiss from him, sliding her hands up and down his back and buttocks and savouring the feel of his warm skin and hard muscles.

'Works for me,' she said, wriggling against him, while at the same time trying to escape from her pyjama bottoms.

'Here, let me.' John flung back the covers, and rolling onto his hip, started stripping off her garment. A second later it went flying across the room, then, with no further ado, he slid a hand between her thighs.

Lizzie arched. She was ready. She was always ready.

'Good grief, woman, you're so wet. So ready...'

'John, you look like an angel, you're as fit as a butcher's dog, and you've got a million squillion quid, what's not to get wet about?' She growled and gasped when he rubbed her.

'And here I was thinking I'd have to coax and seduce you, and you seem to be ready for me to climb on top straight away!'

'I thought you'd never ask!'

His eyes were like blue fire in the lamplight, and his smile provocative. She'd thought he was going to twist around and get a condom out of the beside drawer, but instead, he went on stroking her, redoubling his efforts, sliding his fingers around in her moisture and bringing it to her clit like a gift, making it silky.

'John, I want you,' she groaned, squirming her bottom

around against the mattress, unable to keep still. He didn't miss a beat, even though she was all over the place.

'And I want you to come first.' He stifled further protest with his mouth on hers, his tongue swirling around her tongue as his fingers swirled around her clitoris.

Pleasure gathered, swift and sweet. She grabbed at him, gripping his shoulders, her body stiffening and arching as he worked her. Whimpering against his mouth, she dug her nails in hard as the crisis enveloped her, her sex pulsing and fluttering even while he still caressed her.

She rose to him. One orgasm became two, morphing into each other. As she lay gasping, still all a-spasm, he turned from her in a quick decisive move, pushed open the drawer and brought out the familiar packet. He shook them all over the bed, grabbed one, and in a couple of moments, he was wrapped in latex, ready.

'Lizzie,' he whispered, kissing her face, lips printing tenderness across her cheeks, her brow, even while he was positioning himself and pushing into her.

Oh God, yes, she started coming again, harder than ever even as he worked his way in and began to thrust, his body wild, hungry, almost desperate. Again she clung to him, vaguely aware of the fact that she was tattooing him with more nail marks. Good job she kept them short, for sewing, or he'd have been scarred for life!

Mind whirling with ecstasy, she surrendered to pleasure and his body, making no effort, just receiving, enjoying, loving. With John, she never had to try or struggle. She came easily, repeatedly, copiously. He was her match, her perfect match, just right for her.

And in the midst of her bliss, she felt his climax too. The pounding of his hips, his hoarse cries, the discrete pulse of his semen inside her, and the condom. She moaned, coming again, lost in him completely.

'So, are you going to have a gin, or what?'

'I think I'll give it a miss. Hopefully the "what" we just had will suffice.'

Lizzie grinned at John as she rearranged the covers over them, after she'd retrieved her pyjama bottoms and they'd sorted themselves out in the usual little post-sex dance of nipping to the bathroom, disposing of condoms, and what have you.

'Well, it's made me sleepy…in the nicest possible way.' She turned on her side, looking at him as he lay on his back, hands settled across his middle, staring at the ceiling. 'How are we going to do this? Do you want to snuggle or something? I've never really done the sleeping in one another's arms thing. I don't think it works, really. It's just a load of romantic BS from books and films.'

John turned to her, eyes amused. 'Really? I thought all girls wanted to sleep in the arms of their lovers. Accepted practice and all that.'

'Great in theory, but not at all practical,' Lizzie announced, wanting to be firm on the point. She had a feeling that not crowding John would give him a better chance of sleeping. 'One party or the other always ends up with a crick in their neck or a dead arm, or both. It's not really comfortable. Especially if the man has magnificent, rock-hard pecs like you. A properly designed pillow is much better for the spine.'

'What an incredibly sensible woman you are, Lizzie.'

'Sorry I'm not reacting like love's young dream, but when-ever I've tried it in the past I've ended up with a nadgered neck.' She reached out to touch him. 'And I'd rather stay sound in wind and limb, and be fit for sex, as and when.'

'Don't worry, love, you're preaching to the choir here. I totally agree.' He reached for her hand. 'Just lying next to you is sweetness in itself. Far better than tangling up with each other like a pair of octopi with separation anxiety.'

Lizzie giggled. But she wondered whom he might have tangled with in the past, before prison had changed his sleeping habits irrevocably.

I bet you used to snuggle all the time with Clara.

She kept that thought to herself, though. She had a feeling that thinking about his ex-love wouldn't be in the least bit soporific, so better not to go there. And she didn't want to think about the other woman either.

'Shall we just be quiet, then, and see what happens?'

John turned his head on the pillow. In the semi-darkness his smile was still dazzling. Especially when he leant over quickly, and kissed her forehead. 'Yes, let's do that. Sounds like a plan to me.'

'Nighty-night, then.'

'Goodnight, Lizzie.'

Not quite closing her eyes, she watched him covertly from beneath her eyelashes, wondering if he'd be able to detect that he was being observed with his unnerving, sometimes downright spooky perception.

But this time, it seemed not. His chest lifted as he drew in a deep breath, almost like a diver preparing to submerge, and then settled back down again. His eyes were closed, and his beautiful and ridiculously dark eyelashes cast shadows on his cheekbones. In repose, his sculpted mouth was a thing of beauty.

Looks like I'm the one who isn't going to be able to sleep.

It's like putting a great work of art in the bed next to me, and expecting me not to slavishly admire it.

For a while she just lay there, watching him. He was really trying, but she knew he wasn't sleeping.

'No, I'm not asleep yet,' he said suddenly, eyes still closed, but grinning.

'Didn't think you were, somehow.'

'Don't worry, love. Forget about me. Just relax.' A hand slid across, caught hers and gave it a squeeze. Then, he began to stroke it, slowly, hypnotically, just in the way he might have stroked Alice the cat if she hadn't been out in the grounds somewhere, ranging about, pursuing various furry prey.

The slow rhythm of his fingers was so delicious, as wonderful in its own way as when he stroked her when they were making love. Lizzie's eyelids fluttered, suddenly heavy as lead, and she wondered if he was actually hypnotising her. Perhaps using techniques he'd learnt himself during his therapy, when he'd pursued a 'normal' sleep with the help of a psychotherapist.

Well, it mightn't have worked for you, gorgeous man, but I've a feeling it's going to work for me...

Lizzie's eyes snapped open again. Déjà vu.

Yes, she'd been asleep. John's gentle stroking of her hand had seen to that. But what about him? His hand had slid from hers, so no more stroking. Did that mean the miracle had occurred and he'd fallen asleep too? She was desperate to know, but she didn't dare move.

He had slept with her before. Once, at St Patrick's Road, that time after Brent's suicide attempt. John had definitely nodded off in her bed then, but they'd both been exhausted from a long, eventful night that had run through a complicated spectrum of kinky pleasure at a fetish party right to the pits of desperate fear and anxiety, worrying about Brent.

But now things were different. There were still areas of anxiety – for both of them, she suspected. Nothing quite so acute, though, just their 'couple' stuff.

Turning her head on the pillow, millimetre by millimetre, she stole a glance at him, straining to see him out of the corner of her eye.

Bloody hell, you are asleep, aren't you?

Lizzie knew from their role-playing games that John was a brilliant actor, but something about the relaxed and gentle quality of his facial expression was different. Impossible to fake. He looked even more like a worldly-wise angel than ever, all tension drained away in repose.

Lizzie hardly dared breathe. Even though she wanted to smother his face in kisses, and put her hands on him. It wasn't a sexual thing, just an expression of her wonder and amazement at being with her perfect man.

I love you; you know that, don't you? Even if it's not for ever for us, it's for ever for me. There'll never be anybody else.

John might have been freed from tension by sleep, but she was far from it. She had to keep still. She mustn't do anything to disturb her slumbering prince.

A sobering thought struck her. Would it always have to be like this? Lizzie, on tenterhooks in bed, for fear of waking him up and fracturing his fragile ability to sleep.

Bloody hell…

'You can move, you know. And I'd recommend breathing from time to time too.'

'Oh, you beast! You're not asleep! I thought we'd nailed

it, but you're faking it, after all!'

John's eyes flew open and he rolled onto his side, facing her. Reaching out, he cradled her cheek and stroked it with his thumb.

'Au contraire, sweetheart, I have been asleep. Maybe an hour or two. I checked the clock.' He leant over and kissed her lips gently. 'So, we've definitely made progress.'

'But you woke up again.' She reached for his hand, and wove her fingers with his.

'Yes...I hate to say this, but I think I subconsciously detected your tension.'

'Oh, so it's my fault?' she said, keeping her voice light. Was he blaming her? Gently, tactfully, but still, it sounded that way. He was a man, after all, and even the most adorable ones, like him, had a bred-in-the-bone tendency to believe they could never be in the wrong. 'Bollocks, I should have had some gin, shouldn't I? And then I might have been dead to the world.'

He squeezed her fingers again, and quirked his eyebrows at her in the dim light that filtered through the voile curtains from a high moon. 'I never said it was your fault, Lizzie love. I never would...It's my issue. My thing. My fault.' He paused, and gave her a long, almost wistful look. 'We'll get there, darling. It'll happen. I know it will. And even when I'm not fully asleep, it's still restful lying here next to you.'

'I hope so. I was trying my best not to move about or...um...remind you of anything, you know?'

John gave a soft laugh. 'Don't worry, love, you don't remind me in the least of Jack! There's no way I could ever mistake you for him.'

'I should hope not!'

They lay for a few moments in silence. Could they recapture what they'd had? Both of them asleep at once? Lizzie had an ominous feeling that might be it for tonight. They'd had an oddly prickly little moment there and she felt unsettled. John seemed relaxed, but his eyes were open and he was looking up at the ceiling. Or whatever he was seeing with his mind's eye.

'What are you thinking about?'

Gah, why had she asked that? Why couldn't she leave him in peace, or at least not ask needy girlfriend questions?

He didn't turn her way, but he took her hand and laid it across his midriff, resting his over it companionably.

'About someone else I once tried to sleep with.'

Yikes, now she'd done it. Who was that person? Some flame of his that'd come after his prison sentence, obviously.

Oh God, was it Clara? When they'd had their brief reunion?

'And before you jump to any conclusions, it wasn't Clara.' He gave her a little sideways smile in the darkness, and she'd never been more glad to see it. 'During the time we got back together, she thought my little problem was quaint and rather tedious. She always did like to do the "sleeping in each other's arms" thing, whether the partner concerned was comfortable or not. Probably just another reason why she fucked off and left me.'

Was there bitterness in his voice? If there was, it was well hidden. Lizzie felt again the urge to smash in the face of this insufferable cow who'd hurt and betrayed her man!

'So who was it?' Probably somebody else to be jealous of, but anything was preferable to thoughts of the 'C' word again.

'It was Benjamin.'

'You what?'

A man? After the prison experience?

'Yes, my dear old crush from school, bless his heart.' There was fondness in his voice, but this time, Lizzie couldn't resent it. She knew Benjamin had been good to John, back when they'd enjoyed their passionate fling, and she had a feeling it might have been the same later.

'But I thought…after prison and Jack and all that, well…that you might not have been into men any more.' After the trauma, it only seemed logical.

John brought her hand to his lips and kissed it. 'At the time, I thought that too. But I was glad of Ben as a friend back then. He'd heard about my various falls from grace…prison, my glorious army career, the big bust-up with my father…and he reached out to me. He knew the score with Clara, and because he was a decent guy, who still cared for me in his own way, he made a kind gesture.'

'He sounds nice.'

'He was nice. He still is.'

'But…how did it get to sex?' Sensitive as it was, she suddenly had to know.

'We talked a lot. He knew I needed it and he was a good listener. Because we'd been lovers, I was able to tell him about Jack…and my confused feelings.' His voice sounded haunted. He was reliving those feelings. Lizzie returned his gesture, bringing his fingers to her lips, now, for a reassuring kiss.

'We talked long into the night, on the gin, and I admitted that I wasn't sure whether I'd ever want to have sex again…with a man or a woman. Because we were both tipsy, Ben offered his services, as therapy, and I accepted.'

Lizzie said nothing, not wanting to fracture the delicate

moment, or balk John in his narrative. She hardly dared breathe again, but she let it out in a gasp when she saw that John was smiling.

'And it was good. Really good,' he went on, voice warm as if reliving the sense of relief he must have felt. 'Ben was gentle when I needed him to be, and, well, enthusiastic when I needed that. We were only together for a shortish while. We messed around, played a bit, even fucked a few times…One day we even did a bit of BDSM, more for a laugh than anything. I'd never really thought much about it before then, but that was when I discovered I had a taste for it…and Ben liked it too.'

'Good for Ben! He's done me a service. All my little forays into that area were sadly disappointing until you put me right!'

John laughed, and nibbled her fingertips. 'Yes indeed. That all worked out very nicely, didn't it?'

'Absolutely. But what happened to you and Ben? If you were getting on well? Apart from not being able to sleep together, that is? I guess he was sympathetic?'

'He was. He never tried to force the issue. He said I shouldn't worry, that things would right themselves eventually.' John smiled at her, and Lizzie's heart sang. They would right themselves. She knew they would. They were already partway there. 'But…I sensed there was something else going on with him, and he admitted there was someone else he was drawn to, where he'd been working. A woman. He hadn't asked her out or anything yet. Hadn't even intimated he was interested. But he did like her, and he wanted to be honest with me, first, before he made a move.'

Lizzie bit her lip. It was so bittersweet. John and Ben sounded as if they'd been a wonderful couple, but if they'd stayed together, there might never have been a 'John and Lizzie'. 'Were you upset?'

'No. I was happy for him. I knew what we had was only temporary, just a moment in time, even if it was great. I was glad he'd found someone he might have a future with, and, as luck would have it, it wasn't long after then that I met Caroline again.' There was an odd note in his voice, perhaps a lingering wistfulness, a curiosity, him wondering what a quite different life might have been like. 'And I've always known that, at base, I'm heterosexual more than bisexual. Ben and I both were, and I valued him as a friend most of all.'

'Sounds like he was certainly that. Do you know what happened, with the woman he met at work?'

John beamed. 'Yes, I do. They ended up getting married, and they're still married. Blissfully so. Nobody deserves a "happily ever after" more than Ben. I was best man at his wedding. He'd told her about me, but she's a broadminded lass and it wasn't…isn't…a big deal to her.'

Happily ever after…will we have that? Will we ever get as far as marriage, or has John sworn off it now?

She hardly dared contemplate that can of worms. In fact, those cans…

John's eyes narrowed a little, as if he'd read her thought. He drew her close and gave her a hug. 'And now I've got my own broadminded lass too. Everyone's a winner. Ben and Jessica live in Scotland, but one of these days, you and I will have to visit them. They have a pretty place, by a loch. I think you'd like it, and they'll love you!'

'If you say so.'

'I know so.'

He wanted her to meet people in his world. In the cooler

light of day, she could rationalise this. She was just as good as anybody. She could hold her own. But in the dead of night, doubts circled.

'Lizzie, don't worry. I want to show you off to people. You're my jewel, my star. I want to bask in their envy when they see me with you.' He kissed her brow, her temple, her hair. 'And anybody who doesn't adore you, or "get" you, just isn't worth my time of day.'

It blew her away when he said things like that, but still, her nerves frazzled over it.

'I don't know...'

'Look, let's not think about that now. I've got something that'll take your mind off any anxieties about future socialising.'

Holding her tight, he rolled his hips against her.

Again? Oh, you insatiable devil!

John laughed again. 'Yeah, I know it's a bit of an imposition to expect you to accommodate my horny excesses in the small hours of the morning, but if we go at it spoon style, you don't have to do any work. It'll just be me, in your exquisite pussy, while I play with your clit and make you come.'

'Tempting.'

Who was she kidding?

'But not irresistible, then?' Grabbing her, he rolled onto his back, so she was half lying across his erection. Hot as a brand through his pyjamas, it almost had a life of its own, lifting and pushing against her. As he held her with his hands at the small of her back, she writhed against him, making him groan.

'Actually...yes,' she gasped, twisting her wrist to slide her hand between them, and grip him. 'It is irresistible.

You're not the only one that's subject to horny excess, you know.'

'Ah ha! I knew you'd succumb,' he cried, gripping her by the waist, using the power in his strong wrists and forearms to work her against him. 'So, what's it to be, horny miss? On top? Underneath? Or spoons? Or maybe some devious new variation from your fertile mind?'

'Oh, spoons, I think…I really fancy spoons.' Slithering off him, she turned away, and massaged her bottom against the long, muscular line of his thigh. Her pyjama bottom bunched as she moved to and fro, slipping down.

'Minx! You know how I love the crease of your bottom…I'm almost tempted to…'

'Think again, buster,' said Lizzie quickly, but half laughing also. 'Much as I enjoy that, it's not on the menu without at least a little prior warning.'

John laughed too, his voice husky against the back of her neck as he swept aside her hair to kiss skin. 'We must check our organisers tomorrow. So I can make an appointment to have your beautiful arse soon.'

'Don't mock. You know what I mean.'

'I do, my sweet darling, and you're right.' He nuzzled her shoulder as he rubbed his erection along the cleft of her bottom, 'Now, stay right where you are while I fish in the drawer for a condom.'

'No need. I slipped a couple under the pillow. Just in case.' Well, if he hadn't been able to sleep, they had to have something else to do.

'Naughty girl. Were you counting on my not being able to sleep?'

How easily he read her.

'Just thinking ahead to the possibility.'

As John slid a hand beneath the pillow for a condom, Lizzie hitched and hutched and shimmied and wiggled to get out of her pyjama bottoms. The sheets were tangled around them, though, and while she was still struggling, one leg in and one leg out, the solid presence of John's cock butting against the underside of her bottom told her unequivocally that he was ready.

'Leave it,' he commanded as she grappled with her pyjamas. 'I can get to you quite nicely.' He grabbed her hip, pressing her against him, his cock probing. The latex-clad head jostled her labia, and as she tilted her pelvis, he found her entrance. She felt him reach down to position himself better. 'Lift your leg, baby…Let me in…'

Breathing heavily, she adjusted her position. The angle was better then, and John began to push. Lizzie relaxed, opening herself to his cock, welcoming him in as he gripped her by the hip again to ease the way.

In, in, in…Ah yes, home!

Now it was John's turn to shimmy and work with his hips, swirling for maximum penetration.

'Good girl…Good girl…Oh God, that's good,' he murmured, holding her round the waist so he could control both their positions and fit them together even closer. 'Mm…now, doesn't that feel nice? I'm right in you now.'

Nice? Nice? It was heavenly. He was deep, pressing on all sorts of sneaky little nerve endings as he imposed his shape on hers, creating a snug space for himself inside her body. And it became even nicer when, satisfied with his depth, he reached around her belly and cupped her sex from the front. One long, clever finger wiggled its way through her bush, probed between her sex lips and settled squarely on her clit.

'Oh…oh God,' she cried at the sharp-sweet quality of the pleasure. Captivated by their joshing and by-play, she hadn't realised quite how aroused and agonisingly needy she'd become. One touch of John's finger at her centre and she was right back on the precipice of coming again.

'It is nice, isn't it?' The finger circled, but not too far, staying on point.

Lizzie made a strangled sound, starting to thrash and work herself. Just a little more, a little more…

'Answer me. Tell me if that's good.' His voice was dark, deep, thrillingly husky. In this most vanilla of positions he was still her all-powerful dominant.

'Yes…Yes…It's good. It's so good.' She moaned, long and brokenly, when the pressure on her clit suddenly increased, the rub firmer, the pattern of circling more complicated. 'Oh! Oh hell…John!'

She came, her body clenching and gripping him, her clitoris leaping in a pulsing dance beneath his fingertip. Arching and rocking, she rode the pleasure while John's grip was unyielding, his free hand sliding between her hip and the mattress, holding her in place, keeping her steady.

'Stay still, beautiful girl.'

It was impossible. She was still coming, her body filled with wild energy. She tried, though, half failing, half obeying, shrieking when he assaulted her clit anew with clever, wicked and loving manipulation.

Tears of bliss dripped from her eyes, running sideways onto the pillow. She clasped one hand between her legs, over his, and with the other grabbed at his thigh, holding on tight, fingers digging into the firm, flexing muscles.

Holding her, he pushed in further, seeming to reach places that were impossible, almost part of her soul.

The crisis went on, everything dynamic. Lizzie laughed through the pleasure, mocking everything she'd read, and perceived, about spoons being a gentle and passive position. This was as wild, somehow, as anything they'd done, and yet in reality they were hardly moving. The tiniest action, and reaction, was enormous in sensation.

'Yes! Yes!' John shoved harder. Lizzie seemed to float, her sex and belly golden with exquisite sensation while in her mind, coloured lights seemed to drift up and up, like slow motion fireworks.

'Yes…Yes…' she sighed, smiling, and almost dreaming as she felt him pulse inside her, deep to the hilt at the very limit of his in-stroke.

For a while, afterwards, they lay together still joined, almost breathing in unison. Normality returned, though, as it always did. Lovely…but real.

'I'm lying on your arm, aren't I? Has it gone dead?' Lizzie shifted position, feeling John withdraw, his cock sliding out of her body as he wiggled his arm from under her. She shuffled away a little way, her pyjama bottoms still caught around one leg.

'Just a bit.' He sat up, giving the limb in question a little shake. 'Don't worry; it's waking up again now.' He flexed his fingers. 'See, no harm done.'

Lizzie reached for his hand, drew it to her lips, and kissed it, nibbling the fingertips. 'Yep, seems OK to me.'

Sleepily – well Lizzie, at least – they sorted themselves out again, and lay back down again, side by side. She studied her lover in the darkness. He seemed calm and relaxed, but she had a strong feeling he might not sleep again. Even though she was fighting to keep her eyes open, and already half drifting off, replete, sated.

'Sleep, sweetheart…Don't worry about me.'

His voice sounded so soft and fond. The words wound around her like a protective cocoon, guarding her from all worries and fears. There was plenty they had to face together, and it might not all be easily dealt with. But they were together. That was what mattered.

They were together.

5

Touching Various Bases

John was gone when Lizzie woke up again.

Sitting up sharply, she glanced around the room, then chided herself.

Don't be an idiot; he won't be hiding behind the chair or in the wardrobe. He'll have gone to his own room, long since. You're alone.

Expecting a pang of disappointment, she was surprised. Yes, it would have been super romantic and like a movie to wake up in bed beside him, but she had nothing to feel neglected over. He'd made a real effort to sleep with her last night, and they had even managed to doze together for a while. This wasn't something they could set to rights in one night, and it might be a long time before they achieved it, if they ever did.

But they'd made progress, and John's delicious lovemaking in the night had more than offset any childish whim of hers for everything to be perfect, utterly perfect, all at once.

Fishing beneath the pillow, she located a couple more of the condoms she'd tucked away there, and popped them back in the drawer. Goodness, how many performances had she been expecting? John had the sexual vigour and recuperative powers of a man half his age, but even he was only human, after all.

A soft rap at the door made her grab for her light robe, draped across the bottom of the bed.

'Come in,' she called out, not sure whether it would be John or Mrs Thursgood, or even Mary or one of the other day girls. A quick glance at the clock said it was probably early for the latter, though.

Mrs Thursgood entered with a tray.

'Good morning, Miss Aitchison. Looks like a lovely day today.' She strode over with the tray, then flipped down its little legs and set it on the bed.

Ah, tea. Lovely. And a couple of newspapers, *The Times* and the local weekly rag, as well as a lovely rosebud in a little crystal vase.

'Wow, thanks. This is great!' Before Lizzie could reach for the teapot, Mrs Thursgood was preparing her a cup, just how she liked it. She'd been well briefed by John. 'Thanks for the rosebud. It's very pretty.'

'Oh, that was Mr Smith. He picked it himself for your tray. He's in his office, working already, the silly man.' Mrs T tut-tutted. 'But he says, when you're ready for breakfast, he'll either join you in the little dining room or up here, whichever you prefer.'

Lizzie took a sip of tea. Perfect! 'Oh, dining room, I think, if it's no extra trouble to you. Just some cereal and toast for me, as usual, please. Um…thanks.'

It was still getting some taking used to, this having staff around the place, doing things for her. But luckily the Thursgoods weren't stand-on-ceremony types and they were so nice and discreet that it was gradually becoming more natural to have them around.

A short while later, Lizzie wandered into the small dining room, a casual little breakfast space adjacent to the kitchen. It had old-style French doors that opened on to the garden, and it wasn't nearly as posh and intimidating as the formal dining room, where Lizzie presumed that at some unknown, dreaded date in the future they would entertain.

John rose to his feet as she entered, his golden smile lighting up the room.

'Sleep well, love?' He pulled out her chair for her.

'Yes…eventually. But more to the point, did you sleep again?'

'A bit, yes.' He squeezed her shoulder and bent down to kiss her cheek. Just like a proper, long-standing couple, she thought. 'Thanks to you,' he whispered in her ear, his voice lowered and more intimate in case Mrs Thursgood were to appear any second with coffee and toast.

Soon they were eating and chatting. Comparing notes on articles in the newspapers, mapping out tasks they needed to fulfil now they were home.

'I'm planning to go into JS North for a few hours,' said John. 'Will you be all right on your own?'

Ah, typical man. Assuming that not only the whole world, but specifically that of his woman, revolved around him. Lizzie hid a grin. His confidence and self-assurance were so masculine, and even though he was the most special man in the world to her, he could be a cliché just like any other male.

'Oh, don't worry about me. I thought I might call in and see Marie for an hour or two, and go over what's occurred in my absence. Including the obvious, of course.' She gave him an old-fashioned look, referencing his hand in securing the new premises. 'Then perhaps I'll swing by St Patrick's Road and touch base with Shelley and Brent, if they're around. Maybe have a bit of lunch with them, unless you've got plans?'

Agh, we are just like a married couple.

'Sounds like a good idea, sweetheart. I don't want you to lose touch with your friends.' He smiled, but there was seriousness in his eyes. 'I don't want you to miss anything in your life that you're used to. I want us living together to, well, add more to your life, not take things away.' His little shrug was so boyish, so adorable that she suddenly wanted to leap over the table and ravish him. He looked as edible as the home-made muesli and the country loaf toast they were enjoying, in his navy blue T-shirt and well-worn jeans that fit like the proverbial glove.

'I know, and I thank you for that, John,' she answered with her own seriousness, while trying to squish her ever-present lust for him.

The way his eyes twinkled seemed to suggest he was dealing with the same kind of problems.

'And at least now I can tootle about all over the borough in my swish new Audi!'

'Indeed!' John grinned, reaching for his coffee cup. 'But take the thing for a spin up and down the drive a bit, first, to get the feel of it. When was the last time you actually drove?'

He was right. She hadn't been behind the wheel in a while.

'I shared the driving with Brent and Shelley last year, when we all went to a friend's wedding in Scotland. Brent does have a car, but it's a bit of an old banger, and we've tended to use public transport most of the time lately. Running expenses and all that.' She grinned at him. 'Mind you, now that Brent and Shelley have got such a bountiful new landlord, he can probably afford to put it back on the road.'

'This landlord of theirs must be a true humanitarian. A blessing to society,' said John airily before sipping his coffee in all innocence. 'But I meant what I said, about the test drive. I know I'm an old worrier, but I'd feel much happier if you try out the vehicle first.'

'Right you are, boss,' said Lizzie, winking at him.

A while later, after they'd zipped up and down the drive a couple of times, and taken a spin along the lane, around the nearest roundabout and back to Dalethwaite again, John seemed satisfied with Lizzie's road-craft. In fact, quite impressed.

'Is there anything you don't excel at, Miss Aitchison?' he remarked fondly, unclipping his seatbelt, beside her.

'Not a lot!' Lizzie grinned, feeling pleased with herself. The S3 was a dream to drive. It handled beautifully, was perfectly responsive, and was a miracle of ergonomic driving design. She hadn't actually driven all that many different vehicles, but it made Brent's old Vauxhall seem like a right old rattletrap, and her father's own, older Audi positively antediluvian.

'Even so, take care, love. And check in with me from time to time, eh?' John leant across and laid his fingers against the side of her face. 'It's not that I want to lay down the law to you or keep you wrapped in cotton wool or anything. It's just that you're incredibly precious to me, Lizzie. I couldn't bear it if anything were to happen to you.'

Lizzie gulped, then bobbed forward and took a kiss from

his lips, a long, intent kiss. He was real and warm and alive beside her, and yet, even now, sometimes he seemed like a dream. Especially at moments like these.

'I will, John. I'll take care and I'll drop you a text or two.'

His eyes blazed, and cupping her face, he kissed her back with an almost desperate ferocity. Trapped by her seatbelt, his mouth and his hand, Lizzie shuddered with pleasure, parting her lips to admit his bold tongue.

'Jesus, woman, now I've got a hard-on again!' cried John, laughing as they broke apart. 'I'll have to do a swift bit of biofeedback to get myself back in order again. Either that or make a dive for the downstairs cloakroom and take myself in hand. You really are the most arousing creature, you minx. I swear you gave me tongue then just to get me stiff.'

'I did not!' It might have been a lie, though, albeit subconsciously.

'That's as maybe.' John's expression grew wolfish and twinkling. 'How about a quick blowjob instead? To deal with my little difficulty.' He nodded towards his crotch.

Oh, lordy, what a temptation. Lizzie was a hair away from unclipping her seatbelt, inclining over him and prising out that beloved monster to do the deed.

But only a moment ago, she'd glanced towards the house. Windows were open to air various rooms, and she'd no doubt that Mrs Thursgood and possibly Mary, too, were busy with dusters and polish. But not so busy that they couldn't glance outside and catch sight of the master of the house being given head!

'I know…I know…' He reached for her hand and squeezed it. 'I wouldn't embarrass you, my darling. I was a wicked pig in the orangery yesterday. I'll not put you at risk of compromise again.' He kissed her fingers gently, then furled them around the wheel. 'Now, go on, check in with your friends, and just try to ignore the fact that you live with a horny old goat for a few hours.' Popping open the door, he stepped out, walked around to the passenger window, and when she wound it down, he leaned in to give her one more kiss.

Lizzie fired the ignition, and just before John stepped back to let her pull away, she said, 'Don't worry, Mr Goat, I'll give you that blowjob tonight. Now make with the biofeedback or you'll give Mrs Thursgood and Mary a fit of the vapours.'

With that, she was on her way, watching John laughing in the rear-view mirror as she went.

The coffee in the workroom at New Again wasn't as delicious as that at Dalethwaite Manor, but Lizzie still enjoyed it while she and Marie chatted and caught up. As she'd suspected, her friend had quickly figured out how the new premises had fallen so easily into their laps.

'It was the luckiest day of my life when you walked in asking for sewing work, Lizzie,' Marie said, a happy grin on her face. 'Not only did I get the services of a first-rate seamstress, I also got one hell of a fairy godfather into the bargain!'

Lizzie took a sip of her coffee, not quite sure what to say. It felt weird, still, when people expressed their gratitude to her for John's generosity. Much as she loved to help anyone out, he was the giver.

'He's a very generous man, Marie. He…well, he just doesn't think twice. If it's something that'll make my life easier, or even make the lives of people I know easier, it's a case of money no object.' She reached for her coffee and swigged down a sip. 'It's wonderful, but it's a bit terrifying too. The only thing I have to give in return is myself.' She blushed furiously, realising what she'd said, and put her coffee cup down with a rattle.

Marie laughed, and Lizzie joined her.

'You're a sweetie, Lizzie, and a smart girl too. I'm not surprised he adores you. And I feel very lucky that he's a generous guy with pots of money. If I didn't love my Eddie to pieces, I'd be putting my name forward for John's little black book, just in case you two ever split up.'

Lizzie shivered.

'Not that you will! Not that you will!' added Marie quickly. 'From what I can see…Well…I wouldn't be at all surprised if you don't accidentally become one of your own bridal clients before long.'

'Oh…I don't think so. I'm not sure if he ever wants to get married again. And even if he did, it's…well, it's very complicated.' She sighed, feeling the weight of titles and expectations suddenly bearing down on her. One didn't just marry 'John Smith'. The groom in question was Lord Jonathan Llewellyn Wyngarde Smith, second son of the Marquess of Welbeck, and on his broad shoulders and lusty loins rested the last hope of continuing the family line. Not to mention the eventual stewardship of a famous stately home.

'How complicated? He isn't married already, is he?'

Lizzie had never really told Marie the whole story before, beyond the fact that John was unbelievably wealthy, but now she revealed a little more. Her friend's eyes popped wide at the mention of Montcalm and the title and the somewhat tortuous relationship John had with his family, especially his father.

'Golly, I never realised he was aristocratic too,' said the older woman, 'although it doesn't surprise me. He has that bearing, you know? Like a prince…the lord of all he surveys…well, quite literally, I suppose.'

'He's not a snob! He doesn't act in the slightest bit posh,' said Lizzie, defending him.

'Oh no, he's lovely, but he definitely has a very classy air about him.' Marie grinned. 'Look, if you do get married, please tell me you won't give up work straight away, and that you'll hang out here with us plebs for a while, eh? Can you imagine the cachet that having a bona fide "lady" working in the shop will give us? And exclusively designing for us. The Kissley Magna Mafia will be wetting themselves to give us more business, I tell you! The sky's the limit!'

'Let's not get ahead of ourselves, shall we?'

Lizzie had been dancing around the implications of being involved with John in the longer term. Pretending they didn't exist. Because they scared her. She loved him, but marrying John and becoming his bride meant a different life altogether, in the future. His older brother would be the Marquess before him, but George and his wife, much as they loved their daughter Helen, hadn't been able to produce a son and heir for the title. Which meant that at some time in the future John would accede to the title…and whoever was married to him would eventually become the Marchioness.

Bloody hell! I love you, John Smith, I really do. But I can't be a marchioness, I just can't! It's…mad!

Making a concerted effort to shove that particular piece of insanity into a securely locked mental box, Lizzie smartly changed the subject. It wasn't difficult, because there was masses of stuff to discuss with Marie about the shop, their new projects, and the rather daunting list of appointments for alteration fittings that had accrued during Lizzie's holiday. There were several new bridal enquiries that had come in to New Again while she'd been away too. Marie hadn't even advertised; word of mouth alone was working like a charm.

From being one of the laziest women in the universe, I'm going to have to turn myself into at least as much of a workaholic as you are, John! It'll be a bloody sight easier than trying to become a toff, though.

For all it meant lots of hard work, Lizzie relished the thought of being busy and challenged. At last, she had a solid purpose and direction in her life, something that had once been lacking. She might be unsure of some aspects of her future, but in the moment, she was Elizabeth Aitchison, with a viable career and real self-belief in it. Would this have happened without John? Had he directed her towards this new potential? Or might she still have got there on her own? Either/or, she suspected, but John had probably speeded up the process, and that was just another reason to love him.

'We're going to need more staff, too, when we expand,' pointed out Marie, as they considered the way ahead, with two shops. 'At the very least, we should have a couple, probably more, because at this rate you're going to need help with all the sewing. We need to look in trade journals…see who's looking for work, and who's good! Ideally we need a couple more Lizzie Aitchisons…' She grinned and shrugged. 'But I think you're a one-off, kid. For the shop, though, I have a cousin who's looking to get back to work, and I think she might do well. She's a sensible lass and always looks beautifully put together.'

Lizzie had an idea too. 'There's my house-mate...well, ex-house-mate, Shelley. She's bored to death with temping and she'd love something with more job satisfaction. Shall I sound her out? She's smart and clever, and good with people, and she loves fashion, so she'd be great for the shop.' There was someone else too... 'One of the women that works part time at Dalethwaite does quite a bit of sewing. She's good, too. I'll have a word.' One day she and Mary had chatted for ages about sewing, as Mary made a lot of clothes for her family, and Lizzie had offered her use of the sewing room and its equipment at Dalethwaite, if she ever needed a bit of space to work.

Lizzie was glad that traffic was unexpectedly light as she drove away from New Again. Her head was buzzing. Full of thoughts and hopes and plans...and concerns. Marie's talk of marriage, and what would come with it, had shaken her.

Don't scare yourself, Lizzie. Just keep your mind on the short term. The shop. The bridal commissions. Concentrate on being happy with John in the now, and not brooding and pondering on the future. He might never marry again, even if he does reconcile with his father.

So, no use torturing her head with the dark-looming question of whether he should really marry someone else. Someone more 'suitable'. Someone who was probably still young enough to give him an heir...and who had the perfect shade of blue blood for the job description.

Someone called Clara.

6

All Change

It was weird to be knocking on the door at St Patrick's Road instead of just letting herself in. Lizzie still had her key, but this was Brent and Shelley's personal space now. Hers was at Dalethwaite Manor with John.

'Lizzie! Oh, love, I've missed you so much! What the hell are you standing around out here for?' Before she'd even crossed the threshold, Lizzie was bear-hugged, then hauled inside by Shelley.

'I've missed you too, mate. Really I have.'

She hadn't realised quite how much, though, until she followed her friend into the familiar old kitchen, rubbing cautiously at her eyes while trying not to smudge her eyeliner.

'Let's have a cuppa first, then I'll make some lunch,' said Shelley, already filling the kettle. 'It'll be an inedible nightmare, of course, but at least it'll be a change from the gourmet nosh at your new gaff, eh?'

'A sandwich will be fine, or maybe we could nip out for something.' Shelley's cooking owed more to slapdash enthusiasm than culinary skill, but Lizzie would've been glad to eat bread and jam with her friend.

'You look fantastic. Not quite as tanned as I would have expected, but I guess the sun doesn't shine inside a bedroom, even in Provence,' said Shelley with a wink as they settled down at the table, where Mulder the cat was curled up at the other end. Lizzie wondered what John would say if she let Alice do that; although she had seen him sneaking titbits to the little tortoiseshell on a few occasions.

'Why, thanks, Shell. And you don't look so bad yourself.'

Shelley had lost a bit of weight, but looked well on it, and her short blonde hair was even shorter now, cut in a cute gamine style. And in her eyes there was something mysterious, a bit knowing.

'Well, that's what having a regular chap will do for you, especially a kinky one. You should know.'

Sholto Kraft, obviously.

'So, how's it going with Sholto? Are you...are you still paying him?'

Shelley swirled the tea in her cup. 'No, not any more. After the first couple of "dates" he refused to take money, and he even tried to give me back the dosh I'd already paid.' She looked up, her eyes bright, half excited, half fearful. 'Bit of an argument about that...but we resolved it.' She bit her lip. 'Oh Lizzie, I really, really like him. It's not just the wild sex. I like him as a person. I like just being with him. He's strong and down to earth and he's quite a laugh when you get to know him. Even though he's had the most shit life lately. The most awful luck you could imagine.'

'I'm glad you've found someone, sweetie. He sounds wonderful. As if he's come through the fire, so to speak, and come out a stronger person.' She thought of John, and what had happened in his life. It wasn't quite the same. The two men's lives had been radically different. But the quality of 'tempering' was probably very similar.

'Yes, exactly. I mean, obviously, he's not a fairy-tale prince like your John. In fact, he's pretty much the opposite in some ways. He's got no money whatsoever, especially now he's given up the escorting and he's just doing bar work and stuff. He lost his house, his business…everything really…but he's tough and he's making the best of things, and I guess that's what your John does too.'

'He does…He does…I mean, he's mega rich and all that, but he's had plenty of crap in his life. Being in prison…and…well…someone who he loved betrayed him and hurt him very much.'

For a moment, the old, endearingly nosy Shelley leant in for the juicy details, but then she shrugged. 'I won't pry.' The new, wiser Shelley reached out and laid her hand over Lizzie's. 'But whatever it is, you can work it out with him. I know you can. Now, tell me all about your hols…all the bits you can disclose, that is.' She grinned.

Over tuna sandwiches, the two women chattered and giggled and Lizzie regaled Shelley with tales of the private plane, and the villa and the pleasures of Provence. She didn't expound in too much detail in certain areas, but the glint in Shelley's eye said that she could easily fill in the blanks.

After all, as you say, Shell, you've got your own kinky guy now.

When Shelley was flinging dollops of 'value' Neapolitan ice-cream into cereal dishes, Lizzie raised the issue of her possibly working for Marie, at either the old New Again, or the new shop.

'Not sure if it'd be full-time or part-time, but it'd be better than some poxy office, eh?'

Her friend looked thoughtful. 'Yeah, I'd definitely be interested,' said Shelley as they dug into their dessert. 'Part-time would probably be best. I've picked up some work at the Waverley Metro in town. The Guidettis must've been pleased with Sholto's work at the hotel, because he's been appointed part-time manager at the new place, and he's got me some bar work and admin there too.' She licked her spoon. 'But I don't really think it's a good idea to work all the time with him. We each need our own space, and our own thing, you know?'

Lizzie did. She couldn't just be John's satellite, either. 'Totally agree, mate. Which is why I'm so glad the sewing and New Again and everything is taking off. I might not be a millionaire, but at least I've got a career of sorts, something of my own. I don't want to just be a rich man's WAG.' She stirred her ice-cream, muddying the colours. 'It would be so easy to let that happen with John. I mean, he's not a tyrant or anything, far from it. But he's so used to being at the helm, and he has so much money. If I don't stick up for myself, I could end up as a bird in a gilded cage. Making no decisions...stifled by his sheer generosity.'

'Yeah, I get what you mean,' replied Shelley, stabbing at her own dish. 'Sholto's a strong-willed sod too, so I need to assert myself now and again. Obviously, our money problems are pretty much the opposite of yours, but I would feel the same way, in your place.' She grinned then. 'It'd be nice to do the WAG thing some of the time, though, eh? We're girlies, after all, and we deserve a bit of pampering.'

They laughed then, and spent some quality time seeing who could make up the daftest fantasy about lounging around all day, drinking cocktails and having mani-pedis and vajazzles.

'Brent always claims he'd love that kind of life, but he wouldn't really. Even he seems happier with a job,' observed Shelley, 'although I suspect a lot of his cheerfulness at the moment is down to this hot new bloke of his.'

'Yeah, it's a shame he's not here.' Lizzie pushed aside her bowl. 'I've swapped a few texts with him here and there, but they're pretty skimpy. I would love to know more about this new guy! Brent does sound happy, though…Do you know anything? I don't even know the guy's name.'

The old conspiratorial look appeared on Shelley's face. 'I don't know much either. He's like a clam. He just smiles like the proverbial cat with cream, but he won't spill any details, the beast. It's like there's some big secret about this fella that he can't trust me with. All I know is that he's a little bit older…and if the grin on B's face all the time is anything to go by, he's fantastic in the sack.'

'Well, it looks like we're all getting quality nookie on a regular basis now.' She winked. 'Hell, we waited long enough for our Mr Rights to come along, didn't we?'

'Amen to that,' said Shelley. 'I would like to meet this mysterious man of Brent's, though. I keep encouraging him to bring him home, but he just says "soon" and that he doesn't want to jinx things. I think they mostly meet at the Waverley, of all places. And Brent's taxed the car now, so he drives over to lover-boy's place. Sounds like he has a cottage somewhere, and some kind of "country" job, although that's another thing Brent persists in being vague about.'

Lizzie frowned. She wanted Brent to be happy, and to find the right man, just as she had. But all this mystery was a bit worrying.

'They met at the Waverley? When was Brent at the Waverley?'

'It was one of Sholto's nights working in the bar there, and Brent decided he'd go and have a "talk" with him, taking it upon himself to make sure Sholto was on the level. Which is a bit of a cheek, really…He gets to vet my bloke, but I'm not allowed to see his.'

'Maybe I can get something out of him face to face?' said Lizzie as they were washing up the dishes. She'd suggested they do them straight away, and then had to smile to herself. At one time she'd probably just have left the pots, but clearly some of Mrs Thursgood's domestic excellence was rubbing off on her.

'Yes, I think he's more likely to open up to you. You two were…well, you two were closer.' Shelley squeezed Lizzie's shoulder. 'But whatever you find out, please, please, please…you must share! If you don't, I'll hunt you down and shake it out of you!'

Once she was sitting in the car outside the St Patrick's Road house, Lizzie texted Brent. He'd be at work, of course, but maybe they'd be able to fix up a meeting afterwards. A soft drink in a pub's beer garden or something?

To her surprise, she got an instant answer.

Can you meet me at the garden centre café, about three? I've got a break and I'd love a natter…B.

Wonderful! It was half past two. Plenty of time to get there. About to start the car, Lizzie paused, and sent another text.

Hey, Mr Business, I hear U like getting naughty messages from women? Are you having rude thoughts about yr girlfriend? I hear she's a bit of a raver & goes like a train. Sincerely, an Admirer.

Within a few seconds, a reply shot back to her. Her man

was clearly an accomplished messager; one who could text fast and in proper English too, if he chose to.

You're a wicked person, Admirer, & yes, my girlfriend is a voracious sex-pot. Thanks to you, have got a hard-on in a meeting & have to stay sitting down until my massive cock subsides. Yours, Mr Business. P.S. why not drive over here & sneak under my desk to take a look…or something?

She texted back. *Sorry, I'm meeting another man. Keep motor running on massive cock until I get home.*

That's a given. Adore you, came the reply.

As Lizzie drove, she smiled. She sang along to the 1980s station the Audi's radio was tuned to. She enjoyed her driving. Life was so good!

She was loved by a beautiful man. She lived in a beautiful house with him. He'd given her a beautiful car, amongst many other thoughtful gifts. OK, so they had a few issues. But who didn't? And she and John were both pragmatic grown-ups, not a pair of self-absorbed emo drama queens. They could sort things out between them – and prevail.

Counting her blessings, Lizzie hoped that her friends could be as happy, and thought about Shelley.

'Look, there's something I need to tell you,' the blonde girl had said as they'd hovered with the door open. 'I…I hope you don't mind. But…well, when Brent's away with his boyfriend, I've been inviting Sholto over here to stay with me. It's hard for us to meet, otherwise. I can't afford hotels on a regular basis, not decent ones, anyway, and it seems a shame when I've got a nice place and he hasn't got anywhere. He's in the most crappy digs, and it's a treat for him to have a comfy bed and a bath in a proper bathroom and all that, you know? I hope you don't mind,' she repeated.

Puzzled, Lizzie stared at her. What was she on about?

Why on earth shouldn't Sholto stay over? Even move in, if he wanted to? It wasn't her business to say yay or nay, either way.

'But why should I mind? I'm happy that you're not on your own, love, especially if Brent's out a lot.' She grabbed Shelley's hand and gave it a squeeze.

'But this is your house, Liz.' Shelley gestured towards the hall, and beyond.

Lizzie sighed. God, now she understood Shelley's misgivings.

'But I don't live here. It's your home, Shell.'

'Ah, but your John owns the house, and…and that means it's yours, really.'

'Look, I know this is weird.' She put her hands on Shelley's shoulders. 'Just pretend Oldacre Holdings is some totally anonymous but benevolent landlord with a liberal tenant policy or whatever. If you really do insist that you need my approval, you have it. A million time over, you dimwit! I don't really know Sholto yet, but if you like him, he's a good guy in my book.' She threw her arms around her friend. 'If Brent's OK with it, I'm OK with it. Sholto can move in and live here full-time, as far as I'm concerned.'

Now it was Shelley's turn to blink tears. 'I'm not sure we're quite at that stage yet.' She grinned ruefully. 'But we might get there.'

'Right, then. When you get there, go for it. Why should he live in some terrible rat-hole if he could live in a proper house with you?'

They'd parted with more hugs. And if Brent did have objections, Lizzie resolved to talk him round. It was obvious Shelley was pretty serious about Sholto Kraft.

At the garden centre café, Brent was on his feet as she

approached, and when she reached him, she was wrestled into her second bear hug of the day.

'How the devil are you, you beautiful strumpet?' demanded Brent, as they sat down at a rustic table. He had a fruit-flavoured water waiting for her. 'You look magnificent. A life of luxury, and two weeks in the sun with your own tame billionaire, obviously agrees with you.'

'Not so tame,' said Lizzie, taking a swig of her water, 'And you're looking pretty swish yourself, B. Obviously you're getting something that agrees with you too.'

A broad smile graced Brent's handsome face. His dark eyes sparkled. Lizzie had never seen him look happier. 'It does...It does...So, how was the holiday?' he asked, changing the subject with a blatant wink.

Lizzie supplied more edited highlights, then fixed her friend with a determined look.

'Enough about me. What about you? Enough with the subterfuge and secrecy. Shell and I want to know more about this mysterious new boyfriend of yours. You know all about ours, and all we seem to have gleaned about your bloke so far is that he's a fantastic lover.'

Brent looked away for a second, a slightly bemused smile on his face as he brushed his dark curly hair back off his brow. 'Lizzie, love...I don't know where to start, other than the fact that I think this thing of mine might be pretty serious. Is serious. Really serious. And I'm fairly sure the feeling's mutual.'

'I'm happy for you, B. I'm happy for both you and Shell, because it sounds like she's pretty serious about Sholto too.'

Brent looked thoughtful. 'Well, I must admit that I had my misgivings about that at first, but she seems very happy and he seems to be treating her right.'

'Good. But that's her. What about you? Tell me all about your bloke!'

'Well...Yes...Tom,' said Brent, looking down at his long fingers, cupped around his drink bottle. 'I'm guessing John hasn't said anything, which means that Tom hasn't told him about us.'

Tom? What was he on about? Lizzie felt as if she'd suddenly been parachuted into a different conversation altogether. Then it dawned...

No, it couldn't be. Too much of a coincidence.

Before she could speak, though, Brent went on:

'My Tom is your John's younger brother.'

7

Serendipity

'You what? You must be kidding me. How can that be?'

And yet, the instant she'd heard Brent say the name 'Tom', she'd just known.

'I met him at the Waverley, the night I went to "have a word" with Sholto. He was there, having a drink in the Lawns Bar. He and John were supposed to have met up, but your man was late back from London and went straight to Dalethwaite Manor.'

Lizzie remembered that night. Waiting up, also wanting to 'have a word', but with John, over the purchase of the St Patrick's Road house. He'd mentioned having to give his brother a rain check.

'And you just happened to strike up a conversation with him? That's a bit spooky, isn't it? Did you know who he was?'

Lizzie sipped at her water, still digesting Brent's revelation. It was kind of cosmic serendipity, she supposed. She'd accidentally picked up the older Smith brother – sorry, Wyngarde Smith brother – in the Lawns, so why shouldn't Brent pick up the younger one? If Tom was even half as hot as his older sibling, Brent would have clocked him straight away. And would probably have had a strong inkling he was gay, too.

'I already knew him, love. But not as John's brother,' said Brent quietly. He had an odd look of nostalgia on his face. 'I'd met him before…at Sylvestro's.' Lizzie remembered some of Brent's tall tales about that particular club. She'd even been there with him once. 'We had a one-night stand. A few years ago, before I was with Steve.'

She shook her head, 'You couldn't make it up, could you? How incredibly weird…Long before I'd even set eyes on John, you'd slept with his brother!'

'Just one of those *Twilight Zone* things, love, eh?' said Brent cheerfully. 'Of course, I had no idea who he was other than that. We never exchanged surnames or even numbers that first time. He was just a "Mr Right for the Night" rather than a "Mr Right". In fact, I'd forgotten all about him. But when I saw him at the Waverley, I sort of recognised him twice. I remembered him, and yet he looked familiar in a different way too.'

'Does he look like John?'

'A little bit. His hair's darker, and he's about ten years younger, of course, but there's a resemblance.' Brent's expression went dreamy for a moment. Yes, the Smith men could do that to you. 'It's mainly the eyes. He has the same gorgeous blue eyes as your John.'

Lizzie laughed. 'Well, now I've heard everything. When did you realise? When you got as far as asking him his name this time, I presume?'

Brent grinned too. 'Yes, that's pretty much it. We were on our third date. I nearly fell out of bed when he said he was Tom Wyngarde Smith. And he was as surprised as I was when I explained about you. And how you were this incredible woman his brother wanted advice about because she was too stubborn to move in with him!'

'Who said that? Was it him? Or was it John?' Suspicions stirred. 'Has Tom told John who he's dating? Seems that everybody knows what's going on but me!'

'No, don't worry. Tom hasn't said anything to John. I told him I'd like to tell you first, and he agreed it was best.'

Lizzie stared out at the car park for a moment. Life was bizarre. So full of strange coincidences and interactions. She couldn't help but smile, though.

Good for Brent. And good for Tom. She loved her old friend – and ex-boyfriend – like a brother, and she desperately wanted him to be happy. She wanted the best for him, and if Tom Wyngarde Smith was anything like his older brother…well, he *was* the best. And *he* couldn't look for a better man than Brent.

'So, it's really serious, then?' she said at length, reaching out to fold her hand around Brent's.

His face was a picture of excitement, joy and a touch of apprehension. Oh, how Lizzie knew that state. She felt it every single day.

'Yes…I think so. I think I'm falling in love with him. Or maybe already have fallen.' He hauled in a deep breath. 'He seems to feel the same. He even wants me to move into his cottage with him, on the Montcalm estate. There's a position for me there, on the gardening team, if I want it. It's starting right back to basics, but it'd be the real deal, proper horticulture, not just selling potted plants and garden furniture to yuppies.' He made a vague gesture towards the main part of the garden centre. 'I think I want it…and him…but well, like a certain person of my acquaintance,

I'm prone to dithering when it comes to moving in and commitment. Not to mention getting together with someone who's posh and much better off than I am.'

'Tell me about it! It's bloody terrifying, isn't it?' Lizzie slid off the bench and darted around to Brent's side of the table, to hug him tight. John was her life, but her old friend would always be a soul-mate too. Especially now he faced a future so parallel to her own.

But, as they laughed and hugged, drawing odd looks from fellow patrons of the café, it dawned on Lizzie that there might be one significant difference between Brent's situation and hers.

She was prepared to bet there wasn't a male equivalent of Clara in Tom's life.

'Shall I tell John? Or do you think Tom wants to?' Lizzie had asked as she and Brent had prepared to part, and he was admiring her new wheels.

'Oh, Tom's very easy-going. You tell John, if you want to. Tom won't mind.'

And now, as she let herself in, back at Dalethwaite Manor, she was both nervous and excited at the prospect. She had no idea what John would think of this strange coincidence.

The house was quiet. The Thursgoods had the rest of the weekend off, and were away visiting family in the area. She and John had the house to themselves until late tomorrow evening.

So, where are you, Mr Business? You're not working your people to a standstill on Saturday, surely? Especially if you've still got that hard-on you texted about!

The Bentley hadn't been parked out front, but it could be in the garage. She supposed if this were a romantic novel she'd be able to 'sense' her lover's presence in the house, but she wasn't Mystic Lizzie and certainly didn't have the almost supernatural powers of perception that John himself sometimes displayed.

Unsettled, she wandered through the house after depositing several urgent sewing projects in her workroom. Pausing in the kitchen, she topped up Alice's water dish and put her a bit of food down, then passed through the small dining room, heading for the terrace overlooking the pool.

Yes, time for her daily exercise, and she often did her best thinking whilst in the pool, swimming laps. Gliding through the water, moving on auto pilot, she could let everything just drift through her mind for review. Shelley and Sholto. Brent and Tom. All the other stuff. She who should not be named…

Ten minutes later, Lizzie dived into the pool and hurled herself towards the other end, at her best pace.

The water was the perfect heat, not too warm, not too cool, and the canopy above kept the late afternoon sun off her head. Lizzie loved that the pool had a chorine-free system. She'd never swum in one before Dalethwaite, and the water was pure and clean and silky against her body as she powered through it. Never the most elegant of swimmers, she could still manage a fairly creditable crawl and breaststroke and, untroubled by chlorine, it was far more pleasant for her face when it went beneath the surface as she swam properly.

After quite a few laps at a fairly fast pace, concentrating on nothing but working her muscles and getting her heart rate up, she eased off and moved through the water at a more leisurely speed. Then she engaged her brain.

Brent and Tom. Shelley and Sholto. Her and John. Her house-mates were serious, she sensed, and she knew she was too. Earlier, she'd blithely told herself that everything could be dealt with, but now, some of the 'issues' surfaced, as if they'd been lurking in the depths of the pool and her passage through the water had stirred them up.

How nice it would be just to go on in a kind of happy limbo, living together, loving together, experimenting with sex, just enjoying each other's company. But would life allow them to do that? Or would 'stuff', and other people, soon intrude?

If I said the word, John would maintain our status quo, but is that really fair to him?

There were family expectations. He'd set himself apart from them, but deep down, she knew he'd follow duty eventually, because that was the kind of man he was. He always shouldered responsibility.

And there was Clara.

Lizzie suspected that John's former love would insert herself into their happy bubble world sooner or later. She didn't know how, but she sensed it, being Mystic Lizzie on that score, at least.

I'll not push things. I'll not ask any more questions. I'll just wait, and move at John's pace. I'll accept the good things, and enjoy the man I love for as long as I can.

Pushing her wet hair out of her eyes, she kicked out hard again, splashing inelegantly and speeding up, savouring the sheer pleasure of being young and healthy and living in a wonderful home, to which her wonderful man would soon return.

For now, the realities of life did not exist.

*

As John entered the house, he could hear splashing water. Lizzie was swimming. He closed his eyes, picturing her incredible body in a sleek suit that clung to her beautiful shape.

Not that he needed the idea of her in form-fitting clothes to fire his imagination. She was stunning in everything she wore, whether it be vintage glamour, or jeans and T-shirts, or even her pyjamas. She didn't need to wear peek-a-boo or skintight styles to look sexy, and she looked elegant and arresting in the simplest of outfits. She had an unerring eye for what suited her to perfection.

But even so, it took barely a blink an eye for John to see Lizzie naked. Her body divine and bare, just for him.

His cock kicked hard in his shorts, returning to the condition her text had prompted, earlier. God, he was going to look obscene in his swimming trunks. It was a good thing they were alone in the house for twenty-four hours. Grinning, he hurtled up the stairs, two at a time, imagining Lizzie's tart observations on his horny condition when he appeared at the side of the pool.

Ten minutes later, John emerged onto the patio, walking quietly on bare feet, not wanting to disturb Lizzie. She was still lapping the pool, slicing through the water in an enthusiastic, impressively fast crawl.

He stifled a moan as his cock lurched again. She was a goddess. He could see her shapely body as she moved, perfect in a neat, conservative black one-piece, her inky hair streaming out like a veil as she swept along.

What have I done to deserve you, Lizzie? I want you so much. I love you so much.

That the thought came so easily surprised him. For so long, he'd been confused about love, unsure of it. But now he *was* sure, because that was what he felt about this woman.

She fulfilled all his physical needs, all the desires he'd ever felt, and she made his heart happy in a way that no woman ever had before.

She was as different from Clara as night was from day, and a more complete match for him than any other woman, Caroline included, had ever been.

I could have it all with you, Lizzie. I want *it all.*

As if she'd heard his thought, Lizzie paused at the end of her lap and looked towards him. A grin spread across her face as her gaze flirted towards his groin, and she shook her head, sending water flying from the tips of her hair. Then, still smirking, she struck out, back across the pool towards him.

She could be everything to him.

Friend. Companion. Enthusiastic, imaginative lover.

Wife. His children's mother. Eventually, in the far future, his Marchioness.

But much as she loved him, was the burden of all that really fair to her?

8

Pool Party

'Well, Mr Smith, is that an inflatable banana in your swimming trunks or are you just pleased to see me?'

Lizzie looked up at John, where he stood at the side of the pool. Lord, he was a sight for sore eyes! She never got tired of looking at his body. His lean strength. The perfect proportions of his limbs and muscles. The little bit of sandy hair on his chest. The quite frankly enormous bulge of his cock, dramatically showcased in an abbreviated pair of navy blue swimming trunks. The way it jutted out proclaimed that he was pleased to see her, joking apart.

'Always, darling, always.' Smiling and without a trace of self-consciousness, he dropped down onto his knees, all grace, then inclined forward to kiss her as she pushed herself up, elbows on the pool's edge, to meet him.

Why did it always feel as if each kiss was the first one ever? John's mouth was warm, and lazily demanding, eager but not voracious. His tongue greeted hers, but didn't subdue it, simply swirling and lightly tasting before they broke contact.

'Are you coming in?' she asked, her hand on his shoulder,

pulling him towards her again. 'The water is quite literally lovely. This pool is fab!'

John laughed. 'I'd love to come …' He paused for a wicked Lothario eye-roll. 'But I feel as if I need some exercise first, of the conventional kind. Would you be deeply insulted if I swam instead of fucking you?'

'I'll live,' she replied, pulling harder, 'and don't they always say, anticipation increases the pleasure, or something like that?'

'Indeed. Something very like that.' In a nimble, sinuous movement, John swivelled around and plunged feet first into the pool beside her, disappearing smoothly beneath the surface then bursting up again, spraying water everywhere as he shook his wet curls.

'Mm…that's good,' he said, sweeping back his hair, sleek as an otter. 'I don't think it's doused the banana entirely, but it's probably made him a bit more manageable while I swim a few laps.' Kicking with his feet, he pressed towards her, and took her in his arms again for a slippery wet kiss. Lizzie didn't notice any discernible diminution in the 'banana', though.

'We should have cocktails, shouldn't we? Make this our own personal Club Tropicana, seeing as we have the house to ourselves and can be as ridiculously self-indulgent as we like.' She'd been turning thoughts over in her mind, again and again, but somehow, now that John was here, it was easy to put them aside, and focus on her pleasure in the presence of the man she loved.

'Cocktails?' He looked dubious, then smiled. 'Why not, eh? Let's go mad. I mean, it's so long since we had a holiday, isn't it?' Beneath the water, he reached out and clasped her bottom in a playful squeeze.

Lizzie grinned at him, reaching out for a very light squeeze of her own, testing the banana for ripeness.

'Careful, minx,' he warned, his blue eyes dancing. He looked dangerous, somehow, with his hair slicked back, more sexually menacing than ever, if that were possible.

'We can call this weekend the last gasp of our holiday, then get back to business, business, business…and sewing, sewing, sewing…on Monday.'

'Sounds like a plan,' affirmed John, licking the water from his lips, then reaching for her hand, plucking it from his erection. 'Now, leave this alone for the time being, eh? Or I'll never get any exercise done to keep this ageing and decrepit body in shape.' He drew her hand to his mouth, kissed it fiercely, then released her and kicked away towards the middle of the pool.

'Perhaps you're right, old man. Better get to it. I don't want you to fall to bits before my very eyes, do I?' she shot back.

'I'll get you for that,' he called over his shoulder, then set off at a fast crawl.

'You'll get me anyway,' said Lizzie, not sure he'd heard her, but guessing he knew in any case.

For a few moments, she watched John swim. He was a far better, far smoother swimmer than she was, and totally focused on his stroke. Or at least he seemed to be. Did he, like her, turn thoughts over and over as he did his laps? It was possible. Probable. What was he thinking about? Business? Her? Something or someone else?

Don't go there.

The pool had a changing room adjacent, and she slipped in there to put a widetoothed comb through her hair and change into a dry suit. There was nothing worse than clammy nylon against the skin. She chose a similar suit to the black one she'd been wearing, only this time in dark red, with a navy piping.

Out on the deck again, she surveyed the pool. John was eating up the laps, his pace still punishing. She thought about calling out to him not to expend all his energy swimming, but it probably wasn't necessary. He was infinitely strong, and his stamina was breath-taking. No matter how many times he went back and forth, he'd still have plenty in the tank to see to her.

At the little bar beneath an overhang, she investigated the possibilities for cocktails. She didn't really have much of a clue about mixing them correctly, or what ingredients to choose for a man who usually drank neat gin, but there was a surprisingly wide selection of fixings.

In the end, she poured a slug of rum, a dollop of apple juice, and a dash of red syrup of some kind into glasses filled with crushed ice from the machine, then tossed a couple of cherries, an umbrella and a straw into each one.

Not bad. A bit sweet. John would probably hate it. But perhaps he could chastise her for her poor bartending skills? A heat surged in her belly that was nothing to do with rum. Impatient, she strolled over to the two sun loungers set out on the deck, side by side, and settled down on one, cautiously sipping her drink. Best not get smashed while waiting for him. What John could do to her and for her was best savoured with most of her faculties intact.

Admiring the view, she wondered if John could have been a competitive swimmer. He was fast and smooth, almost machine-like. His laps took half the time hers did, but how many more was he going to do? She shifted position on the thickly padded lounger, feeling the old familiar stirring in her pussy, the heavy clench of desire. The sweet lust which never failed to surprise with its sudden intensity.

Half-hypnotised by the remorseless regularity of John's mastery of the pool, Lizzie blinked when, in a sharp change of direction, she saw him head for the ladder, then haul himself out, dripping. Her gaze zeroed to his groin.

The water and the exercise had taken the edge off his erection but he was still mouth-wateringly substantial beneath the sleek blue nylon. But then, he was always awesome, even at rest. Yum, yum...

Yet, she'd have loved John even if he'd only had a tiny dick. It was the man who owned her heart, not his accoutrements. And anyway, what he could do with his mouth and his hands would more than make up for any hypothetical tackle shortcomings.

'Try this.' She held out the glass to him, watching the quirk of his sandy brows as he took it from her. Clearly, he was doubtful, but still, he took a sip, even before he reached for a towel.

He pursed his lips. He rolled his eyes. He pulled a face that made her giggle.

'It's...divine.' He took another tentative sip as if she'd handed him hemlock.

'You think it's terrible, don't you?' she accused as he sat down on the lounger beside hers, abandoning the glass in favour of the towel.

'In a word...yes.' He rubbed his hair furiously then emerged from beneath the terrycloth with tousled angel curls. 'But I'll drink it because you made it for me, my sweet.' In a gesture of bravado, he snatched up the glass and took another healthy swig.

Lizzie laughed. 'You don't have to.'

John gave her an arch look over the rim of the glass. 'Are you telling me what I can or can't do?'

A shiver of something familiar rippled through Lizzie's middle. The thrill. The harbinger of the game.

'I…I wouldn't presume to,' she said, lowering her gaze.

'Good,' he said. She watched through her lashes as he finished the horrid drink and set aside the glass. 'Now, drink your cocktail and tell me about your day.'

The alcohol in the rum was like tap water compared to the surging excitement that flowed through her veins. She barely noticed its taste as she tossed it back and put down the glass. John arched his brows at her, marking her out as a naughty, intemperate girl.

She summed up her chat with Marie and her lunch with Shelley, yet prevaricated over what had passed between her and Brent.

'What are you keeping from me?' John leant forward, and when Lizzie stole a glance in a southerly direction, she saw that his cock was well on the rise again.

'It's a secret.' She gave him a little smirk, teasing him, licking her lips. Brent and Tom was a very juicy titbit. She could use it to goad John into action. Not that he really needed that. From the way he scanned her, assessing, enjoying with his eyes, promising much…in fact, promising everything, she knew he needed no excuse whatsoever.

'You'll have to beat it out of me.' She lifted her head, defiant, then almost swooned at the fierce metal flash in his eyes.

'Is that a fact?' He reached out, cradled her chin, fingers holding her firmly.

'Y…yes…' Raw lust surged like honey in the pit of her belly, stirred by that odd, irrational longing that ran counter to all her confidence and self-sufficiency. Her feminism. She wanted to bare herself, to bow herself to him. Be exposed and vulnerable. Feel the harsh slap of his hand upon her…upon her bottom.

And yet she still couldn't look away from his eyes. From beautiful pools of blue, midnight now, electric with lust. To be the perfect submissive, she should look away, but he was the potent delicious drug that energised and strengthened her rather than making her pliant.

'Are you sure?' He let his thumb drift across her chin, her lower lip, pressing it down. Instinctively, she drew his thumb into her mouth and sucked on it, letting her glance dart quickly down, towards the immense bulge in his trunks.

'Ignore that,' he said crisply, pressing with his thumb. 'That's not for you. Not just yet, anyway. And especially if you persist in keeping things from me.'

Boldly, she stole another look, and then reached for him. He denied her, though, sliding cleverly along his lounger, putting his magnificent cock out of her reach.

'Do you deny me?' He freed her mouth.

She didn't answer, but stared back at him: *do your worst.*

'A spanking it is, then,' he pronounced, letting his hand slide down to her breast and giving it a rough squeeze through the dark red nylon. Then, lunging forward from the lounger and coming up onto his knees on the deck, he kissed her hard, plunging in his tongue, subduing the tongue he'd already teased with his thumb. While he handled her breast, he held her head with his other hand, compelling her to accept the conquering kiss. He was kneeling, but his dominance and his power loomed over her.

Oh love…Oh my love…

She melted. Ached. She was ready. Ready for anything. Even if it was just more of this rough he-man kiss.

But just as she really thought she was about to melt into a puddle, he drew back, resuming his position on the lounger.

'Stand up and peel down your suit,' he commanded, lying back, resting on one elbow, 'pull it right down...not off...just down to the top of your thighs so I can get at your bum and your cunt.'

'Oh, you're such an aesthete,' she countered, rising to her feet and loving how he was deliciously crude sometimes. The contrast between this coarse talk and his general gentlemanliness made her quiver.

'Uh oh...Naughty, naughty.' He gave her a narrow-eyed trick of a smile and wagged an admonishing finger. 'Now come on, do as you're told.'

Lizzie was trembling so hard, and was so hyped up, that she fumbled with her costume, wriggling and squirming to peel it down her body and into a bunch at the top of her thighs, as he'd specified. Hot blood hurtled around her veins and she blushed in places she wasn't sure were even supposed to blush. With her costume at half-mast she was infinitely exposed, much more so than if he'd told her to strip altogether.

'Touch your nipples,' he commanded. 'Both at the same time. Fondle yourself.'

Lizzie closed her eyes. It was like she was floating. In a different world. Warm silky arousal pooled between her legs, before she'd barely even touched herself, and when she did, she gasped aloud at the sweet-sharp jolt.

It was a battle royal not to circle her hips, jerk herself about, and ignoring her boobs altogether, just rub herself furiously between her legs.

Why hadn't he ticked her off, and told her she was a naughty girl again? It was what she'd been expecting, and heaven alone knew she deserved it. When she'd touched her nipples, she'd moaned out aloud.

To open her eyes, or not to open her eyes? She decided on open, and when she did it was to see John, reclining back and stroking himself through his trunks as he watched her.

Oh, let me do that, she wanted to cry, the sight was so gorgeous, so decadent. But she kept silent. She needed permission to speak, permission to touch, permission to do anything other than that which he'd instructed her to do.

'I'm not seeing much fondling, Lizzie,' he said, voice low as he continued to touch himself. She'd been thrilled to immobility by the sight of his display. 'Pinch your nipples. You know I like to see that. Why aren't you doing it?'

Lizzie bit her lip, agonised by the pain-in-pleasure of the sensation, at war with herself again to keep from pointing out to him that she wasn't a mind-reader. Maybe he sometimes seemed to have that ability, but she had no mental powers and that was a fact.

She had others, though.

Rolling her nipple between her fingers, she put on a show, swaying, getting into it, riding the little hurt and the bigger arousal. Glorying in her own disobedience, she slid her fingers between her sex lips and stroked herself, slicking her clitoris in time to the way she tweaked and tugged at her nipple, making a provocative, syncopated dance of it. Undulating, she was Bettie Page, Queen of Cheesecake, turning on a hundred thousand men in one of her primitive black and white porno flicks. Her sex rippled, almost at the tipping point, as she performed for her audience, the one man who both ruled and adored her.

'God, you're a luscious trollop! You know that, don't you?' His voice was ragged, broken. He was still smoothing his fingers over his bulge and his eyes were as bright as a plasma flash.

'I do, master,' she purred, continuing, and yet at the same time backing off just a little. It was too soon. She wanted this to last.

John made a sound of impatience, and snatched his hand away from his groin. 'Now look what you've made me do, you wicked girl.' He laughed. 'You almost had me out of control there, madam. You almost made me forget that I'm supposed to be tanning that gorgeous arse of yours for you, for keeping secrets from me.'

He sat up, reached out, knocked her hand away from her crotch, and replaced it with his own. His fingers slid between her labia and he rubbed her, edge on, back and forth. The action was rough, casual, and he watched her eyes as he worked her. *Don't you dare, don't you dare*, his blue gaze challenged her, and though she fought him, making a fist and digging her nails into her palm, she couldn't best him and her pussy clenched hard in a sudden, shocking climax.

Swaying, she grabbed at his strong shoulders, digging her nails into him now as she crested another wave, her belly molten with pleasure.

'Oh John,' she moaned, roles forgotten for the moment. And as if he'd forgotten too, he snaked his arm around her waist, to hold her steady.

For a few moments, she just breathed, out of herself, recovering, and then she braced up, widening her stance and standing straight. Snatching her hands away from his beloved body she let her arms hang loose at her sides.

I should think so, said his laughing eyes, though his face was stern.

'You're a wicked slave,' he said in a low voice. She could tell he was fighting not to laugh out loud and perhaps to grab her and hug her and kiss her and bring her off again. They were playing the game, yet not playing the game, although he might still hit hard even if they were only having fun.

She looked at his hand, glistening as he withdrew it from her flesh, and remembered how ferocious it could be, despite its elegance.

'And somehow, madam, you've distracted me from my purpose.' Pausing, he lifted his fingers to his face, and breathed in her aroma. 'Delicious,' he said, then slowly and lasciviously, licked at her silk.

The sight of his flicking tongue made her catch her breath, it was so suggestive. How could she need to come again, when she'd only climaxed barely a moment ago?

'Again?' he said softly. He'd read the lust in her face, her reaction to him. 'Aren't we forgetting something?'

'No, master.'

'I should think not. Now, why don't you lie on your lounger, face down, so we can do the deed?' His tongue peeked out again, sweeping over the firm, velvety curve of his lower lip. Oh, the devil, he was so enjoying this.

Ungainly with her swimsuit around her thighs, Lizzie got down onto the lounger and spread herself upon it like a sacrifice on a slab. She curved her fingers round the top edge, holding on tight, anticipating what was to come. Her toes curled of their own accord against the thickly upholstered cushion beneath her, and she turned her face boldly towards her master.

John sat there, watching her, taking his time, as yet not inclined to move. Again, he cupped his crotch, gently fondling himself. Lizzie was hypnotised by the tiny movements in the tendons in the back of his hand. He seemed intent on stretching out the tension, making her wait, ramping up her reborn desire, and the strange amalgam of fear and longing that preceded a spanking.

After what seemed like an age, he reached for his towel and solemnly proceeded to fold it into a towelling pad, which he set beside her lounger. 'Got to protect the old trick knee,' he said conversationally as he slid onto the towel, on said knee and the non-trick one, next to where she lay.

'There's nothing wrong with your knee, you old malingerer,' she said pertly. 'It's as fit and fabulous as the rest of you.'

John sighed, segueing into his old weary mentor with wayward pupil act. 'Lizzie…Lizzie…Lizzie…When will you learn respect for your elders…and your fucking master! You really are the most useless sub on the planet. It's a good job you're the most beautiful, desirable, adorable woman that ever lived, because as an obedient slave, you leave a lot to be desired.'

She loved the laughter in his voice. She loved the lightness and the playfulness of him. Oh, he'd spank her hard, yes he would. And she might even shed a tear or two. But it'd be fun too. With John, it always was.

His hands settled on her, on her back, on her bottom, fingers spread. Slowly, he caressed her, assessed her, savoured her. Stroking. Teasing. Visiting each inch. Telling her how he cared for her as he sampled her skin and the musculature beneath it.

'Perfect,' he breathed. 'Absolutely perfect.'

Would he use his hand? He most often did. They did use toys and devices, but time and again they returned to the intimacy of skin on skin. Simple. Classic. Uncontrived.

But the way he seemed to hesitate seemed to suggest he might mix it up a bit today. She sensed him casting around, devising something. It didn't surprise her when he reached for one of the rubber flip-flops that she'd been wearing on the poolside.

Ooh, that might hurt. Indeed it would hurt. The flip-flops were quite chunky and substantial. She could feel the weight of the one he'd chosen as he laid it against her buttock, introducing her to it. He let it rest there a moment, then...

'Yowch!'

Before she'd even had a chance to realise he'd started, he'd laid the damn thing on with quite a wallop. It felt twice as solid and substantial as she'd expected it to be, like a length of wood rather than moulded rubber, knocking the breath out of her and instantly filling her bum with heat.

Oh, it hurt! It hurt! Only one spank, and her left bottom cheek was roaring. And at the same time she was already grinding her pussy against the lounger.

'Hush, be still,' he commanded, soft of voice and hard of intent. The flip-flop crashed down on her other cheek and she yowled again, mashing her crotch against the upholstery beneath her as her fingers gouged it too, above her head.

It was either that or push her hand between her body and the cushion, and masturbate as he spanked her. She was tempted to do it. After all, he'd reminded her what a wilful sub she was, so she might as well fulfil his expectations.

'Oh no you don't, madam,' he warned, as if he'd read the thought.

She squirmed again, and yelped too, as he brought the flip-flop down in two fast strokes like thunderclaps, one on each cheek. Oh, the delicious agony!

'How the fuck do you do that?' she demanded.

'What? Spank you? It's like this…' Wallop! 'And this…' Slap, on the other cheek!

'Not that,' she croaked, her voice distorted by the burning heat that seemed to be in all her body, not just her buttocks. Her nipples were aching stones against the cushioned surface beneath her. 'The thing…the way you seem to know what I'm thinking all the time. It's just weird, and a bit scary. Especially if I happened to be thinking something rude about you.'

'How rude?' He slapped again, inciting inferno, and again. 'How rude?' he demanded, pausing, then inclining forward over her, pressing his crotch against her bottom, rubbing himself on her heat. His empty hand curved around her hip, holding her steady as he massaged her with his cock. That hurt too, but she lifted herself, pressing back against him.

'Oh…just stuff. About what a horny pervert you are, and how colossal that thing is that you're jamming against me.'

But it was more than that, and more scary. He could see her heart, when sometimes his was opaque to her.

'Sweetheart,' he whispered, as if he'd read that thought too.

For a few moments he just rested against her, enjoying the stimulus of the warmth of her punished bottom cheeks on his aroused flesh. Then he swirled his hips again, rubbing, rubbing. Was he going to come?

But then, he straightened up. 'I'm going to spank you for just a little longer, my darling, because the way you wiggle and moan, and the gorgeous cherry glow in your bottom, is so divine. And then you're going to tell me what this secret thing is you're keeping from me.' He laid the flip-flip against her right buttock, as if retrieving his 'sighting' of it. 'Because despite your claims that I read your mind all the time, missy, I have absolutely no idea what the devil it is.'

Between gritting her teeth, and groaning, Lizzie smiled. She'd completely forgotten about Brent and Tom for the moment, but it was nice to know something John didn't know, for a change.

9

The Secret Thing

What was it, this secret? John had no clue, and he didn't care. His whole focus was Lizzie. Her peerless body. The way she moved. The skin of her bottom so pink. Her bold, sweet, happy spirit, playing the game with him, easing all his anxieties.

Even as he watched, she undulated against the thickly upholstered lounger, massaging her crotch as if she was so full of erotic energy that she couldn't contain it within herself. The thick mass of her coal-black hair slid on her shoulders, still damp, and the muscles of her back flexed. Her buttocks were tense and hot, marked a little by the rubber sole of the flip-flop.

He wanted to kiss them. He wanted to mark them more. He wanted to come all over them, pearls spattered across rose.

Enough prevaricating, man!

He brought the flip-flop down and she yelped, squirming hard. Magnificently, though, she gripped on to the top edge of the lounger, fingers digging in. A lesser woman would have grabbed her own flesh to ease the ache, but Lizzie held fast. He brought the sandal down again and she only gasped this time, controlling herself, controlling him.

'God, woman...I can't fight it any more...' Grabbing at her hips, he lifted her up. She hissed as his fingers caught the edge of her redness, but she didn't resist and allowed herself to be draped, sideways, half across the lounger. 'I don't have a condom handy...we'll have to extemporise. A bit of rubbing...a bit of wriggling...Do you think you'd like that? Don't worry, though. I'll get you off.'

'I have every confidence in you, boss man,' she purred, looking over her shoulder, her eyes wild.

With a growl, he flung himself across her, pushing down his trunks and pressing his aching cock against the heat in her bottom. The sensation was piquant, fabulous, feverish, and her gasps, and the way she hissed through clenched teeth, were like strands of super-pleasure winding themselves around his flesh. His body clamoured at him to go for it, take what he wanted, to rub and frott himself against her in blind, greedy lust.

But no! No! There had to be pleasure for her too, or his own release would be empty.

The lounger creaked ominously as they rocked against it, but still held up. John reached around beneath Lizzie's smooth belly, his fingers zeroing in on her pussy, wiggling in amongst the soft dark hair and finding her clit. He jerked harder, using the momentum of his body to work for him and for her too, a gallop of pressure and friction, cock and fingers, heart and soul.

'Yes! Yes!' he chanted, pretty words lost in the intensity. But he didn't have to flatter or sweet-talk her, or even dirty-talk her, because she knew he cared for her. For all her talk about not being able to read him, he was certain that she could.

And he'd praise her to the skies when he got his mind back, afterwards.

Climax barely took a few moments. While molten fire seared its way down his spine and enveloped him, his cock jerked and bucked, disgorging semen onto her rosy pink bottom in haphazard spurts.

'Lizzie…Lizzie,' he crooned, brain gone, functioning on auto.

But still, love actuated his fingers. Love and pure instinct. He couldn't think, but he could still rub her, still caress her, and he almost sobbed as she cried out his name, coming too.

Lizzie prised John's hand out from beneath her. It must be going to sleep with their combined weight pressed upon his wrist. She smiled when John wiggled his fingers to stir the circulation, and then straightened up, behind her. Liberated, she knelt up too.

His mouth settled on her shoulder. A soft kiss, almost a salute.

'Are you OK, sweetheart?' His breath ruffled her hair.

Was she all right? Hell yes! Even the hot glow in her spanked bottom was already morphing towards pleasant heat, and the sweet memory of submission, rather than out and out pain. Obviously it'd be a bit sore when she sat on it, or accidentally knocked against something, but John was so skilled, with both hand and implement, that he'd never once hurt her in a bad way.

'I'm fine…I'm good.' She reached around and touched

herself. Yes, sore, but not agonising. 'A bit sticky, for obvious reasons, but otherwise, nothing that won't fade sooner or later.' She gave him a sultry look over her shoulder. 'And the orgasm was very nice indeed. Very nice.'

'Good.' He looped his arms around her belly and she felt his cock against her bottom again, quiescent against the glow. Not that it was likely to stay that way for long, knowing John. He had a young man's recovery powers, and an almost infinite appetite for pleasure. 'Maybe we should both cool off in the pool again?'

He gave her a brisk kiss on the side of her neck, then stood up behind her, urging her up too. As she turned to him, he peeled his swimming trunks all the way down and stepped out of them, lifting his sandy eyebrows at her provocatively as he straightened up and kicked the garment away.

'Well, we've got the place to ourselves. Let's swim in the buff, eh?'

But what if someone called? Some unexpected visitor. A tradesman or something?

Still she grinned, though, and reached down to where her suit was still bunched around her thighs.

'Let me,' said John, sinking down gracefully and easing the suit down her legs, then letting her step out of it as she leant on his shoulder for balance.

It seemed uniquely piquant to be standing naked here, in the daylight, even in this, their own private space. They'd swum naked in France, in the villa's pool, and visiting a plage privée, but this was different, the north of England, the place where they conducted their everyday lives.

John smiled again, his eyes telling her he understood how it seemed to her. Reaching for her hand, he kissed it, then touched her face, sweeping her still damp hair back from her brow.

'Dive…or drop in?' he asked.

'Oh, drop in, I think…with this.' She brushed her fingers against her simmering bottom, the jolt of contact creating a tiny new plume of nascent desire.

John led her forward and they slid smoothly into the pool, together. The water was divinely cool against her spanking, and she looked up at the blue sky through the translucent UV-filtering roof over the pool. She'd thought the villa in the south of France had been paradise, but this, their home, was Shangri-La.

Anywhere with John was the perfect place to be. Despite complications, despite issues, anywhere with him was home. Was right.

They trod water for a while, lazily flapping arms and legs, in just sufficient movement to keep them afloat. Lizzie closed her eyes, focusing on the contrast between different degrees of temperature. The gentle, moderate blood heat of the pool; the ebbing fires in her bottom. She imagined John, floating in the same way, eyes closed, and then got a surprise when she opened her eyes and found him watching her, speculation in his gaze.

'Ah, the secret,' she said. 'I promised I'd tell you, didn't I?'

He beamed. 'You did. You told me I'd have to beat it out of you, and I fulfilled my part of the bargain.'

Drawing in a deep breath, Lizzie stroked her way closer to the side of the pool, and secured a hold on the lipped edge. This was going to take some telling, even though she suspected that John would find the news a pleasant if ironic surprise.

'I'm not quite sure where to start with this…But you

know I mentioned that Brent had a new boyfriend?' Beside her, also holding lightly on to the lipped edge, John nodded. 'And you mentioned to me that your brother Tom had a new man in his life too?'

John blinked, then laughed softly.

'Well, fuck me!'

'I would if we had a condom handy.'

John aimed a little splash her way. 'Yes, that, obviously. But really, Brent and Tom? How on earth did that come about?' He smiled and moved forward, clearly eager for the details. 'I had no idea they'd ever even met.'

He's pleased. He's really pleased.

Lizzie wondered why she'd had any qualms about telling him. Brent's life was Brent's life, and Tom's life was Tom's life, and there was no reason why John shouldn't consider Brent an entirely suitable man for his brother.

'They actually met long before you and I ever did, believe it or not.'

As they floated lazily in the water, Lizzie recounted the story as Brent had told it to her. The one-night stand. The chance meeting in the Waverley. The realisation by both men that they wanted more.

John was silent for a moment when the story was done, and Lizzie felt a pang of disquiet, only to have it banished when he grinned broadly.

'Well, I never would have predicted this one, I must say, but I wish the pair of them well. Brent's been through the mill, and Tom's taken some serious shit from the family over his sexuality, and stood up to them. I'm happy they've found each other again.'

Lizzie surged forward through the water and hugged him and kissed him. The resulting commotion unsettled their buoyancy and they both ended up sinking beneath the water, only to burst up again, laughing and spluttering.

'I'm so glad you're pleased,' she said, panting and wiping water out of her eyes. 'Brent's a good man…and your brother sounds lovely. I'm happy they've found each other too.'

'Everyone's a winner!' announced John roundly. 'Shall we get out of the water now, dry off, and then celebrate in absentia that your friend and my brother have got together? With another of your cocktails or maybe a bottle of Champagne?' With a grin on his face, he moved towards her, gliding smoothly through the water, and then kissed her on the lips. 'And some condoms, perhaps?' he added, winking outrageously.

'Well, that's a bit weird, Mr Smith,' she shot back, but couldn't help grinning back at him. How would she keep a straight face when she next saw Brent, knowing that she'd toasted him getting a new boyfriend with Champagne…and a shag?

'Ah, but as you know full well, sweetie, I'm a very weird man.'

'True. But that's a good idea, the Champagne. And the other thing.'

'Mm…the other thing,' said John, giving her a quick, splashy kiss, then hefting himself easily from the pool, powered by the strength in his arms. 'Do you think you can manage the other thing, with a tingling red bottom?' Turning and reaching down for her, he hoisted her out effortlessly too.

Standing naked on the deck, looking into his face, Lizzie winked. 'I'll manage somehow. There isn't much on the face of this sweet earth that would keep me from the other thing with you, boss man.'

'I didn't think so,' said John, stealing another kiss.

Later, lying face down on the bed, and enjoying the afterglow of quite a lot of the other thing, Lizzie gazed at John, lying beside her.

Was he asleep? His eyes were closed. He looked relaxed. They'd made love a couple of times since the pool. First, with John sitting on the bench in the changing cabana downstairs, and most recently here in bed, with Lizzie on top, riding him furiously. Both times, he'd been scrupulously careful to avoid stirring up the furore in her spanked bottom, although now it was barely more than a simmering, nostalgic glow.

The flat screen television on the far wall was on, but with the sound low, and neither of them had really been watching it for a while. Twisting, Lizzie reached for the remote and snapped it off, having no interest in the rather lurid true crime show.

'I was listening to that.' John smiled, but didn't open his eyes. Lying naked against the pale bedding, he looked like a debauched angel, his blond curls awry, his body gleaming. Lizzie eyed his cock. It was currently somnolent, but she knew it would barely take more than her blowing on it to make it start to rise, all over again.

'No you weren't.'

'All right. I wasn't.' His blue eyes snapped open and he rolled onto his side and laid his hand possessively on the small of her back. A swirl of desire seemed to rouse beneath his touch.

'You weren't sleeping, though, were you?' she prompted.

'Not really.' His thumb moved over her skin. 'But dozing a little, I think. We're getting better on that score now, aren't we?' He smiled at her, a little, tentative, strangely vulnerable smile.

'Yes, I think we are. We'll get there, lover, I know we will…One of these days…or nights. It'll happen when we hardly realise it. We'll both wake up in the morning like a perfectly normal couple who've slept the night together.' She rolled onto her side, feeling a twinge or two from her punished bottom, but relaxing into the sensations, embracing them. Catching John's hand as it slid from her flank, she kissed his fingers.

'Not too normal,' he said with a twinkling grin, his blue eyes fiery.

'Perish the thought,' agreed Lizzie.

'I tell you one normal thing we might do,' John said, drawing his hand from her mouth, and bringing her hand to his for a reciprocating kiss. 'We could have Brent and Tom over for a meal next weekend, perhaps. Maybe make a bit of an afternoon of it? A pool party or whatever? Would you like that?'

Lizzie considered the notion. On one hand, it would be fab, like the old days, hanging out with Brent. But on the other, ooh, entertaining, scary. Especially having to put on a good show for her lover's brother. A brother who still lived in a stately home – well, at least some of the time – and who, unlike his sibling, hadn't entirely abandoned his aristocratic heritage.

John laughed softly. 'Well, I can tell from the hesitation that you've got qualms. But you shouldn't have them. Tom won't bite. He's the sort of person nobody ever feels nervous with…and I can't imagine how he could possibly fail to adore you on sight!'

'Reports of my adorableness have been greatly

exaggerated. Especially by horny old goats who are banging me.'

John shook his head. 'You are adorable. And I won't hear otherwise,' he said firmly, assuming a mock reproving tone. 'And even though we two brothers mostly admire the desirable qualities in different sexes, Tom's a man of discerning taste in beauty and character, just like I am.'

'Well, if he's as daft as you are, I'm sure he and I will get on like a house on fire.'

Lunging forward, John cupped her face and kissed her hard, a stern, masterly kiss.

'If I hadn't already spanked that lush bottom once today, I'd give it another going over. You really are the most provoking, smart-mouthed woman.' Not allowing her to get a word of answer in, he kissed her fiercely again.

After a tussle, they broke apart, and brushing her hair from her face, John said, 'Seriously, Lizzie, there's nothing to worry about. My brother is a very sweet guy, and he's far easier to get along with than I am. He's got a sense of humour, and before you say anything, he's not in the least bit stuck up. He cares even less about having a title and all that than I do. He does love Montcalm, and the family, despite the obnoxious way the old man's treated him in the past, but he's just an ordinary bloke in a lot of ways. I think you'll really like him.'

'If he's anything like you, I know I'll like him.'

It was the simple truth, despite her nerves. John's face glowed as he stared at her, strangely befuddled, as if she wasn't the only one unsure of herself and with doubts about her desirability and suitability to be loved.

'Thank you,' he said softly. 'And you will like him. Let's fix something up for next weekend, eh? We could have a buffet. A barbie, even. Very casual, very easy, no ceremony. We could all just slop about in shorts and bathing suits, and eat too much and drink too much. Brent and Tom could stay over…We've got masses of room.' He leant forward, very intent. 'And remember, you don't have to do anything at all but enjoy yourself. The Thursgoods will be here to do all the cooking and hospitality stuff. You don't have to lift a finger, sweetheart.'

Despite her initial qualms, Lizzie felt a sudden excitement. Eagerness. She'd missed seeing Brent every day. She wanted to know how he was getting on with this man he so obviously cared about. And she was curious about John's brother.

But there was one thing that still bothered her.

'Could we invite Shelley and Sholto to this beach blanket barbecue extravaganza too? It doesn't seem fair to leave Shell out of this, somehow, and if she comes, I want her to know that her bloke is welcome too.'

'Of course, you ninny! The more the merrier!' John reached over and tousled her hair playfully. 'This is your home, love. It's yours to invite whoever you want to. Your friends are my friends now, you know that.'

He made it sound so easy. Perhaps it was easy? Although there were friends and people in his life that she would still be anxious about for a long time yet, perhaps for ever.

No, don't go there. Don't think about her. Or his parents. Live for the moment!

John's eyes narrowed, as if he'd sensed the thought, and he moved closer, embracing her, silently reassuring. The warmth of his body, and the waft of his breath against her neck, renewed her confidence.

'So, who's going to invite whom? Shall I invite Brent and

tell him to bring his boyfriend?' She grinned at him as they drew apart. 'Or will you invite Tom and tell him to bring *his* boyfriend?'

John sat up, and reached for his phone on the bedside table. 'What say I invite Tom and Brent, and you invite Shelley and her friend Sholto?'

'What, now?'

'No time like the moment.' John was already scrolling through his address book. 'And it gives them time to clear their calendars.'

Lizzie burst out laughing. 'Well, I'm not sure Shell has much of a calendar to clear, Mr Business Tycoon Man...But you're right. She and Sholto both do bar work. At your Waverley Metro, I might add. So it'd be handy for them to have time to rearrange shifts if they need to.'

John waggled his eyebrows at her as if to say, 'Of course I'm right!' while his phone's call tone beeped.

'Hey, brother of mine, how do you fancy a pool party at Dalethwaite Manor next weekend? I understand your new boyfriend is a friend of my girlfriend, you sly devil. I think it's about time we all got together for the formal introductions and whatever. What do you say?'

John's instant, beaming grin said the reaction was positive.

10

Brent and Tom

'So...we're invited to a party,' said Tom Wyngarde Smith, beaming as he set his phone on the bedside table. 'Should be interesting. I'm really looking forward to meeting this incredible woman who both my brother and my boyfriend constantly rave about.'

Brent sat up too, not quite sure how he felt about the prospect of the weekend to come. He loved Lizzie. He always would. But he loved Tom too. He couldn't imagine how either one of them could not like the other, really, but life was weird sometimes, and you never knew what could happen. Especially things like ending up in bed, at the Waverley Grange Hotel, on a late Saturday afternoon, with a man you once had a one-night stand with – who also turned out to be your best friend's boyfriend's brother!

Tom had picked Brent up from the garden centre in his rather manky old Porsche at the end of his shift, and whisked him away here to the Waverley. The plan had been to have a healthy walk in the grounds, then early dinner, then bed. But somehow that had morphed into bed first, something Brent didn't mind in the least.

'You'll like Lizzie,' he said, studying Tom's handsome face. 'Really. She's kind and fun and very intelligent, though she plays it down. And she's astonishingly beautiful, something else she won't believe when you try to convince her of it.'

Tom pursed his lips, those firm, shapely lips that were so quick to curve in a generous smile. Was he worried? Over Lizzie? Bloody hell, was he jealous? It seemed incomprehensible, and yet, Brent considered his own insecurities. The ones he'd always had, and the new ones, out and about with Tom, who was every inch a stunner in his own way as his elder brother was.

'Look, I can't deny that I've been with women in the past, and not only when I was an escort. I love Lizzie.' He reached out, and grabbed his lover's hand. 'She is beautiful. I still think she's gorgeous. But I love her as a friend now. Sex was good when we were together, but we both knew we weren't really suited that way, not deep down.'

Tom laughed. His face lit up. Oh hell, that smile. John Smith had it too. It was a knockout. Beneath the sheet Brent's cock started to stir again, even though they were fresh from pleasure. He could get a hard-on just from Tom's smile, never mind the rest of his magnificently fanciable face and body.

'I'm being a twerp, aren't I?' said Tom. 'A nervous nelly, spooking over every desirable person of either sex that I think you might be lusting after.'

Brent swallowed. For a moment, emotion blocked his throat. It awed him that Tom could feel just the same way he did, and think of him as just the kind of ultimate lover that he considered Tom to be.

'Yes, you're an idiot. You're the one I want. But if it's any comfort, the twerpishness is pretty mutual.'

His heart thudded. He smiled back at Tom. He felt giddy. *This is it*, his heart beat out in a tattoo. *He's the one. Really the one.*

Not having to say anything, they fell into an embrace, Tom subsiding onto the pillows, on his back, strong, but, for the moment, yielding.

'She's good for John, you know, your Lizzie is,' said the older man, when Brent lifted his face for a moment, gasping for air. 'I don't think he's ever been this happy in his entire life. I mean...I've only spoken to him on the phone, but it's in everything he says, in his tone of voice. He's different, but in the best possible way.' He gave a quizzical lift of his brows. 'Probably sounds weird, given my brother's success and wealth, but I think Lizzie is the making of him, I really do.'

Brent considered his lover's words. 'Well, I don't know your brother all that well, so I've no frame of reference, but when I've seen them together they seem well matched. As if they're meant to be together.'

Tom's hands slid over Brent's back. The touch was intimate, and yet a little distracted. He had more to say about his brother. Brent didn't push for more kisses; he prepared to listen.

'John hasn't had a "steady" woman for a long time, and when he did have one, well, you wouldn't believe the complications. Considering that he's the looker of the family, Goldilocks has had the most tortuous luck with women!'

'Goldilocks?' Brent smiled. John Smith was a looker, and he did have the most remarkable blond hair. Not as gorgeous as his younger brother's thick, wild brown locks, but lush, just the same.

'Childhood nickname. Both George and I have dark hair. Well, George is getting a bit grey now, but it was dark once. We take after our mother's side of the family, and John takes after Pa, who's always had a bit of a lion's mane, even if it's shock-white now.'

Brent would have liked to find out more about the rest of the Wyngarde Smiths, these blue-blooded men with titles, lineage and the whole shebang. He hadn't met them as yet. Tom's cottage was on the edge of the park, a fair distance from the main house and formal gardens. But there might – would – come a time when it was unavoidable. If he took the job, at least, he'd very probably encounter members of the family when he was working. But it could be much more than that. Hell, he might be facing exactly the same quasi 'in laws' issues that Lizzie had ahead of her.

'So, John's women, what about them?' John Smith's romantic history was something he needed to know more about; because it impacted on Lizzie's present and future, and her happiness.

Tom grasped his hand, and the two men lay on their sides, facing each other.

'Well, for long enough now, he's only really had short-term relationships. "Affairs", I suppose you'd call them, although they'd barely merit the term. He just wasn't interested in anything serious, after Clara…even after all these years. And being married to Caroline…'

Brent had heard these names mentioned in passing before, but he and Tom hadn't really touched on Tom's brother's love life all that much. They'd been too busy enjoying their own.

'Caroline was his wife, right? And Clara…a girlfriend? Fiancée? What?'

Tom heaved a sigh. 'Well, I would have said she was the love of his life, until recently, but now Lizzie's obviously taken that crown.' He frowned. 'The trouble is…Now that she's lost his love for good and all, Clara might decide she wants it again, especially if she knows he's with someone else. She's like that.'

Brent kept silent, waiting for more. He felt that Tom was right about Lizzie's status with her man, and the idea that this woman from John's past might hurt her was chilling.

'Clara was…is…poison. Beautiful poison. She fucked my brother over big style.' Tom made a sound of exasperation, his words confirming Brent's fears. 'Jonny is the strongest, toughest, smartest man I've ever known, but love can make even otherwise intelligent men into total idiots.'

Against his will, Brent tensed, and Tom laughed. 'Fret not. That is not the case with us!'

The sense of carousel, of elated giddiness, surged again, but Brent made a conscious effort to settle, stay quiet, to pay attention.

'Clara chucked John over, just when he needed her. And then she fucking well did it again, years later, when he thought they were both older and wiser and had a real chance.'

Brent found it hard to imagine any woman chucking over John Smith. He had everything, looks, money, innate charm. Just like his brother.

'Seems hard to believe, someone dumping your bro.'

'Exactly,' responded Tom. 'But Clara was…is…Clara. Always looking for the bigger, better prize, or whatever. And the first time, well, he was the second son…and a jailbird. Not the greatest catch. So she broke up with him by default. Just never visited him, never replied to letters and was gone by the time he got out.'

'What a mare.'

'You said it!' Brent sensed there was clearly no love lost between Tom and John's ex-lover. 'Not sure why she dumped him the second time. She was technically between husbands then, and John was fairly loaded by that time.' Tom paused, as if for effect. 'Knowing Clara, she was probably paying him back for marrying her mother.'

Brent felt his jaw drop, and knew he was gaping like an idiot. 'What the fuck? What are you on about?'

'Oh, I guess you didn't know. Which tends to suggest that Lizzie doesn't know either.' Tom's eyes widened.

'Know what?'

'That Caroline, John's ex-wife, is Clara's mother.'

'Jesus fuck! How the hell did that come about?'

Brent listened, rapt, sex with his gorgeous boyfriend almost forgotten, as Tom told the tale. The story of how Caroline had always fancied her daughter's beautiful, golden boyfriend, and when Clara had treated John so badly, the older woman had done a crazy and also bizarrely compassionate thing. She'd asked him to marry her, in exchange for making him a rich, rich man in his own right.

'No, I'm almost certain Lizzie doesn't know that,' Brent said when Tom fell silent. 'She knows about him having an ex called Clara, who was shitty to him, but if she'd known about a tangled web like this, she'd definitely have told me.'

'I think you're right,' said Tom, reaching out to touch Brent's face. His fingertips were strong, yet the touch was feather-light, suggesting, prompting.

Brent's libido stirred, yet still this mad revelation gripped him. 'I wonder why he wouldn't tell her? I mean, it's quite a big thing, really.'

Tom's fine-featured face grew thoughtful. 'I…I think maybe it's some kind of Achilles' heel. I think John sees his entanglement with Clara as a kind of weakness now. And he's a proud man. He's strong and confident and very clever. It's human nature, and masculine ego, to want to be seen as all-powerful to the woman he loves, and his history with Clara undermines that. It doesn't make him a bad person to want to hide the screw-ups of his life, and be the great hero, the invulnerable warrior, for his woman.'

Brent laughed softly, then turned his face to kiss Tom's palm. 'You're a very smart man, lover. You should be a psychologist, or a counsellor or something. I hope you're not trying to analyse me all the time. I think you'll find that I'm perfectly aware of my own shortcomings. And…well…after cocking up my life a fair bit thus far, I'm actually quite comfortable with them.'

Before Brent could catch his breath, Tom lunged forward, grabbed him by the back of his head, and kissed him hard, very hard. It was a wild kiss, but affectionate too.

'I like you just the way you are, man.' he said as they broke apart. 'Shortcomings and all…In fact…' The older man drew in a deep breath. 'I love you, Brent. You know that, don't you? All this talk about a job at Montcalm…and the cottage and all. I just want to be around you as much as I can possibly be. I want us to be together. Properly. A couple.' His mouth twisted in a wry grin. 'We'll just have to build up to it very carefully, very cannily. The old man knows I'm gay, even though he chooses to ignore the fact. This will be putting it right in his face, though, and I don't want him to have another of his turns. But I think we'll be OK with a bit of finesse.'

Brent shook. His body wouldn't stop trembling. They'd been circling around this, since almost the moment they'd come together again. But this was Tom's most overt declaration so far.

You're everything I want too.

'I know it's quick. And if it's too soon for you, I understand.' Tom's voice sounded almost breathy, and Brent could see, wonder of wonders, that his lover was trembling too.

He laughed. He couldn't stop himself. It was an expression of pure joy.

'Not too soon for me!' he cried, wrapping his arms around Tom, and answering the wild kiss he'd received with one of his own. 'I fucking knew it the moment I saw you again. I just knew it, man. That first time, we weren't ready. We had to go through stuff…At least, I had. But now I'm ready. Completely ready.' He gave Tom a steady look. 'Of course, I'll play it low key in public. Don't want to cause you family grief. But between just the two of us, I'm yours, Thomas Wyngarde Smith, for good and all, as long as you want me.' He kissed his lover again, a soft, sweet kiss. 'I love you, Tom. I love you.'

They kissed again, rolling around, devouring each other, the kisses all-embracing. It was all emotion, yet sex too. Their bodies surged together beneath the sheets, cocks rubbing against each other, more haphazardly than with intent, but deliciously pleasurable and exciting all the same. Tom slipped onto his back, his hands sliding possessively around Brent's buttocks, increasing the pressure, increasing the friction, his legs coming up, presenting his erection to Brent's in the cradle of his pelvis.

Oh, this was so good. So sweet. They'd already come off a while ago, rocking and rubbing their cocks together, stroking each other to climax. But now Brent wanted and needed more, the closer communion, and he knew without having to be told that Tom wanted that too.

'Please…have me, love. Fuck me,' Brent whispered, offering himself. They'd never felt the need to discuss who did who, but Tom had naturally assumed the role of the dominant partner.

'You're beautiful,' answered Tom, his voice unsteady. 'I love the way you feel when I'm inside you…It's perfect…but…I…'

Oh dear God.

Brent almost threw himself at Tom, kissing harder, almost on fire with love. Blown away that this beautiful prince of a man would offer himself. His cock was a rod of steel, forged hard by desire and emotion, ready to enter, to possess.

'You're sure?'

'Yes, completely,' said Tom, smiling as they drew apart.

Brent was all of a dither. He laughed at himself.

Shape up, man! Be a stud! That's what he wants.

'OK, then, gorgeous…Let's get to it.' He kissed Tom again, then pushed at him, urging him to roll over. 'I'd like you this way. I want to see that hot, tight arse of yours as I'm pushing in. I want you to be touching yourself as I fuck you. Stroking your rod.'

'You say the sweetest things, lover.' Tom laughed, complying.

As his lover moved into position, Brent cast around and snatched the towel flung across the end of the bed. Things might get messy, with lube and spunk, and nobody wanted to get either of those on the twee chintz bedding of the Waverley. Although God knows how much spunk got spilt on a regular basis in this den of iniquity.

He nudged at Tom, nodding at the towel. This wasn't going to be the most elegant procedure. In fact, as they shuffled around, getting tangled in their limbs and the towel, rearranging themselves, it all got a bit haphazard. But they laughed, and got sorted, and pretty soon, Brent was pressing the head of his latex-clad cock to Tom's anus.

It was a tipping point, the first time for him, with Tom. Strong as he felt, his eyes filled with tears. He blinked them away, but one dropped on his lover's back as he inclined over him.

'Go for it, big boy,' encouraged Tom. Brent knew that somehow, he'd felt the tear, the hesitation. 'Go for it.'

Brent pushed. Tom was tight, the ring so very snug, so resisting. Brent could almost taste Tom's tension. It was a familiar, beautiful fear, even as desired as the act was. So he spoke softly to Tom, plying him with nonsense love words, anything to help him relax. To amuse him too, to make it fun, because fun always gentled the way. And it worked, because Tom grinned over his shoulder, looking back at him.

'You really are the most loveable dickhead, you know.'

'I should think I am!' said Brent with a laugh, pushing with that head of his dick, passionate and ironic. His reward was Tom's body yielding to him and letting him in.

He slid home. Deep and home. Home, more than physically. He bent over Tom's back, putting skin to skin, while he was lodged inside his lover. He kissed Tom's skin, beyond words, loving the tight heat surrounding his cock.

'Oh man,' sighed Tom, adjusting his position, going onto one elbow as he reached beneath him.

'Yes!' encouraged Brent, eager for his lover-man to pleasure himself.

They rocked and swayed. Brent began to thrust, keeping it smooth, even though the temptation to go maniacally wild was huge. Tom, around him, was delicious. Heaven on earth. He groaned, keeping it sleek and steady, swinging his hips in a light arc, in and out, in and out.

'Oh yes, man, yes, do me! Do me! Do me! Do me!'

Right over Tom now, like a second skin, Brent let go, thrusting, thrusting hard, losing his control. His body escaped him and on his last scrap of control, he kissed and kissed again, pressing his mouth to Tom's mad, brown curls, tears dropping onto the lush silkiness of them.

Hips on auto, he thrust and shagged and fucked. Tom was with him, loving the furore, gasping, grunting, burbling love words of his own, barely supporting himself while with his strong right hand he pumped his cock in time to the beat of Brent's possession.

It could not last long. It was too fabulous. Brent shouted, his cock pumping semen into the latex that contained him, while he reached beneath, folding his fingers around his lover's fingers to feel the pump of his seed, free and unfettered, spurting over their clasped hands onto the towel beneath.

With a great sigh, a sigh that Tom echoed back to him, Brent collapsed over his lover. For a few moments, they lay joined, sticky and happy, then they each rolled to one side and settled as spoons, smiling, lost for words, but not needing them.

A while later, fresh from a shared shower and more fun

– mutual masturbation beneath the teeming water – Brent stepped into fresh boxer briefs from the overnight bag he'd brought with him. 'Do you think I should tell Lizzie about Caroline and Clara when I see her?' he asked Tom, who was buttoning his shirt. The two of them had agreed on a meal in the hotel's restaurant, then an evening walk, then back to bed. Shagging was great, wonderful, the best, but somehow doing other things too had acquired a precious new aura of togetherness.

Tom paused, pursed his lips. 'I dunno…perhaps not. I think we ought to let John tell her the full story. In his own time.' His slender fingers went back to work on his buttons. 'I understand his hesitation, but he'll tell her sooner rather than later. He's a decent man. He doesn't like keeping secrets. Not really.'

'I wonder how she'll take it?' mused Brent. 'It's a bit of a shocker.'

She'll probably take it quite well, though, on second thoughts. Lizzie was strong and pragmatic, not a wimpy, weepy woman who behaved like an emo.

'She sounds quite a grounded character,' said Tom.

'She is,' Brent agreed. 'She's got a lot of sense.'

Tom came over to him, and embraced him. 'Don't worry. They're both intelligent. Both grown up. I think my brother and your friend have some ups and downs ahead, but they'll get there. I'm sure of it. I know my brother. He's made mistakes, but he does learn. That's his great strength. And your Lizzie sounds like his perfect match.'

She is. She is.

Brent smiled as they completed their dressing and set forth from their room, together. Always together. From now on.

As he was sure Lizzie would be with her John, before long.

Tom smiled back at him, and took his hand, as they walked.

11

The Perfect Hostess

'Don't worry, you'll be the perfect hostess, Lizzie. You look divine, and you don't have to do a thing. Mrs T has got every food angle covered, and Thursgood will sort everything else. All you have to do is enjoy yourself.'

Gah, easy for him! Swanning back home after being away most of the week, and completely used to sophisticated parties to start with. John was so suave and self-assured, he could fit in and probably be an honoured guest at every gathering he'd ever been invited to. When had he last experienced a single nerve at all, the blasé git?

I'm being really stupid. It isn't as if the Queen's coming round for a burger or a burnt sausage. These are all my friends, plus John's brother, who's apparently a sweetheart anyway. And Shelley's bloke, who I'm sure is also a fairly normal human being. Well, sort of…

It was all under control. It would be fun. She had to calm down.

John came to her, across the room, and stood behind her as she frowned into the mirror. With his hands on her shoulders, she felt the twanging of her nerves settle. Ever since she'd first met him, she been aware of this hypnotic way he had, and how it affected her, and now he was using it to cool her fears and make her relax.

'See...Don't we look a fabulous couple?' He smiled at her in the mirror, his eyes wise and blue as he did something amazing with his thumbs that unzipped the tension in her shoulders like a miracle cure.

He was right too. They did look great. And seeing the heat in John's eyes only affirmed what she knew in herself. At the risk of being big-headed about it, she looked a knockout in her newly finished red and white flower patterned sundress. It was something she'd had half done in a dress bag, not sure when she'd have an opportunity to wear it, but she'd completed it during the week for the party, in spare moments.

In fact, she'd been sewing like a maniac altogether this week, with John away several nights on business in Belgium. It'd been a perfect time to catch up on a lot of New Again alterations and some original commissions too. She'd worked so hard and, with help from Mary, she'd almost got ahead of herself. And the intensely focused concentration, the Zen quality of really getting in the zone with a garment, was the ideal panacea for missing the man she adored and yearned to be with.

'If you were some fancy air-head of a mistress, you could have come with me,' he'd said, when suited and booted and just about to leave, 'but as you're a businesswoman yourself now, as well as a highly sought-after craftswoman, I can't just drag you off with me whenever I want to, can I?'

'No, you can't,' she'd asserted, just a teeny-tiny part of her psyche wishing she could just chuck everything up and travel with him. The main bit of her, though, was newly proud and thrilled that at last she did have a career and purpose of her own, a great partner to work with in Marie, and that her days of bumbling through life, not amounting to very much, were a thing of the past.

John didn't define her, but she loved him ever more each day for helping her to achieve her potential. It sounded like a cliché, but it was true.

She smoothed her hands over the full skirt of her dress, and the vivid, quite garishly patterned fabric that just somehow worked and looked adorable. With her hair in a ponytail, and her lips tinted and eyelashes dyed, she'd nailed a look that was both casual and prettily party-style at the same time. Especially with her diamond earrings to add that extra touch of glamour. If you were going to entertain your mates in a five point two million pound mansion house, there was no point in holding back on the bling, was there?

And the man standing behind her, whose hands now slid around her waist, just looked like a god and a million squillion dollars rolled into one, it was as simple as that.

You devil, you know how fab you look in blue, don't you? She grinned at him.

'Yes, I think we look pretty nifty, Mr Smith.' Observing his answering smile, she squeaked when he pulled her closer and she felt him, hard against her bottom.

With a hard-on or not, John too cut exactly the right figure for a laid-back weekend party. His suit was soft, mid-blue linen, with a slightly darker shirt. She wasn't sure what the weather had been like in Belgium, but he still had a bit of his light, south of France tan, and the combination of that, and his blue clothing, made his eyes flash as bright as a pair of aquamarines.

If the guests hadn't been arriving any minute, Lizzie

would have suggested that he take off his fabulous blue suit, and the rest of it, and that he ravish her furiously on the bed, in very short order. She almost did it anyway, but just at that moment, there came the sound of crunching gravel, a vehicle drawing up on the drive outside.

'Shit. Damn. I was just going to suggest that we strip off again and have a quick fuck,' said John with a soft laugh. Great minds thought alike, but then, there wasn't often a time when they didn't want to make love.

With a pat on his hand, Lizzie shook herself free of John and hurried to the window. A taxi stood idling below, with Shelley standing waiting while the tall man beside her paid it off.

The mysterious Sholto Kraft.

'So that's Sholto, then,' Lizzie said quietly to John, who'd come up beside her.

Sholto Kraft was tall and muscular, with brutally short hair. It was a hard look, and made harder by black jeans and T-shirt, and a boxy black jacket. His face was all tough lines too, but Lizzie felt a rush of relief when the man smiled at Shelley in a gentle, thoughtful way. Lizzie's friend was currently staring up at the frontage of Dalethwaite Manor, and didn't see the fond expression, but it spoke volumes about how the man at her side felt about her.

'Looks a bit hard-core, doesn't he?' whispered John.

'Yes,' agreed Lizzie, 'but…I dunno…I think they'll be all right together, don't you?' She turned to him.

'I think you're probably right, sweetheart. Now, shall we go down and meet him, just to be sure?' He reached for her hand and held it in both of his. It was his power grip, giving strength to her, with his touch and with the expression in his eyes that said, *we're in this together*.

'Absolutely. Game on!' Not letting him let go of her, she made for the door. No shillyshallying and forever checking her face, hair, dress, whatever, allowed.

Down in the entrance hall, Thursgood was just ushering Shelley and Sholto in the general direction of the pool.

'Lizzie!' cried Shelley, hurling herself forward. The two women had seen each other in the week, meeting with Marie to discuss Shelley's part-time job at New Again, but Lizzie had a feeling her friend was just as nervous now as she was. Hence the almost desperate over-enthusiasm.

Lizzie returned the bear hug, her own embrace of her friend just as full-on.

'I'm so glad you're here, Shell,' she said. 'Really I am. And you too, Sholto.' As she and Shelley detached, she held out her hand to the tall, austere figure standing a little way behind her. 'We've never met…I'm Lizzie, obviously, and this is John…my…'

She turned to find him close, smiling. God, he was so at ease, the devil. 'John Smith, Lizzie's boyfriend. Pleased to meet you.' He shook Sholto's hand briskly, then gave Shelley an air kiss worthy of an A list red carpet. 'Good to see you again, Shelley, welcome to Dalethwaite Manor. Shall we all head for the pool and get a drink?'

Lizzie and Shelley exchanged 'eek!' looks as they made their way through the house and out onto the deck.

Was there a bit of an atmosphere? Two alpha males, head to head? Lizzie monitored the two men as John handed out beer for himself and Sholto, and she automatically prepped two white wine spritzers for her friend and herself. Probably better not to get too blasted too soon.

Lizzie's heart thudded through a bit of nervy chat about

the house, and God almighty, the weather, then Sholto said to John:

'That's a nice car you have out front there. A Bentley Gran Turismo?'

'Yeah, I like it,' John replied. 'It's very smooth. I don't drive myself a great deal…Sometimes it's handy to be driven, when I'm prepping for a meeting, but I do like the Bentley for general A to B…Want to take a look?'

'Cool. That'd be great.'

'Back in a bit.' John grinned over his shoulder as the two men headed in the direction of the front of the house.

'Thank God for cars!' Lizzie grinned at Shelley. 'Blokes all seem to have an inner petrol head, thank goodness. It's like the universal language they can all speak when they're at a loss.'

'Thank God for John,' said Shelley with feeling. 'I was a bit nervous coming here. I mean, not that Sholto's weird or anything. It's just, well, he can be a bit prickly sometimes, with the stuff that's happened to him, and I was a bit worried he'd take against John because he has so much money and he's so successful and everything…and he owns the house I live in.' She lifted her glass, and clinked it to Lizzie's. 'But I think they're going to be OK, fingers crossed. He seems quite relaxed, and John's such a great guy. I can't imagine anybody not getting on with him. He's like…ultra-charming, but not too OTT and smarmy with it.'

'I'll tell him that,' said Lizzie with a grin.

'Oh, don't!'

'You're right. Probably best not to,' observed Lizzie. 'John's far too aware of his own gorgeousness already. And it never does to encourage a man to think he's God's gift. Even if he is.'

The two laughed and sipped their drinks. Shelley stretched out on her lounger, like a contented cat. Lizzie was happy to see her friend so relaxed.

'It's fab here, Lizzie. You're very lucky. Glorious house. Glorious man.' Shelley shrugged and kicked off her sandals, pointing her toes. 'But at least I'm partway there. I've got the bloke...and even if St Patrick's Road isn't Dalethwaite Manor, it's home, and it's...well...safe, thanks to John.'

From the other side of the house came the sound of the Bentley's engine firing up, followed by some aggressive revving. And then even more revving.

'They'll be in seventh heaven now,' remarked Lizzie. 'Boys with their toys, poring over carburettors and tappets and big ends and stuff.'

'Sholto's more of a biker really, although he doesn't have a bike at the moment. He might get one again, though, now things are looking up a bit. He managed to pay off most of his debts with his escorting money, and now he's got a steady job at the Waverley Metro, and I've got regular money coming in, so we're not doing too badly.' For a moment, Shelley frowned. 'If only he'd move in full-time at St Patrick's Road, and give up his horrid digs completely.'

Lizzie eyed her friend. *Ah, still some tension there...Just like me and John.*

'You'll have to work on him. He'll come around. Even these take-charge types can mellow eventually.'

The two women chatted idly for a while. It was such a peaceful afternoon. Lizzie couldn't imagine why she'd been nervous. When John and Sholto returned they were talking easily. Motorbikes, it sounded like, with John apparently considering purchasing one. Lizzie hid a grin, her mind filling with her pervading fantasy of leather trousers.

'Fancy a swim, Shell?' called Sholto after a few moments, and when Shelley roused herself and the two made their way to the changing cabana, John took her place on the lounger next to Lizzie.

'Seems like a sound man,' he said, sitting sideways on, facing her where she lay stretched out. 'I think Shelley will be OK with him. I wouldn't worry.'

Lizzie gave him a provocative look over the top of her sunglasses. 'Ah, so he's passed the John Smith character assessment, then, has he? That's good to know. Although, knowing Shelley, if she likes him, it wouldn't matter in the slightest if everybody else thinks he's a total git.'

As she sat up to face him, John reached for her hand. 'I hope I can rely on that degree of unswerving support from you. You haven't forgotten we're visiting your parents for your dad's birthday next weekend? You will still like me if they think I'm a total git, won't you?'

For a fleeting moment, a look of almost boyish vulnerability crossed his face, and Lizzie drew his hand to her lips and kissed it passionately. 'You know I like you. I love you, you dickhead! And I don't give a monkey's what my parents think of you.' She kissed his knuckles again. 'But having said that, I know they will like you. What's not to like? You're as charming as the day is long and you've got obscene mountains of money! My mother at least is amazed I've done so well for myself.'

'You know what I mean,' he said, his blue eyes still serious.

She did. It was the age difference again. But she wasn't having any of that sort of talk from him any more!

'Don't be ridiculous, John. And don't go there. How many times do I have to tell you, it doesn't matter to me, and it doesn't matter to me what anybody else thinks, either?' She gave him a very fierce look. 'Just as long as you can manage without your Zimmer frame for the duration of the visit, Methuselah, I don't think anybody will notice you're ninety-six.'

'Cheeky mare!' The grin, the dazzling golden wonder-grin returned, and with it surged Lizzie's ever-simmering desire. If only they didn't have guests. She'd have dragged him up to the master bedroom and begged him to make love to her.

But just as she was about to lunge forward, and steal a quick, hot kiss, at least, before Shelley and Sholto returned from changing, the sound of voices issued from the interior of the house, rapidly approaching. A second or two later, Thursgood ushered Brent on to the deck, and alongside him strode a man who could only be Tom Wyngarde Smith.

'Goldilocks, you old bugger, how the devil are you?' demanded the newcomer as John shot to his feet and approached his brother. 'This is one sweet gaff you've got here.'

The two siblings embraced, as Brent, smiling and looking very dapper in chinos and a white shirt, came over to give Lizzie a hug.

'Looking fab as ever, Mizz Bettie,' he said, putting his arms tightly around her.

As they all drew apart, Lizzie had the chance to quickly study John's younger brother, and was powerfully struck by their family resemblance. The two men were the same height, and roughly the same build, although Tom was a touch on the skinny side. Where John's hair was golden, Tom's was light brown, but they both had the same wild curls. Tom's features were slightly sharper than John's but they both had the same brilliant blue eyes. And the same killer smile, she discovered, as Tom approached her, beaming.

No formal handshake for Tom Wyngarde Smith, it seemed. He swept her into a hug almost as enthusiastic as the one he'd shared with John.

'Lizzie! How wonderful to meet you at last!' He let her go, but ran his hands down her arms to take hold of her hands. 'You're even more gorgeous than John and Brent have described to me, and believe you me, they both described you as the very last thing in ultimate female beauty and grace. Bettie Page for the twenty-first century…and they're exactly right.'

'Yikes,' was all she could say. Oh, he was lovely. Every bit as drop-dead fabulous as his brother. Lucky Brent!

She turned to John, grinning. 'Goldilocks?'

John rolled his eyes, and Tom reached out and ruffled his hair. 'Suits him, doesn't it?' he said, winking at Lizzie.

Lizzie grinned back at him. 'Indeed it does. In fact, his golden locks were what caught my eye in the first place, across a crowded bar. That and the outrageous way he ogled me.' She gave John's brother a bold look. Might as well grasp the nettle. 'I'm guessing that John's told you pretty much how we met. About our slightly unorthodox first date?'

'He did…and I think the old devil was damned lucky to find such a delicious, clever woman who was prepared to play along and outwit him at his own mad games.'

John gave his brother a mock-stern look. 'OK, so we met under rather unconventional circumstances. Can we get past that?'

'Of course,' said Tom, giving his brother another hug,

then reaching out to grip Lizzie's hand. 'I can't imagine an unconventional meeting turning out better.' He turned from both of them, and smiled at Brent. 'Except maybe mine with this guy. Now, is there any possibility that a man can a get a beer in this joint? I'm dying of thirst!'

'Well, we've got beer, wine, cocktails if you want them, and plenty of soft drinks.' John gave his brother a wink. 'And of course there's that big old trough there, too, if you're desperate.' He nodded to the gleaming pool, rendered sky blue by its tiling.

As Tom made a beeline for the refreshments, John shook Brent by the hand. 'Good to see you, Brent. Welcome to Dalethwaite.' He slid an arm about the younger man's shoulder. 'Weird how life turns out, isn't it? But I'm glad about you and my brother...Really...He's a good man. I'm happy you're together.'

Brent looked a bit flummoxed, but his smile was irrepressible. 'Thanks...He is a good man.'

As her old friend wandered off to join his lover and get a drink, Lizzie studied John closely. She couldn't be sure, but she'd always sensed a lingering touch of edge between John and Brent. Understandable, really, as she'd once been Brent's girlfriend for a while. It must've been a bit odd for John, to be around someone else she'd slept with.

But now that awkward edge was gone. John was relaxed, and his expression, as he watched Brent and Tom rummaging through the drinks cooler, was contented. Openly approving. Thank God for that.

Shelley and Sholto emerged from the changing cabana and more introductions were made. Lizzie noted that her friend's colour was a bit hectic, and she smiled to herself. A few naughty shenanigans in the changing room? Why not…? Crikey, if she hadn't been the hostess with the mostest, she might have dragged John in there next. He looked totally edible in his blue linen suit and with the sunshine making his hair doubly golden.

As she yearned for him, he turned suddenly and gave her a long, hot look, as if he'd read her thought from afar. The fire in his eyes promised that they'd get their turn, later.

The afternoon flowed easily. Her qualms had been groundless, and despite their varied backgrounds, the members of the party seemed to gel nicely as a group. The food and drink was perfection, thanks to Mrs T, and nobody seemed to object to John's 1980s music either.

After a while, she retired to a lounger with a glass of iced water, John by her side on the next one along. He'd shed his jacket and rolled up his sleeves, and he looked chilled out, yet mysterious, wearing his shades. Everyone else was in the pool, and engaged in a noisy and rather peculiar hybrid of tag and water polo. Lizzie had no idea of the scoring system, but judging by the shouting, Sholto appeared to have amassed ten thousand points already and they'd only been playing around fifteen minutes. Tom, who'd been the one to devise the game, was doing atrociously and apparently already in negative figures.

It's idyllic. If this is 'entertaining', I could do it every weekend.

But not next weekend. A trickle of unease ran through her. John was wonderful, but meeting parents was meeting parents. Still, her father's birthday party was a far less daunting prospect than any future visit to Montcalm, even though she'd be subject to cross-questioning by just about everybody at her parents' house: her father, her mother, her sisters Nikki and Judy, and her grandparents – and probably most of her aunts and uncles and her father's friends and colleagues too.

But, having survived that, would she go to Montcalm any time soon? And as what? Friend? Girlfriend? More than that? Best not to dwell on it. Just face things when they arose…That made better sense.

Even though they were beneath the canopy now, the beating sun was warm. But still Lizzie shivered.

'Are you OK, love?'

She turned and discovered John watching her, sunglasses dangling from his fingertips.

'Yes…fine…In fact, better than fine. This is lovely, isn't it?' She made a sweeping gesture, encompassing the pool, the people, the laughter.

'It is, and I told you so.' John leant over and kissed her cheek. 'But you shivered just now. You're not cold, are you?'

'It's nothing. I was just thinking about visiting my parents again. I mean…I know it'll all be fine, but I'm still nervous, you know?'

The kiss turned into a hug, body contact for reassurance. The dizzying deliciousness of John's cologne was enough to distract anyone from their worries.

'We'll be fine. We'll be together,' he said simply.

And Lizzie felt better.

They lay back on their loungers for a while, watching the 'game'. Lizzie was just wondering about attacking the buffet and scoring some of Mrs T's mouth-watering barbecued chicken, when Thursgood approached John from inside the house.

'There's a phone call for you, sir. I would have taken a message, but it's Mrs Pemberton, so I thought you'd like to take it.'

Lizzie shot up on the lounger. Pemberton. Wasn't that John's ex-wife's name?

John didn't actually frown, but he looked puzzled. 'That's fine, Thursgood. I'll take it in the office.'

None of my business. None of my business.

But when John leapt lightly to his feet, he turned, and offered his hand to her, drawing her up. He didn't speak, but he seemed to be expecting her to come with him to take the call.

'It's OK.' She tried to demur. 'I'm sure you've got lots to talk about with Caroline.'

'Probably, yes,' he said easily, his fingers firm on her hand, insistent. 'But nothing that can't be said in front of you, sweetheart.' When she got up, he flung an arm around her waist and urged her along with him as he headed for indoors, and the office.

'This'll be a nice chance for you to say "hello", Lizzie. Caroline is a wonderful woman, and I'm sure you'll get on famously.' He gave her a sparkling smile. 'And after all, you've met one member of my family today, so you might as well meet another...sort of. Don't be scared.'

But as they entered the office, to take the call, she shivered again. Easy for him to say!

12

The Former Mrs Smith

'Caro! How are you? How nice to hear from you again so soon. Nothing amiss, I hope?'

As he pressed the button for speakerphone, there was a hint of wariness in John's voice that Lizzie hadn't expected. She knew he was fond of his ex-wife, and she didn't begrudge him the bond he must still have with Caroline, but she had the strangest feeling that something else was bothering him, something else that might be related to Caroline. Or might not.

'No, nothing amiss, John, darling. Sorry to call you out of the blue like this. I do hope this isn't an inconvenient time?'

The high-end phone had a crystal clear speaker, and the voice that issued from it was low and warm, with not quite a cut-glass accent but refined in a gentle sort of way. If Lizzie hadn't known Caroline was seventy, she'd have pinned her as a much younger woman.

'Not at all. Not at all. Just enjoying a quiet weekend party, with Lizzie and a few friends. Tom's here too.' He glanced at Lizzie, nodding. 'Lizzie's here with me now, by the way. We have you on the speaker.'

Panic whirled. Goodness, she'd have to speak to John's ex now. Obviously she was nice, but still.

'Hello, my dear,' said Caroline. 'I'm so sorry to interrupt your party like this. I do hope you don't mind. I…' The older woman hesitated. 'I was hoping to drop in and see you and John this afternoon. We're over for a few days, and Ralph is at some dreary regimental reunion thing. I'm only about twenty minutes' drive away, but if you're entertaining, I wouldn't dream of intruding.'

Lizzie didn't stop to think. 'Oh, please, do come! It's only a casual pool party thing. With a bit of barbecue and a few beers and a bit of wine and swimming and stuff, but you're more than welcome. Please come. We'd love you to join us.'

John slid his arm around her waist in a fierce hug, and he kissed the side of her face. *Thanks, love*, he mimed, smiling.

From the other end of the line, Caroline laughed. 'Well, I'm not sure about the swimming, but a glass of wine and some barbecue sounds perfect. I'd love to join you. Thank you so much for asking me.'

'That's wonderful, Caro. We'll see you soon, then,' said John. 'Do you have directions?'

'Oh yes, we'll find you. We have satnav, of course, and Fenton has the navigational instincts of a homing pigeon. He can find any place, anywhere. I'll see you in about twenty minutes, then, darlings. So looking forward to meeting you, Lizzie. Ciao!'

The line went dead. Oh, crikey. What to do now? Lizzie felt like she had to 'do something', make some special preparation – but what?

Oh hell, I'm going to meet John's ex-wife!

'Don't worry! Don't worry!' John's arm tightened

around her, and he guided her to the sofa that was set in a bay-window niche.

'Of course I have to worry,' she shot back at him. 'It's your ex-wife, John! How can I not be nervous?'

He cupped her jaw with his fingers and made her look at him, gentle, but firm. Very firm. 'I understand, love, really I do. Would you believe that I've sometimes felt a bit nervous around Brent? Because he knew you first, and loved you.'

She'd wondered. Yes, she'd wondered. 'But you're fine with him now? I mean, today…It's been great, hasn't it?'

'Yes, he's a good guy, and I'm glad he's with Tom.' He laughed. 'I'm over my insecurities now.'

Lizzie twisted in his grip, and quickly kissed his hand. 'The difference is, I was never married to Brent. You and Caroline must have been much closer.'

'Yes…and no. What we had was good, but predicated by so many different issues. It was hardly ever a simple "boy meets girl", believe me.' He looked away for a moment, a frown pleating his brow. 'And there're complications. Well, a complication. One that I've not told you about yet.'

What complications? What?

'What do you mean?' Lizzie's heart fluttered. John's face was so tense now, stressed. For once he looked his age. 'Is it something you can tell me about now?'

John slid his hand down her arm, and then took both her hands in both of his. 'Yes. In fact, I must tell you now, even though it'll seem very weird to you. Downright peculiar, to be honest. But I have to tell you now that Caroline's on her way. I wouldn't want you to be embarrassed, not knowing.'

What the fuck is it, John?

'OK. Lay it on me,' she said quietly, bracing herself.

'I blame myself. I should have told you sooner. Who

Caroline is.' He pursed his lips, then seemed to brace up, stiffen his spine. 'Hell, there's no way of making this sound less weird than it actually is.' He took a deep breath. 'Caroline is Clara's mother, Lizzie. In a nutshell, I went from the daughter, to the mother, then the daughter again. When Clara wasn't there after prison and the army, and when Ben and I parted…Well, Caroline was there, and she was warm and kind and she made her offer. And we got married.'

Lizzie mind whirled. Clara? Bloody Clara again…and her mother?

John heaved a big sigh. 'I knew it. You're revolted, aren't you? You think I'm a creep and a pervert. Some kind of bed-hopping sex addict freak who jumps from one woman, to her mother…and then back again. I knew it would hurt you!' His blue eyes were full of agony.

Still reeling, Lizzie got a grip on herself, and a firm grip on John's hands too. It was hard to take in, this new revelation. Difficult to get her head around. But he was also exaggerating, making it sound sordid. She didn't know the full details, but she knew enough about John to know it wasn't really like that. The damned bitch Clara, he'd loved her deeply and she'd hurt him and betrayed him. Who knew what anybody would do in circumstances like those? What would she have done? If she'd lost John, sought comfort elsewhere…and then seen a chance to be with him again?

'But you said Caroline was a friend of your mother's?'

'She was. She still is, despite everything.' He looked away for a moment again, towards the window. 'And she was there for me when Clara wasn't. When Clara had cleared off, Caroline was an angel, kind and gracious. We'd always flirted in a light-hearted way, but we became closer friends, and it developed into something deeper. I was alone. I'd failed in the army. Ben was in a new relationship. Caroline saw that we could be good for each other, and that was when she made her offer, the bargain we struck.'

'Yikes.'

'Yikes indeed.'

'And after you and Caroline split up…then Clara came back? Had she just been biding her time? Waiting for your marriage to end?' Had her Nemesis decided to claim what was hers, perhaps to thumb her nose at her own mother? God, what kind of woman *was* Clara?

John's face hardened. 'I don't know. I really don't know. Perhaps she was biding her time, but not to be with me. I was a "filler" man until her next target became free. I think it amused her mightily that I'd been with her mother. She's always been stupidly competitive with Caroline. I suppose she thought she'd "stolen me back", even though it was because of Ralph that Caroline and I parted amicably.'

The pit of Lizzie's stomach went cold. She was sure of her love for John, and sure that he loved her too. But this woman from his past was a piece of work, a force to be reckoned with.

What if she decides she really wants him again? What if she takes it into her head to steal him back from me? Just to see if she can do it…

'What's wrong?' John was staring at her, scanning her face, monitoring signs and interpreting them.

'I…Well, it's just a bit of shock…Caroline and all that. And Clara…'

John slid his hands around her hands again, raised them to his lips and kissed them. 'I should have told you this sooner, shouldn't I? When we were on holiday, and talking and sharing. I should have been more open then.'

Yes, he probably should. But they'd already come a long, long way in a relatively short time. When they'd first played their escort and punter games at the Waverley, she'd never expected to discover any of his mysteries. She'd barely even known that he had any.

'Yes, you should. But you're a man with a lot of baggage, John. No matter how honest you want to be, I guess it's just not…practical…to just dollop it out all at once.' She gave him a level look. 'You have to dispense it in manageable portions.'

'You make me sound rather clinical. Calculating.' John tipped his head on one side, looking a little sad.

'No, not that. Not really. But I know you have to have a cool head to do what you do, and be successful. You wouldn't be who you are, otherwise, would you?'

A shadow-play of emotion passed across his face. Were calculations being performed now? Was he thinking of some way for them to get past this difficult moment?

'True.' He touched his tongue to the centre of his lower lip. It was an unconscious act, but it always got her going. Despite everything, despite Clara and the weirdness and the imminent arrival of Caroline, she wanted him.

'I can't help but feel this makes you think less of me somehow.' He frowned. His hands felt tense around hers.

'No. Don't be idiotic. Of course not,' she cried. 'It's a bit odd, admittedly, but it's life, isn't it?' She drew in a deep breath. 'You'd have to do something pretty damned horrific to put me off you. You know that, don't you, you dummy? The slack I'm prepared to cut you measures in light years.'

Men! Even the strongest and most über-alpha dominant

ones were subject to self-doubt. She had to show him it didn't mean a thing. Even if it did.

Plunging forward, she planted a kiss on his lips. A tactic that always worked.

And it did this time, because when she drew away, the shadows across John's face had become a smile. *The* smile. The golden smile.

Bingo! She dived forward for another kiss and this time got one back, John ascendant. His hands rose to her face, cradling it, holding her, compelling her with his lips and tongue. Her own tongue answered, duelling. All the molecules of her body stirred, primed by him in the space of a few heartbeats.

No! This was mad! Caroline would be here any minute.

Yes, said her body, and her heart, speaking to his.

'We shouldn't,' she gasped, without the slightest bit of sincerity.

'Oh yes, we should,' he replied, kissing again, hard. 'Or at least I should.' His blue eyes were bright and sly as he parted their mouths and he looked at her. 'You don't have to do anything, my goddess; I'm the one who owes you. So I'll do the giving.'

'But the party...' she began, a token protest.

'There's nothing to worry about. The party is perfect and you're perfect. And you need something to take your mind off my stupid torrid past and the idiotic things I've done. I need to do something to relax you.'

Devil! He didn't have to say what. The way he looked her up and down, his gaze gravitating suggestively towards her loins as he flicked out his rosy tongue, said it all.

'Oh, no you don't. Don't go there, John. There's no time. I'll be all flustered.'

What a little liar she was. She didn't care now if his entire family were heading up the drive in a fleet of limousines, Marquess of Welbeck included.

She made a just-for-show attempt to pull away, but his hand was firm around hers, and she couldn't help but laugh. That smile, that wicked tongue of his, they were all he needed to prime her engine and start a process with only one resolution.

'You'll look even more beautiful if you're flustered.' He lunged forward and gave her a ferocious kiss, owning her, goading her, exacerbating her madness.

I should resist. This is bonkers. How long have we got? Fifteen…twenty minutes?

But the motor was running now, and that madness was let slip like the dogs of crazy lust. She could no sooner turn back now, than stop breathing. What the hell…? Shelley's face had been awfully pink when she and Sholto had emerged from the cabana.

If Shell can steal a quickie, so can I!

'It's all right. I won't mess you up or do anything to spoil your pretty clothes,' murmured John, sliding his hand down over her breast and squeezing her through the colourful cotton of her dress, and the light summer basque she wore beneath it.

'You'd better not,' she growled, remembering a time when he'd made a similar promise, in his room, at the Waverley. And he hadn't either, apart from the necessity of buying herself a new pair of knickers from the hotel boutique.

I love you, whatever you've done, you evil sex-monster!

Yes, an evil sex-monster who looked like a gilded angel from the hosts on high; although angels didn't usually lick their plush, sensual lips in such a downright provocative and lewdly suggestive way.

He kissed her again, letting his lips travel from her mouth, to a tender spot beneath her ear, then down to her throat. Dipping down, he kissed her collar-bone, then as deeply into her cleavage as he could get, tongue stroking and teasing.

'What are you doing, you beast?' she demanded as he kissed his way down her inner arm, even though she had a shrewd suspicion. His mouth moved from the crook of her elbow to her wrist, and then, in a sudden flourish, he sank to his knees in front of where she sat, and grabbed her right ankle and kissed that too, then her calf, and then...ooh, the inside of her knee, pushing the full froth of her petticoats out of the way as he went.

Oh dear God...Yes!

'John, you mustn't!' she cried, knowing he'd translate it quite correctly as, Y*es, yes, yes, John, you must!*

'Yes, indeed I must,' he said, as if he had one of those universal gadgets from *Star Trek*. 'Now, let's get your knickers off so I can get my face between those fabulous thighs of yours, and lick your cunt until you completely forget every terrible thing I've ever told you about myself.' His eyes flashed, sapphire, sky, ocean. 'Come on, woman, hurry up! Let me at you!'

'You're outrageous!' She tugged at his hair, more play than threat, teasing a beautiful golden curl between the tips of her fingers. But setting him free, she reached down and snuck her fingers into the elastic of her knickers and started to tweak at them.

John completed the task, slithering them down her thighs, over her knees and off over her ankles, without even hooking them on her shoes. Oh, he was so clever!

He didn't speak, but his eyes and his smile were a litany of seduction and wickedness. Without hesitating, he plunged in, plying his way through her bush, then parting her labia.

'Mmm...your most precious jewel,' he murmured, blowing on her clit, 'a pearl beyond price. More lustrous even than those rocks in your ears.' He looked up and winked, nodding at her diamond earrings.

'Oh, don't talk bollocks, John, just get on with it! We haven't much time.'

He laughed out loud. 'Such a lady.'

A thought passed through her mind: maybe...one day? Then his mouth met her pussy and thoughts didn't stand a chance.

He went in wildly. Licking. Sucking. Playing and toying and teasing and taunting with his tongue. Long, drawn-out finesse was notably absent for the moment. His goal was to get her off and do it quickly.

But John was still an artist. Still divine. Float like a butterfly; sting with pleasure – like Lucifer incarnate. Within moments, Lizzie was hissing obscenities at him through clenched teeth, coming like a train, just as she'd described to him in her text, the other day. Keeping quiet was the devil's own struggle, but if she didn't at least try, she'd end up letting out a scream that would be heard the length and breadth of the garden outside...and around the poolside. Pulling hard on John's golden hair, she punished him for his greed, for his provocative mouth and for being irresistible and untameable, despite everything. Every goddamn thing.

But when he looked up at her, his eyes were the jewels beyond price, brighter than her diamonds with happy, playful triumph. She grabbed him by the ear and tweaked it.

'You wicked, fucking devil,' she said, unable to keep the love out of her low, shaking voice. 'I expect you want me to service you now.' She glanced downwards. He was huge in his trousers.

'Actually no,' said John, springing up as if he were totally unaware of his erection. 'I only wanted to remind you that I care for you now, love, and to let you know that the past is just the past, no matter how torrid.' He gave her a slow smile, and shrugged. 'And it is my punishment for crimes past and present to go without. As you so rightly point out, sweetheart, we don't have much time, and I'm sure you want to nip away to the bathroom and "freshen up" now, as they say.'

'I certainly do,' she replied as he drew her to her feet. 'I could do with a shower, but there's no time. Your ex-wife, and your ex-girlfriend's mother, will be here any moment!'

'Why not put your swimsuit on and dive into the pool instead? That'd freshen you up.' He kissed her cheek, with a kind of salacious chasteness that made her want his mouth on her pussy again, and a lot more besides.

'No, I'm not greeting Caroline in a bathing costume. She'll be judging me enough without me having flesh on show.' She tried to pull away from him, to stalk off towards her bathroom, but he held on tight.

'Ah, but your flesh is lovely, beautiful girl. Just the right amount, all in the most perfect of proportions.' Though his eyes still twinkled, he looked more serious. 'Caroline won't be judging you, Lizzie. She's not like that. She's a good woman. One of the nicest people I know. And you and she will get on like a house on fire. Because you're basically the same. Intelligent, level-headed and warm-hearted.'

Not like her daughter...

Lizzie shuddered. John frowned as he let her go, and she knew he'd felt it.

'Now, don't worry, go and do what you have to do.' He gently urged her with a pat on the backside. 'And I'll do what I have to do.'

Lizzie arched her brows at him.

'Yes, that,' said John, arching his own brows back at her. 'I will if I have to. But it'll probably go down of its own accord, with a bit of the old biofeedback. Now, hustle, gorgeous! We don't have much time.'

'Whose fault is that?' called Lizzie as she paused at the door, then scooted along the corridor towards the staircase. It was her fault as much as his, really. If she'd really and truly wanted to stop, John would have done so. He'd only given her what she wanted and needed; pleasure as a panacea, a reassurance.

Ten minutes later, as spruce as she could make herself and in a fresh pair of knickers, Lizzie dashed through the house, heading for the front door. A glance out of the window had revealed a beautiful blue vintage Rolls-Royce already drawing up, and John standing on the gravel waiting to open the door.

Calm down, Lizzie. Cool it. She's just a human being, even if she is John's ex-wife and Clara's mother. No need to get in a flap.

Slowing her pace, she walked out of the front door, in time to see John embracing a tall, stately woman with short, softly styled pepper and salt hair. She had her eyes closed and she was hugging him back, her affection obvious.

So this was Caroline. Mother of the dreaded Clara and also John's former wife. A well-preserved woman of seventy, wearing a gorgeously tailored lightweight trouser suit in a soft shade of antique rose. Lizzie almost laughed as she observed them. Caroline reminded her a little of a favourite actress of hers, from the television. Someone who played a character as warm and cheerful and generally all-round good-hearted as John claimed his ex-wife was.

Were appearances deceptive? Lizzie sincerely hoped not.

As John released her, Caroline looked over his shoulder and smiled. Instantly and unguardedly. Her eyes were kind. Just like the actress's.

'And you must be Lizzie. How lovely to meet you.' The older woman surged forward, her movements light and swift and energetic. Before she knew it, Lizzie found herself being hugged with not inconsiderable strength. It was the easiest thing in the world to hug back. And to mean it.

'I'm so grateful to you for letting me intrude on your Saturday afternoon. Especially when you're entertaining,' said Caroline as she let Lizzie go. Instantly she slipped her hand through Lizzie's arm, clearly a person who gave physical contact easily.

'I'm glad you could come. You're very welcome,' said Lizzie, realising that within the space of a few moments, she meant that too.

They walked through the house together, arm in arm, Caroline remarking on the airy elegance and beauty of the rooms they passed through. Lizzie caught John's eye, and he nodded as if to say, *I told you so, I told you you'd get on.*

On the poolside, Tom got a ferocious hug too, and the others a warm smile and an easy handshake. Lizzie could see Brent and Shelley watching her closely, as well they might on discovering Caroline's identity. But Lizzie beamed back at them to let them know that despite the oddness of the situation, all was well.

Caroline settled down on a lounger, and within minutes it was as if she'd been with them all afternoon. She chatted with John about business while watching the resumption of the tag-water-polo-murderball match. Lizzie brought her some food and wine, and as she settled on a lounger beside the older woman, they fell into conversation.

'That's a beautiful dress, so fresh and summery. Did you make it yourself? I chatted with John on the phone a week or so ago, and he told me about your designing and dressmaking, and the boutique you work in.' Caroline smiled. 'He's so very proud of your achievements, Lizzie.'

Still a little on edge, Lizzie instinctively went 'shields up'. Her own mother still had a tendency to patronise, when it came to her sewing. But almost as quickly, she realised Caroline's remarks were genuine, completely without side. Even on so short an acquaintance, Lizzie was drawn to the older woman, warming to the honesty and candour in her.

'Yes, I'm quite proud of myself too. For a while, I was a bit aimless in life, but I really feel I've got purpose now. I've always loved clothes and sewing, so it's good to be using my talents properly at last.' She smoothed her fingers over the bright cotton of her skirt. 'John's helped. A lot. With the dress agency and everything, but with encouragement too. I think he's given me a lot of extra confidence.'

'He's a very shrewd man, and a kind one too.' For a moment, Caroline looked far away, a bit dreamy; perhaps a little troubled too. Was she thinking of her daughter? 'And it's obvious he cares for you, my dear. A very great deal.'

'Um…Yes…I think he does.'

'Of course he does.' Caroline set aside her glass and

got to her feet, straightening up with ease, not at all like a seventy-year-old woman. 'How about you showing me around the house a little, my dear? It's very beautiful and I'd love to see more of it –' she glanced across to where John had just emerged from the cabana in his trunks '– and John seems about to hurl himself into this game, whatever it is.' She paused. 'That is, unless you're planning to join in too?'

'I had a good long swim this morning. A proper one, not all this farting about and splashing like big kids.'

Caroline laughed, and offered Lizzie her hand to help her up. 'Good. Let's look around, shall we?'

Uh oh, are we heading for some sort of heart to heart? Perhaps a kindly warning?

At first it seemed not, and as they walked through the ground floor of the house, Caroline's praise of the rooms, especially the orangery and Lizzie's workroom, only reinforced to her how very wonderful it was to live there. But when they reached the upper floors, and her bedroom, Lizzie sensed that now was the time.

'This is an exquisite room,' said Caroline, and then took her time as she wandered from dressing table, to bed, and from window to window. 'What a lovely view. Shall we sit a while, so I can catch my breath?'

Oh dear.

Lizzie took her place beside the older woman, repetitively rearranging the folds and fullness of her skirts. She knew now that she liked John's ex-wife – in fact, she liked her very much – but the moment was still nerve-wracking.

Caroline looked a bit tentative too. She glanced towards the bed. 'Perhaps I'm prying too much, my dear, but do you and John actually sleep together? I only ask, because he simply couldn't get to sleep with anyone else in the room when we were married. We maintained separate bedrooms…Even though…' The older woman's cheeks were a little bit pink. 'Even though we did have a normal married life in other respects. At least at first…We were always more friends than lovers, although I must admit I was very deeply infatuated with his beauty.'

'Me too.'

Caroline laughed and reached out to squeeze her hand.

'But it's not just that. Not just that he's so handsome and rich and all that,' Lizzie went on quickly. 'I love him. He's a wonderful man. Funny…a bit of a challenge sometimes, I must admit. But he's everything I ever dreamed of. I know that sounds a bit drippy, and a bit melodramatic and OTT, but when I sit down and work out how I feel about him, well, that's it.' She hesitated, aware that she was babbling like a fool and that her cheeks were hot. 'And yes, he does sleep here, some of the time. I'm not sure he's slept a full night with me, but I think he gets a few hours' sleep, most nights. So, that's progress, isn't it?'

Caroline beamed. 'It's wonderful! I'm so happy to hear that. I mean, it's obvious to me that he loves you very deeply, my dear. And he deserves that love. He's waited for it a long, long time.'

Lizzie blinked furiously, and the older woman slipped a hand in the pocket of her rosy jacket and pulled out a crisp, laundered handkerchief trimmed with lace, and passed it to her.

'I feel such a fool.' Lizzie sniffed and blotted her eyes, feeling terrible that she was putting mascara splodges on a very expensive handkerchief.

'No, you're not.' Caroline hugged her. 'You're a lovely girl in love with a lovely man.'

'I know…I know…It's just I'm…well, the future, you know? I think I want it all, but "it all" comes with a lot of other stuff. A very different life. I'm not sure I'm fitted for it, and I'm not sure John even wants that anyway. He's never said as much, but I get the feeling he doesn't plan to marry again.'

The older woman nodded. 'Yes, marrying John brings responsibilities, but you love each other, and you'll be able to support each other through whatever you're faced with.' She squeezed Lizzie's hand again. 'And really, his family are quite a decent bunch, apart from his father…who more or less banned me from Montcalm after John and I married. He actually waved his shotgun at John.' She shrugged expressively. Lizzie knew the tale. 'But his mother is still one of my oldest friends, and I know she'd welcome you ecstatically. You wouldn't be able to do any wrong in her eyes, for finally taming her most difficult son. Well, as much as is possible…And as for Welbeck, well, the old bastard doesn't really like anybody, and least of all me. But he'd probably embrace you happily because you're young enough to produce an heir. Which I so obviously wasn't.'

It was Lizzie's turn to laugh, but it came out a little high and shrill. Caroline gave her a shrewd look.

'But I think I know what worries you more, my dear. Apart from his family and dynastic implications.'

How could she tell this lovely woman about that deepest fear? The fear of Caroline's own daughter.

'John was over Clara long, long ago, sweetheart. And they were never really right for each other anyway, even though I know John loved her at the time.' She looked away for a second, her lips pursed. 'But she treated him abominably, and that's why I…I made my own play for him. To punish her. And to give him a chance to punish her too.'

For a few long moments, Caroline seemed to be thinking, drawing in deep breaths. 'You must think it's a very strange state of affairs. John being with Clara, and then marrying me...and then, afterwards, going back to her.'

'It is a bit weird,' admitted Lizzie, and Caroline turned back to her with a smile.

'She behaved appallingly. Betrayed him in the most hateful way, when he'd sacrificed so much for her. She didn't deserve him.'

Good grief, did Caroline know the true story of the accident too? The secret knowledge, told to Lizzie by Rose, the only other living witness, that Clara had been driving the car that fatal night?

'Ah...Yes...John has never told me the full story of the night of the accident. He's too chivalrous. But I have my suspicions.' She looked into Lizzie's eyes, her own bright and perceptive, and suddenly very sad. 'I see that I was right. I might have known.' Tears glistened in her eyes, and silently Lizzie handed back the crumpled handkerchief so Caroline could dab too. 'I won't ever say anything, though, sweetheart. I won't let him know that I know, and Clara would never admit it, of course. She's probably convinced herself that it happened the way everybody else believes, anyway.'

How torn she must be. Clara is her own daughter, and yet she knows all her child's faults, and suffers for them.

'I do love Clara,' Caroline went on. 'Despite how it might seem. I still feel guilty, because she's my daughter and in some ways I quite deliberately tried to hurt her by marrying John. But I know how selfish she can be, and

at that time I hated her too, for what she'd done to him.'
She smiled at Lizzie anew. 'John is much better off with
you, my dear. With you he can be happy, and that's what
I want. I only wish Clara could find a man who's right for
her too. There was one…A man I think would put up with
her skittishness and with whom she'd have a good life…'
Caroline shrugged. 'But she's too stubborn to see him in
that light.'

Curious, Lizzie asked, 'But what about her husband?
Isn't she happy with him? John says she lives in South
America now.' Disquiet stirred. As long as her Nemesis was
far away on another continent, she could put her out of
sight, out of mind. But if Clara was on the loose, well, that
was troubling to say the least.

Caroline let out a sigh. 'No, I think that's probably over.
He was too old for her, really. Both her husbands have
been…And she had affairs.' The older woman stared out
of the window again, frowning. The day was beautiful, and
golden, but somehow there were also shadows now.

'Oh…' was all Lizzie could manage, trying to quash her
qualms.

Suddenly, Caroline grasped her hands very hard. 'Lizzie,
I do fear that Clara might be setting her cap at John again. I
could see it, a little while ago, when John visited me in New
York. Clara was there too, complaining to me about her
husband, and I could see by the way she looked at John, and
the way she acted…I know her. I saw her plying her wiles.'
Her hands tightened around Lizzie's. 'You must believe
me, dear, he wasn't interested. Not in the slightest little bit.
But still, I fear my daughter could make trouble for you.
She's planning to return to England, with my grandson. She
might already be on her way.'

I must not be cowed by this. I must not go ballistic. John does love me and I love him. She can't touch us.

'Oh…right. I didn't know Clara had children.'

'Yes, a boy. Charlie,' replied Caroline, with a wry smile. 'He's a sweetie. Bright as a button. And for all her faults, my daughter does love him dearly, even though she's not the world's best mother.'

But even as she wondered vaguely which of Clara's husbands Charlie belonged to, Lizzie knew what she had to do herself, in order to combat the threat of her lover's powerfully determined ex. She shuddered. It would be the best thing…The most unequivocal. To be as sure as it was possible to be of their relationship. But, would John ever be ready for that step, or even want to take it? She wasn't even sure of it herself…

'I think you know what you should do, don't you, Lizzie dear?' said Caroline softly.

Did John's ex-wife have the same mind-reading powers he did? It almost seemed so.

'I'm sure it's in his mind,' the older woman went on. 'It would only take a word, a hint from you, that you want it too…And that way, Clara would know that her fantasies of getting him back were hopeless and empty.'

Lizzie nodded, but her thoughts were whirling.

It was the next step…but was it a step too far for John?

13

The Next Step

As John watched the Rolls-Royce pulling away, and waved to Caroline, his thoughts whirled.

Get a grip, man. How old are you? Fifteen?

He knew what he had to do. He knew what he wanted to do, and needed to do. But still, it was a huge step. He gambled with millions in his business life, but it never felt like this. The only sure, steady anchor was Lizzie's arm tucked in his, and her warm, fragrant presence at his side. He smiled at her, more to reassure himself than her. She was his confidence.

He was in turmoil. Good turmoil in a way, but even so.

'That all went well,' said Lizzie, her smile bright. She was shaken up too, despite her composed demeanour, and the gracious, natural way she'd just said farewell to Caroline.

Her smile made him smile. God, he was so proud of her. He always was, but today more than most days. With awesome poise, she'd met two very important people in his life, and they'd both loved her, instantly. She'd shown no nerves and no uncertainty, even though he knew she'd been feeling both.

A beautiful, easy-going hostess, she'd helped everyone enjoy themselves. He was the one who'd felt awkward, always fighting his rampaging desire for her, all through the afternoon. Never had his powers of self-control been taxed so hard. Was that why he was in such an idiotic stew now?

'It was a wonderful day, love, and you were amazing.' He spun her round and kissed her. They had serious issues to confront, heavy 'stuff'. But his mind and his body shied away from that, zeroing in on unfinished business that was easier and simpler. He could still imagine the luscious taste of her pussy. He wanted to taste it again, and do much, much more, even though he knew that plunging into sex now was just a way, albeit a very beautiful way, of avoiding thornier discussions.

'Thank you, Mr Smith. You weren't so bad yourself. Everybody had a great time, especially Brent and Shelley and Sholto. Thank you for putting them at their ease.' She kissed him back, playful nibbles around the edge of his mouth. Oh, God love her, she was right on the same page. Going for the sexy stuff, just like him.

'And you made Caroline love you. I knew you would. Thank you for being so kind to her. It must have been awkward any number of times over.'

Lizzie gave him a steady look. 'It was easy. She's a lovely woman. I really like her.'

He knew other words were on the tip of her tongue, but either through tact, or perhaps anxiety, she didn't utter them.

'Shall we go inside now?' he said, taking her by the arm.

Everyone had gone. Caroline had been the last to leave. Lizzie had urged her friends to stay the night, but both Brent and Tom, and Shelley and Sholto, had politely declined. John had a feeling that both the other couples felt as he did. They were at that stage when it was important to be in their own particular space, in order to be truly intimate.

Intimate. Intimate. Intimate. That was what he wanted to be. Now. Mad lust galloped through him, the urge to grab Lizzie and fuck her right there, on the hall floor. His cock stiffened. It would be a displacement activity as much as lovemaking, and she'd know that, but she'd still be up for it. And the Thursgoods had retired for the evening.

No!

He'd make love to Lizzie, long and slow…or wild and fast…or both…later. There was another matter to be dealt with first. Something he couldn't put to one side, not even for the ineffable pleasure of fucking Lizzie. Caroline's benign prompting had only crystallised something that had already been in his heart and mind, but not acknowledged. Perhaps as far back as that first fateful night at the Waverley Grange.

He'd experienced what the French called a *coup de foudre* that night – love at first sight – and he'd begun changing and growing, as he'd fallen deeper and ever deeper under Lizzie's spell.

He stopped Lizzie in the hall, and pressed a chaste kiss to her forehead. 'You go up, love. I'm just going to check all the doors and the security. I'll join you as soon as I've done that, and had a shower.' He stole another kiss. 'Keep the bed warm for me.'

That look of comprehension passed across her face. She understood. He needed a bit of space to order his thoughts. Before…well…before what they probably both knew was coming.

'OK, see you in a little bit.' She squeezed his hand, then hurried on and up the stairs, almost making him groan at the provocative sight of her sleek legs making her petticoats flounce as she ascended.

'Marry her, you idiot,' Caroline had said. 'Marry her and love her and be together for ever. She's wonderful. She's right for you. She's the one.'

His ex-wife had buttonholed him in a quiet moment, drawing him aside while Lizzie had been in the pool with her friends and Tom.

John had been nonplussed. Not because Caroline was saying something he didn't want to hear, but because, as ever, she was so absolutely and completely right.

'Get engaged as soon as you can, Jonny. The sooner the better.' His ex-wife's frown had spoken volumes about her own conflicted feelings. 'You…You do know that my daughter might be harbouring ideas that she might be able to get you back, don't you? She's getting a divorce from Ernesto and she's coming back to England with Charlie. I know what's in her mind, even if she doesn't know I know. It was patently obvious in New York.'

They'd spoken further, quietly, John confirming Caroline's suspicions. She'd begged him to act, alarm on her face, although to her credit, as the party had reformed, she hadn't shown even a hint of it. Even though Lizzie wasn't her daughter, they were much alike in that.

And now he prepared to follow Caro's advice. As he checked the house, he rehearsed little speeches in his mind, laughing silently at himself. He'd brokered hundreds of deals, subtlety and guile his most potent weapons. He'd pushed and he'd achieved his goals through what amounted to sheer force of personality. He was a winner. The ultimate achiever. A force to be reckoned with. But faced with love, and the possibility of cocking things up completely, he was as gauche as a boy again. A fresh, hopeful boy, though; the lad he'd once been before his illusions had been shattered.

With about twenty different versions of his 'speech' in his head, and freshly showered and shaved, he strode to the bedroom. No faltering now, even after he'd frowned in the mirror, prodding at his laughter lines, then grimaced even more, swearing that there might even be a few grey hairs amongst the gold. The night was chilly after the gorgeous day, but the pyjamas and robe he wore were his shield and his armour.

Bloody idiot. You're not going into battle. Even if she wants nothing to do with marriage, she's still here, isn't she? This is solid and enduring, what we have already. Clara can think what she likes, but there's nothing she can do. She can go fuck herself!

He smiled at his own absurdity as he pushed open the door to the master bedroom, his heart and, inevitably, his cock, rising at the sight of Lizzie in bed.

His love was bundled up too, wrapped in a shawl over a T-shirt and soft pyjama bottoms. She was flicking through a copy of *Draper*, but he could tell her attention wasn't really on it. Catching sight of him, a smile lit her face as she battled too, facing their shared preoccupations.

'Shall I light the fire, love?' he asked, approaching. 'It's a bit nippy tonight.'

'No, it's OK. I'll be warm when you get into bed.' Flinging aside her trade magazine, she held back the covers for him invitingly.

He flung off his robe and climbed in beside her, heart thudding, loins thudding too. Without make-up, she was fresh and exquisite, her black hair brushed and loose, so shiny. Her heart was in her eyes and he almost gasped aloud.

God, I'm the luckiest man alive.

'So?'

'So?'

They both laughed at once.

'I suspect we're both probably singing from the same page,' said Lizzie, twisting to face him, tucking her legs to one side. His angel, yet total woman, total sex.

'Yes, and that would be the hymn sheet as written by my ex-wife.'

'That's the one.' She smiled at him. He could see her nervousness, but a sheen of excitement too, and his spirits soared.

Oh God, he was nervous too. Like the adolescent he'd once been, barely able to reign in his emotions, his hormones. But she was with him. He could ask. He could ask and know that he wouldn't be refused.

Lizzie sat very still, although inside every bit of her was jittering. John's eyes were level as he looked at her, but there was the same out-of-control energy in them too. For once, it wasn't primarily to do with sex, even though she hadn't been able to ignore his partial erection.

This is it. The next step. The big one.

She felt like Neil Armstrong on the ladder. One small step, a few simple words. One giant leap into a new ball game, a new world.

'What Caroline said is right, love.' John's voice was low, and both measured and taut. Alarm rose in her, then ebbed when he smiled. That golden smile of his, happy but laced with anxiousness now. So boyish. 'The simple fact is that I love you, Lizzie. I can't imagine a life without you now, and for me, it's for ever.' He reached for her hand and folded it in both of his, the hold light as if she were precious and fragile. 'I never thought I'd say this. And I never have said it before, not in so many words. But I want to marry you, love. Will you marry me?'

It was a question. A supplication. But his blue eyes were filled with intense power. Stunned by the words out loud, despite them being exactly what she'd expected, Lizzie almost laughed. He was the unstoppable, irresistible John Smith, and as ever, on the cusp of a critical 'deal', he'd deployed his most effective bargaining tools, his fabulous glamour and his hypnotising gaze.

She opened her mouth, wanting to scream the words *Yes! Yes! Yes!* despite her qualms, but somehow her lips and tongue wouldn't work. They probably wouldn't function properly for a kiss either, but she shot forward anyway, and aimed her mouth at his, taking one.

Surprised for a split second, John gasped, then responded, lifting one hand and sliding it into her hair, cradling her head. It was a sweet kiss, a gentle kiss, but when they drew apart they were both panting as if they'd been passionately embracing for hours.

'Is that a "yes"?' The mesmerising expression wavered, and Lizzie pressed forward again, giving him another, very quick affirmative kiss.

'Yes, it's a "yes".' Crazy shivers wracked her body. Shock of a kind. It was stupid but suddenly she couldn't stop shaking. Or laughing.

John darted for her sliding shawl, then swathed it back around her shoulders, enclosing her and it in a hug. He laughed too and they rocked together.

'It is a bit mad, isn't it?' he said as they settled. 'But I'm serious. I do want to marry you, Lizzie. I know we can be happy, and have a good, good life.' He looked serious for a moment. 'But I also know that there are complications, implications, and I'm putting a god-awful responsibility on you.' His hands enfolded hers again. 'I'll do everything in my power to smooth the way for you, my love, but I can't think of a woman on earth who's more up for the challenge of taking me on.'

God, it was a challenge. Hell, yes. But this was John. Her John. The love of her life, he'd be worth it. The vista of the years ahead started to unreel in her head, and the shakes threatened again. But she quashed them. *One step at a time, idiot. One step at a time.*

She smiled at him, and he smiled back, then they were kissing again. And as their tongues duelled, a wicked little imp inside her murmured.

Up yours, Clara. Put this in your pipe and smoke it. You can't have him now.

As they drew apart again, John gave her a sharp, knowing look. Oh, damn him and his empathy. He'd sensed the direction of her thought, if not the actual words. She waited for him to mention her *bête noire*, but he didn't. He didn't want to spoil things. The issue of Clara would no doubt loom again soon, but this was their moment, unique for just the two of them, and his ex-lover just didn't belong in it.

'The family stuff, the title stuff. We don't have to do any of it, you know. Not if you don't want to.' His eyes twinkled. 'There might be the odd social thing, Christmas, birthdays and whatnot. But only on your terms, love. Otherwise, we just keep our own household, here at Dalethwaite, and live our lives as we please.'

He was offering a safe way, an easy way, and yet perversely the rockier path, with its huge challenges, had a strange appeal. Hadn't John been the wildest challenge of her life, when she'd first seen him, grinning at her over his glass of gin in the Lawns Bar? She hadn't been a coward then, and she wouldn't be one now. There were tests ahead, big ones, but the longer she knew John, the less she wanted to turn away from them.

'But…um…What about children? Won't your dad be counting on some? From us, that is?'

Yes, that was a biggie.

Lizzie had never been one to coo over babies, but she didn't actively dislike them either. She'd just never really pictured herself in mother mode. Well, at least she hadn't until certain little rogue notions had begun to sneak up on her lately.

'Children, yes.' John blinked. Were his own thoughts on the matter just as nebulous as hers? 'We'll have to have some, I think. Unless you're violently opposed to the idea? If you are, the old man will probably get his shotgun out again and ban you from Montcalm too. But if he does, well, we'll deal with it.' He took her by the shoulders. Tightly. As if using the pressure to make her believe him. 'It's what you want, love, not what he wants. If the title goes, the title goes. I don't care about anything but you.'

Oh God, what a responsibility. Never mind Neil Armstrong, she felt like the Duchess of Cambridge now, with the succession and the throne of England depending on the fruitfulness of her womb.

'Don't worry,' said John, his voice firm, strong. He pressed his lips to hers again, briefly but passionately. 'You'll never have to do anything you don't want. I hope

I've never made you feel that way, and I mean it most of all now, believe me.'

She did. His eyes said it all. The real strength was there, more than in his voice or his lips or his hold on her shoulders.

'It's not that I don't want kids. I quite like them. But I just hadn't envisaged having them for a while, you know?' And now more than ever, when she finally had a job she enjoyed, and a man she wanted to enjoy a rampant, untrammelled sex life with. For a few years ahead at least.

John smiled. Happy. Relieved? Wasn't he ready yet either? Would he ever be?

'There's plenty of time, Lizzie. Plenty. You're only young, and hell, even I'm not quite in my dotage.' He nodded, almost to himself, as if thinking on the fly. 'Look, I do suspect that if my father at least knows there'll be kids eventually, that'll make him happy. And then perhaps he'll relent and start to quite like his black sheep again.' He laughed, giving her a hug, then sliding his hands all the way down her arms to clasp hers. Lifting her hands to his lips again, he covered them with kisses. 'So, we're sorted, then, Miss Aitchison? We're engaged?'

'Yes, I think so.' It was still stunning, still hard to grasp the momentous nature of what they'd just agreed to do. 'But is it officially or unofficially?'

John pursed his lips, thinking again.

'A bit of both, maybe? Let's tell a few people. Local friends, the household, etcetera . . . but wait and tell the respective parents face to face. It's not as if either lot lives right on our doorstep. I would like to ask your father for your hand formally, next week.' He quirked his sandy eyebrows at her. 'Much as I play that black sheep role, I think there's still a bit of the traditionalist in me, you know?'

Oh, hell. Her parents. She'd been so busy worrying about John's parents, and their aristo expectations, that she'd somehow managed to completely forget her own parents, the forthcoming visit, and how they'd respond to the news!

John and her mother had seemed to get on well on the phone, so that was a good sign. But there was still the issue of her marrying a man roughly the same age as her father. There was a big difference between them being OK with her dating an older man, and confronting her family, in a fait accompli, with John as their future son-in-law.

'You're worrying again,' he said softly, rubbing her hands as if she'd complained of them being cold. 'We'll face them together, love. Together. And I'll overwhelm them with my charm and good looks and my enormous mountains of money.' He beamed at her. 'Because, let's face it, apart from my advanced years and general decrepitude, I'm a sound financial prospect as a husband.'

'Twit!'

'Not to mention the fact that their daughter will be marrying into the nobility, and what parents don't secretly aspire to that for their offspring?' He winked. 'Even in these libertarian, egalitarian times.'

As an avid reader of *Hello!* and *OK!*, especially the doings of the royal family and assorted toffs, her mum would be thrilled by the idea of her daughter's ennoblement. Lizzie wouldn't have been at all surprised if her mum hadn't already been poring over back issues, and other resources, trawling for details of John's lineage, and his noble, blue-blood family.

'I think my mum will be over the moon at me being Lady Something. Even if you were already in a bath chair.'

She winked back at him. 'Not sure about my dad, though. He's more of a republican.'

'Well, I shall look forward to debating ideological issues with him when we meet, then.' John leant forward, cradling her face, and kissed her again, a slow, sneaky kiss this time, tongue flicking at the seam of her lips.

Despite everything, Lizzie smiled inside, savouring his taste. Now the big step had been taken, it looked like John was set on guiding her to simpler, sweeter waters. The part of their relationship that was just them, and so much less full of complications.

Sliding her arms around him, she subsided back against the pillows, pulling him with her.

14

Celebration

It was like sinking into a delicious familiar space. Warm, safe, known; but still dangerous and exciting in its own way.

The next big step had been taken. Now it was time to celebrate. John's hand settled on her waist, her hip, reacquainting itself. It had been a long afternoon, and his touch was like fire after all those hours of having to behave for company at the pool party. His cock had been behaving itself for company too, but not now. It was hard and insistent, jabbing against her as he lay over her, kissing and kissing and kissing.

'So, Milady Lizzie of Dalethwaite Manor, are you up for it?' John growled, sneaking his hand under her T-shirt and cupping her breast imperiously. 'It's been bloody agony all today, keeping this rogue in check...' he swirled his hips '. . . while watching you swan about looking like a sex goddess. It makes life very difficult for us lower orders who adore you.'

Ah, it was like that, was it? As he kissed her again, Lizzie smiled inside, remembering a game they'd once played, not all that long ago, in this very room.

'You're a very vulgar and forward ruffian, you are. Getting above your station, my lad,' she reproved him, laughing as she reached down and took a less than ladylike hold on his cock. God, it was like iron. She was amazed he'd managed to keep it under control for so long, but then he did have special powers. 'And as for this?' She gave him a little squeeze. 'Rubbing this disgusting object against me, what are you thinking? Have you no respect for your betters?' She tightened her hold, infinitesimally, prompting a happy moan.

'I'm sorry, ma'am. I can't help myself. I've been checking out your tits and your bum and your sumptuous thighs for hours.' He rocked his hips, pushing himself against her hand. 'It tends to have this effect on me. I don't know why.'

He closed his finger and thumb on her nipple, rolling it, taunting it.

'Uh oh, behave yourself!' she said sharply. The authoritarian effect wavered a bit, though, and she gasped when he did it again, her own fingers releasing his erection. 'Paws off, underling!'

'But, ma'am, I thought you were enjoying it?'

'I shall enjoy what I want to enjoy, and in my own good time. Now strip off and show me the goods, you insolent pleb!' She needed breathing space, or she'd be throwing open her legs to him without any preliminaries, and surely an engagement – of sorts – deserved a little more than that to mark it!

And one should never waste the opportunity to make John undress for her.

'Of course, milady.' His grin was facetious. Adorable.

John sat up in bed and unbuttoned his pyjama jacket, making quite a performance of each button, and of the way he slowly parted the panels and slid the thing off his shoulders. Lizzie's fingers tingled with the urge to grab at him, he was such a feast. Body lean, yet strong, lightly golden. Mm, that little dusting of sandy hair on his chest. Mm, mm, mm, that enormous tent in the cotton fabric of his pyjama bottoms.

'Come on. Move it! Stop teasing,' she instructed, clenching her fist, out of his sightline, aching to reach for him again.

'Are you sure? It's not really the sort of thing for a refined lady's eyes, you know?' Slowly, slowly, John ran his tongue over his lower lip, making Lizzie nearly launch herself bodily at him.

'I'll be the judge of that.'

'Very well, milady. If you're quite sure.' His eyes were dancing. His long fingers splayed across his crotch, highlighting the offending object, not masking it.

'I'm very sure. Now stop shilly-shallying about.' She tried to give him a haughty look, but it came out as a grin. A grin and a leer of female hunger.

With a sinuous grace that Lizzie genuinely envied, John unknotted the cord of his pyjamas, lifted his bottom from the bed, and slid the garment down. The action made his cock bounce up as it was released, swinging in pure temptation.

'Good grief, man! Have you no control over that thing?'

'None whatsoever, ma'am. It gets that way every time I'm anywhere near you. I have to nearly hypnotise myself to make it go down.' His gaze locked on hers, and he laid his fingers on himself, slowly stroking, and fondling. Showcasing. Proud of his body.

He was raw temptation. Like a male odalisque, presenting

himself to her, nominally passive and yet infinitely powerful. She'd never quite control this fabulous man, no matter what game they played, and she didn't want to. His dominance was perfect to her, based as it was in infinite kindness and humanity.

'Are you sure you don't want to touch it, ma'am?' His grin was wicked, as irresistible as the sturdy reddened flesh in his grip. 'A bit of *noblesse oblige* for the poor randy serf?'

Tweaking her shawl around her as if she were trembling in horror, Lizzie gave him a stern look, while at the same time extending an experimental finger. 'I really don't know. It looks a bit of a monster, to be honest. You country types always have whoppers. I can't imagine how you could possibly get that…um…thing, where it's supposed to go. It looks far too large for purpose.'

John's cock was as hard as tropical wood. Hot. Full of intense male energy, even though he still held it so lightly. He let it rest in his palm, as if he were indeed her feudal underling offering his tribute to her. Lizzie ran her fingertip up its length, right to the sticky tip. Pre-come bathed the rounded head, colourless silk making it shine.

'Ah, but even a delicate lady like you should be able to accommodate it, ma'am. It might be worth a try, if you were so inclined to sample it.' John's long dark eyelashes fluttered as she flicked her fingertip around the under-groove.

'It's so large and crude.' She folded her fingers around him in a firm grip again, loving the bareness where before there'd been cotton cloth. 'I really don't know why you think I'd subject myself to it, you impudent peasant.'

'Because you ladies of the manor are all alike.' His fingers closed around hers, taking control of the grip. 'You flounce about acting all refined, and complaining about men being crude and animal…but really you love it! You can't get enough. You're insatiable.' Their gazes locked. Lizzie's heart revved up. Desire ground like a stone wheel in her belly. 'It's no wonder your husbands have to take the whip to you sometimes, or spank you.' His tongue snaked out again, sly, and provoking. 'Fiancés too. If they've any sense, they'll start as they mean to go on. Lay the law down before their womenfolk get too bossy. Or too randy.'

'I don't know…That sounds barbaric!' God, he was getting stiffer by the moment. His entire body was a column of heat and strength, radiant. She had him in the palm of her hand, but in the greater sense, he had her in his. Exactly where he wanted her.

'Oh, I don't think so. I don't think you think that at all, milady.' John's eyes glittered. His whole demeanour was sultry, but tricky. 'I think you like a strong man to sort you out. Someone to take you in hand.'

'Impertinence!'

'No. Truth,' he purred, his voice soft yet rough. He reached down and unwound her fingers from around him, then, swift and confident, he caught both her hands in both of his and pressed her back against the pillows, holding her arms above her head by the wrists. Imposing himself upon her, he used his lean form as a full body caress, nipping at her throat, her jaw and her ear as he massaged his bare cock against her still-covered thighs.

'You like that, don't you, milady?' he sighed into her ear, still rocking. 'You like having some poor, besotted man do all the work for you, half out of his mind with lust?'

'Yes. I do,' she gasped back at him, her hips rocking against his.

'I thought so.' John laughed, a low happy sound, and

with a last nip at her ear, he sat up. Lizzie made as if to sit up, and wriggle out of her clothes – she was wearing far too many – but he admonished her, 'Oh no you don't, Miss High and Mighty. Stay exactly where you are. Don't move a muscle.'

'But, J-'

'But nothing.' He silenced her with another fierce, possessive kiss, and a hard thrust of his tongue, then sat up and cast around for his pyjama bottoms. What was he up to? Of course, they were the classic, English gentleman's kind, and she watched him unthread the cord from the waistband, then pull it taut before her eyes as if exhibiting its sturdy, unsnappable quality.

Lizzie quivered, tingling goose-bumps of anticipation popping up over her skin.

He was going to bind her. Her servant-lover had become her lord and master in the blink of an eye, and he was going to secure her. So she couldn't touch him, but he could make free with her. Handle her. Pleasure her.

Quickly, deftly, he looped the cord loosely around her wrists, and threaded it through the brass bed-rails. Smiling and triumphant, he knelt at her side, a figure both divinely beautiful and obscene with his ruddy, jutting erection poking up from his groin. Lizzie's mouth watered, longing for a taste of him, yearning for the chance to worship him with her lips and tongue.

His glance followed hers. 'I might let you. If you're a good girl.' Slowly, insolently, he fondled his cock, his head falling back as he worked himself and savoured the pleasure of his own touch.

'Please, John.'

The words were breathy. What was she asking for? For

him to touch her? To let her suck him? For him to fuck her? All of those, probably, but the anticipation was suddenly agony. She needed…everything.

He went on stroking himself for a moment or two, shimmying a little, then, with his hand still on his flesh, he returned his attention to her.

'Very well, one little suck, then.' He moved up close to her, sliding a hand beneath her head, cradling and lifting it gently up from the pillow, then inclining half across her, to present the head of his cock to her lips. 'But don't go mad. I'm not ready to come yet.' His eyes narrowed as he looked down on her, dark lashes drifting low as his silky glans pressed against her mouth. 'You've driven me crazy all day, sashaying around as lady of the manor, so now I'm going to drive you crazy too, and make you wait.'

Holding her head in one hand, bracing himself on the bed-rail with the other, he pushed in, a shallow, measured thrust.

Lizzie squirmed her hips, even though he held her face still. He tasted clean and salty and wonderful. The head of his cock was heavy on her tongue, feeling even bigger than it actually was, its presence his complete ownership – albeit temporarily – of her.

'Give me some tongue.' His voice was rougher. He seemed to swell. He was so close that his body was her world.

She was dominated by the thrust of his erection, the sleek shape of his narrow hips, his smooth skin, toned muscle, and the pubic hair, sandy gold. Obedient, she licked and lapped at him, but mindful of his instructions she controlled her urges. Difficult, because she wanted to suck him dry.

Laughing and groaning, he cursed, turning the air blue.

He called her names, but every word, every profanity, was bright with joy and love. His love for her.

'Enough!' he cried, as, gasping, he jerked his hips, forcing her to relinquish him. Lizzie's eyes nearly crossed. His cock was huge in front of her face, shiny where she'd anointed him. 'You're too damn good at that, milady...trying to get the better of me.' He flashed her his devil of a grin and lunged forward, taking a rough, wild kiss. He'd be able to taste himself on her lips and the thought of that turned her on even more.

It probably turns you on too, you kinky sod!

'I've got to have you, love,' he said more gently, peppering softer kisses across her face, circling her lips with them. 'I've got to finish in you.' More kisses. Her jawline now, and her throat. 'But I'll get you off first, beautiful girl. It's the least I can do for my fiancée.' He winked at her, then started his way down her body, pushing up her T-shirt above her breasts, his mouth skipping over the bunched cotton to naked skin again, kissing and tasting as he went.

'I should think so too!' she protested, then wriggled wildly again when his mouth latched on to a nipple, sucking hard. 'Aren't...? Aren't you going to unfasten me?' She rattled the bed-rails as he slid his hand into her pyjama bottoms and cupped her pussy, squeezing hard as he assailed the tip of her breast with his naughty tongue.

'Oh, in a little while,' he replied, then lapped her teat, and nipped it, making her legs flail. 'I like you like this. At my mercy. I've been at yours all day, watching you drift about being the belle of the party, making everybody love you, and deliberately taunting me with your gorgeousness.' His mouth closed around her nipple again, but he was still looking up at her, his eyes dancing with light.

Lizzie struggled with the pyjama cord again, a token gesture. She didn't really want him to untie her. Being bound was thrilling, a delicious part of the game. She jerked her hips, though, coaxing him, enticing him, compelling him to stop playing around and give her clit some attention.

Dominant and in charge, with her at his mercy, he still obeyed. A strong, clever finger wiggled its way through her pubic hair, settling right on target. Lizzie yelped at the sudden sharp surge of pleasure, of yearning fulfilled.

Half coming, she groaned, 'Oh God, yes!'

'Yes indeed,' murmured John against her breast, his finger flicking hard, below. Working.

'More…Oh, more, more!' gasped Lizzie, working in sync with him, rocking to the strokes of his finger. Within moments, the longed-for climax hit her, intense and dazzling, her pussy clenching furiously. John reared up, abandoning her breast so he could stare into her eyes as, barely missing a beat, he twisted his wrist and slipped fingers inside her, taking up the pleasuring of her clit with his thumb.

'Yes, milady,' he said, mock facetious, smiling down archly at her. 'There's always more for you. I never tire of seeing your face when you come.'

No smart remarks came to her. Her mind was blank. Her whole body throbbing to the beat of her orgasm; one fixed point, her fiancé's blue gaze. He took her up, again…and again…Would it go on for ever?

In an instant of clarity, she caught her breath. 'John, please, I want you inside me. Fuck me. I need you to fuck me.'

He didn't answer, but withdrew his hand. In a graceful

swoop, he bent down, pushed her pyjama bottoms halfway down her thighs, and pressed his lips against her sex, more an action of fealty than of eroticism. Then, twisting, he pulled open the bedroom drawer and fished out a handful of condoms, flinging the lot on the bed, and snatching one up again.

'I should bloody well think so!' Lizzie protested. She was still shaking all over, but her brain was working again, at least for a few moments. 'Are you going to untie me now too?' She pulled at her bonds, wriggling her hips.

'Soon,' said John, rolling the contraceptive on. An errant thought flitted through Lizzie's mind.

I should go on the Pill, so there'd be no need for one of those. Especially now we're engaged...

But now just wasn't the moment to get into that. It was something for another time, a cooler time. But she still wondered why he'd never suggested it, making love without condoms. Perhaps that would change now.

'Well, you'll need to take these off for me, then.' Banishing her inner debate, she churned her thighs, flexing them against the pushed-down elastic of her pyjama trousers.

With a grin, and his latex-clad cock bouncing, he divested her of the garment, tossing it aside. Firmly, he parted her thighs, making the path open for himself. 'Gorgeous,' he murmured. 'What a divine view.' Then he plunged his face greedily at her crotch, and opening her sex with his thumbs, he licked at her clit.

'John! You fuck! You said you'd fuck me!' Sensation swirled, she was so sensitised already, almost back to orgasm.

'So ladylike,' he said, smirking up at her, but with one last, long, insolent stroke, he withdrew his mouth from the field of ecstasy and gracefully hustled his body into position. 'But

I still love you.' Resting on one elbow, he adjusted himself, resting his glans at her entrance.

With a long, deep kiss that tasted of her body, he pushed in, sliding his shaft in as his tongue danced with hers.

The sensation was like effervescence. She was bottled between his cock and his tongue, filled, possessed. And gathering pleasure was like some delicious fizzy beverage, pressure building and building as he thrust and kissed and she rattled again at the bed-rails with her secured hands. Only her legs were free, and she hooked them around the back of his, to strain and arch and push against him.

She was on the brink. Teetering. Ready to ignite. But she needed something.

'Let me loose, John. Do it now!' she growled, breaking the kiss.

He looked down at her, eyes wild, half out of it, close to his own crisis. Then he plunged back into her, and into the kiss, but at the same time, resting on one elbow, he reached up and worked the knots, freeing her hands with just one of his.

Just like a boy scout.

Lizzie half giggled, half panted. Hysteria and pleasure ran alongside each other.

'Minx!' John gasped, almost laughing himself as she wound her arms around him and slid her hands down to clasp his pumping, flexing buttocks.

'Horny beast!' Canting up her hips, so he could get deeper, she dug her nails into his bottom to goad him on. He answered by pounding harder, hissing through his gritted teeth as she scored him.

'You're a cruel bitch, Elizabeth Aitchison!' he accused, then kissed her again, harder and more hungrily, his usual fabulous accuracy wild and messy as he pounded and pounded, diving into her.

Lizzie rose to him, flying again, pleasure effortless. She cried his name again and again, the words half-mangled as her body gripped and gripped him, pulsating.

'Oh, hell, Lizzie, yes!' shouted John, coming with her. Simple clichéd orgasmic outpourings, but everything to her, ringing with love as he climaxed.

Chests heaving, hearts thudding, they clung to each other, drifting until gradually they got their breath back. John hauled himself off her and flopped on his side, hand searching and finding hers and lacing their fingers together as if he couldn't bear not to be entwined with her, at least in this sweet, small way. Gripping back, Lizzie smiled, blinking sudden tears, the simple handclasp as precious as the gorgeous sex.

'It's a good job we don't have to go to work tomorrow,' she said presently, still not quite back in herself. 'I'm knackered. I won't be able to walk, or if I do, I'll be bow-legged.'

John rolled on his side, smiling. 'Don't worry, I'll still fancy you if you're bandylegged.' Matter-of-factly, he rolled off the spent condom and Lizzie reached for a tissue from her bedside box to wrap it in. Sitting up, John tossed the little bundle in the direction of the adjacent waste bin, mouthing, 'Yes!' when he scored an easy hit.

Lizzie supposed she should find her pyjama bottoms, but she couldn't be bothered, for the moment. Instead, she snuggled up to John. He wouldn't complain if her crotch and her arse were still bare.

'So…that's one way of celebrating an engagement,' she said, stroking his chest. His smattering of soft body hair was damp still, with sweat, but she liked the feel of it, and the slightly foxy, raunchy smell of both their bodies.

'Probably the most popular one,' observed John, his hand over hers. 'I'll bet ninety-nine per cent of newly engaged couples mark the occasion with a glorious shag.' He rubbed his face against her hair, nuzzling. 'But not one of those engaged guys is as lucky as me.'

'Or the girls as lucky as me. If you don't mind the mutual admiration society.'

'I don't mind it at all, love.'

They lay quietly for a little while. Lizzie tried not to think of anything but the moment, and the feel of John's body against her, so warm, so sure. Stuff – their issues – tried to bubble up, but she squashed it down firmly. Not now. They'd deal with them when the time came; there was no need to spoil this beautiful golden hiatus of perfect peace.

Eventually, John stirred. Kissing her face reverently, still holding her against him, he sat up. 'I'm awfully thirsty. Banging the living daylights out of the woman you love can do that to a man. Would you like me to bring a drink to bed for you, love? We can have Champagne, if you like? Or water. Or even tea…Just say the word.'

Hell, yes, thinking about it, Lizzie realised she had a raging thirst too. 'Water would be lovely, I think. Lots of ice.'

'Sounds perfect. I'll go and get it. I won't be long.'

As if he couldn't bear to stop touching her, John hugged her again, then put her from him, with obvious reluctance. His smile for her was the wonder-smile, but dazed too, as if he couldn't quite believe what'd happened. As if he were as stunned as she was. Stunned to be engaged. But happy too, unabashedly happy, thank God!

Still grinning, he sprang from the bed, grabbed up his robe and belted it quickly. At the door, he looked back at her, and seemed to give a little gasp.

Yes, lover, I'm real, she wanted to say.

Are you?

15

The Ring

When Lizzie returned to the room from the bathroom, she found John sitting cross-legged on the bed, in his reassembled pyjamas. He was sipping straight from a bottle of mineral water, and there were more bottles in an ice bucket on the bedside table, along with glasses on a tray. One of his iPads lay on the bed in front of him, and leaning over it, he was swiping through pages.

'Mm, heaven,' said Lizzie, as she took a long draught from a bottle herself. She'd sipped a little water in the bathroom, but it didn't have the same frosty deliciousness. 'What are you looking at?' She set the bottle aside as John did the same.

'I've got something I want you to look at.' John swiped through some pages on the iPad, then paused, staring down at the device. Lizzie couldn't quite see the screen, but for a moment, he seemed deep in thought, frowning slightly.

'Do you remember I told you about an aunt who let me have my bequest from her early, in order to pay for Rose's care?'

Lizzie nodded. She loved what John had done for Rose,

whose mother had been killed, and who'd been left badly injured by Clara's dangerous driving. He'd made sure that Rose had been given the very best medical treatment, and therapies, and he'd tried to do everything he could to ensure that she could lead a fulfilling and productive life, even though she'd never walk again.

'Well, as her favourite nephew, she also set aside a family heirloom for me. A ring that I might give to my fiancée on our engagement.' His long fingers tapped the edge of the tablet. 'It's documented for insurance purposes, and I thought you might like to take a look at it. It's in the vault at my London HQ, but if you like it, I'll get Willis to send it up by secure priority courier.'

Crikey. A ring. Idiotic as it seemed, she'd never even considered the traditional symbol of engagement. Just the idea of being with John was precious enough, somehow.

'OK, then.' She nodded to the iPad. Why did he seem oddly reluctant to show it?

John turned the device around. Lizzie gasped.

Even simply as an image on the Retina screen, the ring was dazzling. Exquisite. Not at all what she'd expected, but much, much more lovely. Nestled in a bed of dark blue velvet was a delicate, beautiful vintage piece, Art Deco if she wasn't mistaken, a sizeable marquise-cut diamond, surrounded by rubies, surrounded again by smaller diamonds.

'Oh John, it's gorgeous. Just gorgeous. I…I never imagined I'd ever have a beautiful ring like that. It's awe-inspiring.'

'You like it?'

'I bloody love it, you idiot! It's breath-taking.' As if she might be able to feel its radiance, she touched the screen, making a fingerprint.

'Intrinsically, it's nowhere near as valuable as your diamond earrings, but, well, I was very fond of Aunt Constance, and I'd like to honour her wishes.' He pursed his lips. 'But only if you're happy with it. If you're not, we'll choose something. We'll go down to London, to Asprey or somewhere, and choose together.'

Lizzie frowned, puzzled. 'Why wouldn't I want it? It's glorious, and I'm very touched that you'd want me to have a special family ring.' She blinked, all the more moved as she thought about it. If only John was as sure. What was bugging him?

For a moment, he closed his eyes, and tipped his head back. It was almost as if he was trying to shake something from his mind. A worm of unease stirred in Lizzie's middle.

'It's the ring I was planning to give to Clara,' he said quietly. 'We were never formally engaged. She was hard to pin down about it. But she had seen the ring, and I know she liked it.' There was unease in his eyes too as he looked at her. Pain, even? Oh God, did that still hurt him? Even now? 'If…If that puts you off it, because it would have been hers, you don't have to have it. We'll get something brand new. Together.'

Clara. As ever. Those long blue-blooded fingers had reached out again, sneaking their way into everything.

For a second Lizzie faltered, and the request that yes, she would like a new ring, hovered on her lips. But then…

No! It's a wonderful ring. I want it! She's not taking the ring from me and she's not taking John from me either. She had her chance and she chucked up the most wonderful man. She's an idiot, not someone to fear or change my choices for. Sod her!

'I like this ring, John.' She put another fingerprint on

the iPad, and looked up at him. 'It's sublime. It's the one I want. Clara had her chance, and this is my chance. I'm not going to pass it up.'

John beamed, relief and, yes, admiration, in his eyes.

'You'll have it on Monday, my love,' he said quietly, as if greatly moved. 'That, and anything and everything else you want. Just say the word.'

Lizzie took the iPad from him and set it aside. 'I've got everything I want.' She reached out and cupped his face. 'You, John. You're all I'll ever need.'

As she so often did herself, he turned his face and kissed her palm, then took both her hands in his, leant across and kissed her on the lips. Up close, his blue eyes shone with a sharp glitter that might just have been a hint of a tear.

'Me too, love. Ditto,' he whispered against her lips, then kissed her again.

Words, somehow, seemed inadequate, but the quiet, sweet, uncomplicated kiss spoke eloquently. It wasn't to do with sex, just a gentle marking of their agreement, an acknowledgement.

They were together. It was the real thing. The big thing. And they weren't going to let anything, least of all anybody's exes, stop them moving forward.

For a while they just lounged against the pillows, talking about the ring, and John's aunt, who'd gifted it to him. Aunt Constance, who'd been kind, and who, Lizzie suspected, had been as bowled over by her beautiful nephew as most other people were.

In a natural lull in the conversation, though, a thought occurred.

'What about Caroline? You were married to her. Didn't she wear the ring?' Lizzie had noticed Caroline's impressive jewellery. A diamond the size of an asteroid and matching wedding ring. A couple of very beautiful and huge rings on her other hand. Had she worn the diamond and ruby treasure too, at one time?

'No. She didn't,' said John after a while, his fingers gently smoothing over Lizzie's shoulder. 'We never discussed it, but I think we both knew our marriage wasn't for ever. And we accepted that. Also, I wasn't exactly rolling in cash at first, and she was. She bought herself a rather nice emerald to celebrate our arrangement, and she still wears it.' Out of the corner of her eye, Lizzie saw him smile. Fondly. She didn't mind that, because she liked Caroline and she'd been good to her beloved when he needed it. But what about Ralph?

'Doesn't her hubby mind?'

'No, Ralph's a sensible, down-to-earth guy, and their relationship is rock solid. I think he's happy that I made his wife's life pleasurable for a while.' He laughed softly. 'I was her sort of fill-in husband, a placeholder for him.'

'Well, if you put it like that. It makes sense. Weird...but sense.'

John cradled her face, making her look at him. 'It's fate, love. Maybe Caroline and I knew that the right woman, "the one", would come along for me, if I waited long enough.'

An evil worm of disquiet whispered in her ear. Had he been saving the ring, hoping Clara would eventually come back to him? Which she had done, even if only for a brief fling, not marriage.

No, don't go there.

'No, I wasn't saving it for her. At the time, I never thought I'd see Clara again, at least not in any way other than socially.' His thumb moved against her cheek. Gentling her? Or distracting her? 'And when we did get together, I…well, I did entertain the idea of marriage, but I'm still not sure I'd have wanted her to have Constance's ring.' He hauled in a great breath, as if perplexed.

'Why? Because you subconsciously suspected she might do the dirty on you again?' She spoke softly. She didn't want to be confrontational, least of all now. But she couldn't spend her life being scared of a name, much less the woman herself.

John sighed. Not sadly, just wryly. 'I wouldn't have admitted it at the time, but yes, you're right. Stupid me wanted to believe that we might marry; but deep down, the me who'd been through the mill was wiser, knowing she'd probably fuck me over again, just as she did before.'

'There's nothing wrong with hoping, is there? Hoping for the best, and believing things might turn out.' She placed her hand over his, then turned her face so she could kiss his palm.

John smiled, his eyes warming and losing that vaguely clouded look. 'No, there isn't. You're very wise, my love. It's the best way to live.' He leant forward, and kissed her on the forehead, then, sliding his hand around her shoulders, drew her back with him, to lie against the pillows. The iPad slid to one side, on the bedclothes.

'I wonder what everybody will think of our news?' said Lizzie, snuggling in closer. 'I mean, obviously a certain person won't be too pleased, but what about everybody else? Caroline will be chuffed, I guess. She pretty much engineered it.'

John grinned. 'She's in raptures, love. I just emailed her before you came in, and she answered straight away. I think she was waiting to hear the news.'

'Good. I like your first missus very much. I mean, I know we only met this afternoon, but she feels like a kind of auntie somehow, or a fairy godmother.' John's arm tightened around her, a squeeze of approval. 'She waved her magic wand today, and voila!'

'Tom and Brent are thrilled too. I just texted Tom. Told him not to say anything up at the big house just yet, though.'

Lizzie laughed. 'Honestly, Mr Smith, you're acting far more like an excited little girlie over this than I am!'

'Not so much of the "girlie", madam,' John growled. 'If you don't watch it, I'll show you who's the girlie and who isn't.'

'Promises, promises. But seriously, I'm glad to hear about Tom. I thought he might be pleased. He's lovely, and I'm so happy he and Brent are together. You don't suppose, perhaps, that they might be next, do you?'

John seemed to mull the idea over. 'It wouldn't surprise me. They make a great couple, so comfortable with each other. I'd be glad to hear it, if they decide to make a commitment.'

'Me too.'

Lizzie was just about to say more when the bedroom door, which had been open just a crack, swung wider and Alice the tortoiseshell cat prowled in. The little feline had been out and about in the park most of the afternoon, having put in an appearance beside the pool, and found the splashing of murder-tag-water-polo not to her liking. She'd accepted her rightful homage, and some fussing, then quit the scene. Now, she leapt onto the bed and crept up between Lizzie's and John's stretched-out legs.

'Well, that puts paid to any further "celebration" for the time being,' observed John, reaching down to stroke the cat's ears and receiving the reward of a loud thrumming purr.

'Looks like she approves too,' said Lizzie, also stroking Alice. 'That's good to know.'

'That just leaves my family, and your family, and Shelley and Mr Kraft,' continued John. 'We'll see your mother and father next weekend, and perhaps my lot the weekend after.' He gave a great, theatrical shudder. 'And maybe you could text or call Shelley now? Or is it too late?'

The clock on the mantelpiece read 1 a.m.

'I'll text her,' said Lizzie, sitting up and reaching for her phone on the bedside table. 'I won't call. You never know what she and Sholto might be up to. I'd imagine they're very sexually adventurous, not like us staid old engaged people.'

'If this cat hadn't settled in, I'd show you staid, young lady!' said John with a saturnine smile.

What to say? Lizzie debated a moment. Shelley would be pleased for her, she knew, but news like this marked a watershed in her relationship with her friend. They'd been close as close for quite a while; the two of them – and Brent – against the world. And now that configuration was radically changed.

It's John and me against the world now. And probably Brent and Tom, too. But how about you, Shell? Is it you and Sholto? I hope so, and if it is, I hope it works out for you.

Tapping quickly, she decided to keep it simple.

You won't believe this. I'm engaged!!!!! I'll phone you for a natter tomorrow, or in the week. But just wanted to let you know. Love and kisses, L

She pressed send, and smiled at John as she set aside the phone.

'That's it, then. Everybody who needs to know at this stage knows. I'll tell Marie when I go into the shop on Monday. What shall we do now?'

'Well, I think that as soon as this cat moves her furry butt we should make love again.' John pressed his thigh gently against Alice's tortoiseshell flank, but to no avail. 'But until then, maybe we could make a few plans?' He leant over and kissed Lizzie on the cheek, while stroking the cat.

'Plans it is, then,' Lizzie affirmed.

Heck, this was scary…but exciting!

Shelley stared at the screen of her phone, feeling a little thud of 'something' inside her. What was it? Happiness for her friend, yes. Maybe just a little envy, obviously. John Smith was absolutely loaded, and Lizzie would never ever have to concern herself with money worries ever again. Wistfulness? Yes, that, but not about the money.

She glanced across at Sholto. They were sitting on a bench in the party quarter of town, the Piazza, looking out onto the canal. Night-life was still in full swing as Sunday morning waxed, and loud but largely good-humoured posses of clubbers and other animals were milling about across the broad concourse, making their way from the venues that were closing towards the ones still open.

What would Sholto think of this news? Shelley almost hesitated to tell him. He'd enjoyed the pool party at Dalethwaite, that was obvious, and everyone had got on well together, despite them being such a disparate bunch. But since they'd left in the taxi, he'd lapsed now and again into the deepest thought, sometimes with a slight frown on his tough-hewn face.

Shelley had expected that they'd go straight back to St Patrick's Road, on leaving the manor house, and they had done. But when they'd reached the house, Sholto had asked the cab to wait, and they'd dropped their bags with their swimming gear, and then jumped straight back in it, heading for town, and a drink at the Waverley Metro. Even though neither of them had been due to work there that evening, Shelley had still liked the idea. She always did. She loved the buzz of the Metro, and the crowd it attracted. Even on a normal night, there was always an electric atmosphere. On a fetish night, it made her heart trip just to walk in there.

Unable not to take his job seriously, Sholto had checked in with Greg, who was duty man tonight. There was nothing to worry about, though: takings were up, the vibe was great, as always, and there'd been no incidents. Shelley and Sholto had a couple of drinks, and boogied to a couple of numbers on the dance floor, but then, by unspoken agreement, left after a last word with Greg.

'What is it?'

With a jump, Shelley realised Sholto was staring at her curiously, although she'd not spoken a word about the contents of the text. 'Is something wrong?' He nodded to her phone.

'Er, nothing, really. In fact, it's good news, actually.' Should she tell him? She could still sense that trickle of an edge in him. He had something on his mind, something to do with the afternoon they'd spent, despite how much fun it'd been.

No use keeping things from him, though. 'It's from Lizzie. John's just proposed…and she's accepted,' she said, shoving her mobile back into her little cross-body bag.

Sholto nodded, apparently unfazed. 'I had a feeling that might happen soon. Didn't you? It's obvious he's besotted with her, and she with him. And there's nothing really standing in their way, so why shouldn't they get hitched?'

His voice was smooth and even, yet Shelley, growing

more attuned to him by the day, could almost taste the tension.

'I suppose not,' she said, wanting to slide along the bench, closer to him, so she could put her arms around him. Reassure him, although about what, she wasn't precisely sure. Money, she guessed. All he'd lost, and not just the money. Maybe she'd suggest a little session when they got in. Something to take his mind off things. He'd given her a few playful slaps on the bottom when they'd been changing in the cabana at Dalethwaite, but it'd just been larking about, really.

'There's nothing to stop them really,' she went on. 'I mean…there's the age gap and everything, but they don't seem bothered by it, so why should anybody else be?'

'That's nothing,' said Sholto, almost dismissively.

'What's wrong?' asked Shelley, mirroring Sholto's earlier enquiry.

He was quiet for a few moments, staring out into the Piazza in a way that said he didn't see either the place, or the people.

'I just wish I could give you all that,' he blurted out, his voice hard-edged. 'I could have done once. Well, certainly not to that degree. But we could have had a nice place, a secure future, a comfortable life, with a bit of spice round the edges.' He turned to her, his green eyes full of familiar shadows. 'You know I want to, don't you? I know I've not said it in so many words, but I've fallen for you, Shell. I want us to be together. Properly, you know?'

Shelley's heart beat hard, a thud on her own behalf now. In light of Lizzie's news, was this…Was this Sholto's version of a proposal?

She slid along the seat, not stopping to think, but just

circling her arms around him, beneath his jacket. It was getting chilly now, and his powerful body seemed all the warmer for it.

'I don't want all that, Sholto. What Lizzie's got is a full-on fairy tale, a bit over the top, really. I know she'll be happy, and she'll take to it like a duck to water, because John will be there beside her.' She tightened her arms around her man, for emphasis. 'But it's not really what I want. OK, a little bit more money would be nice, but we're doing fine, aren't we? We've both got steady jobs. Doing stuff we enjoy, at last. And we've got a decent place to live that costs us next to nothing.' Shooting forward, she pressed her lips to his jawline, nuzzling, trying to relax the tension in him. 'And…well…we've got each other, and that's all I really want, not millions and big houses and titles and whatnot.' She kissed again, then, hardly able to breathe, she went for broke. 'I just want you, Sholto. I know you might not be ready yet, but I just want to put this out there in the meantime. I love you.'

Barely daring to look at him, she did so, nevertheless. And her batting heart leapt again. His green eyes were warm, full of wonder. 'Oh, Shelley,' he murmured, then pulled her against him, kissing her hair, his hands sliding up and down her back, almost as if she were Mulder the cat and he was stroking her.

Was it just affection? Or was it more? It was certainly something, and it felt good.

Somehow their mouths found each other, and they kissed hard. It was a hot kiss, a sex kiss, but more, deeper. Shelley wanted her man, as she always did, but there was something else. An awareness that she'd put herself out there, in a vulnerable position, revealing her emotion, and for once in her life, it hadn't been a mistake. It'd been the right thing to do, and Sholto had liked it. Did like it.

As his hand slid up her ribcage, she almost moaned. His hands were big, nearly all-encompassing, but they had a gentle touch too. His massage skills were amazing. He could go light; he could go in hard. And both were good. It was the same with sex and BDSM play. He could beat her fiercely, when she wanted it. And caress with breath-taking finesse when she wanted that instead.

He could be tough and taciturn too, or as kind and considerate as an angel.

Somewhere outside their little zone of togetherness, an amiable, ribald voice cried out, 'Go on, my son!' and Shelley laughed in the kiss, aware that they were putting on a show.

When they drew apart Sholto's green eyes were bright, full of desire, but a lust tempered with tenderness. He grabbed her by the hand and drew her to her feet. 'Come on, woman, let's fuck.'

Shelley gasped, but she was right with him, and when Sholto marched her across the Piazza, she hurried along beside him, grinning. She knew where they were going. They'd been there before.

16

Shelley and Sholto

There was a narrow little alley, tucked away between two shops, on the way to the bus station. They'd found it once whilst looking for a shortcut, and in the shadows, hot for each other, they'd kissed, then it'd spiralled out of control and they'd fucked up against the wall. Shelley had hardly been able to believe that they'd done what they'd done – but the next time they'd been that way, they'd done it again!

Within moments, they were sidling into their secret place like a couple of spies surreptitiously scoping out a dead-letter box. Sholto grabbed her and backed her up against the none too pristine brickwork. Shelley didn't care, though, and now less than ever. This was her Sholto, the man she respected and loved. He might not be the superstar that John Smith was, but in his own way, and for her, he shone.

Their mouths met, and their tongues twined and battled. Picking up where he'd left off in the Piazza, Sholto slid his hand up her top, pushed aside her bra and cupped her breast. The caress was rough and eager, lacking in the finesse of which she knew he was eminently capable. But it was just what she needed and wanted. Her heart sang when he grunted with satisfaction at the touch of her flesh, and she felt his kiss shape into a smile against her mouth.

She yelped when he squeezed her nipple, and a shot of sensation sped from his fingertips to the niche between her legs. He squeezed harder and she rubbed her crotch against him. 'Horny little bitch,' he growled, sounding happy and pleased. 'Pull your skirt up and touch yourself,' he commanded, still pinching her breast tip, his free hand flat against the wall beside her head.

Shelley sprang to obedience, hauling up her flirty summer skirt and pushing her hand into her pants. She was swimming with lust for him already. Hell, yes! She rubbed herself as Sholto assailed her tits, pinching one, then the other, and back again.

'Bring yourself off, Shell. I want an orgasm out of you. Now. Don't disappoint me.'

So masterful. It was easy. She worked her clit like a madwoman, and while she did, he abandoned her breast and thrust fingers into her mouth, so she could suckle them.

It only took a moment or two, and she nearly bit down on him, coming hard, and fast, in great wrenching waves. She tried to keep quiet, but she couldn't. Uncouth noises issued from her lips, garbled by the obstruction in her mouth. They sounded loud too, stark over the voices of people passing the end of the alley. Out of the corner of her eye, Shelley glanced that way, half-fearful someone would hear her and come to investigate, half hoping, that someone would come to watch. The idea of some unknown person...man...seeing her come made the pleasure skyrocket.

Drawing his fingers from her mouth, Sholto kissed her through the tumult, then murmured, 'I want you, babe.

I'm going to fuck you now.' Nonsense words for a genuine emotion. 'Now, take your pants off.'

Swaying on shaky legs, Shelley obeyed him, and just as she was about to stuff her knickers in her pocket, Sholto grabbed them and flung them away down the alley. 'Bare for me now,' he said, in triumph, and she could feel him fishing about in the back pocket of his jeans for a condom. Then, turning slightly away from the entrance to the alley, he unzipped and worked his cock out of his fly and underwear.

Bashful, eh?

Shelley smiled. Maybe her hard, bold, tough boyfriend had his shy side after all. For herself, she didn't care, right at that moment, who saw her; although perhaps soon, very soon, she might not want to show off, but to keep her nakedness exclusively for her man. And whatever he might eventually become to her.

'Put the rubber on me.'

She complied, sinking to her knees on the roughly concreted surface beneath her. Quickly, she rolled the condom on, then sucked his glans a bit through it, not really liking the rubber flavour, but joyous to please him.

'Enough of that.' He grabbed her by her shoulder and hauled her up, pushing her back firm and flat against the wall. Flexing his knees, he dipped down, and at the same time, lifted one of her legs, to open her wide. Shelley felt blindly, instinctively, for his cock, and taking him by the tip, she guided him to her entrance, hitching a little this way and that, to notch him there.

Then, with a roll of his hips, and a mighty shove, Sholto Kraft pushed his way magisterially into her body.

*

Laughing, gasping, throwing her head back with joy, Lizzie cried out, riding her orgasm, and riding John.

Alice the cat had leapt off the bed and gone, as mercurially and unexpectedly as she'd arrived, and in a sudden, intense need to take John by surprise too, Lizzie had climbed astride her new fiancé and rubbed herself against him, massaging his cock with her crotch. Pleasures of the flesh were so much easier to deal with than 'the future' and within seconds, the inevitable had happened, and they were fishing for a condom and making ready.

In a wild happy bounce they'd thrown themselves at each other, as hungry and eager as if they'd not made love for weeks, much less barely an hour or so ago.

'Lizzie, Lizzie, Lizzie,' chanted John, his hips jerking as he came in her, and she folded herself down over his beloved form, and kissed his lips.

'Well, I've always prided myself on my sexual stamina,' said John cheerfully, a little while later as they lay beside each other, 'but since I met and started shagging you, my darling fiancée, I seem to have reached a whole new level of virility.' He took her hand, and conveyed it to his lips for a short, sweet kiss. 'And believe you me, love, I'm certainly not complaining.'

'Me neither.' Lizzie pressed her lips to his smooth bare shoulder. 'Although I must admit I'm a bit too knackered now, for getting into those plans you mentioned.' She looked at him, more seriously, meeting his eye. 'Do you think you'll be able to sleep?'

'I'm certainly going to try, sweetheart. And don't let me stop you either, if you're tired now. There'll be all the time in the world to make our plans.'

A stir of disquiet surged in her mid-section. Plans. It

sounded so serious. So grown up. And a little part of her was still coming to terms with the reality of being engaged to John Smith, multi-millionaire and aristocrat. It was like nothing she'd ever imagined for herself. It was like a movie, but suddenly, quite real.

'What exactly did you mean by plans, apart from the obvious? Um…length of engagement. Where and when we get married etcetera, etcetera?'

John gave her a long, steady look. 'Well, I would say "don't worry your pretty little head about it all", but I'm fairly sure I'd get a sizeable smack in the chops if I did.'

'You would indeed.'

He laughed. 'So, as I said…Other than putting the respective parents in the picture, we'll do everything at your pace, Lizzie. And however you want. Big do, small do, it's entirely up to you. I'm not even sure whether I can get married again in church, as a divorced man, but if you'd like to, we can always have a blessing instead, along with a civil ceremony.' For a moment, he paused, and bit his lip. 'Actually, daft as it might seem, I'm starting to find the thought of wedding preparations quite exciting. Is that a bit girlie of me?'

Lizzie's heart turned over. Aw, bless him. 'I think it's rather sweet, boss man. I…I haven't really thought about the idea of weddings myself all that much. Well, not until lately, when I started work on the first New Again bridal gown, and the other commissions. I'd always imagined having some kind of quickie wedding, if I got married at all, but now I'm starting to like the idea of something a bit more elaborate, you know?' She kissed his shoulder again, tasting a hint of salty sweat on his skin. 'Nothing major on the Wills and Kate level, but the proper thing, a proper wedding. White frock and all.'

'You'll look gorgeous in a big, fluffy meringue of a dress,' John said, with a grin.

'I'm not wearing a meringue! But I've got some ideas.' She had, too, but it was early days, and she'd no idea how she was going to find a suitable pattern to adapt. 'And I shall be making it myself, whatever it is.' She had to be firm on that. She was still Lizzie, who made her own decisions, and many of her own clothes, even if marrying John made her into a very rich woman.

'I wouldn't dream of suggesting anything else,' he said quickly. Too quickly?

'Well, you did say we'd do everything my way,' she pointed out, mock-nipping him, 'and that's my way.'

'OK, OK.' He reached around, slid his fingers under her chin, raising her face to him. 'But you'll be my wife, Lizzie, and my fiancée first. There'll have to be some changes. Just practical ones. You'll need bank accounts, credit cards of your own, all that jazz. And perhaps you could put your business relationship with Marie on a more formal footing?' He paused, and Lizzie sensed that suddenly John Smith, powerful business mogul, was with them, fused with John, the beautiful lover. 'I'd like to buy the entire New Again business for you as an engagement gift.'

Lizzie sat up sharply. 'No way, John! It's Marie's business. I work with her as a partner. I don't want to be a boss!'

John was quiet for a moment. 'I'm sorry, Lizzie. I'm getting grandiose ideas again. Trying to buy everything and steamroller you.' He sat up alongside her, and drew her hand to his lips. 'You're very wise, my darling. You know what's right for you. Much better than I, or anyone else does. I promise not to put pressure on you.' He kissed her hands again, his lips expressing acceptance. He was a great man, a dominant man, acknowledging his equal now, just as she'd specified. 'But if you ever do need funds, or any kind of resource or business advice, anything, just say the word. I'm here for you now. We're partners too. And I've got your back.'

It was a heavy moment, an intense moment. He loved her and he wanted the best for her, but he was so used to having his own way. 'I know, John. And I appreciate that.' She leant forward and pressed a kiss to his cheek. 'You've got my back…and the rest of me too. And I think we've made progress here…At least you did ask me first this time, about the business.'

She winked at him, and he threw his arms around her. They hugged. This sort of issue would always resurface between them, and there would be contretemps. It was just the way they were. But they'd deal with it too…because that was what people who loved each other did.

'Enough with all the heavy stuff,' said John as they broke apart. 'Let's try and sleep now, my love. It's been a big day. A very big day. We'll talk tomorrow. Now we have to rest.'

Rest, yes. Easier said than done. Not sure whether she'd be able to nod off, never mind her beloved with his long-standing sleep problems, Lizzie still lay down beside him, hoping for the best.

And despite everything, despite the momentousness, despite the qualms, despite the wonderfulness, she nodded off, her fingers still lightly entwined with John's.

Shelley clamped her knees together. It was a summer's night, but even chillier than when they'd set off from the Piazza.

And at this hour the naughty cool breezes kept finding their way up her skirt as she sat on the bench. Her knickers were lying somewhere amongst the muck and grunge of the sex alley, and no matter how much she liked them, no way was she picking them up from the ground.

'You're cold,' said Sholto, making her jump. For a big man, he had a knack of being able to sneak up unawares, especially on people who were deep in thought to start with. 'Here, take these.' He handed her two insulated cups from the coffee machine on the bus station concourse, then shrugged out of his jacket. Settling it around her shoulders, he took a coffee cup back from her, and popped the lid.

'Now you'll be cold,' Shelley countered, starting on her own coffee. For vending machine witch-brew, it was surprisingly good. Beside her, Sholto didn't seem to be displaying any signs of being cold, though. No goose-flesh on the skin of his magnificent biceps and forearms.

'I'm fine,' he said easily. 'How about you? Not feeling the draught, are we?' He nodded in the direction of her groin.

She laughed. 'A bit, but it was worth it.'

'Wasn't it just?' Sholto winked. He looked happy. Happy in an unalloyed way that made Shelley's heart sing to see it. The troubled man she'd first come to know as an escort, at the Sorrel Hotel, here in town, was gradually being replaced by a new, more at peace with himself Sholto. The fact that she'd helped him to get there filled her with wonder, and a great sense of pride.

'I'll buy you some new knickers,' he went on. 'Something lacy and frilly, or perhaps leather or rubber, if you prefer?' He grinned salaciously. 'I might not be able to buy you a mansion house or a car or diamonds, but I can spring for a nice pair of pants.'

'How many times do I have to tell you? I don't want all that stuff.'

'I know, babe, I know.' He seemed so much less up tight about it now; less, even than before. It was almost as if the wild, haphazard, but strangely tender sex in the alley had sealed something between them. Been a watershed of some kind. 'So, did you enjoy our celebration shag, then?'

'Well, if you couldn't tell, you must have been well out of it yourself,' she pointed out. 'It's a wonder we weren't reported by someone in the Piazza, and the police sent for.'

'I was in heaven, Shell,' he said simply. 'I always am with you.' He took a sip of coffee, as if fortifying himself. 'I meant what I said before, about us being together, you know. And, well, for what it's worth, I love you too. We can make a go of it. If you'll have me.'

'Of course I'll fucking well have you, you idiot!' Taking Sholto's cup from him, and setting it aside, with her own, Shelley hugged him. Her heart was overflowing.

They kissed again, gently this time. Another sealing of their pact. Words didn't seem to be necessary, and when they broke apart, and saw that the last night bus that would take them to the end of St Patrick's Road was pulling in, they rose as one, and walked towards it, hand in hand.

'One thing, though,' said Sholto as they took their seats, 'when we're a bit more established, and we've saved a bit, let's buy the St Patrick's Road house off His Lordship. I know it'll involve a mortgage and all that, but I'd like it to be ours, at a proper going rate price, not as some grace and favour gift of Lizzie and her billionaire, no matter how decent a guy he is.'

There was a quality of hope in Sholto's eyes. He was offering a commitment. A tougher route for them. But a shared one. And a goal she'd be prepared to work harder than she'd ever worked to achieve.

She drew in a deep breath. 'OK. I'm cool with that. To be honest, I'd prefer it.' She darted forward and planted a quick kiss on Sholto's smiling mouth. 'Although, maybe we could still hope he names a slightly low-balled price, eh? Nothing stupid and patronising, but a bit on the bargain side?'

Sholto gave her a long look. She almost started to worry. But then he smiled again, broadly, shaking his head. 'OK, OK, just to please you, babe. I won't complain if we get it as a snip. But apart from that, we pay our own way, right?'

'Right!' concurred Shelley, snuggling up to the side of her strong, stubborn, irredeemably proud man, and knowing it was exactly the place in the world that she should be.

Not even Lizzie's fairy tale could be as wonderful as this.

17

Power Couple

Lizzie looked up from her sewing.

Your sixth sense must be catching, Mr Smith.

Even though she hadn't heard the smooth-driving limousine pull up, she knew John was home. He'd been out and about today, travelling a fair distance to meetings, so he'd been chauffeured, as he usually preferred when he had to prepare for negotiations. He had a new driver nowadays, seconded from a local luxury travel hire firm that he'd recently bought out. Jeffrey, his old driver, was London born and bred, and hadn't wanted to relocate his family to the North, so John had put some capital into a Thames-side premium car maintenance garage that Jeffrey and his brother were now running with great success.

You're a good man, John. You always take care of everybody. Most of all me.

Part of her wanted to leap up, and fly down the stairs to greet him, but the rest of her thought that if she did that every single day from now on, it was pretty soon going to start seeming slightly demented, and juvenile, and not in the least bit ladylike. So, she just took a few deep breaths, completed the last bit of hand finishing on the section of a bodice she was working on, and then started neatly folding the garment.

But she'd barely got it tucked away in her sewing bag when the sitting-room door flew open, John strode in and, in a heartbeat, threw himself down onto the settee with her and was kissing her as if they were a pair of sixteen-year-olds who'd been apart for months, rather than two working people who'd spent only the length of a normal, if slightly lengthy, business day separated.

John obviously hadn't got the memo about trying to play it cool and act like a grown-up power couple!

Lizzie laughed, hugging him back and giving in to her urges, which were, as so often, to smother his handsome face with kisses and grope him slightly.

'That's more like it!' John drew back, grinning at her. 'I thought you'd come charging down the stairs to greet your new fiancé, and instead you're sitting here as prim and buttoned up as Miss Marple, busy with your needlework as if butter wouldn't melt in your mouth.' He took her hand, lifted it to his lips and kissed it, then nibbled the tips of her sewing fingers. 'If you're not careful, I might have to spank your bottom for lack of enthusiasm.'

Lack of enthusiasm? Good grief, she'd have torn his clothes off and jumped on top of him right now, if she hadn't thought that Mrs Thursgood would knock at the sitting-room door any minute, asking if they wanted tea. There was nothing quite as desirable as a golden god of business at the end of the day, still in his perfect Savile Row suit, but looking just ever so slightly tousled and frazzled around the edges.

'I was practising for being a lady,' she answered, giving

him a mock-haughty look. 'You know, showing a bit of reserve and decorum and stiff upper lip and all that, don't you know, old chap.'

John cradled her face. 'You don't have to be anything other than what you are already, Lizzie. Not for me. You're absolutely perfect as is.'

Lizzie's heart pounded. She felt as if her world were whirling. Sometimes, it still all seemed like a dream.

'At the risk of sounding like a soppy mare…Well…ditto,' she whispered.

'Oh Lizzie.' Flinging off his suit jacket, John launched himself forward again, kissing hard, subduing her with his tongue. Lizzie wound her arms around him, dragging him yet closer.

That was, until a hard object jabbed her in the ribs. A hard object located in a more northerly part of his anatomy than the usual hard object that jabbed into her, although she'd noticed that he had a hard-on too.

'Oops, yes, forgot about that.' John drew away, reaching into the pocket of his waistcoat and bringing out a small, burgundy-leather-covered box.

A ring box. Oh God, his Aunt Constance's ring. Delivered by secure courier during the day.

Instead of flipping the box open, John slid gracefully off the settee and on to his knees in front of it, and then undid the tiny catch, popped up the lid, and displayed its contents to Lizzie.

'I know I've already asked you once…but…Miss Elizabeth Aitchison, will you do me the enormous honour of becoming my bride?'

Words seemed to be glued to the tip of her tongue. She couldn't form them. Not only was she swept away by the sweetness of John's new, kneeling proposal, but the ring he offered to her was...was...amazing!

'Nothing to say, love? Don't you like it?' The note of anxiety in John's voice freed her from the spell. How could he possibly believe she wouldn't like something so beautiful? Or even have the slightest second thoughts, despite everything, about marrying him?

'Oh John, it's divine! It's just the most gorgeous thing I've ever seen.' *Apart from you*, her heart appended. 'It's...It's so much more beautiful than the image on the iPad. And...um...it's a lot bigger too!'

Aunt Constance's marquise-cut diamond was probably the biggest gem Lizzie had ever seen in real life, surrounded by square-cut rubies, and with smaller diamonds set in white gold, or was it platinum, on the shoulders. John had described it as less valuable than her own diamond earrings, but Lizzie found that hard to believe. It was a sublime work of the jeweller's art and simply had to be priceless.

'Yes, I think you're right about that,' said John, slipping the ring from its velvet bed. 'It does seem bigger than I remember. But don't worry, love, you've got the lovely, elegant hands to carry it off.' Gently, he took her left hand, lifting her ring finger so he could slide the exquisite jewel on.

It was huge. It was dazzling. Despite its antique provenance, it was a delicious chunk of mega-bling. But somehow, it also looked right. At home on her finger. Fitting perfectly, as if made for her.

'Thank you,' she whispered, a tremor in her voice as the central diamond wavered and scintillated, made more dazzling by the lens of sudden tears. 'Oh John, thank you. It's wonderful...wonderful...I'll try to do your aunt's memory proud. I...' Overcome, she pressed her lips to the glorious gem. It felt strangely warm, almost alive to the touch.

John blinked. Was he feeling the same? Lizzie grinned at him, watching him purse his lips, fighting for control. 'She'd be very happy, Lizzie. She wanted me to find a good woman to love, and now I have!'

They fell back into an embrace. Just hugging, just savouring the loving closeness, nothing sexual. Pressing her face into John's shoulder, glorying in his warmth and the solid, real presence of his body, Lizzie imagined she could still see the ring on her finger, as well as feel its light weight, resting against her skin.

I'm engaged. I've got the ring. Oh God, it's all true.

Holding him tight, she felt a shaking. Was it her? Or him? She was just about to ask when a knock came at the door.

'The traditional toast,' whispered John with a smile, before calling out, 'Come in!'

Thursgood entered with an ice bucket and glasses on a tray, the door held open by his wife.

'Thank you, Jim. Thank you, Sheila,' John said as Thursgood set down the tray on the sideboard and, at a nod, expertly opened the bubbly, not spilling a drop. 'I wanted you both to help us celebrate our engagement.'

John, having sprung to his feet, handed around the glasses. 'To my beautiful fiancée, Lizzie! Gracious, smart, and bloody brave too, to take on a challenge like me!'

Lizzie blushed as they all clinked their glasses.

'Lizzie!'

'Miss Aitchson!'

'Miss Aitchison!'

The Champagne was reviving, and despite its heady bubbles, it steadied her.

'Thanks, everyone,' Lizzie said after a good sip. 'And to John. Also brave, to take *me* on.'

They chatted for a few moments, the ring being duly admired and the Thursgoods offering the congratulations of the entire staff, before preparing to retreat.

'Take a couple of bottles of Champagne from the cellar for yourselves, will you?' said John, nodding to the bottle. 'And make sure each member of staff gets a bottle too. I'd like even the ones who aren't in today to get a chance to celebrate.'

When they were alone, Lizzie darted across and kissed John quickly. 'That was a nice thing to do. With the Champagne.'

'Well, I'm happy and I'm lucky and I want to share it with people around us. Those "few" we mentioned are . . . Well, more than a few now.' He smiled; a strangely gentle little smile yet also, aglow, excited. 'I'll arrange for some to be sent round to St Patrick's Road, and to Buttercup Cottage too. Oh, and Rose and Hannah like a drop of bubbly too. Better send them some as well. I think they'll be pretty pleased for us too.'

'I've a feeling they will,' said Lizzie, but she was puzzled too. 'Buttercup Cottage, who lives there?'

'That's Tom's place. In the interests of familial harmony, he doesn't actually live at Montcalm itself, most of the time. The old man finds it easier to ignore the fact that my brother is what he is that way.' John took her hand, and kissed it, his lips brushing the diamond ring. 'It's a very nice little place on the edge of the park. That's where Brent will be living, well, probably already is, I should imagine.'

Again, Lizzie was reminded that it wasn't just her life that was changing. Shelley and Brent were both moving on too. Six months ago, who would have thought it? How bizarre life was. How fast it could change.

Her first week as an engaged woman was crazy. So much happening. So much to do. And she really hadn't expected so much 'financial' stuff.

Suddenly she had new bank accounts, new credit cards, although still in her own name. They'd decided not to think about actual wedding dates until both sets of parents had been visited, and their reactions gauged. Lizzie had tried not to protest on discovering the opening balance of her newly set up current account; nor when she was presented with her credit card. A black one of her own, to match John's. It still all seemed completely surreal.

But she did speak up when her fiancé announced the engagement gift he intended giving her.

'I know you won't let me buy the entire business as your gift, but I've made the Kissley Magna property over to you,' he'd said, over breakfast, all booted and suited for a three-day trip to Scandinavia to look at several construction projects. 'The shop on the village green is yours now, free and clear, to do with as you wish. I'd also like to stand the cost of the shopfitting.'

Oh John, you're doing it again!

'John, that's too much! Even Marie doesn't own the shop in town outright. I don't want things to be…be awkward between us.' Marie had been almost beside herself with joy when Lizzie had announced her engagement news, and the entire day at New Again had become decidedly festive, with the older woman discreetly whispering the news to anyone who happened to be browsing in the shop at the time.

'They won't be,' John answered, giving her a steady look and reaching for her hand. 'I've spoken to Marie, and she's delighted. And I said I'd point out to you the fact that Marie brings an established business, customer base and retail experience to the table, which is perfectly balanced by your raft of skills and the material assets you can now offer.'

Lizzie took a deep breath. He was so generous, but still oh so controlling. She was going to have to find a way to get used to that. It was a fact of her life now. But by the same token, he was going to have to get used to another fact of life. Consulting her...as an equal.

'You're taking over again, you monster.' She gave him an old-fashioned look. 'It's not that I'm ungrateful...I'm incredibly grateful, and I love you for making so many things possible for me. But I thought we'd decided you were going to consult me about big stuff like this? No more fait accompli moves without asking me about them first. Equals, remember?'

John frowned for a moment, then shrugged. 'I know...I'm hopeless, aren't I? Mea culpa, mea culpa...' His look of guilt morphed then, into an irresistible blend of boyishly shame-faced and self-assured 'like a boss' smug. The way he waggled his blond brows at her made Lizzie half forget what she'd been laying the law down about. But only half...

'And don't do that, either. Trying to bamboozle me with your gorgeousness, just to get your own way, Mr Smith!'

'You're the one that's gorgeous, Miss Aitchison. I just want to give you all the things in the world...because you're worth it!' He winked and ran his free hand through his hair, like he was in a shampoo ad. But then his beautiful face grew more serious. 'But I hear you too, love. Consultation first. No more guerrilla tactics and pre-emptive strikes, I promise.' He inclined over her hand, raising it to his lips for a fierce little kiss, as if sealing the pledge. 'Equals,' he whispered against her skin.

It had been hard to say goodbye to him, knowing he'd be away three nights and not back until the day before their trip to her parents. Sleeping together was gradually, so gradually becoming more natural. There were still times when she woke in the night, and found John either sitting up and reading, or lying open-eyed in the darkness. But equally, there were times when she woke up before him in the morning, and found her sleeping prince at rest, slumbering peacefully.

She spoke to her mother on the phone. She spoke to Caroline. She spoke to Rose, and to Hannah, Rose's carer who'd become her life-long lover. She even chatted at length to Tom, not just about her own news, but his relationship with Brent. She didn't reveal her engagement to her parent, though, not yet. If she said anything to her mum, the celebration on Saturday would be all about herself and John, eclipsing her father's birthday completely.

It was impossible to resist wearing her ring, though, even though she made a point of not flashing it about. John had encouraged her to wear it, even though she'd take it off again at her father's party, until John had formally 'asked' for her.

'Oh my God! It's…It's gobsmacking!' Shelley had announced, over a small celebration lunch in their favourite bistro in the Piazza.

'Yes, it is rather wonderful, isn't it?' said Lizzie, running her thumb over the central gem, nervously polishing it. 'I keep thinking I should wear a glove over it, for safe keeping, you know?'

'Looks perfect on you, though.' Shelley's eyes were a bit misty. 'It's like a fairy tale, you and John. I'm so happy for you. He's a wonderful man, and I don't only mean the money and the manor houses and title and whatnot. Or the movie star looks. He's good guy, with it.'

'Yes, I think so.'

'And I'm glad you're properly engaged. I'm glad it's official and you're going to be married.' Shelley's voice was brisk. 'That way, that bitch of an ex you told me about won't get any more stupid ideas about getting him back!'

Yes, that was true. Lizzie had been trying hard not to think about the fly in the ointment. Clara. The one who may, or may not, have inadvertently prompted the engagement in the first place. She still experienced niggles of disquiet over that. It was hard to hear them over the noise of excitement, of plans, and the roller-coaster momentum of her new life rolling out before her, but they were still there.

'I hope you're right, Shell. I really do. I still do worry a bit about her…to be honest.' Still her thumb circled over the ring. 'I know I shouldn't, but I do.'

'You've nothing to worry about.' Shelley took her hand, calming the action. 'John loves you. He adores you. It was blindingly obvious when we were at Dalethwaite. He has eyes only for you. It's like you're the sun of his world.'

The sun? How strange. That was how she always thought of him. Golden. The shining radiance in her world.

Her hand stilled. She laughed at herself. A fiancée's collywobbles, that was what it was. She smiled at Shelley, warmed by her friend. No matter what happened, they must never drift apart. Sliding her hands around Shelley's in return, and realising she was mimicking John's reassuring double-handed grip, she opened her mouth to thank her friend...and then realised something. Something that if she hadn't been so bloody self-absorbed, she'd have noticed sooner.

'What's this?' She touched her finger to the exquisite antique ring on Shelley's finger. Her engagement finger. It was a garnet, rosy and pretty, flanked by tiny matched diamond chips.

Shelley beamed. 'Well, I'm not exactly engaged like you. In fact, I might never get married. But this is my Aunt Mae's ring, that she gave me a while back. It's sort of...um...a symbol of commitment between Sholto and me.' She fondled the rich, wine-coloured stone. 'One day, we'll get a new ring, but this will have to do for the moment.'

'Oh, that's wonderful! You know, I had a feeling about you and Sholto too, when I saw you together.' Lizzie reached out and squeezed her friend's shoulder. 'I'm so happy for you two...and for Brent and Tom as well.' She paused, grinning. 'I wonder who wears the engagement ring in that relationship, or whether they both get one?'

'I guess we'll soon see,' said Shelley, with a grin, reaching for her glass. They were drinking water, as Lizzie had to drive, and Shelley was about to work her first afternoon at New Again, but somehow that day H_2O had the sparkle of Champagne.

Friday soon sped around. The days were busy, even if nights without John were harsh. Lizzie filled her time with New Again business and with sewing. The shop in town was going from strength to strength, thanks to some new advertising they'd now been able to afford, and in Marie's opinion, the growing word of mouth trade they were attracting, not only thanks to the sewing commissions Lizzie had taken on, but also a certain curiosity value. To capitalise on this, Marie had hastily organised a little coffee and cake morning, to celebrate her new business partner's engagement. All their 'key' customers had been invited and they'd brought their friends, and those friends had told their friends – in a rapidly snowballing effect. The shop had been crowded all day as the coffee morning lasted well into the afternoon. Which, Lizzie reflected ruefully, amounted to far more than just telling 'a few local friends'. Still, in his happiness, John seemed to be having the same problem as she was keeping a partial lid on things, what with sending celebratory Champagne to all and sundry.

'They've all come to stare at me. And the ring!' Lizzie wasn't sure she was easy with the notoriety, and yes, the staring, but in an odd sort of way she also welcomed it. As the unknown girl from nowhere, marrying one of the country's wealthiest men, and the scion of an aristocratic family to boot, being looked at would be a fact of her life from now on, so she had to start getting used to it, sooner rather than later.

And as Marie had pointed out, having a titled lady, and a billionaire's wife, as joint owner of New Again was amazingly good for business!

Someone Lizzie had been particularly happy to see at the little party was Angela Cox, the harried young wife who she and John had delivered a dress to on the day he'd purchased Dalethwaite Manor.

'Congratulations, Lizzie. I knew it! I knew you'd marry him! It was obvious that day that you were meant for each other. Even in the midst of my own chaos, I could see that.'

The two women hugged, and Lizzie listened with pleasure to the outcome of the cocktail party, for which she and John had helped Angela prepare.

'It was a roaring success,' the other woman said, grinning. 'The advice about the gin really helped, and everybody raved about how great I looked and how cool my dress was.'

Lizzie gave her another quick hug. 'I'm so glad. But your husband didn't need to impress the boss after all, did he? John tells me he's working for him now, at JS North. I'm so pleased your hubby followed up on that.'

'Oh God, me too! It's changed everything for us. Ollie is a hundred per cent happier in his work now, and he's earning more too.' She leaned in closer. 'We're well and truly over our rough patch now. It's um...like a second honeymoon. But I'm still going to take a part-time job. Just something for me, you know? I was talking to Marie, and she said with the new shop and all, you might be looking for some more staff here?'

Taken aback for a moment, Lizzie suddenly realised something. She had the 'yea or nay' to hire and fire. 'Well, yes, we are.' She paused, thinking fast. Her instinct about Angela was strong. The other woman looked happy and confident, and her outfit was perfectly put together. She obviously knew what suited her, and had an eye for colour. 'Why don't you come in one day next week, and have a trial afternoon, to see how you like it? Obviously you know the vibe here, as a customer. I think you'd do great, but you won't know until you try it.'

'That'd be amazing. Thank you! I think I could do a great job for you, Lizzie. God knows, I love the clothes here.'

The two women chatted for a few moments more,

Angela clearly over the moon, but eventually Lizzie excused herself and nipped into the back room.

Oh God, I'm a boss now. I'm going to have to learn to hack it. Be more like John.

She poured herself a glass of water from the tap, and sipped it, calming down. She could do this. She could be John's mate and match, steering her own career just as he ran his immense business empire. Their compatibility was so much more than just sex. They could be that power couple, sustained by love. They could!

18

His Daughter's Hand

The bride at the altar-rail was very lovely, but John's attention was more on the simple, understated, exquisitely elegant dress she wore than the happy young woman inside it.

Glowing pride filled him, making him smile.

My Lizzie made that. It's the work of her hand, her supremely talented hand. By means of her gifts, she's made this girl's day wonderful. Or at least helped it to be.

On his return from the continent, Lizzie had said, 'How would you feel about attending a wedding tomorrow morning? I think we can squeeze it in, and still be at my parents' house for mid-afternoon. It's Serena, the first ever New Again bride. I made her dress for her, and she's invited us to the ceremony. She wanted us at the reception too, but I had to give our apologies for that, because we have to be at Dad's birthday thing.'

And now, it gave John a strange frisson to be here, as part of an engaged couple himself, knowing that sooner or later, he and Lizzie would be standing before a congregation too, taking their vows.

Scary. But exciting. More exciting than he'd ever have believed possible before he'd met the beautiful woman at his side. His first wedding had been ultra-quiet, an enjoyable day, but with no pomp and ceremony and very few guests.

But this time, it would be different. Lizzie would have every wonderful thing that she wanted as a bride. She was his dream princess and he longed to show her off.

'Doesn't she look lovely?' she whispered, tucking her hand in his arm during a momentary lull in the proceedings. 'The dress really works, doesn't it?'

'It's exquisite, love. You did a perfect job. But you'll look better.'

'Don't be silly.' She pinched his arm.

'I mean it. Nobody could possibly be a more beautiful bride than you'll be.' He put his lips close to her ear, admiring the cute little vintage 1950s toque she had pinned to her dark hair. It was a perfect match for the lightly fitted, elegant but oh so sexy pink dress she was wearing. 'And if you persist in denying that, minx, we'll have to pull into a layby somewhere on the way to your parents' house, so I can spank you for wilfulness.'

Lizzie gave him a silky smile, and just murmured 'Hush!'

God, he was her slave. Gladly and utterly.

'Oh my God, is that the billionaire, then?'

Lizzie had been sitting quietly in a corner of the terrace, with a weak Pimm's, keeping a low profile at her father's party and away from the small but swirling *mêlée* of neighbours, family, and fellow academic types who were chatting in the garden. The afternoon was as perfect as it could be for a birthday party, but after the initial introductions there was only one thing on her mind.

John and her father, at the far end of the lawn, by the herbaceous border, talking earnestly. Man to man.

Oh shit! Oh fuck! This is it ... He's 'asking for my hand'!

And now her two sisters, Judy and Nikki, had just arrived, sharing a car as they were both at the same college, just a year apart. They'd plonked themselves down on either side of her at the rustic table, obviously intent on grilling their elder sibling.

Nikki, the youngest and most outspoken, had asked the big question.

'Yes, that's John.'

'Well, considering he's probably Dad's age, he looks pretty fit to me,' observed Judy. 'What do you think they're talking about? It all looks very intense.'

'He's gorgeous,' chipped in Nikki again, 'but honestly, Liz, he *is* Dad's age, by the looks of it. How on earth did you get hooked up with such an old man? Well, older ...' Nikki frowned, and then went shamefaced when Lizzie gave her a look. 'I mean, look at Dad. He really looks like Hot Dad today, quite young and fit for him, and to be honest, they do sort of look the same age! Only difference is that your John looks like he should be in the movies and Dad looks like a professor who's just pretending to be a movie star in that shirt.'

'Thank you for those observations, Nik. And I'll have you know that I never even think about John's age at all. He seems like a young man to me and, as you'd say, he is fit. In every possible way. And I'd rather have him than whatever scruffy nerd you happen to be hanging around with at the moment.' She focused on John, down at the bottom of the lawn. Thank God, he was laughing, and so was her dad. Nearly matched in age they might be, but they were getting on OK, and there were no signs of sudden shock and horror from her parent.

'And as for the shirt,' she continued, 'that's my pressie to Dad. Or part of it. He liked it so much he changed into it straight away.' She gave Nikki another look, but smiling. 'That's one of the big advantages of being with a rich older man. You can buy nice things for the people you love.'

The new shirt was one of half a dozen she'd chosen for her father, from the summer prêt-à-porter collection of John's shirt-maker, and her parent had indeed been thrilled to bits. Not quite as much as he'd been with the book John had presented to him. A very rare first edition of her Dad's favourite obscure Victorian poet, Alfred Ratcliffe. Lizzie was amazed he'd been able to obtain it at short notice, but that was probably down to instructions to Willis or Martin, or the legendary concierge service provided by his black credit card, after John had quizzed her about her father's speciality.

'Fair point,' observed Nikki.

'He is rather lush, Liz. Me, I don't care how old he is. I'd do him,' remarked Judy.

'Jude!'

'Judy!'

Lizzie swivelled around to see her mother, who'd joined them, standing behind her. Mrs Aitchison looked as nervous as her eldest daughter felt, her eyes on the two men talking at the end of the garden.

'Well, with any luck, nobody else will be "doing" Mr Smith ever again, apart from your sister. If those two are discussing what I think…What I hope they might be discussing,' said the older woman crisply.

'Oh hell, he's not doing the "asking for your daughter's

hand in marriage" thing, is he?' asked Nikki. 'Nobody does that nowadays. It's archaic. And it's not as if Liz isn't shacked up with him already, is it?'

'Very tastefully put, sis, but with John being so ancient and decrepit, he's also a bit old-fashioned in other ways too,' replied Lizzie. Her heart was thudding, but she couldn't help smiling. Her father looked pleased. John looked pleased. The conversation was obviously going well. 'Despite the fact he doesn't exactly hang out with them any more, he does come from a very traditional family. I'm sure Mum's told you that he's a Lord, as well as a multi-millionaire.'

This revelation was cause for much mirth between her siblings, and accusations that Lizzie might become too posh to have anything to do with them after she was married. Mrs Aitchison shooed the girls away, and Lizzie's heart sank a bit. Judging by the look on her mother's face, she wanted a 'serious talk' too.

'So you are going to marry him, then?'

'Yes, Mum, I am. I love him. It's as simple as that.' She put her hand over her parent's hand. Was her mum shaking? 'I know it's…um…not what any of us expected for me, and there are going to be challenges, to say the least. But I want to be with John, and he wants to be with me. And like I said, at heart, I think he's a traditionalist, so that means marriage.'

'Are you sure, darling? He's a lovely man, and he couldn't be more eligible. I really like him, and clearly your father thinks he's first rate.' Mrs Aitchison bit her lip. 'But just look at the two of them together.' She gestured towards John and her husband, who were shaking hands, now, with the older – only just – man slapping the younger on the back. 'They're contemporaries. They're virtually the same age. You're marrying a man old enough to be your father,

Elizabeth. Are you sure you've really thought this through?'

'Yes, I have. And it comes back to this…I love John, Mum. He's a wonderful man, and when I'm with him, I don't think about our ages at all. He seems as young as me, and I know you'll pooh-pooh this, but I have grown up quite a bit since I met him. I feel much more confident since I've been with John. I know you and Dad thought I was a bit of a waster and a drifter, but I'm not any more. I've got the man I love, and he's given me purpose and belief in myself, as well as his love. Surely you see that?' She squeezed her mother's hand tight.

A great smile came across her parent's face, and shaking off Lizzie's hand, she enveloped her daughter in a hug. 'Yes, sweetheart, I think I do see it. And I am happy for you. I've never seen you look so confident and so poised. You…you look as if you've found yourself,' she whispered then drew back, still beaming. 'I know neither you nor John need your father's permission, or my permission to marry. But you've got it, Lizzie. You've got it absolutely.'

Lizzie looked back at her mother. She did have doubts. The shadows were still there in her eyes, but bless her, she wasn't going to make any more of a deal about the age gap. At least not to her daughter's face.

And there wasn't going to be much time for it now, anyway. John and her father were striding back up towards the party, still talking, still smiling. In a weird moment, all conversation seemed to still amongst the assembled friends, family and colleagues – as if it wasn't just Lizzie, her sisters and her mother who'd been hanging on the outcome of that man-to-man chat at the bottom of the garden. The discussions between her father, whom she loved despite their past differences, and her man, her lover, her fiancé. In the sunshine, John looked like more of a golden god than ever, the light glinting on his blond curls matched only by the brilliance of his smile, so sweet and reassuring, and focused on her now.

He winked. All was well.

'Well, my friends,' announced Professor Aitchison, smiling at the assembled company, 'I'm thrilled to announce that we have another celebration to observe today, not just my humble birthday.' Lizzie grinned back at her dad as he looked across at her, nodding. 'Most of you won't know John here.' He gestured to the man at his side. 'But I hope you'll soon get to know him, because he and my daughter Elizabeth have just become engaged!'

A general excited chatter erupted across the party, all eyes darting from John, to her, and back again, as she rose from her seat with her mother and made her way to the men. All hints of nervousness fled away, to be replaced by relief and happy pride as John took both her hands in his and leant across to kiss her.

His lips were like heaven, even in just this fleeting gesture, and this assertion of their status. And the way John smiled at her as he pulled back was so focused, so intimate between them, that she almost gasped. They were at the centre of the party, yet alone together for a moment. It wasn't sexual, but an intense communion, the two of them against the world.

People rushed forward, and all became a whirl of congratulations, introductions, and well wishes. In a momentary lull and to gasps of stunned admiration, John retrieved from his pocket the ring Lizzie had been wearing all week, and quickly restored it once again to her finger, kissing her again to seal the moment.

'I'm sorry we've derailed your birthday, Dad,' said Lizzie a little while later, feeling a bit like visiting royalty when she and John were circulating separately, accepting good wishes.

Her father gave her a hug. 'Think nothing of it, Elizabeth. I'm thrilled for it to be so, and incredibly happy for you, sweetheart. I like John very much. You've chosen very well.'

Lizzie met her father's eyes. His expression was shrewd. 'You don't think he's too old for me?' she asked, suddenly anxious. 'I'm not just marrying him for his money, you know.'

'Of course you aren't. He's a charming man. Very warm, and surprisingly unaffected, given his background. I think you'll be very happy together. I think being with someone older is very good for you.' He nodded to himself, as if marking an internal debating point. 'I know you and I have had our differences in the past, about the way you've conducted yourself...but I see a new Elizabeth today. A woman of confidence and purpose, as well as a woman in love. Your news today has been the best birthday gift of all. Even better than the fabulous shirts and the Ratcliffe, although I must say, I was delighted to receive those too.' He plucked at the fine cotton of his gift.

'Thanks, Dad. I'm so glad you like John and approve, despite the ages. I think Mum's still a bit worried, even though John's so massively eligible and all that.'

'Oh, don't worry, she'll come around. You're just the first of her chicks to get engaged. She's bound to be a bit broody over you.' He paused, looking reflective for a moment. 'Although she might be a little nervous about the prospect of your new in-laws, Elizabeth. You know my feelings on that matter, but I think your mother might still harbour misdirected awe at meeting members of the aristocracy. Don't worry, though, I'll put her right.' He winked.

Something to consider, thought Lizzie later, as she and John took their leave. Anticipating a fairly boozy afternoon, he'd booked them rooms at the village's rather nice vintage pub-come-hotel, and parked the Bentley there so they could walk over to her parents' home. A good thing too, because when a couple of cases of chilled Champagne had arrived at the party, delivered in a refrigerated van from a local high-end supermarket, both she and John had enjoyed several glasses toasting her father and themselves.

As they waved and called out their goodnights along the lane, Lizzie shivered. She wasn't really cold. It was just a reaction. The excitement. The utter relief of John being accepted so happily by her family. An awareness that the more difficult introductions still lay ahead.

'You're cold,' said John, slipping his jacket off and draping it around her shoulders.

'Thanks, love.' As his hand enclosed hers, some of the wibbles dissipated. Strength seemed to flow from him to her, giving her fortitude. With him at her side, she could handle anything.

Still, it was better to air her thoughts.

'I think that might have been the easier set of parents, you know. No offence.'

John was quiet for a moment as they strolled along. 'In some ways, yes, perhaps. But in other ways, I wouldn't say there'll be much difference.' He gave her a reassuring smile. 'Like I told you, my mother and father will be so thrilled that I'm finally marrying a suitable girl of childbearing age that it wouldn't matter if you were cross-eyed, had green hair and chewed gum all the time.'

'Well, seeing as how I don't have or do any of those, I should be all right, then.'

'You will be. Don't worry.' His voice was assertive, no nonsense, that of John the decision maker, confident in his choices and his chosen path. But was he really so assured of her welcome at Montcalm? 'I know my family and I know you, and they're not really so stuck up and entrenched in their class that they wouldn't love you. Nobody in their right mind wouldn't love you, Lizzie. You're perfect! Believe me. That's definitive. I have spoken.' He flashed her the wonder-smile.

'Well, in that case, yes, I am perfect.' She grinned back at him. 'This way now…' She pointed to a narrow footpath, flanked by bushes, leading off the main lane along which they'd been walking. 'It's a bit dark and we'll have to watch our step. No street lighting here. But it's a quicker way back to the George.'

She led the way along the path, a route she'd taken so many times in her younger days, but suddenly made magical and mysterious by the presence of the man escorting her. There was damp in the air, the smell of leaves and mulch. Today had been bright and sunny for her father's party, but yesterday there had been rain and the soggy aura of it still lingered here, making their footing muddy.

Halfway along the path, John drew her to a halt.

'Mm…muddy paths through woods. Does that bring back memories?' Pulling her into his arms, he kissed her fiercely, and she responded. It had been agony behaving themselves all day in front of her parents and her family, and their friends.

But oh yes, those memories. A rainy afternoon in the park at the Waverley. Scrabbling through undergrowth, a willow switch, a fallen tree. Happy days. He'd thrashed her bottom, and oh how it had hurt. And yet, barely able to remember the pain, she had a perfect recollection of the delicious pleasure afterwards, and of riding John to orgasm in that soggy grove.

Against her body, as she kissed him back, his cock was iron-hard.

'Jesus, Lizzie, I want you,' he growled as they broke apart, gasping. 'It's been bloody torture today, wanting you, fighting to control myself. Imagining what's beneath those pretty pink skirts, and longing to plunge myself into you.'

Lizzie laughed, shimmying against him. It was madness. John was a force of nature when he was roused. 'My mother would have had a fit if she'd known you were having such randy thoughts. I don't know where she gets these ideas that I shouldn't be sleeping with you or anything, but she does have them. It's ridiculous really, given that I was only just born in wedlock myself. Conveniently premature, you might say.'

'She'd be scandalised if she knew what I was thinking now.' John's eyes flashed like blue stars in the gloom. 'Planning to drag her beautiful daughter into the bushes and shag her senseless, engagement ring or otherwise.'

He kissed her again, tongue going in deep as he tugged at her skirt, then rummaged amongst her petticoats so he could caress her bottom and thighs.

'So beautiful…So beautiful…' he murmured, stroking her, his fingertips sliding expertly into her groove from behind, touching her sex.

Lizzie churned herself against him, tantalised and frustrated by the near contact. His fingers were close to her clit, but not quite brushing it. She stood on her tip-toes, trying to tilt her hips so she could get some stroking action.

'Hold your skirt up…Let me get at you…'

It was madness. They were on a public path that was well used, even in a smallish village like this. People cut through here all the time, on their way between the George and a couple of other pubs and the houses along her parents' lane and a small residential development in the same direction.

Yet still she did it, and John switched his approach, pushing his hand into her knickers from the front, finding her sweet spot instantly and starting to rub and rub, even as he kissed her again, harder than ever. Lizzie clung to him, moaning and rocking. She wanted to drag him into the bushes, and to throw herself down in the mud and muck so he could mount her.

As pleasure gathered between her thighs, she was almost on the point of doing it, even though what last shreds of sanity she currently possessed were shrieking *no, no, you mustn't*. This wasn't the rainstorm of that day at the Waverley, but everywhere was still damp. Within moments they'd be plastered with mud and twigs and God alone knew what else, and this was a village where her father had a respectable reputation, and the conventional George was not the crazy, risqué Waverley, where naughty behaviour was actively encouraged.

If she and John were to stagger into the pub covered in filth and leaves, looking as if they'd just been bonking in the undergrowth, word would get back to her parents, and that would embarrass them.

Even then, though, she almost groaned the words, almost hauled John by the hand into the bushes so he could finish in the time-honoured fashion, with his beautiful cock thrusting hard inside her.

But a high, clear shout and a whistle coalesced the shreds of her wits with a jolt.

'Freddie! Freddie! Come here, you bad dog!'

Like lightning, John withdrew his hand and patted her skirts back modestly into place, just as a boisterous black and white spaniel charged towards them from the direction they were heading, paused a moment to pant eagerly at them, and then dashed off down the lane behind them. Only to be followed by a middle-aged woman, short of breath, dashing in his wake.

'Oh, I'm so sorry!' she cried, clearly embarrassed. 'He just won't behave himself. He didn't jump up, did he?'

'No, it's fine,' said John, and Lizzie was forced to smile. He was so cool, so composed. 'Would you like us to help you catch him?'

'No, I can manage. Thank you. He'll probably stop at the other end of the lane and wait for me. He's not a bad dog really…just young, you know?'

'He's very cute,' said Lizzie, in an effort to sound normal and not let the woman think she'd interrupted anything. 'A lovely dog.'

The woman bustled on. 'Yes, he's a sweetie really. I just hope he didn't startle you both. Have a good evening.' Then she scurried out of view, calling for Freddie again.

'Good evening,' called out John, towards her voice.

When their new friend was out of earshot, Lizzie burst out laughing. John hauled her into his arms, laughing too.

'That was a close thing,' he murmured in her ear, then kissed her neck.

'An unbelievably close thing,' gasped Lizzie.

It was true. She'd been almost on the point of coming. It had faded now, discombobulated by Freddie and his mistress, but close to John, feeling his strong body pressed to hers and breathing in his intoxicating cologne over the smell of leaves and the damp night, it would only take a moment to get there again.

'Ah…I thought so. Do you want me to finish you?' He breathed deeply against her skin, teeth grazing her neck as if he were a blond Dracula. He wouldn't actually bite or suck, though, because they were having an early lunch with her parents tomorrow, and he wouldn't make a mark that they'd see.

So tempting. So very tempting. Her pussy quickened. The forbidden and the riskiness were an aphrodisiac. But this was her parents' village, and word would get around.

'Yes, but back at the George, hot-stuff. We're a respectable engaged couple now, and we have to behave with a bit of decorum.' She nuzzled his neck, and did a bit of biting of her own, nipping his earlobe.

'Decorum, my arse,' said John, grinning in the darkness. 'You make me feel like a mad young lad who can't keep his hands off his girlfriend.' He paused, running his hands up and down her body, through her clothes. 'But the beds in the George are a lot more comfortable, and far less muddy than rolling in the undergrowth. So, come on, let's go!'

Heedless of the shadows and the unknown footing of the path, they set off at a run, hand in hand, eager to touch each other.

19

That Lingering Worm

Coffee and a croissant in the beer garden of The George Arms was a very pleasant thing of a Sunday morning. Nibbling a bit of the flaky confection, Lizzie glanced up at the window of her room, glinting in the gentle sunshine.

Last night, they'd plunged into that room and thrown themselves at each other. For all John's talk about comfort, it'd been speed that'd been of the essence after a long day of abstinence. Within seconds, she'd been on her back on the bed, still in her dress, knickers flung across the room, while John powered between her legs, thrusting and shoving with very little of his usual erotic finesse.

It'd been a wild fast ride that had ended in a wild fast orgasm, with both of them biting their lips to keep in their shouts. For such a venerable old pub, that looked so solidly built, the George had extraordinarily thin walls; and no special soundproofing such as the wicked Waverley boasted.

This morning they'd stifled their cries of pleasure with kisses, the love slower and more leisurely; more exploratory and more repeated, yet with the excitement geed up by a few lazy slaps to Lizzie's bottom. Though the bench beneath her now wasn't exactly soft, she could barely detect the aftershock. It'd been play, lightly applied, that she'd invited to increase her enjoyment rather than as any form of punishment.

John was relaxed now, sipping his coffee, reading a newspaper. Every now and again, he'd wink at her over the top of it, and grin.

They'd both slept well. And spent almost all the night together, even though they each had a room. Tired out by the excitement of the day, and the now-resolved anxiousness of introducing her fiancé to her parents, Lizzie had found it easy to nod off. With John beside her, at least for a little while.

And he'd been there when she woke up.

'Wow, were you able to sleep all night?' She'd reached to stroke his handsome face as he blinked his way awake.

'Sort of...' He sat up, golden hair all a-tousle. 'I lay awake for a while, thinking about the day, and how well it went.' He looked at her intently, even though his eyes were still a bit sleepy. 'I was so nervous, love. So very nervous.'

How could that have been? He'd looked so assured, so cosmopolitan, the king of all he surveyed in his beautiful blue-grey summer suit, effortlessly charming her family and making them love him on sight, almost to a man or woman. 'Nobody would have known,' she said, kissing his cheek. 'You looked as cool as a cucumber...although, also, incredibly hot.'

'Years of practice. Years of practice.' He sat up. 'But I did spend some time reflecting on the day last night, and I thought I'd better slip away to my room and see if I could get some sleep. For the drive home, you know?'

Lizzie smiled at him. Sometime in the night...he'd come back. 'So what happened?'

John ran his hand through his already untidy curls. 'I couldn't sleep there, either. So I came back, and about ten minutes later, I must have nodded off.'

'That's wonderful!'

'We're getting there,' he said softly, reaching for her.

And now, here at their al fresco breakfast table, he looked relaxed. Well rested. Being able to sleep together in a strange bed was good progress. Pretty soon, with luck and a bit of patience, his nocturnal phobias might become a thing of the past, and they'd sleep together the whole night through as a matter of course. The shade of prison after dark, and all the entrenched irrationalities and fear would be banished, or at least their hold on him would be minimal.

And if that issue could be conquered, so could her own uncertainties. Her concerns about 'fitting in' when John was reunited with his family, and the sense of awe she felt, contemplating a future she'd never in a million years have anticipated for herself.

And...that other pervasive, lingering worm of doubt that still gnawed at her. The woman-worm who bore the innocuous name of 'Clara'.

I might have to meet her soon. She's in England, and her mother says she's set her cap at John again.

'What's wrong, love? You're frowning?'

Lizzie looked up from her half-eaten croissant and discovered John watching her. Apparently his paper was not as absorbing as she'd thought. Should she dissemble? Say it was nothing?

'I was just thinking about what Caroline said. About Clara being in the UK.' She picked up a flake of croissant, eating it without tasting it. 'I…I guess she'll be contacting you before long. Wanting to meet you.'

A shaft of pain, and what looked like guilt, darted across John's face, as shadow across the sun. 'She has phoned a couple of times. I should have told you. I meant to tell you.' He threw aside his paper and the pages slithered and slid, falling on the floor. He made no move to pick them up. 'But each time…you always seemed so happy, so relaxed. I didn't want to spoil things.' Rising gracefully, he came around from his side of the rustic table and sat down beside her on her bench. 'She's my past, Lizzie. Not a part of my life now, or ever again. I know that. You need to know that. Even if it might take her a while to accept it.'

Lizzie frowned at the idea of Clara's phone calls. Would she have preferred to know about them? She had no idea. Was she upset with John for concealing them? Again, she didn't know. Everything about him that she was sure of told her that any concealment on his part was to ensure her own happiness, an attempt to deal with an issue before it became an issue.

But did Clara see it that way? Gut feeling told her this woman she didn't know had an agenda. A single-minded goal in life. She could understand that.

Knowing John, and loving him, she couldn't give him up herself. And it stood to reason that Clara might feel the same way, even if her motivations were twisted, and perhaps more self-serving or self-deceiving.

We're two women who want the same beautiful man. I should feel sympathy for her, not hatred.

'You're right to be angry with me for not being totally straight with you.' John took her hand, folding it into both of his. 'I'll not conceal anything again.'

'I'm not angry, love. I'm not even angry with her,' said Lizzie, recognising a truth, 'and if the roles were reversed, I might have kept quiet too, if I thought I could make a situation go away without spoiling things in the process.' She gave him a fierce look, a look to show him her love. 'Neither one of us is perfect, John. And it'd be unrealistic to expect that neither of us will screw up ever again. I mean...that's life, isn't it?'

Love side-swiped him. As it did, again and again and again. This woman he adored was amazing, and would never cease to be amazing, as drenched as she was in a wisdom and compassion far beyond her years, as lovely on the inside as she was on the outside.

'I love you,' he said, throwing his arms around her and hugging her to him, not caring that the action attracted the interest of other breakfasting residents at tables nearby. Nothing mattered but holding Lizzie, and loving her.

As they drew apart, she didn't speak, but she didn't need to. It was all there in her eyes, and the sweetness of it almost made his own eyes prickle.

'At the risk of this getting boring, you're the wisest woman I ever met, Lizzie. And I thought Caroline was smart.'

'I take that as a high compliment, love,' she said with a grin, 'Caroline *is* smart. And she's a lovely lady. I really like her.'

'But not so much Clara,' he said, giving her a wry look.

'True. I don't know her, but from what I do know of her, I can't see me warming to her all that much. But I think I understand where she's coming from, John.'

She shrugged, even the roll of her slim shoulders utterly graceful. He watched her straighten up, squaring herself, wise and ready to move on. She glanced at her watch. 'Eek, I think maybe we ought to go and smarten ourselves up, ready for this early lunch/brunch type thing of Mother's, eh?' Touching his arm, she stood up. 'We'll have more time to discuss…um…other stuff, and how we might handle it, when we're back home.'

Perfection. She was perfection. And knowing her, he felt a better man.

He rose to follow her, but the sound of his phone forestalled him. Tapping his pocket, he considered ignoring it, but almost on auto-pilot, he drew it out to answer it. The mobile number was unfamiliar, but still a chill of unease gripped him. He pressed 'answer'.

'John Smith.'

'Oh, Jonathan, I'll never get used to plain "John Smith". It doesn't really suit you at all. Too mundane, darling.'

'Clara. Hello. How are you? I didn't expect to hear from you again so soon.'

He'd known. That premonition. It was uncanny. He took a deep breath, fighting his instincts. The urge to be curt and rude in a way that wasn't his style. He mustn't let her get to him. Especially with Lizzie staring at him, fighting her own fight and trying to look casual. She gave a little flip of her fingers, indicating she'd leave him alone.

He dived forward and grabbed her by the hand, even as Clara spoke.

'I don't know why you'd say that, Jonathan. I told you I'd be coming over to the UK soon and you said that we'd have to get together.' Clara laughed, and John's grip on Lizzie's fingers tightened. He had a feeling he might be hurting her, but she didn't flinch, she just shrugged and stayed where she was. Frowning.

'Indeed I did,' he said, thinking fast. He didn't want to see her again. He didn't trust her, and he knew from their meeting in New York that for him there was probably no way back to just a harmless friendship. And that wasn't even what Clara wanted. 'I didn't realise you'd be over here so soon. Where are you staying?'

'You don't sound awfully pleased, Jonathan.' Her voice was warm, but delicately reproving. Flirtatious. Just as she'd once been, acting as if nothing had happened. Nothing at all. 'I'm staying at Mother's London house…' A pause…Was it significant? 'I'm with Charlie.'

'Charlie?' With a gentle pull on Lizzie's hand, John resumed his seat, and she sat down next to him, watching his face.

'My son, silly.' Clara laughed. 'Don't tell me you've forgotten about him.'

What the hell do you mean? What are you trying to say?

'Of course not. But doesn't his father mind you traipsing him about the world?' Charlie's father was Robson Hertingstall, an American financier who Clara had been involved with, unbeknownst to John, even while they'd been having their own 'reunion' affair. Clara had been 'punishing' Robson with time apart, telling him she was unsure about marriage.

What a fucking idiot I was! I never saw it. Too blinded by hope and infatuation. Idiot. Idiot. Idiot.

'No, not at all, Robson has been very generous and decent. Did I not mention that he's paying for Charlie to be educated in England? So he doesn't lose his heritage?'

The disquiet he'd felt moments ago surged in his gut. There was more to this. He was sure of it. Much more.

'No, you never mentioned it, Clara. It isn't as if we've had much contact lately. Our lives grew apart years ago.' He tried not to sound too harsh. Or show his unease to Lizzie. Her keen eyes were monitoring him, reading him. She was attuned to his emotions in the way Clara never had been.

'Well, we can rectify that now, can't we? I've left Ernesto for good. I shall be living in the UK for the foreseeable future.' There was no sadness, no distress in his former love's voice. She sounded excited and confident. 'There will be plenty of opportunities for us to become good friends again.'

Damn her! The way she said good friends sounded exactly like lovers.

'Yes. Friends. Of course.' His tongue seemed frozen. He, the man who'd always been able to talk his way into any deal, out of any tight spot, and into any woman's bed. He was devolved almost to stuttering adolescence. Hating, hating, hating his own feeling of weakness, and hating that Lizzie should see him floundering like this. Even though he knew her sympathy would be complete...

Or would it? She too was only human. All this kow-towing of his, to Clara, must be painful to the woman he loved.

'Perhaps we could all meet up for dinner when I'm next down in London?' he said, desperately pulling himself together. 'Lizzie and I, you and Charlie, and Caroline and Ralph? I'm right in the midst of a variety of critical negotiations at the moment.' He rolled his eyes at Lizzie, silently owning up to the fib. 'But in a few weeks it would be good to get together. Perhaps you could ask Charlie if there's any special place he'd like to dine? We could make it a big treat for him.'

There was silence at the end of the line. He could imagine Clara trying to re-group, working out how to return the conversation to intimacy. He prepared to steel himself, buoyed up by a sudden gentle caress of Lizzie's fingers around his.

'Why yes, of course,' said Clara, finally. He could tell she was juggling her emotions too. Was she disappointed? Or was she hiding an even greater determination? 'I do know that you're a busy man, Jonathan. And of course, with a new relationship…' She let the words dangle. A challenge. John wondered whether to tell her he was engaged, but held back. His parents should know first, and he doubted Clara would keep it to herself. 'We'll get together in a few weeks. It'll be fun! I'm dying for you to meet Charlie. I know you'll adore him.'

Charlie again. This Anglo-American boy. There was such an odd note in Clara's voice when she said the lad's name. Almost gloating. Smug. John closed his eyes, pushing away thoughts. Lizzie's fingers tightened around his.

'I'm sure we will. I'm sure we will. But, I'm sorry, I do have to go now, Clara. I have an early lunch appointment with some friends. And a bit of a drive.' More lies! 'It's been good to chat. We'll talk again soon.'

'Of course we will. And I'm so looking forward to it. Ciao! I'll see you soon. It'll be wonderful. Phone me!'

The line snapped dead. Just like that. It felt as if he'd almost imagined the whole conversation. He let out a long breath as if he'd been holding it. Perhaps he had?

*

The fingers of Lizzie's free hand tingled, filled with the urge to reach out and smooth away the frown from his forehead. His eyes were dark with shadows. He looked torn and troubled. If Clara had been right there with them, Lizzie would have given her a damn good talking to. It was true what she'd said earlier, that she was more sorry for the woman than anything. But her primeval instinct was to nurture her man, and ease his troubles.

And right now, John obviously had troubles.

'Golly, that was spooky,' she said, keeping her voice light. No need to show him she was at least as rattled as she was. 'Fancy us talking about Clara like that, and her actually ringing you at that very moment.'

'Spooky, yes. But then, she always did have a knack for that.' Lizzie watched him make a conscious effort to banish the frown from his face. He grinned. A quirky grin, but a start. 'I think she's probably a witch.'

Lizzie laughed. Nervously. 'I think you're right, love. Er...what did she want? I know it's not really my business.'

John raised her hand to his lips and kissed it passionately. 'My business is your business, Lizzie.' He breathed deeply. 'Caroline was right...I think Clara's got it into her head that she wants me back. And I'm pretty sure she believes she can get me too.'

'She'll have to fight me for you first!'

'I know, and you're younger and stronger. If it came down to pure fisticuffs, you'd win, my love.' He kissed her fingers again. 'You'll always win. You and I are it, together now. For good and all. You know that, don't you?'

She did. In every normal circumstance, she had no doubt in him. Not a speck of it. But Clara was a wild card and the tension in John's fine jaw suggested that he suspected…something. Should she pry? Or let him work it out in his own time?

'I do, John. I do.' She hesitated. 'But I do think we, or at least you, should meet her, and tell her that face to face, so she stops harbouring hopes. I think it'd be easier on everybody that way.'

'You're right, love,' said John, his face relaxing, his eyes growing lighter. 'That's the only way. It won't be easy, but I should probably meet her privately. A lunch. Somewhere. And lay down the way things are, once and for all.' He gave her a very level look. 'Will you be OK with that? With me meeting Clara? If you're not, we'll find some other way to handle it. But let's get Montcalm out of the way first. Let's make us totally official then I'll speak to her.'

Primitive Lizzie screamed, *No, no way!* But sensible Lizzie knew she should, and could trust John, even if she would never trust this as yet unmet rival of hers as far as she could throw her.

'Yes. Yes, of course. I agree. That's the best way, John. The only way.' She didn't mention issues of trust, except with her eyes. 'Hopefully we'll still be able to have that dinner all together, though, for the little boy's sake. In a week or two, when we've been to Montcalm and your family have got over the shock of me, and we've started making our wedding plans.'

'If I've told you once, I've told you a dozen times, my family will adore you!' he cried, giving her hand a reassuring rub. 'But yes, we will still do that dinner. Clara is nothing if not resilient. And in a bizarre sort of way, I'd like you two to meet.' He laughed wryly. 'God knows, you might even like each other. Now, come on, we need to get ready for lunch with your parents now. I think I've made a good impression there, but I don't want to spoil it by being late today.' He winked.

Lizzie rose and they walked swiftly inside, still hand in hand. Solid. Together.

The lingering worm of doubt still wriggled, but she told it very firmly that it didn't stand a chance. Happy couples dealt with exes all the time, and she and John were as happy as any. Happier – and tougher – than most.

Getting past the 'Clara' issue would be uncomfortable. Might even be painful. But they could do it, and then move ahead, facing new challenges, stronger than ever.

And next weekend, Montcalm was the first.

20

Montcalm

'Turn the music off now, please. I need to prepare myself.'

Frowning and clicking off the Beach Boys on the iPod, John slid the Bentley to a halt. They'd just been let through the main gate at Montcalm, and greeted with enormous enthusiasm by the gatekeeper there. The sight of the wayward Lord Jonathan was clearly a source of huge excitement and novelty. Especially as he had a woman with him.

With the engine turned off, John turned to Lizzie. 'There's no need to prepare, love. Just relax. Enjoy yourself. Nobody's going to be judging you. You're a most honoured and welcome guest.' He leant across and kissed her cheek. 'And it's not a state visit. Hardly anybody's here. George and Rosemary are away sailing with some friends and Helen's in London.' Indeed, he'd done everything to keep their first visit to Montcalm as low key as possible, picking a time when his older brother and his wife weren't in residence, and their daughter, his niece, was away too. 'It's just my mother and father, and Tom, who you know already. And Brent's invited to lunch too, so you'll have one of your best friends in all the world on hand as well.'

I'm being silly. I can do this. John sailed through meeting my lot, didn't he? And that was a big birthday bash, not just Mum and Dad.

Yes, last weekend had been a triumph. It'd been clear that John had been accepted at the party, and that everyone had loved him.

As they were leaving, her father had said:

'In principle, I still abhor both the aristocracy and the plutocracy of money, but personally, Elizabeth, I like John very much and I thoroughly approve of him for you.'

Her mother had said:

'I still think he's too old for you, darling, but if you're going to be with an older man, he's the one I want you to be with.'

Her sisters had no qualms.

'Are you sure he's not a movie star?' Nikki had enquired.

Judy had said, 'Well, anybody who buys you a pair of diamond earrings the size of two birdbaths is all right by me!'

The only black spot in the whole weekend had been Clara's phone call. And despite what she'd cheerfully agreed to, Lizzie still wasn't sure she ever wanted to meet John's ex. The idea daunted her even more than meeting his parents.

'Yes, I know. I'll be OK,' Lizzie said, snapping back to the present, and smiling at John. There was tension in his handsome face too, the faintest of dark shadows beneath his eyes. Goddamn Clara had affected him, Lizzie knew it, and today had to be as much a pressure situation for him as it was for her.

His father.

There was a big difference between the buffer of correspondence, or even a phone call or two, and the reality of the last black sheep coming home to meet his parent face to face.

'You'll be OK too,' Lizzie said softly, matching his cheek kiss with one of her own. 'Remember, you're bringing them what they want. Well, after a fashion…The prospect of a healthy young wife, at least.'

John gave her a despairing look. Over the course of this last week, they'd gone over and over again how the class issue did not matter. Lizzie still felt that it might, but she tried not to make too big a deal of it. It was certainly easier for John to ignore it; as the one born to privilege, it was a part of him, no matter how he tried to deny it.

But he smiled. 'One look at you and every fatted calf on the entire estate will be slaughtered. I'm bringing home a magnificent prize.'

'Ew! I'm not so sure about the calves, but I get what you're saying.' She shuffled in her seat, feeling as if she was atop a Soyuz about to take off. 'Shall we proceed to Manderley, then?' She nodded to the wide, winding drive ahead, flanked by trees. It was the big daddy of the long and lovely drive at Dalethwaite Manor. Montcalm would be huge compared to their own little domain, but Lizzie was glad she'd had the preparation of living at Dalethwaite, with staff and a domestic 'establishment'. It was a much easier transition this way, than if she'd still been pigging along in a semi in St Patrick's Road.

'I think you'll find Montcalm is more like Downton Abbey than Manderley,' remarked John, firing the engine and setting the Bentley rolling. 'It's actually built very much in the style of Highclere Castle. What they call Jacobethan revival. Victorian built, but as an over the top fantasy of Elizabethan and Jacobean influences.'

'I know that!' Lizzie shot back at him, grinning. 'I've looked at the website and Wikipedia and all that. I wanted to be ready so I don't make a twit of myself.'

'I've told you. Don't worry.'

'I'm not.'

'I think you are.'

'A bit, then. But I'll try not to.'

This went on a little longer while the sleek car sped up the drive. The way to Montcalm was far longer and far twistier than the drive at Dalethwaite, and they passed in and out of the natural tunnels formed by mature trees several times. It was just when Lizzie was wondering whether they were ever going to emerge that the Bentley burst out of the shadow into light, still with a long, winding way ahead of it.

'Bloody hell! It's huge!'

'It is a bit, isn't it?' Despite the magnificent house ahead of them, tall and towered, standing on a rise, dramatically silhouetted against the skyline, Lizzie still turned to John. There had been such a note of yearning in his voice, something that sounded like both happiness and sorrow.

The car slowed. And for once, John's eyes weren't scrupulously on the road. He was staring at the house, hungrily, eating it up with his eyes. As she watched, he bit his lip, as if containing great emotion, then huffed out a breath, applied foot to accelerator and returned his total attention to driving.

He's missed it. He's really, really missed it. All that talk about his heritage being meaningless. That was all bollocks. He loves his old home, and he loves his family.

'It's beautiful, John. Pictures don't do it justice at all. The way the light hits it makes the stone glow.' The house was mellow, but fancy. Tall windows glittered. 'I love

Dalethwaite with all my heart, but Montcalm makes it look like a garden shed by comparison.'

'I'd forgotten how breath-taking it can be,' said John quietly. 'Even though I grew up here. It's as if I dreamed it, somehow, being away.'

Poor John. Life was weird. And bloody fucking Clara, she was to blame. If she hadn't done what she'd done, that night so long ago, driving under the influence of drugs, this need never have happened. John would never have been estranged. Would never have had to give up the joy of this lovely house.

But then, you'd never have been here with him.

For a moment, Lizzie felt tearful and confused, not sure if she was happy or sad. But then, suddenly, as they saw a dark-dressed figure appear outside what was obviously the grand front door, she pulled herself together.

You're here now, Aitchison, you idiot. Things happened this way, you're with John, and he loves you.

Clara was both her arch enemy, and the woman she should be most grateful to in all the world. How bizarre was that?

As they neared the door, a couple of other men appeared, running smartly from around the corner. Footmen? Did Montcalm have footmen? Lizzie was quite relieved that they were wearing dark trousers and waistcoats and white shirts, not some elaborate Ruritanian livery. That would have fazed her. The butler wore a dark, sober suit and a black tie, no tailcoat.

When the Bentley was at a halt, and before they'd even unbuckled their seatbelts, the car doors were opened for them, the butler stepping back respectfully at her side, yet clearly alert to assist her should she require it.

'Thank you,' said Lizzie, emerging. 'Thanks very much.'

'Welcome to Montcalm, miss. I hope you had a pleasant journey.'

'Yes. Yes, thanks, we did. We don't live very far away, though.'

'Indeed, miss.'

John appeared at her side. 'This is Brewster, Lizzie. He's a genius. He can do anything.' A strong arm slid around her waist; her love, giving her strength and bolstering her up. 'Brewster, this is Miss Elizabeth Aitchison. You'll be seeing her here regularly from now on. With me.'

A look passed between the two men, and Lizzie got the impression that Brewster understood pretty much everything.

'That's wonderful to hear, milord.'

Milord? Oh God! Oh hell!

She'd almost forgotten.

Beside her stood Lord Jonathan Llewellyn Wyngarde Smith. He wasn't just her John any more.

As if he'd heard her, John flashed her a look. 'It's still me,' he said in a low voice, giving her a squeeze.

Lizzie opened her mouth to answer, but at that moment, a woman appeared in the doorway, hurrying forward. She was stocky, but dignified, dressed in light tweeds and solid, sensible shoes, her white-grey hair coiled in an old-fashioned style. Her face was lined, but still beautiful, the shape of cheekbone and jaw unmistakeable, as was the dazzling, overjoyed smile.

The Marchioness of Welbeck. John's mother.

'Oh Jonny, Jonny!' The Marchioness surged forward, moving vigorously to fling her arms around her son and hug him tight. 'Oh, my darling, beautiful boy. I'm so glad you've come home.'

To her shock, Lizzie realised that the woman embracing her returned son, and being embraced back just as hard, wasn't at all what she'd expected.

Nincompoop! Of course she's not the same age as your own mum! John's the same age as your mum!

A simple fact of years. The Marchioness was a contemporary of Caroline, probably older. She was at least seventy, possibly quite a bit more.

The love, the joy and the relief in the older woman's face were like the sun, though, a beatific glow. Her eyes were closed, but there was a tear or two at their corners. Her lost beautiful boy had returned, the son Lizzie strongly suspected was her favourite of the three.

Was there a tear in John's eye too? His face was a mask of stark emotion. Happiness, but tinged with regret, palpably, that this had taken so long. But he drew back, beaming his wonder-smile – only to have it reflected back from his mother.

Lizzie hung back as the two regarded each other, the reunion beyond words for the moment. And then, stepping away from her son, the Marchioness fixed on her. And darted forward again.

'And you must be Lizzie!' she cried, almost as if Lizzie were equally as long yearned for. 'Oh, my dear, I'm so glad to meet you.' Before there was time to be nervous, or get flustered and do something mad like curtseying, the older woman grabbed Lizzie in a hug almost as fierce as the one in which she'd held her son. 'So very glad…so very, very glad.'

It was impossible to resist. Lizzie hugged back. Her own

family were loving enough, but not hugely demonstrative. She hadn't expected this at all. She'd pictured aristocratic reserve and clipped accents. The Marchioness's voice was refined, but warm and joyous.

Then the older woman set Lizzie away from her at arm's length, and looked her up and down, eagerly cataloguing her. 'Oh, my dear, you're so lovely. So very beautiful. Jonny is a very lucky man.'

'Thank you…' Eek, agh, the title! What did it say in Debrett? 'Thank you, Lady Welbeck.'

'Oh, nonsense, call me Jane. We've waited for you so long, darling, let's not stand on any kind of silly ceremony.'

She knows. I'm not wearing the ring, and John says he hasn't said anything. But she knows all the same.

They'd decided to go in low key, and assay the mood at Montcalm before making any big announcements. But judging by the eager look on Jane Wyngarde Smith's face, they didn't need to announce anything.

'Thank you, that's very kind. I've been ever so worried about making some idiotic gaffe,' Lizzie went on. 'In all the time I've known John…Well, he's just been John to me. Just an ordinary person. Well, not ordinary ordinary, you know what I mean.'

What in God's name am I babbling about?

But her hostess gently touched her arm. 'Oh, exactly. There's never been anything ordinary about Jonny, but I do know what you mean. Now, shall we have some coffee? Or perhaps a nip of sherry? When you've seen your room, of course. Do come this way.'

'Coffee would be lovely.'

Oh lor, the Marchioness herself was to be her escort. In a heartbeat they were climbing a grand, wide, carpeted staircase together, leaving John behind them talking to Brewster and the footmen. He'd waved to her when she'd reached the gallery, blowing her a kiss as her hostess began to point out a few particularly fine family portraits, drawing her attention to the likeness some of them bore to John himself. There was a succession of bold, handsome golden-haired men in Victorian, Georgian and even Cavalier attire. Brilliant blue eyes stared out at her, again and again. 'Montcalm is a Victorian fantasy, of course,' the Marchioness said, 'but there have been Wyngarde Smiths on this land almost since Tudor times.'

In a corridor leading off the main gallery, Jane opened a door and showed Lizzie into an exquisitely beautiful room decorated in tones of rose and burgundy. The furnishings were rich, but a combination of modern and older pieces, expertly chosen to harmonise.

'The Rose Room,' said Jane with a flourish. 'One of our prettiest. I think you'll be very comfortable here.' As she strode across to open the window a little wider, one of the footmen brought in Lizzie's weekend bag and set it on the top of a low chest.

'It's gorgeous! I love these colours.'

'Yes, it's not long been renovated, along with a number of others.' The Marchioness's wrinkled face twisted in a wry little smile. 'And you'll find a nice little bathroom through there.' She pointed to a panelled door. 'We had the plumbing system of the whole house replaced a few years ago…Thanks to…Well, I think you know who.'

The older woman drew close, laying her hand on Lizzie's arm, looking into her face, intently. 'My dear, I know you must know something of the situation between Jonny and his family. But we do all know to whom we owe our comfort and the continued upkeep of Montcalm. And our privacy...Very few families nowadays are able to live in houses like these, mainly as private homes. Even my husband knows that, although he chooses not to speak of it. But underneath, he's as profoundly grateful to Jonny as the rest of us are...and, in his own bull-headed way, enormously proud of him.'

There was such a look of pride and love in Jane's eyes that Lizzie couldn't help but clasp the hand that lay on her arm. 'John...or should I say Jonny...? He's an amazing man. You *should* be proud of him. I am.'

Jane beamed. 'Wonderful! Wonderful!' she said, briskly vague. 'Now, my dear, I'll leave you for a little while to powder your nose and all that. Just come down when you're ready. We'll take coffee in the Red Salon. That's along the corridor back the way you came, then to your left, and looking down, you can't miss it. But if you're unsure, just ring the bell and someone will come along and show you the way.' She gave Lizzie another quick hug. 'See you in a little while, Lizzie.' With a satisfied nod, she strode away, out of the room, closing the door quietly behind her.

21

Meeting the Marquess

It was easy to find the Red Salon. You'd have had to be blind to miss it. Lizzie paused on the gallery, looking down, just taking a moment to compose herself. Thus far, things weren't too scary. She'd no doubt that the Marchioness could be as stately and aristocratic as the next toff, but at the moment she seemed to Lizzie more like a kindly aunt or granny than a terrifying prospective mother-in-law from a vastly different social class.

And she seems to want me here. Really want me here.

Lizzie held her station another moment or two, smoothing down her dress, and the hem of her toning cardigan. Not sure what to arrive in, she'd chosen a very simple but quite elegant 1950s-style frock, in a small blue print; one of her own making that she'd run up quickly during the week when she really should have been doing New Again work.

It was no use trying to be something she wasn't, she'd decided. She'd kept her signature style. And if Jane Wyngarde Smith's reaction had been anything to go by, she'd made the right choice. John had smiled too, approving her choice of outfit when they'd set off.

And yet, as Lizzie looked down, she couldn't help admiring her hostess's tweeds. Even shivering with nerves and awed on arrival, she'd noticed them. Beautifully cut, soft and light, in a subtle heathery blue.

Heck, one day I might wear something like that.

She imagined herself older, clad in a tweed skirt and jacket, and sensible shoes, her hair in an elegant coil, and suddenly couldn't help grinning like a twit. She was almost looking forward to it. If she hadn't got a suitable pattern in her vast collection, she'd find one, make the outfit in secret and then spring herself on John as a surprise, dressed as a country lady.

Pulling herself together, she stepped out smartly and made her way down another of Montcalm's wide, gracious staircases. John had been standing in front of the empty fireplace, discussing his father's health with his mother, by the sound of it, but he strode forward immediately to greet her, his eyes alight.

'OK, love?' he said in a low voice, leading her to the place of honour on a wide, no doubt priceless, brocade upholstered settee beside the Marchioness. In a flash, she had a cup of coffee in her hand, prepared just how she liked it, strong and delicious.

'I'm sorry Augustus isn't here to greet you too,' said Jane. 'His health is up and down a lot these days and I suspect –' she glanced at John '– that he's probably just as nervous about today as either of you two have been. And that's affecting him.'

Lizzie half expected John to refute the suggestion, but he looked thoughtful. 'Perhaps you're right, Mother. I've spent so many years with my festering resentment of him, that somewhere along the line, I forgot to remember he's human. And that I've inherited every bit of his stubbornness myself.' He drew in a deep breath, as if the weight of those years was suddenly heavy.

'He's never stopped loving you, Jonny,' said his mother, reaching out her hand to her son, who stepped forward to take it, and squeeze it. 'Oh, he's hated you too. That's his bloody-minded way. But I really believe we're past that now.' She turned and smiled at Lizzie. 'Especially now Lizzie is here.'

A spasm of anxiety made the coffee taste like mud for a moment, and sharp-eyed Jane seemed to see it. 'Don't worry, my dear,' said the Marchioness. 'Don't worry at all. You simply have to live your life with Jonny, and be happy. That's all you have to do.' The older woman's kind smile was beautiful, and Lizzie almost gasped, seeing John in her face, her expression.

'Well, that's no hardship,' she said, grinning back at the pair of them.

The moment had been intense, but clearly a consummate hostess of decades, Jane turned the conversation to lighter topics. Talk of the house, of Tom's new plans for the home farms and the rare breed livestock; questions about Lizzie's sewing, about New Again, about the new bridal shop.

Lizzie could see Jane dying to ask more.

'I do plan to make my own wedding dress when the time comes,' she said, grasping the nettle. 'I thought something along the lines of Grace Kelly's gown, when she married Prince Rainier of Monaco. Simple, elegant, refined, you know?'

'Oh, my dear. How wonderful! That would suit you perfectly.' The older woman hesitated. 'This does mean…doesn't it? What we're so desperately hoping…'

'Yes, Mother,' said John, pulling a footstool from the side of the hearth, setting it in front of Lizzie and his mother and subsiding gracefully onto it. He fished into the pocket of his jacket. 'Lizzie and I are engaged. We…' His eyes flashed to Lizzie. 'We were just waiting for the right moment to tell you, but this seems to be it.' Reaching for Lizzie's hand, he slid on the ring.

For the second time in an hour, Lizzie was hugged breathless by a Marchioness, and then by her son. Jane chatted joyfully, reiterating again and again how happy she was, clearly as all a-flutter as Lizzie felt.

'We shall have Champagne with lunch!' The Marchioness turned to her son. 'Jonny…Will you tell your father now? Please…It'll mean so much to him.'

'I was planning to have a quiet word with him first. You know, open up lines of communication face to face. Letters and phone calls between us aren't quite the same.'

The Marchioness rose to her feet, drawing Lizzie up too. 'I know you're being cautious, Jonny. Considerate, too. But I do feel that this news is the very best thing for him. The best gift you could give him.'

A few moments later, they were being ushered into the Marquess's bedroom. On the threshold, Lizzie pressed her hand to her chest. Her heart was bashing so hard, it felt as if it had to be visible: thud, thud, thud. John reached for the hand, grasped it tight and squeezed it. In his blue eyes, Lizzie saw the nerves, just like her own, and somehow that helped.

The Marquess was propped up on a day bed, by the window. At first, Lizzie thought he didn't look too ill, but then she saw oxygen nearby, and a raft of medications on a tray on a side table. Ominous. Lizzie guessed there was a nurse within call.

But the man himself was full of life, fiery life, despite his health problems. And, oh crikey, he was handsome. For a man of eighty, he was breath-taking. The genes, the genes...This was where John got his looks!

'Well, well, well...' The Marquess's fierce blue eyes flashed, brilliant and hypnotising, the mirror of his son's. His mane of white hair was far longer than John's but had the same wild, precocious curl, still thick and full, despite his years. 'The prodigal returns at last.' The bright gaze flicked to Lizzie, and suddenly a rakish smile flooded the old man's face. 'And goddammit, he's brought Bettie Page with him!'

As if energised, the Marquess sat up straighter, tutting at his wife, who rushed forward to adjust his pillows. He reached out his hand towards Lizzie. 'Come here, my dear, let me see you. I'll thrash out my differences with that sod soon enough –' he said, nodding at John, his look reassuringly benign '– but you're the one I want to see now. Come closer.'

Lizzie felt the gentle pressure of John's hand on her back like a boost of energy. Her confidence rose. She walked towards the old man on his couch, and John drew up a chair beside his parent for her.

The shrewd eyes narrowed. 'I take it you do know who Bettie Page is?' He lifted his hand in an indicative gesture, pointing out Lizzie's thick, carefully coifed black fringe and the long pageboy style brushing her shoulders, and her 1950s dress. 'All this is deliberate, isn't it?'

'Yes, your lordship. If it wasn't, I might not be here. I think it was "Bettie" who most caught John's eye when we first met.' Standing beside her, John squeezed her shoulder.

'I'd have come over anyway, Bettie or no Bettie,' he said.

The Marquess's scrutiny was intense, but she noticed his eyes flick to his son's momentarily. Was there a faint look of approval there? Possibly...

'I should think so!' said the Marquess. 'And by the way, young woman, I'm "Welbeck" or "Augustus". I'd prefer the latter.'

'Oh, I'm not sure I could...'

'I'll have you thrown off my land if you don't!'

Shock froze her, even with John's fingers against her shoulder. Then she saw it. The electric blue twinkle in those uncannily familiar eyes. The genetic sense of fun, that even an old and cantankerous man still possessed. Augustus was John, and sounding uncannily like his son, he laughed.

'Only pulling your leg, Bettie. Call me whatever you feel comfortable with. The Old Sod if you must.' His expression gentled. 'But just...be here...Now, tell me a little about yourself. I'll deal with this reprobate later, but you're the important one now.' He reached for her left hand in a surprisingly strong grip, and raised it. 'Good! Capital! Pleased to see this here.' He nodded at the ring, and flashed a look at John. 'Getting it right at last, Jonny. Thank God for that. I thought I'd probably shuffle off this mortal coil first.'

What followed was an unexpectedly easy 'interview'. The fact that she was young, and so obviously of childbearing age, clearly made her a person of worth in the unreconstructed Marquess's eyes, regardless of her background. Although that didn't stop him questioning her.

'One of three girls?' He frowned.

'But I have quite a few male cousins! My father is one of four brothers. And my mother has two brothers.'

'That's more like it.'

Lizzie flashed a look at John, who seemed to be trying to avoid laughing.

'Stop sniggering, you young shit!' the Marquess shot at him, but his expression was warmer than his words. 'So, Bettie, I understand you work. Tell me about that.'

Lizzie launched into a description of New Again, and how she'd come to be part of it, and what she did.

'Pretty frock,' commented Augustus, when she told him she'd made it herself. 'Now, obviously, I'm interested in when you'll stop working…and start producing…but I know women prefer to have a career these days.'

It was bizarre. It could have been grotesque. But Lizzie could feel the old man's pain, and the weight of dashed hope and disappointment over the years. Some of that was John's fault – it had to be faced and admitted – but also some brought about by the misfortunes of Augustus's elder son George, and his wife.

'I'd like to work full-time for a couple of years,' she said firmly. She felt for Augustus, but she had to have her own life too, and she sensed he'd respect that. 'But after that, well, it would be nice to start a family. And I can still design and sew afterwards too. I mean…' She glanced around her, at the beauty of the room, and the entire magnificence of Montcalm beyond. 'It's not as if we're going to be short of a bob or two, so I won't have to do everything alone. I'll have a bit of help.'

'Fair enough, my dear,' said Augustus, taking her hand again. 'I think I can hang on that long, and this devil will give you all the help you need. Or I'll personally get up off my sick bed and horsewhip him until he pulls his weight!'

They spoke a little more, then the Marquess seemed

to be tiring. 'Now, my dear, you go down and have a spot of lunch with my wife, and my son and I will have our discussion.' He gave John a very old-fashioned look, that almost made Lizzie giggle. She'd seen that look from John, so many times. 'Jane, come along, take this lovely young woman and feed her up well. She's got a nice figure, but a bit more meat on those curves wouldn't go amiss.'

John came to the door with Lizzie and his mother, and gave them both a hug. 'Don't worry. You've put him in a good mood, love. You go and enjoy your lunch. I'll be OK.'

And as she and the Marchioness made their way down to the dining room, Lizzie rather thought he would be.

A most difficult hurdle, maybe the most difficult, was behind them.

22

Interlude

'You don't think they wish I was Clara, do you?'

Where had that question come from? Lizzie hadn't meant to voice it, but the Champagne at lunch had loosened her tongue, and taken the brakes off her remaining subconscious fears.

She and John were out for a stroll. By unspoken agreement, they'd both needed time to themselves, together. Lunch had been a very jolly meal with Tom and Brent there too, and congratulations all round. The Marchioness and Brent already seemed to have bonded.

'To the manor born, eh?' Brent had said, giving Lizzie a hug. 'You fit right in, like Cinderella into the glass slipper.'

'Welcome to Montcalm,' his lover had said. 'You do know you've done Brent and I a huge favour, don't you? With the black sheep shedding his grubby fleece to become the beloved son again, nobody's going to make a fuss about me "getting engaged" too.' He winked at Brent.

The Marchioness had been chatting away merrily with her gay son and his lover as Lizzie and John had left for their stroll. Lizzie was thrilled to see Brent as happy and accepted as she seemed to be, although she wasn't quite sure what Augustus's thoughts on the matter would be.

So why, when the day was turning out to be such a spectacular success, had the spectre of Clara suddenly risen again?

'No. They don't,' said John, his voice crisp and decisive. The Champagne didn't seem to have affected him. 'Maybe once they still harboured hopes that Clara and I would get together and marry. Probably for a long while. Both she and Caroline are still family friends…Well, my mother's friends. The old man has probably forgiven Caroline now, at last.' He paused, drawing her to a halt, looking down into her eyes. 'But now…Now they see that you were the one worth waiting for. The right woman for me.' He kissed her hand. 'The true princess who finally came along and kissed me back to life.' They fell back into step, meandering in the general direction of a folly John wanted to show her. 'And in all honesty, even Mother, who was always fond of Clara, would be the first to admit that she's flighty and unreliable…and can be cruel. And, of course, my mother doesn't even know the half of it.'

Yes, the second time Clara had walked out on him. Dashing John's hopes, and his pride too, when he realised he'd only been a diversion, for sex, while Clara had been teasing and snaring a bigger, better prospect, her American billionaire.

But we've got the last laugh. We have…

As they vectored towards the folly, a neo-Grecian construction nestled amongst trees at the edge of the park, clouds slipped in front of the sun, and the skies darkened. Lizzie laughed.

'Yikes, we start talking about Clara, and suddenly the

sun goes in and it looks as if it's going to rain. If this was a movie, that'd be a cliché.'

John laughed. 'Yes, there should probably be a clap of thunder right about now. But stop worrying, love. She can't touch us now.' He looked up at the sky, held out his free hand. For a moment, Lizzie saw him back in the grounds at the Waverley, assaying the rain, that day they'd played spanking games in the dell. 'It is going to rain, though. Could be a downpour…Come on, let's hustle and get to the folly.' He tugged on her hand, then released it. 'I'll race you!'

John was always going to beat her there. He often ran for fitness, whereas she preferred to swim each day. But she decided not to run as fast as she could; something in the twinkle in John's eye told her she might need her energy for other things. It had been another of those days of behaving themselves, and that was tough, with John looking so glorious and edible in one of his soft grey-blue suits and a darker toning shirt. He was even wearing a sharp tie, out of deference to his parents, although he'd pulled that off now, and stuffed it in his pocket.

The folly was small, but ornate, built from gleaming pale stone like a mini classical temple, with a pillared portico flanking a fairly solid oak door. John stood waiting for her, beneath the under-hang, hands in his pockets, grinning.

'You owe me a forfeit for not really trying,' he announced as she reached him, then hauled her enthusiastically into his arms. 'God, this business of being on best behaviour for the parents is killing me. This's twice we've had to do it, and it doesn't get any easier the second time around.'

'Then stop messing about, will you!' Lizzie reached up and cradled his head, drawing his face to hers. 'Here's your forfeit.' Exerting pressure, she compelled him to kiss her.

This! This was more intoxicating by far than the Champagne. Happiness fuelled by the relief of finding herself accepted at Montcalm. Crazy lust, but imbued with depth and wonder by the challenge of the years that lay ahead.

This was simple and beautiful. And hot. John's tongue in her mouth, thrusting. His hands roving her body, rucking up her skirts, grabbing at her thighs and bottom. She was ready, so ready for him, in the blink of an eye.

'I want you,' he gasped, taking the words she would have uttered and giving them back to her.

'Here?' She asked, but she knew the answer. It was mad, but they had to. They had to christen Montcalm as their own, and here, away from the house itself, seemed the perfect place to begin. Here they were just John and Lizzie, not Lord Jonathan and Lady Jonathan-to-be.

'Yes,' he growled, kissing her hard again, then swirling round and reaching for the ornate brass doorknob. It turned easily and John flung the door open, to reveal the inner chamber.

It was a scruffy dive, for all its exterior glamour and classicism. Dust lay thick on the floor, and leaves had got in from somewhere, and piled up in the corners. A door to another chamber stood ajar, slightly, and in the centre of the room was a cluster of decrepit furniture. A bashed-up divan, two easy chairs, a low table. Some yellowing newspapers lay on the table, and an empty mineral water bottle on its side.

'Does somebody come here?' Leading John forward, Lizzie picked up a paper, and saw a date from around two years ago.

'It's a bolt-hole of Tom's. From the time before he moved

into his own cottage. He told me he used to come here to get away from rowing with the old man.' John leaned down and thumped at the divan, and dust rose. He rubbed his fingers, surveying the grime. 'It's on the list to renovate properly, but the main house has always taken precedence.'

Lizzie looked at the divan. It was grubby. 'We'll get our clothes filthy if we roll around on there.' The patterned fabric of her dress was pale, as was the blue of John's suit.

Her fiancé beamed at her. 'Well, we'll just have to take our clothes off, then, won't we?'

'Oh John, we can't!' It was an empty protest. The urge to strip was unstoppable. She'd been so prim and buttoned up all day, but now she wanted to be wild.

'Yes, we can.' John's voice was low and thrilling, and in the shadowed interior of the folly, his brilliant eyes were lambent with lust. 'In fact…I command it. I'm your lord and master now, young woman.' He nodded to the ring on her finger. 'Or near as dammit.' He moved forward and cupped her chin, forcing her to look into face, his beautiful face. 'Now do as you're told.' He was trying to act stern, but his fight against a happy smile was all but lost.

'Perhaps you're right, milord,' she answered, her own lips quirking. 'You know best.'

'Of course I do.' He gave her an admonishing look at the sound of the title, something in his bearing changing as he became Lord Jonathan again, the aristo he truly was. Lizzie had seen it the moment he'd walked into Montcalm – the subtle difference, an aura, bred in the bone – and despite the egalitarian tendencies fostered in her by her own father, she'd liked it. Liked it very much indeed. Lord Jonathan was every bit as hot, and just as much her love, as plain John Smith was.

She gave him a bold look. He might be what he was, but she was his match. 'Oh, you love it really, don't you? You've missed it...being Lord Muckety-Muck with adoring lackeys tugging their forelocks and hanging on your every word. Being the golden boy of the family.'

His eyes gentled, and he laughed softly. Lizzie knew he accepted his own foibles. 'OK, yes, I have a bit.' His grin widened. 'Now, stop shillyshallying about. Clothes off, trollop!' He stepped back, and crossed his arms, his eyes on her unwaveringly. To watch the show.

Lizzie's mind flew back to their early days, not really all that long ago, but seeming distant because they'd travelled so far together. He'd been the sexy master then, just as he was now...But she'd known nothing else of him at the time.

Now she did know him, and he was a hundred times as sexy, and as masterful.

Carefully, she set her bag on one of the chairs, then attacked her cardigan buttons, before shimmying out of it. Frowning at the dustiness, she folded it inside out, then undid the zip in the side of her dress. Thus released, she undid the small buttons down the front, and then, plucking at the full skirt, drew it off over her head, revealing herself in her bra and petticoat.

About to fold the frock, she saw John's hand out-held, and let him take it from her and fold it. He did a perfect job, even though he didn't once take his eyes off her, following her every move as she eased off her petti and handed that over too.

Ridiculously nervous, she hesitated.

'All off.'

Quickly, and not as elegantly as she would have liked, she peeled off her undies and tossed them in the general direction of her folded clothing, then kicked off her shoes.

Oh God, she was standing naked in the centre of a folly, in the grounds of one of the greatest country houses in northern England. Someone might come by, some gamekeeper or groundsman or whatever. He might notice a flicker of movement, of pale flesh through the dusty windows – and conscientiously decide to investigate.

John looked at her. A long comprehensive look, as if re-cataloguing the body he now knew so well; the physical domain of which he was now lord and master, in their games.

'Oh, my love, that's a view I'll never tire of.' He let out a gusty breath, then seemed to galvanise himself. 'Now, come on, lie down on that couch and play with yourself while I strip for you.'

'With pleasure!' Cautiously, imagining she could feel the dust grains, Lizzie complied, stretching out her legs, and resting her head on one arm behind her neck, in the style of a Venus or Goya's naked Maja, while with the other she touched her pussy. She was wet and ready: no surprise there.

'I hope so,' said John, nodding in approval, his gaze tracking her fingers. His own first action was to reach into his inner jacket pocket and fish out a condom package, and with a flourish, toss it in Lizzie's direction. It landed on her belly, an inch from where her hand was at work.

'Ooh, your lordship, what would your mam say if she knew you'd had condoms in your pocket all the time?' Lizzie gasped. Her clit was so sensitive; she was almost there already.

John gave her a wicked look. 'I'm sure she'd be

scandalised. Now, make yourself useful, and get that unwrapped. I've waited too long, ogling you in that sexy flowery frock. I need to be inside you.'

In a series of swift, deft actions, he began to undress, dealing with his shoes and socks in a way that was more elegant than any man had a right to be. Next came shirt and jacket, not quite so neatly folded as her clothes, and dumped right on top of them, haphazard. Within a heartbeat he was stepping out of his trousers, then his underwear.

Oh hell...Oh hell...

She would never tire of this view either. The lean, well-shaped body, toned but not overmuscled. The smooth, firm skin. The heavy, but eager cock. He was already pointing right at her, ruddy tip gleaming.

'Lordly,' she remarked, grinning back at him, tearing open the condom wrapper as he advanced towards her and knelt on the edge of the couch to be enrobed.

Jutting forward his hips, he let her roll it on him, and then he seemed to pose for a second, teasing her with the goods.

Devouring him with her gaze, the years seemed to unfold before her, and she imagined a time when he was not so trim, and yet she would still find him utterly sexy. It was a long way off yet, but even so, she knew she'd love him and want him. Heck, even when his face was as lined and hawkish as his handsome father's, and his golden hair turned as white as snow.

And he'd want her. She knew it. Even when she wasn't as shapely; when her figure had probably spread a bit from having children, and there were streaks of silver in her black hair.

'What are you thinking about? Should I be insulted? You

looked miles away then for a moment.' John leant forward, then moved over her, smiling.

'Don't worry, it was about you.' Parting her legs, she put her hands on him, urging. 'I was just thinking that I'll still fancy you when you're an even older git than you are now.'

'Thank you…I think,' said John, positioning himself. 'Are you ready, love? I'm feeling too selfish and horny to indulge in much foreplay. But don't you worry…' He pushed, long and true and sure. 'When we're back at Dalethwaite, just the two of us, you'll get all the elaborate, protracted, kinky lovemaking sessions that your heart, and your delicious pussy, desire.'

Lizzie gasped, filled with him. At last. They'd made love beautifully last night, but it still felt like a century since this unique, gorgeous feeling. Even as her body shimmered in welcome, John took his weight on one elbow, wiggled his hand in between their bodies and sought out her clit.

His finger circled. 'Yes, don't you worry, my love. We'll be the king and queen of perv again. A full programme of everything…' He pressed hard, just to the side, ooh, just where she liked. Her sex fluttered. 'Spanking, bondage, whatever you like. I'll tan your gorgeous bottom with flip-flops, leather slippers, even that old blue ruler if I can find it. And we'll use every little gadget in that chest of wickedness of ours.' Angling his hips, he pushed in deeper, finding another, even sweeter knot of nerves. 'I might even buy a pair of leather trousers, if you want me to.'

'Oh…ah…Oh goody…' Almost there, almost there. Her hips swivelled of their own accord, but John kept contact, moving with her. Their rocking bodies stirred up dust from the venerable upholstery and it drifted around them.

And some of it went up Lizzie's nose and she sneezed

violently, came violently, and started laughing so hard she couldn't stop, even while her pussy clenched and clenched in waves of bliss.

'Bless you!' cried John, laughing too, then a moment later, he bared his teeth, his hips hammering as he joined her, coming hard and pounding like a train.

It was the silliest, wildest, most inelegant mutual orgasm, resolving in uncontrollable laughter and stereo sneezing fits, until eventually they lay in a heap on the rackety old sofa, chests heaving in unison, bodies streaked with dust.

'I love you, Lizzie,' sighed John, when he'd regained his breath. 'I love your body and your heart and your mind…and I promise that next time I do something about it, we'll be in a proper bed. A nice clean bed with crisp perfectly laundered sheets…and no dust!' He smothered her face in kisses, dust notwithstanding. 'Hopefully, I'll be able to sneak into your room tonight. I'm quite sure Mother actually expects me to, given that she knows we live together.'

'I'll look forward to the sneakage, Lord Jonathan.' She snuck in a kiss or two of her own, in between his. 'And in case you were in any doubt, I love you too.'

'I never was…' Kiss. Kiss. Kiss. '…in any doubt.'

A short while later they were walking back across the park, heading for the house. The threatened rain hadn't arrived, but the sky was heavy, and the clouds lowering.

Lizzie tucked a little tissue-wrapped parcel into her bag. It wouldn't do to leave used condoms lying around in the folly.

Watching, John gave her a wry grin. 'I've been wondering…Now we're engaged, we might try not using those.'

Lizzie's eyebrows shot up to her fringe. Finally!

'No, I don't mean no birth control at all. That's a given. No children yet…' He took her hand as they walked. 'But I wondered how you felt about the Pill? Only if it suits you, of course. I'm sure Richard would be able to refer you to a specialist to advise.'

Sir Richard Spillsey, their doctor now. Lizzie wasn't sure how she'd feel discussing birth control with him, but a female doctor would be fine.

'I…I'd like to give it a whirl. I'd like to…um…' Oh for heaven's sake, why so shy? After the things they'd done. 'I'd like us to be skin to skin, you know?'

'Me too, love, me too…I've wanted it, God knows, but somehow I've never felt I had the right to ask, in case you felt I was putting the burden of responsibility on you…' John's voice was ragged as they halted, looking into each other's eyes. 'I'll get myself checked out again, of course. I've always done safe sex, and had regular HIV tests. But sometimes you never know. There have been instances of malfunctioning condoms, and now I want to be doubly…to be trebly sure…rather than put you at any kind of risk.' For a moment, he looked distraught, and she leant across and up, to kiss him.

'You're not putting a responsibility on me, John,' she said, her lips still close to his. 'I don't see it that way. I see it as a sharing of control.' She gave him a serious look, and saw him get the message immediately. 'And I'll get tested too. I've only ever done safe sex, but if you're getting tests, I want to. It's only fair.'

He kissed her long and sweetly. He didn't speak. He didn't need to.

'Come on,' he said. 'If we hurry, we might get some tea. Otherwise, it'll be time to change for dinner.'

A sporty open-top Mercedes stood on the gravel drive in front of the main entrance as they approached, giving Lizzie a momentary qualm. More visitors. Or more family? She told herself not to be silly. She could hack it; she had John by her side.

'Whose car is that? Have your brother and his wife come back? Or your niece?'

John frowned. 'I don't know. I don't know what they're all driving these days. Doesn't look like George's style, though. He's very much a Range Rover man. Could be Helen's, I suppose.' His hand tightened around Lizzie's. It was only infinitesimal, but there was a tension there. Out of all proportion to the idea of meeting his relations.

In the entrance hall, Brewster intercepted them. Had he actually been waiting for them? Lizzie had the strongest impression that he might have been, although there was no question of such a dignified figure simply loitering about.

'Excuse me, your lordship, your mother asked me to let you know that two new guests have arrived.' The man paused delicately; a face that Lizzie guessed was almost always a picture of impassivity showed faint signs of discomposure. What the hell was going on?

'Guests, Brewster…Who?'

John didn't look impassive either. In fact, he looked worryingly rattled in a way Lizzie had never really seen before, as if that weird sixth sense of his was pinging out of control.

What is it? Who is it?

She suddenly had the most awful premonition, as if she too had John's almost prescient powers. Her chest felt tight, her whole body unsettled.

'It's the Condesa Sanchez de la Villareal, milord, and

her son. The Marchioness thought you'd probably prefer to know immediately on your return. They're taking tea in the Red Salon.'

Oh hell! Oh bloody hell! It was Clara.

23

Clara...and Son

John's face was like a mask.

Shocked as she felt herself, Lizzie feared for him. He looked vaguely ill, and she grasped his hand in both of hers, holding it tight. His eyes flashed to hers, a torment of shadows, but just as quickly as the dark moment had arrived, he got control again. She could see him bracing up, straightening his spine, regaining composure.

Does he still care for her? Even now? the demons of doubt whispered in her ear.

'You know, I had a feeling something like this might happen,' he said quietly, twisting his wrist so he could hold Lizzie's hands in his. 'But I thought I was just being alarmist, and idiotic, so I didn't say anything.' He sighed. 'But it seems my premonitions were spot on after all. Unfortunately...' His eyes darkened again, scanning her face. 'Are you all right, sweetheart, you look a bit pale?'

Lizzie laughed; pure nerves. She sounded like a hysteric. 'I was just thinking the same about you. Bloody hell, aren't we a pair?' Her heart was bashing. She tried to calm it. John loved her, not this woman from his past.

And still the butler was standing a few feet away, silently waiting for some kind of answer.

'Thank you, Brewster,' John said, his armour of self-assurance fully returned. 'Thank you for letting us know. We'll join them presently.'

'Very well, milord.' The butler strode silently away, something in the stiffness of his back telling Lizzie that he wasn't all that pleased by Clara's arrival either.

'I think I need a few minutes to "freshen up", as they say, before we join them.'

What a massive understatement. Perhaps a week spent 'freshening up' would be better, and hopefully by then, her bête noire would have upped sticks and moved on, with any luck to an entirely different continent.

'Me too.' John mustered a grin. 'I can't say that I'm pleased she's here, but we were planning to meet her sooner or later, with Caroline. She must be massively curious about you, and Clara's never taken kindly to having to wait for anything. Perhaps it's better to get it over with now.' He shrugged. 'Like ripping off a sticking plaster. Grin through the pain and feel better afterwards.'

'Yes, you're right.' John's attempt at a joke cheered Lizzie up. You didn't call someone you still loved a sticking plaster!

John gave her a hug. 'You'll be fine, darling. We're together. You're my fiancée and before long you'll be my bride. And she's just a woman not a ten-headed monster.'

Lizzie let out a shaky laugh. 'That's what I'm trying to tell myself.'

'Come on, let's tidy ourselves up, and then we'll make a grand entrance together,' said John, leading her towards the staircase and shrugging as they ascended. 'I'm being fucking ridiculous, aren't I? I'm a man, not a mouse!' He grinned at her, boyish for a moment. Shamefaced.

'Oh, yes, you are a man, Lord Jonathan. I can vouch for that.' Thoughts of the folly stirred Lizzie's spirits, a delicious intimacy that shot strength through her veins.

Ten minutes later, nominally freshened, and managing to keep calm by not really thinking too much, Lizzie emerged onto the landing to find John leaning on the opposite wall waiting for her, posed between two ancestral portraits that both looked a bit like him, despite the unfamiliarity of the costumes. As she closed the door, he pushed himself off the wall and came to her, reaching for her hand. Had he been practising biofeedback? He seemed completely composed now.

'Ready?' he said, taking her hand. 'Concerted front, eh?'

Lizzie's heart turned over. He knew her anxiety, and probably still felt it himself, but together, they were stronger. A team. She followed along, feeling stronger.

Their footsteps were soft on the thick carpet runner, and as they approached the gallery, the sound of conversational voices drifted up from the salon below, their owners as yet unaware they were being approached. As one, John and Lizzie slowed down, like a pair of covert operatives on a recce.

The conversation seemed to be about school fees.

'They're absolutely exorbitant. I really don't know where they get the figures from, especially the so-called "extras",' said a low, beautifully modulated female voice. 'But, it's the school Jonathan went to, so it must be first class. I want the very best for Charlie, and I think he could be really happy there if we can secure a place for him.'

That's her. Clara. The ex from hell. My arch enemy. Oh fuck her, if she looks as good as she sounds, she must be ten times as bloody gorgeous as in her photos!

The Marchioness made some reply, but Lizzie barely heard it. Hanging back, she stole a peek over the rail, moving slowly, as stealthy as John at her side.

Two women sat on either side of each other, on one of the wide red sofas, with tea things on a tray before them. The Marchioness was sipping hers, and to Lizzie's eyes, the grey-haired woman looked tense, and very far from the joyously happy mother she'd seemed earlier, almost giddy at her favourite son's news.

The cool, collected creature at her side had suddenly thrown a massive spanner in everyone's works.

And Clara was cool. A relaxed figure, slim and elegant, she wore what Lizzie recognised, even from her high vantage point, as a powder blue, distinctively braided Chanel suit. Couture, no doubt, too. Made especially for her, not like the single prêt-à-porter item that had fleetingly passed through the hands of New Again last week, only to be snapped up the same day it had arrived.

A glossy cap of dark, nut-brown hair nodded in time to a remark from the Marchioness, the cut immaculately styled. Lizzie couldn't see Clara's face from this angle, but everything about the woman's bearing and the graceful movements of her hands suggested supreme confidence in her own good looks.

'Come on,' mimed John, with a shrug. They had to go. They couldn't hide like naughty schoolchildren up here.

What did you expect, nitwit? Some sexy siren loaded down with bling and clad in skimpy, low-cut tightness? Of course she doesn't look like a chav. She's an aristocrat, just like John. She belongs in a place like this.

Perfect marchioness material.

Lizzie's feet faltered. She suddenly saw a mental image of herself. Who was she kidding that she'd got her own look right for today? Wearing a dress she'd made herself, and all done up to look like a 1950s pin-up star?

Ridiculous nincompoop. You look like exactly what you are: a total outsider in this world.

'I love you,' whispered John as they reached the head of the stairs, and both the Marchioness and her companion twisted in their direction.

'Ah, there you are,' said the Marchioness, her lined face troubled.

'Jonathan,' said Clara, her face tranquil and composed, her eyes solely on John, as if no one but him existed.

Not sure quite how her legs were working, Lizzie descended, one hand on the banister, the other a bit sweaty in John's. She could see nothing but that face.

In the flesh, Clara was beautiful, utterly beautiful, there was no two ways about it. Not flashy, not what Lizzie would have termed drop-dead gorgeous, but just as quietly and classically lovely as the Googled pix had suggested, with large, lustrous eyes, a straight, elegant nose and a soft pink mouth, barely made up. She had to be at least forty, but she didn't look it at all; she was an archetypal English rose, ageless, and a perfect product of the privileged upper class.

Not rising from her seat, Clara put out her hand, as if unshakably confident that John would take it as she angled her flawless face for a kiss on the cheek. Which John gave her.

Atavistic jealousy surged in Lizzie's middle, but just as quickly, she got a hold of herself. Of course John would greet Clara that way; that was the way they did things here.

It would look weird if he shunned his former lover's touch completely.

'And you must be Elizabeth? How lovely to meet you.'

As John retreated, it seemed almost as if Clara expected another kiss of fealty, but Lizzie was a frozen doll, and couldn't bend. She did manage to put out her hand, though, and from somewhere, she found herself smiling, perhaps even looking calm.

'Yes…I'm Elizabeth Aitchison, very pleased to meet you. You must be Clara.'

The words *I've heard so much about you, and all of it bad* seemed to hang in the air as Lizzie managed to shake the cool, slender hand in hers quite firmly.

'Yes, for my sins.' Clara's smile was pleasant and natural. There was nothing in it that Lizzie could interpret as antagonistic, yet still she experienced an edge. 'I'm sure Jonathan has told you all sorts of tall tales about when we were impetuous youngsters together, but you mustn't believe half or even three-quarters of it.'

I know it all, you bitch. You hurt him. How can you be so blasé?

'Oh no, John has been the soul of discretion. You mustn't worry.' She managed another smile. God, even a grin! How the hell was she going to keep this up? It was going to need the performance of a lifetime.

Lizzie allowed herself to be guided to the settee opposite, where John took his place at her side. They exchanged the most fleeting of glances, intel passing between them, and as it did, Lizzie recalled certain conversations. Neither the Marquess or the Marchioness really knew quite how Clara and John had parted, that first time, when he'd been to prison. John had shouldered the blame, and given people to believe that the split had been mutually agreed, and any fault was his, in his fall from grace. Lizzie wasn't sure if his parents knew that he and Clara had been together again later; but even if they did, they didn't know details. John would have been chivalrous, yet again, taking on the black mark of being seen to be in the wrong.

For a few moments, there was a bit of breathing space, a welcome to and fro over teacups and milk and sugar that gave Lizzie time to regroup. Time to observe John, beside her, as well as the woman he'd once loved.

Although he smiled, and seemed easy and urbane, Lizzie could see clues. A faint tension in John's jaw; a pinch at the corner of his eyes. He wasn't comfortable, although he too was putting on a bravura performance, projecting a relaxed aura. An aura for her, she sensed, and for his mother, who Lizzie suspected was also masterfully controlling a state of anxiety.

The only person who seemed serenely unruffled was Clara, who chatted as if she visited Montcalm every day, praising the home-made biscuits and cake, admiring a painting on the wall that had been apparently newly acquired, and waxing lyrical over how wonderful the garden was looking, in late summer bloom.

But into a lull in the conversation, John suddenly said:

'So, Clara, were you just passing today? It seems odd that you should arrive at Montcalm on the very day that Lizzie and I are here. Especially as I'm not exactly what you'd call a regular visitor.'

There was a beat of silence. Was that a slight pucker of a frown on Clara's smooth, white brow?

'Actually, I'm here because you're here, Jonathan. I'm travelling around a bit now I'm back home for good, calling on a few friends with Charlie, before his new term starts. I was planning to drop in and visit you at Dalethwaite Manor, but when I rang up, the fabulous Thursgood told me you were here.'

'Really?'

Lizzie couldn't help herself. Out of Clara's sight-line, she touched John's hand. The tension in him was more palpable now. She knew he could control it – a poker face was second nature to him when negotiating, and it was what made him so formidable a businessman – but it hurt her to know that he was so troubled. Clara did still get to him, and Lizzie did not really want to dissect the reason why.

'Yes, it's all worked out beautifully, hasn't it?' Clara smiled, unfazed. Or apparently so. She was either the coolest of cool customers, or a world-class actress. Lizzie tried to control her own surging resentment, and smiled back.

'Yes, indeed,' she said.

'Especially on such an auspicious day.' The other woman's clear grey eyes flicked to Lizzie's left hand. 'I've always admired that ring and it looks wonderful on you, Elizabeth.'

Fucking hell! The bitch, she's rattled me so much I'd almost forgotten why John and I are here!

'Congratulations, Elizabeth…and Jonathan, dear. I hope you'll be very happy.' Clara went on, turning to Jane and still smiling: 'Such wonderful news. Both you and the Marquess must be absolutely thrilled.'

'Yes…Oh yes,' said the Marchioness, with a good deal of feeling. Lizzie could see that the older woman's fingers were tight in the handle of her teacup, and she feared for the pretty porcelain. 'Augustus is delighted. Perfectly delighted.'

Lizzie had always thought the expression 'you could cut the atmosphere with a knife' was an exaggeration, but now, she wasn't so sure. The air in the lofty, spacious room suddenly seemed thick and oppressive, laden with the weight of questions, relationships and personal histories bearing down on them. What had passed between this beautiful, aristocratic woman and John was such a tangle, not only because of the tortuous on and off and on again love affairs they'd shared, but with the added bizarreness of John being married, at one time, to Clara's mother. To Caroline, who was Jane Wyngarde Smith's great friend.

Fighting to find some innocuous, happy, non-contentious remark to make, when there were probably none to be found, Lizzie almost welcomed the sound of hurrying feet along the gallery above them. Someone young was running along the magnificent Aubusson carpet runner that John had probably paid handsomely to be restored; someone was heading their way.

It could only be Charlie, Clara's son. Obviously he and his mother had been invited to stay over too, and the lad had been up in his room.

But, as the newcomer descended the grand staircase, two steps at a time, the air that had been oppressive seemed to turn to ice around them – and a cold claw of a hand gripped at Lizzie's heart.

'Oh…hi!' said Charlie, rushing across to the grouped settees with a grin on his face, and a look of eager interest in the two people who'd appeared in his absence.

'Hi,' said Lizzie, mustering her own smile, even though her face felt paralysed. As if in slow motion, she turned to John, and saw the identical shock writ large on his beloved features. For the second time in an hour, he actually looked thunder-struck, completely taken aback, his poker face undone.

Charlie was a sunny, handsome youngster, not tall, but lithe and lean and wiry in his baggy jeans and equally baggy white T-shirt. Lizzie wasn't good at guessing ages, especially of children, but she judged that he could be about eleven, or twelve, or thereabouts.

What she did know was that one day, this boy would be a breath-taking stunner, and set female hearts racing wherever he went. His smile was a wonder and he had brilliant flashing eyes. Familiar eyes.

Eyes just as blue and jewel-like as the stricken man sitting at Lizzie's side, coupled with the very same angel's halo of curly blond hair.

Oh no…

'He could be mine. I don't know.'

John sat cross-legged on Lizzie's bed, in open shirt and old jeans and barefoot. It was about eleven o'clock, and even though they'd nominally turned in early, each to the separate rooms his mother had assigned them, he'd knocked on her door just a few minutes ago.

Lizzie had never been more glad to see him. Even though it was a council of war he'd arrived for, rather than passionate lovemaking.

'Is he the right age? I mean…could he have been conceived when you and she were together the second time?' It all seemed to be about timing.

'If he's twelve, yes, it's possible. But we used condoms.' John ran his hand through his hair, making it look even more like Charlie's flaxen curls than ever. He was still in a kind of shock, more perplexed than she'd ever seen him, yet trying to keep it together. For her sake, bless him.

Their conversation after the folly came back to her. 'Could there have been an exploding one?' The night was quite warm, and she wore pyjamas and a robe, but she still shivered.

A spasm of pain crossed John's face. It was as if there were words he didn't want to utter. 'It's...It's possible. We had a lot of sex at that time. A helluva lot. We fucked like rabbits. There might have been a torn condom I never noticed.' Eyes like broken blue stars, he reached for her hand. 'I'm so sorry, love.'

His skin actually felt cold, and Lizzie raised his hand to her lips, kissing it as if they might warm him. 'You don't have to apologise to me. You loved her. You thought you were going to be together. You didn't even know I existed then. And even if you had done, I'd only have been a kid at the time.' She kissed his hand again. 'What I can't understand is, why, if she was pregnant and she knew it was your child, did she still go ahead and marry Robson Hertingstall? If she'd cared at all for you, she should have married you.'

John's face twisted. Bitterness, a hotter emotion this time, but again, almost visibly, he quelled it and shrugged. 'At the time, he was the better prospect, and who knows, she may have cared for him just as much. Perhaps more. And to keep him she had to pretend the child was his.'

'Oh, this's such a mess,' Lizzie blurted out, then wished she hadn't. John was having the crappiest time of it already. But still, this was crappy for her too. Too crappy to keep inside and play the martyr.

The evening had made martyrs of the pair of them. Dinner had been a nightmare papered over with polite sociability. The only bright spot had been Charlie himself. Whatever his parentage, and his complications, he seemed uncomplicated, a sweet and amiable personality. Miraculously, given his mother's history, he was a golden child: funny, but with good manners, and smart. Remarkably grounded for his young age, he seemed unscarred by his mother's flighty procession of men and marriages.

He's probably turned out well because he's John's. He's got his father's strength; it's in the genes.

That thought had pretty much extinguished Lizzie's appetite, and she was sure that everyone around the table, with the possible exception of Clara, had been grateful for Charlie's engaging chatter about his summer spent at Robson Hertingstall's English racing and thoroughbred breeding stables.

His mother seemed to be enjoying a quiet, understated satisfaction from the hand grenade she'd thrown into everybody's weekend.

Clara's unwitting bombshell, the boy who could be John's son, obviously loved the outdoor life, and horses. He'd been spending a lot of time at the establishment near Newmarket during the holidays, rather than in South America with his mother, or visiting his 'father' in the States, or even seeing his grandmother, Caroline. To Lizzie, it seemed a slightly strange carry-on, but it didn't appear to have done Charlie any harm. Clearly, he'd been well looked after by the stable manager and trainer there, Arthur Something or other, and the housekeeper who took care of him.

In fact, it was all Arthur this, and Arthur that, and very little mention of the man he believed to be his real father. And no mention of the Conde Sanchez de la Villareal, his step-father.

Charlie's cheerful enthusiasm for horses – and Arthur – coupled with his unabashed opinions on television, music and computer games had just about made the meal bearable. Things might have been better if Tom and Brent had joined them, but the duo were no doubt blissfully unaware of what was going on, and under the impression that John and Lizzie would be having a lovely 'wedding' talk over dinner with the Marchioness.

As for the Marquess, Lizzie had a shrewd feeling that he hadn't even been told that Clara was at Montcalm. She'd heard John and his mother talking in hushed tones, and she wondered if they'd decided not to upset the old man with potentially disruptive news.

'Yes, it is a mess, alas,' said John, softly. 'I don't know what her object is in bringing him here, but I have an awful feeling it's to use him as leverage, goddamn her. To get me back, now that she's made a mess of things with her Argentine count.' He sighed, a low, plangent sound that seemed to come from the very pit of his soul. 'If he is my son, she probably believes he's her trump card.'

Lizzie wanted to shout and scream and break things, but that was no answer. She drew in her own deep breaths, scrabbling for calm, and to stop her mind running in circles.

But the truth was, she could see things with crystal clarity.

Clara *did* want John back. He was the good prospect now. Probably richer than either of her husbands, and . . . well . . . he was John, so beautiful, urbane and sexy. Was Clara playing on the horrible possibility, the suspicion that Lizzie kept squashing and squashing, but which could not be dealt with swiftly and cleanly like that sticking plaster?

The possibility that, despite everything, John had never

completely been able to expunge his feelings for his first love.

He's my perfect man, you bitch. But I suppose you think you can sweep in and take him…because you're the mother of his son.

Despite her attempts to hold it together, Lizzie's eyes misted. John's glance shot to her face when she dashed at the gathering tears and sat up straight, her spine stiff.

With a growl, he lunged forward and grabbed her in his arms. 'I love you, Lizzie. I love you completely. And whatever she has to say, I'm yours now. That's set in stone. It can't change.' His blue gaze seemed to bore into her like a laser. 'I have no feelings whatsoever any more for Clara. Nothing. Nada.'

'But what about Charlie?' muttered Lizzie into his shoulder. Agonised, she thought of her own parents and the rough patch they'd once gone through; marriage rocks that as the eldest, she'd been aware of and experienced keenly.

But her mother and father had got back together again, even though it had been touch and go. Her mother had told her later that the reunion had been solely for the benefit of her sisters and herself at first, although later, the Aitchisons had found a way to love each other again, and were a happy and devoted couple now.

That could happen with you and Clara, my love. If you got married for Charlie's sake. You loved her once…

Her heart screamed, but she kept it inside. John seemed to hear it, though, because he made her look at him.

'Set in stone, love. Don't ever forget that. Nothing she says can change that, and I will work something out, if he's mine.' He shrugged again, rolling his shoulders as if trying to release real physical tension. 'But I'm not so sure he is.

I do like the lad. He's a good, bright kid, but I don't feel a connection.'

'But that might be because you barely knew he existed until now.'

John looked as if she'd slapped him. As if what she'd said was possible.

'Well, I can't begin to know what's what until I've talked to her. I must go down. I don't want to, but I have to face my demon.' He laughed, a wry, harsh sound.

'Yes, it's no use us stewing up here, while she's down there, gloating and spinning her webs like Spider-woman or something.'

Clara had drawn John aside, after dinner, asking him to meet her in the Red Salon, later. It'd been a discreet move, but Lizzie suspected that Clara had intended her to hear.

John smiled darkly. 'I'd better go,' he repeated. With a last squeeze of her hand, he released her, and slid off the bed. He looked like a man going to the dentists or some other unpleasant ordeal, rather than have a discussion with a woman he'd once loved.

'I'll wait here. Come back straight away, though... Afterwards. I want to know everything as soon as possible. Even if it's not good news.'

John paused. 'I'd say come with me, love, but I doubt she'll disclose anything meaningful if you're there. She just won't say what she really means, or what she really wants. It'll be all light and airy, Clara the charming, Clara the gracious, for your benefit. She won't show her true colours.'

'It's all right. You need to have this out with her one to one.' Lizzie leapt off the bed, and stood against him, her fingers spread over his heart. 'I trust you, John. I trust you to tell me all afterwards. No secrets between us now.'

'I love you,' he gasped, hugging her tight. 'I love you, I love you, I love you.'

With a last embrace, he turned and strode from the room.

Barefoot into battle, in the Red Salon.

24

Showdown in the Red Salon

'So, what's this all about?'

Clara looked up sharply, as if she hadn't heard John's bare feet on the stair carpet. Or it could just be a ploy? She was full of these tricks, he remembered, little strategies to get the upper hand.

'Why so combative, Jonathan? We're old friends...so much more than old friends. And yet you come charging down here as if you're spoiling for a fight.'

The woman he'd once loved had prepared the scene well. The Red Salon was softly lit now, creating a flattering ambience, and she was dressed for bed, in a silk wraparound dressing gown and matching nightdress. It was a demure ensemble, in a flattering dark rose shade, but even though it revealed nothing of Clara's body, it suggested much.

Intimacy.

'I am spoiling for a fight. I want to know why you chose to come to Montcalm on this particular day, and why you brought your son with you.' He strode across the room, ignoring her subtle indication that he share the sofa with her, and stood with his back to the empty fireplace, trying not to glare. Despite what he'd just said, aggression was a poor tactic. 'It can't be a coincidence, Clara, and you can't believe for a moment that I'd think it was one.'

'Won't you have a drink, Jonathan? Let me get you one.' She started to rise.

'No. No, thank you. I'd prefer an answer.'

He watched her schooling her face into one of her inscrutable icon-like smiles, making him wait. 'I simply thought it would be a good opportunity for you to meet Charlie.'

'Why now? Why would I need to meet him, other than by chance?' Trying for inscrutability himself, he slid his hands into his jeans pocket. It was either that or clench his fists. The situation was surreal. Clara was acting as if nothing had happened. As if there'd been no betrayal. As if they'd been lovers only yesterday.

'Oh, Jonathan. Don't be obtuse. You know why.' In a measured movement, she reached for her glass, and sipped her gin and tonic. It was she who'd started him on gin, all those years ago, and in perversity, he'd decided never to drink it again. But then later, he'd decided he missed the clean, juniper bite of the spirit and decided it was absurd to cut off his nose to spite his face.

'Pray enlighten me.'

'Because Charlie is your son, and I thought you'd better be made aware of the fact before it was too late. Before you do something silly.'

The words had far more impact than they ought to have had. It was like being hit. Hit in the face, and filled with the need to strike back. Not so much at the woman in front of him, but at life, and fate. Intellectually, he knew that the likelihood that Clara was lying was high, but on a gut level, it seemed as if a hammer had fallen, a hammer heavy enough to knock him to the ground.

Reeling inwardly, he summoned self-control. And the other great source of his strength.

Lizzie. Oh Lizzie…whatever happens, I've got to resolve this without hurting you. Or hurting you in the least possible way.

The thought of her beauty and composure granted him composure too. He could almost feel her with him, warm and close.

Crouched behind a pillar on the gallery above the Red Salon, Lizzie almost toppled back onto her arse.

Idiot. You should never have followed him. You knew it was going to be awful.

Almost as soon as John had left her room, Lizzie had crept out after him, keeping her distance. She knew it was monumental foolishness and childishness to eavesdrop from up here on his confrontation with Clara, but she'd lost the battle with her own good sense at the very first skirmish.

And now all her silly little hopes that the presence of John's ex and her son here might still actually be a pure coincidence were shattered. It was everything they'd feared. And even if it wasn't, the fact that Clara was prepared to go to such lengths at all was still a blow.

'What do you mean, something silly?'

John's voice was low. Even. Beautifully modulated. The more aristocratic timbre Lizzie had noticed as soon as he'd arrived here at Montcalm was back in full force. Austere and subtly cutting.

'Before you commit yourself elsewhere, instead of to your son.'

Instead of answering, John strode to the sideboard and poured himself something colourless from a decanter. Gin. He must be rattled. Lizzie had never known him to drink in response to stress, not really. If anything, he avoided alcohol in such situations, preferring a clear head.

'In case it's escaped your memory, we used condoms when we were last together,' he pointed out, returning to his station by the fireplace, and taking a single sip of gin before placing his glass very precisely on the mantelpiece.

Lizzie wanted to run down and stand beside him, his spear carrier, but she knew he was right to face Clara alone. At least that way he might get some answers, of a sort.

I should go back to bed. This is stupid.

Yet still she lingered.

'Condom's aren't infallible, darling,' said Clara, adjusting her position on the settee, leaning back. Displaying her poise. 'Remember that time in Scotland, all those years ago, when we had a scare?'

'But if you discovered you were pregnant with my child, why didn't you want to marry me?' John demanded, ignoring the invitation to reminisce. 'Wouldn't that have been the obvious thing to do?'

'I didn't realise I was pregnant until I was married to Robson. I thought it was just a little irregularity. I…' For the first time, the woman sitting below seemed to falter. 'I wasn't sure what to do. So I pretended Charlie was premature. But I knew he was yours as soon as I saw him.' She paused, sipped her gin. 'Luckily Robson's mother and sister are both blonde, so he didn't look like a cuckoo in the nest.'

Lizzie watched John run his hands through his hair, those blond curls, so very like Charlie's. 'But when you split from Robson, why didn't you approach me then? Surely by that time, I was rich enough for you?'

Lizzie almost laughed. Ooh, bitchy. Such bitter humour.

'I'd already met Ernesto.' For the first time, Lizzie detected a touch of the shamefaced in Clara's demeanour.

John reached for his drink again, turning away. 'And now that's over, you're at a loose end again and, finally, after all these years, you think you'll give me a whirl again,' he said, over his shoulder.

'Don't make it sound so sordid, Jonathan. It's not like that. It's just the right time. The right time for you to meet Charlie, and to be his father at last. I'll soon be free, and you're not yet committed.' Lizzie sensed a stiffening of resolve. 'You always said you wanted to marry me, Jonathan. Well, now is the time to make it happen.'

John spun towards her, and Lizzie almost thought he might smash his glass in the fireplace like a Cossack. But instead he just stared at the seated woman with a look of raw astonishment on his face.

We both know what she's after, but it's still gobsmacking to hear it, isn't it, love?

'Don't be idiotic, Clara. I love Lizzie. I love her with all my heart. I plan to be with her for the rest of my life.'

A torrent of relief sluiced through Lizzie's heart. He loved her, she knew, but hearing him almost roar it out was like knocking back a jolt of that gin. Intoxicating, despite the situation.

'But you once loved me, and felt that way about me. You could feel that way again, if you gave us a chance.' Was Clara's self-belief cracking? Was there a strident edge to that low, melodious voice?

'I did love you. I loved you crazily. But I'm not sure

we'd ever have been happy, and what we did have seems insubstantial now. Faint, like a faded dream.' He paused, and from her vantage point, Lizzie saw the ghost of a smile warm John's face. 'While what Lizzie and I have is Technicolor, rich, full of life. Like never before.'

'Of course it's Technicolor,' cried Clara, snapping, 'you're nearly forty-seven now, and she's what, twenty-two? Twenty-three? Of course she feels like fun to you! What man isn't flattered by the attentions of a pretty younger woman? But you're not an ageing rocker, Jonathan; you're a man with responsibilities. Not to mention the fact that you need the right sort of woman.'

Bloody cheek . . . but she's right.

In every aspect the woman below was far more suited to these surroundings than Lizzie knew she herself was.

'We're straying from the point,' said John, teeth gritted. 'What you need to understand, Clara, is that even if Charlie is mine – which I still doubt – and even if you and I were to marry, you would eventually become the Marchioness of Welbeck when I succeed George, but Charlie can never be the Marquess. We would have had to have been married at the time of his birth for that to happen.'

Lizzie frowned, and felt a plume of probably premature triumph. She'd wondered about that, but knowing next to nothing of peerage and inheritance, she'd feared that Charlie as a ready-made male heir for Montcalm was Clara's strongest card.

'I thought there might be some act of Parliament or something.' Clara sounded more petulant than disappointed.

'No, Clara! There isn't. And even if there was, I love Lizzie and she's the woman I'm going to marry. The next Marquess after me will be her son.'

Clara rose to her feet, moving jerkily now. 'But I could give you more children, Jonathan. I'm still young and healthy. I could give you a future Marquess, and Charlie could have his real father around and we could be a proper family.' She appeared as if she might dart forward, and hurl herself at John, but the look in his eyes seemed to stop her in her tracks.

'No, no and no. Even if Charlie is mine. No. If it turns out I am his father, I'll support him, and expect joint custody, so that I can help him and guide him and be a friend and a father to him. But I'm not marrying you, Clara, and that's that.'

'Well, then, you shan't have custody or rights or anything!' Clara whirled away, her beauty made suddenly ugly. 'I'm his mother. I'll just say that Robson is his father, which is what everyone believes anyway. That way you'll have no rights whatsoever, Jonathan. I'll make sure that you never see him again.'

'But what if a blood test proves he's mine?'

'There will be no blood test,' Clara cried. 'When did you become so vulgar and petty? I can't believe that you won't take my word…That you won't trust me.'

'Trust you? Trust you? Can you hear yourself, Clara? Look at what you've done in the past when I've trusted you. I've no reason on earth to trust you ever again.' John's voice was ragged now too. He was at the end of his tether.

'Growing older has made you small-minded, Jonathan. Or maybe it's spending time with women half your age. You need a partner of your own age and your own class… especially when you eventually become Marquess.'

Lizzie expected an angry retort, but instead, her beloved just sighed. 'I'm marrying Lizzie. Whatever happens. There's an end of it.'

'You'd turn your back on your own son?'

'Not willingly, and not happily. But you give me no choice.' There was sorrow there, and Lizzie ached for him. If the unlikely was true, what was he giving up for her? Too much?

'You have a choice. Choose me.'

'No. I don't want you, Clara. I choose Lizzie.'

'Then there's nothing more to say.' The older woman straightened her spine. She had such grace, even now.

'No, there isn't. I'm tired. I'm going to bed.' John moved away from the fireplace, heading for the stairs, and Lizzie began backing away from her hiding place, treading softly on the carpet.

'You go there, Jonathan. Do you manage to get any sleep with her? Or do you still have those tiresome "issues"? I can't imagine your conscience ever letting you sleep peacefully with anyone ever again. Not when you're prepared to abandon your own son.'

'Fuck you, Clara.'

He was moving swiftly now, and Lizzie darted for the end of the corridor, just making it by the time she heard his footsteps on the grand staircase.

Idiot. He'll know anyway.

Halting, she walked towards the staircase, not away from it, and John's wry smile, when he reached the top and spotted her, made her wonder if he'd known of her presence all along.

She held out her arms and he walked right into them, hugging her tight.

25

Discovering the Truth

The next morning, Clara – and Charlie – had gone, after a night during which John and Lizzie had achieved little or no sleep.

On that point at least, her beloved's ex had been correct.

For a couple of hours they'd discussed the conversation in the Red Salon, returning again and again to the chief question.

Could Charlie really be John's son?

'I think it's highly unlikely. Especially as she went ballistic at the mention of blood tests,' John had said, lying beside Lizzie in the darkness. 'But we can't rule it out. Not yet. Not until we've sussed out a few facts…which shouldn't be too difficult.'

He sounded calm and confident now, but Lizzie had seen him shaken, down in the Red Salon.

'Really? Where would we start?'

John caressed her hand, rhythmically, a kind of almost Zen, repetitive activity, as if to help him think. 'The simplest way would be to ask Caroline when Charlie's birth date was. She and Clara haven't been close for a long, long time, but at least she'd know when her grandson was born. But the trouble is, she's holidaying with friends now, in the Caribbean, and if I contact her over all this, I know it'll upset her.' Lizzie met his eyes, glittering in the soft light from the open curtains. 'I will, though, if you want me to. She'll understand.'

'No, don't spoil Caroline's holiday. She was nice to me. And the fewer people are affected by this right now, the better. I know Clara's arrival has already upset your mother...and possibly your father.'

After much discussion, they'd agreed that John should set his London PA Willis to the task of research. 'Martin's a damn good researcher, but Willis is better. He's a genius at ferreting information from the most obscure sources, when preparing dossiers on business associates, so it should be an easy task. And in the event he can't find out, there are agencies he uses that, well, shall we say, have somewhat esoteric methods of prising facts from where they can't usually be prised.'

Sunday at Montcalm had been tense. Everyone slightly out of sorts. Some a bit confused. Had they all simply imagined that Clara and her son had been there?

Charlie and his mother had left early, before the rest of the household had risen for breakfast and church. Apparently they'd been 'expected' somewhere, with friends Clara had omitted to mention the previous day.

John saw it as a good sign, and Lizzie hoped he was right. If his ex-lover had felt her position was unassailable, surely she'd have stayed to fight her corner?

After lunch, they'd set off home on the fairly short drive back to Dalethwaite.

'Please visit us again soon,' the Marchioness had urged,

with an intensity that spoke of her confusion and doubt. Lizzie had promised to do so, hoping, hoping.

The Marquess had been more blunt.

'Don't let me down, girl. I'm counting on you. I haven't got long, and I want to see you and that sod of a son of mine down the aisle before I go, at the very least.'

Again, Lizzie had promised, still not sure, inside, that she could fulfil it.

What if Charlie was John's son? Wasn't it better for him to be part of a family? A proper family, with his mother...and his father?

The thought of that was agony. She'd live if it happened, of course she would. She wasn't Clara, who only seemed to be able to function with a man to keep her.

But if she lost John, she would never love again. Ever.

'I know what you're thinking, love, and it will never happen.'

Lizzie's head shot up. After another sleepless night, she'd been half nodding to sleep over the breakfast table. Her body was yearning for rest, but her mind was unable to let go of the awful concept of John marrying Clara.

'I will never, ever marry her. How can I? I love you.' The mauve shadows under John's eyes reflected his lack of sleep too. By mutual agreement, they were both going to be working from Dalethwaite today – if they could keep their eyes open, that was. Lizzie's intention was to research some designs and catch up on some sewing jobs, helped by Mary, who had proved to be a godsend with her accomplished dressmaking skills. Her fine workmanship made her the perfect assistant, and she had a great flair for detailing. She was working full-time for Lizzie now, and another daily girl had been set on to cover the vacated domestic position.

John claimed he had files and portfolios to read through, in his office, and meetings that could be Skype-conferenced.

In reality, both of them would probably sit staring into space, waiting to hear from Willis. It might indeed be as easy as discovering Charlie's date of birth. If he wasn't as old as Clara claimed he was, then that was that. The simple answer.

And yet, it still troubled Lizzie.

'Shouldn't he have a proper family? It seems so hard on him, the way Clara's lived. Husbands…other men. Charlie living with other people. Shouldn't he have some stability in his life?'

John reached for her hand. 'If he's mine, I will take responsibility for him and, regardless of what she says, I will gain joint custody.' His blue eyes were intense and, suddenly, full of questions. 'But only if you want that, love. It'll mean you becoming a mother, or a part-time mother, long before we planned that to happen…' He hesitated. 'It's a lot to ask, I know.'

It was. A son who was already almost a teenager?

But she didn't hesitate. 'Don't worry, boss man. I'm up for it. He's a great kid. I'm sure he and I could rub along together quite nicely.'

John leapt up from the table, came around to her side, and knelt down beside her, enclosing her in his arms.

'You, young lady, are a miracle. It was the luckiest day of my life, that night you walked into the Lawns Bar, you know that, don't you?'

Lizzie leant into his embrace. With John, anything was doable. They could deal with anything life threw at them. 'Ditto,' she said softly, 'it was my lucky night too.'

A busy morning in the sewing room was good therapy,

and surprisingly there was no staring into space. There was a lot to do, even with Mary to help her. One or two of the alterations were quite tricky, and the two women conferred, working out the best ways to achieve a pristine result. It was far easier to frown and re-pin at the tailor's dummy than endlessly go over the prospect of Charlie being John's son, again and again.

Lizzie and Mary were chatting idly over their coffee break, and Lizzie was just wondering whether to call Shelley, and give her a précis of the new situation, when John walked into the sewing room.

He knows. He's got an answer.

Lizzie scrutinised her lover's face. He looked thoughtful, but her heart leapt. The little lines around his eyes had softened.

Charlie isn't his.

'Hi, Mary, how's it going?' he said, giving the other woman one of his devastating smiles. 'She's not working you too hard, is she? She can be an awful tartar sometimes.'

'No, Mr S. No problem. I love the work. I'm glad of the opportunity,' said Mary with a dreamy smile, still clearly not immune to John and his glamour.

'I wonder…Would you give us a minute?' continued John. 'There's just something I need to discuss with Lizzie.'

'Rightie ho, I'll take this into the kitchen and drink it with Mrs Thursgood.' Mary grabbed her coffee mug, and sped from the room.

John took the seat she'd vacated, at the pattern-cutting table.

Lizzie pre-empted him. 'He's not yours, is he? I can tell by your face. You look sort of relieved, but a bit…well…maybe a tiny bit disappointed too?'

John smiled. 'I can't keep a thing from you, can I?' He reached for her hand, folding it in his. 'And no, Charlie can't be my child. Willis spoke to the secretary at St Wilfred's, my old school. Charlie's date of birth was listed on the pre-registration documents. He's only just eleven. He would have to be at least twelve to be my son.'

So, that was indeed that. The news seemed oddly anti-climactic. It had been Clara's last throw of the dice…and she'd failed. Lizzie felt a strange, vaguely sisterly sympathy for the other woman. There was no triumph in this new revelation at all, nothing to gloat over.

'She couldn't really have believed that you wouldn't soon find out Charlie was too young to be yours, could she? I mean…I don't know her, but she doesn't seem, well, stupid enough.' She rubbed her thumb lightly against John's palm. He might still need some comfort. 'I know she wanted me out of the way, so she could have you, but it just seems more an act of desperation than wickedness, you know?'

John sighed, staring at their joined hands, then looking up. 'You're right, my love. It was an impetuous act, not true badness. Not really.' He lifted her hand to his lips. 'Her marriage to Ernesto had failed, and before that her marriage to Hertingstall, and other relationships. I guess she thought she'd tried to go back, back to the beginning, to resume a relationship where she'd once had all the power. But the world's changed, I've changed…Her expectations were unrealistic rather than out and out foolish, I guess.'

They sat for a few moments in silence, then John said, 'Your coffee's going cold, sweetheart,' and released her hands. Lizzie took a sip of the strong, reviving brew then offered the cup to John. He took a long, grateful gulp.

'So, what now, boss man?'

John shrugged. 'I'll have to see her again. Privately. I need to do this in a kind way, but she does need to know it was all madness and it's all over, once and for all.' Lizzie could see him thinking, planning. Focusing on the practical and the expedient. 'I think, perhaps, at Caroline's London house. You could come down with me for a few days. If Marie can spare you. You've never been to my London flat, and it's about time you saw it. It's rather nice.' He grinned. 'Maybe you and Caroline could do some fashion, get some ideas? While I have a sit-down with Clara. Then Caro can take care of her afterwards...she might need her mum at a time like this, even though they aren't the closest.'

Lizzie wanted to hug him. Embrace him for his compassion. Clara had hurt him, and tried to hurt him again, but he wasn't vindictive.

Sliding off her chair, she drew close, and she did hug him.

'Yes, there's this fabulous big dress agency in Knightsbridge I'd like to visit. The Pandora. I'd love to see how they operate, have a chat, get ideas for New Again. I know Caroline doesn't have to buy clothes secondhand, but she might find it interesting too.'

'Actually, she's very canny. She'll be looking for bargains.' John's arms tightened around Lizzie's middle, the pressure saying much that simple words probably couldn't.

In a part of his heart, Lizzie knew he'd wanted Charlie to be his. Not for Clara's sake, but his own. For a moment, she didn't know what to do, or say.

Then John smiled. 'This is the news we wanted, love...so shall we celebrate?' He grabbed her tighter, his hands sliding down over her bottom, grabbing her through her light cotton trousers, his touch telling her he'd banished his what-if moment. For her sake. 'Do you think Mary would mind if we had rather more than a minute? I desperately want to whisk you upstairs and fuck you like a maniac. What with all this upset, we haven't made love since the folly at Montcalm, and I'm feeling a bit deprived.'

'Mary's a woman of the world. She'll understand.' Lizzie drew John to his feet, leading him forward, loving the wicked gleam in his beautiful eyes and the sudden rise of his erection in his jeans. 'But let's hurry, we don't want to be flashing that thing at her, even so.'

They pelted up the stairs, pausing to kiss, pausing to grope.

But in the little passage leading to the master bedroom door, Lizzie stopped, looking into his eyes. Time for her own moment of seriousness now.

'I think there's a part of you that really did want him to be your son, isn't there? I know that, and I don't mind.' She raised her hand, touching his thick golden hair, superficially so much like Charlie's, but not his. 'If…um…you don't want to wait quite so long…I…'

John's eyes glittered. Glittered with a hint of tears.

'I adore you, Lizzie. That you'd make that offer… it blows me away.' He snagged his lower lip for a moment, then smiled. 'But I think we should stick to our plans, give you time to enjoy your work with Marie, and the business.' He paused, and kissed her mouth with infinite tenderness. 'And when the time comes, love, it'll all be worth waiting for. He…or she…will be worth waiting for, just you see.'

They kissed, hard, then John threw open the bedroom, dragged her through, and backheeled it closed behind them.

'And in the meantime, we can always get plenty of

practice!' he announced roundly. 'Now, come on, get your clothes off, beautiful Miss Aitchison. I'm dying here!'

'With the greatest of pleasure, Mr Smith. I thought you'd never ask.'

26

Meeting Miss Page

She looked like a goddess, the woman at the bar. Really. The glow from the downlighter made her hair shine like black satin, and her skin glow as if illuminated from within.

He'd been watching her all day, unable to tear his gaze away from her. She wore a slim black dress now, with diamonds at her throat and ears, although earlier, she'd been clad all in white.

White, so symbolic. Not of virginity, far from that. But of the purity of heart that shone out of her; the sweet integrity he could sense, even from across this room.

He ought to stop staring, but he couldn't. She was so his type. The only type he'd ever really had, or would have. For ever. While she was momentarily distracted, smiling at the rather brutally handsome bar manager, he grabbed a feast of her, possessive that even for a second her attention was on the other man, chatting and calling him 'Sholto'.

She was young. Breath-takingly young, but she had presence. A confidence and composure that went far beyond her years. She was lovely too, with even features, lustrous dark eyes, and a red-tinted mouth so sumptuous it made his cock stiffen and ache just to look at it.

Not yet able to see it properly, hidden by the bar, and by other patrons enjoying themselves, he imagined her body.

Perfection. She was as alluring as a pin-up goddess. Trim, but not skinny. Lovely breasts, shapely hips and a neat waist that looked perfect in her nipped-in vintage dress. To his great joy, someone moved away from the bar, and he could see her better, observing the way her black frock clung to the sleek lines of her thighs. His cock leapt again, imagining those gorgeous thighs clinging to him, gripping him tight.

As if she'd heard his lascivious thought, she looked his way, her eyes assessing him, cataloguing him. Did he meet her discerning standards in a mate? Knocked sideways by her beauty again, he wanted to summon the barman and buy her a drink, but it was already too late: she was heading his way, confidently prepared to claim her prize.

'Hello. I'll join you, then, shall I?'

Her voice was low and melodious, her face wreathed in an impish smile. He nearly fell off the stool, stunned by her, and happily recognising her opening gambit.

'Hi,' he answered, trying to breathe deeply without appearing to do so.

She's made you into a crazy man. But there's not much point trying to hide it because she can read you like a book.

Close up, she was dazzling, a brighter star than the diamonds she wore, the gems that sparkled in her ears, at her throat and on her finger. The pert smile widened and she licked her rose-stained lower lip in a way that almost made him moan.

'Well, I would offer to buy you a drink, boss man, but I'd rather take you up to my room. I hate wasting time.'

Direct. So direct. But then, she always had been. Even when they were playing the most complex of games. He slid off the stool when she took him by the hand, tugging him forward and starting to lead him from the bar.

'Sounds good to me,' he said, trying to gain the upper hand, yet knowing it was useless at this juncture. There was a time and a place for being a master, but tonight wasn't it. 'But before we go, what's your name? You look familiar.'

'You can call me Miss Page.'

Ah, Bettie Page, the famous pin-up girl of the 1950s. How well he remembered first noticing that likeness.

'Thanks, Bettie. You can call me Jonathan.'

'It's "Miss Page" to the likes of you, Jonathan,' she replied haughtily as they reached the lift.

'Yes, Miss Page.'

She was a goddess, a queen and empress. Well, a lady at the very least, as of today. As she sashayed into the lift car, then turned to face him, leaning provocatively against the far wall, he experienced a weird sense of double vision.

He seemed to see not the black dress, but that exquisite white gown she'd worn earlier. Fitted, elegant, demure; long, narrow lace sleeves and a full, puffed skirt. A gauzy veil granting mystery to her fabulous beauty, and not hiding it in the very least.

Was the double vision from joyful tears, now, as then? Her slow smile acknowledged them, seductive yet also sweet.

'So, do we do the elevator scene?'

'I don't know. You're in charge,' he replied, answering her smile with one of his own. He remembered every second of the night when she'd said that.

Before she could make a ruling, the short lift ride was

over and the doors sprang open again. Grasping his hand, knowing what she wanted, she drew him from the cab and led him at a smart clip towards the room they'd share.

Ah, the chintz-clad madness of the Waverley Grange Hotel. How he loved it, even though they could, if they'd wanted, have chosen a far more luxurious venue. But this kitsch yet homely room meant far more to him than any of the most exclusive boutique accommodations, or any of the five star hotels he owned himself.

This was where an adventure had once begun.

As the door closed, she crossed to the bed, and tested the mattress. Satisfied of its resilience, she turned to him, her brilliant eyes commanding.

'I don't want anything fancy. I just want you, Jonathan. I've been watching you all day and it's been driving me crazy. I can't imagine what the guests would've thought if they'd known what I was thinking every time I looked at you!'

'Ditto,' he said softly. It'd been hard. And if it weren't for biofeedback, he'd have been hard too, at the most inopportune moments.

Kicking off her high black shoes, flinging herself down sideways on the bed, yet still managing to look every inch a lady, she gave him the once-over, that all-encompassing look that seemed to strip him bare for her perusal. Her glance drifted over him, assessing him through his clothes, then settling at his crotch where he was already massively rampant.

'Undress for me. I want to see what I've committed myself to for good and all.'

'Very well.' His fingers went to his lapels. *Good God, was he shaking?*

'And be quick about it,' she commanded.

'Yes, my dear.' He started to hurry, aware that her mock-stern expression seemed to suggest he should have said mistress.

Though he wanted to please and impress her, he stripped quickly. He didn't want anything fancy either, just to be with her. In her. Within moments he was naked, his clothes flung about. She extended a gracious hand to him, urging him forward, and when he reached her, she took hold of his cock.

Oh…Oh God. Her touch. She caressed him lightly, her delicate seamstress's fingertips examining his length, his girth, toying with the sensitive head.

'All mine now,' she said, eyeing him from beneath sultry lowered lashes, 'All mine for ever.'

The way she handled him made it impossible to frame an answer. He simply nodded.

'Make love to me, then.' Winking roguishly, she shuffled into position on the bed, wiggling up her slim skirt as she went, to reveal his reward.

The sight of her made him have to fight for control. She wore an exquisite thong, fashioned from black silk and lace, that barely covered her pubis. He almost just plunged in; it would be easy to just push the scrap aside. But even as he climbed onto the bed, to get between her thighs, she wriggled and shuffled again, tweaking the flimsy garment down and off, before flinging it away.

'All yours,' she purred, parting her thighs.

Again the urge to plunge crested, but he contained himself. She deserved more. Almost trembling with lust, he slid his fingers to her sex, parting the ebony curls and her labia, to find her clit.

'Oh God,' she groaned, writhing. 'Ooh, yes…' She squirmed around, working herself on his fingertips, her thighs shifting and tensing, her beautiful face a mask of raw sensation.

'Yes, yes, yes,' she chanted, and against his touch, her sex rippled in a swift orgasm. 'Please, oh John, please…' Still coming she reached for him, grabbing for his flank, his hip, to guide him between her thighs.

Satisfied of her pleasure, he surged forward, fitting himself to her, finding his goal, and hers. With a hoarse groan of his own, he slid into her, his heart almost stopping at the great wave of emotion that matched his pleasure.

His. His bride now. Closer than close. With no barrier, physical or otherwise, between them. Her heat was like paradise; her silky readiness pure joy. Almost laughing with happiness, he accepted the fact that this would not be long, protracted, complicated lovemaking. Just swift, crazy, ecstatic, messy, married fucking. Just a few wild thrusts to bring them both to their peak.

'Oh hell, yes, Lizzie, I love you!' he roared, powering into her, the pulse of his semen echoed by the clench and clasp of her pussy around his cock.

'I love you too, John. I love you, love you, love you…'

Tears came again then, for them both, and the laughter too.

There was a lamp still on in the room as Lizzie opened her eyes, and came up to rest on her elbow. She was glad of the light, to see her sleeping angel.

It was still hard to believe he was her husband now. This fabulous, beautiful man, the love of her life.

And he slept so peacefully. He mostly did nowadays.

OK, there were still some nights when he couldn't nod off, but the worst of his sleeping issues were a thing of the past.

He looked young too. Absurd as it sounded, she could almost imagine he looked younger than he had when she'd originally met him, despite the many months that had passed since they'd first been in this very room together. John was forty-seven now, but even if to say he only looked twenty-seven was a bit of a stretch, to Lizzie's eyes he could certainly pass for middle thirties.

'Lord Jonathan Llewellyn Wyngarde Smith,' she mimed. 'Lord and Lady Jonathan Llewellyn Wyngarde Smith...Far out!' She suppressed a giggle. She still couldn't get her head round some things. Perhaps it was as well that John virtually never used his title, because she wasn't sure she'd ever get used to the one he'd conferred on her.

Of course, one day, she'd have to. But that was the future, the far, far future, and they'd face it together then.

Why aren't I tired? I should be knackered! It's been insane today.

Yes, it had been a long, complicated, but wildly, dementedly happy day.

First their civil ceremony in the banqueting room at Borough Hall, then a brief limousine journey to Montcalm for a blessing in the family chapel there, guests travelling behind them in a convoy of luxury coaches. After that, the official reception and sumptuous wedding breakfast in a grand marquee on the lawn, and now, finally, this mad, noisy, anything goes evening disco party for all-comers here at the Waverley Grange Hotel.

It was uncanny how, when they'd been planning the day, they'd both started to suggest this bash to each other, almost at the same moment.

'How about spending our wedding night at the Waverley too?' she'd suggested.

'Hell yes! I was just going to say the same myself.'

And this was that night. It had seemed as natural as breathing to recreate their first meeting, after a fashion. Neither one of them had needed to prompt the other. It'd just happened, as poignant and romantic as it'd been crazy and fun.

Oh, John, I love you so...

It was still hard to believe she was married to such a dish. She was tempted to pinch herself as she gazed at him, convinced she'd been the absolute envy of every single straight woman at all the series of proceedings today. He'd taken her breath away in morning dress, and she'd caught females blatantly admiring him again and again.

Even Shelley, a little bit, despite having her own man at her side. Her own husband. As, to everyone's surprise, a month or two ago, she and Sholto had quietly tied the knot with no fuss or palaver. Lizzie hadn't even known until the night before, when her friend had rung to ask her and John to be witnesses.

Today's wedding party had been full of happy couples. Shelley and Sholto married. Rose and Hannah, who were also planning to wed as soon as they legally could. Brent and Tom, happily anticipating the same.

Caroline and her husband Ralph, thrilled to bits. John's old friend Benjamin, flown in from Scotland with his wife and kids.

And the entire Wyngarde Smith clan, all of them over the moon. Lizzie still felt a bit weepy herself, recalling the unabashed tears of joy. John's elder brother, and his wife, John's niece, all happy for him. His mother, the Marchioness, glowing, and even the old man himself, who'd actually been well enough to attend the blessing and a bit of the wedding breakfast.

Speaking of the old man, there had been one rather sticky moment over the Champagne, when Lizzie had noticed that a conversation between the Marquess and her father seemed to be lurching dangerously towards an ideological fracas. But she'd been able to step in, quite diplomatically she thought, to remind both them of what they had in common: that on this happiest of days, they'd each managed to marry off a 'problem' child. She and John were going to have to keep a close eye on those two at future family events, though, and steer them towards interests that they passionately shared, such as art, English poetry and the classics. Especially as her father had apparently been going to karate lessons lately, and no matter how infirm he was, the Marquess could still handle a shotgun! But between her and John, and her mum and the Marchioness, they should all be able to keep the peace between the two patriarchs somehow.

Dalethwaite Manor and New Again had pretty much shut down for the day – both the existing shop and the new Bridal Boutique – because members of staff from both places were part of the festivities, especially the two Ms, Mary and Marie, who were in charge of helping with Lizzie's dress, along with the gowns of her sisters and Shelley as her attendants. Quite a lot of the shop's patrons had been keen to throw confetti too, and Marie had expressed no qualms about losing a day's business, because the Princess Grace inspired wedding gown, and quite a lot of the female guests' outfits too, all provided the best possible shop window for New Again Bride.

One person not at the wedding was Clara.

Lizzie had never asked John about his meeting with his ex, but he'd offered the information voluntarily.

After initial anger at being confronted with her foolish deception, Clara had capitulated. Utterly. John had described his ex as being almost relieved, as if a weight had been lifted from her, and a long-endured tension released. Lizzie imagined him hugging the woman he'd once loved. Comforting her. Yet the thought had held no threat. Her faith in her beloved was absolute.

In a spirit of letting bygones be bygones, Lizzie had wondered whether to suggest they invite Clara to the wedding, but before she could even discuss it with John, Caroline had alerted them to the fact that her daughter was racing to the altar herself, hard on the heels of her quickie divorce.

'I'm sure it's just a bit of one-upmanship, my dear.' John's ex-wife had sounded cheerful. 'But I'm happy to pay for a big bash for her, just to be sure she's out of John's your and hair at last. And in hopes that she's finally found the right man. I think Arthur's pretty much got the measure of her.'

And here it was, in a celebrity mag, actually out today, which Lizzie had snagged at the hotel's gift shop. She smiled, handing at least the small victory of being married first, to her rival.

The former Condesa Sanchez de la Villareal marries trainer of Derby winner!

On the front page, the bride looked fabulous in Atelier Versace, posing with her new husband and her son.

They're so alike. He must be Charlie's father.

Both man and boy had the same smile, the same blond hair, and the same blue eyes, evident even in the magazine pic. And what was more, handsome Arthur Fletcher even bore a passing resemblance to John. Both were golden-haired alpha males, and generally similar in height and build. The racing trainer was a little bit older, though, and more weather-beaten and outdoorsy looking, but it was easy to see how Clara might have thought she could pass Charlie off as John's offspring when really he was Arthur's son.

Good luck to you all! I hope you don't need it too much, though.

Lizzie's eyes drooped. She hadn't thought she was tired, but the day had finally caught up with her. Moving with infinite care, she set aside the magazine and snuggled up to her husband.

Rats! He stirred. She'd woken him.

'What do you want now, woman?' Laughter was rich in John's voice as he snapped awake. 'Do I have to service you yet again? I really ought to spank you, never mind fuck you. Waking me up after such a long, rigorous day, you trollop!'

Lizzie leant over him, looking down into his beloved face and his gleaming blue eyes. 'Rigorous? You should try having to wear a meringue and a fifteen-foot train for hours. It was a good day, though, wasn't it?'

'The best,' he said emphatically. 'I always thought that if I ever did have to have a big wedding, I'd hate it. But I didn't. I loved every minute of it.' A surprised grin played around his lips. 'Especially when I saw you walking towards me in that glorious dress.'

Yes, that moment. The best. John standing waiting for her, joy and wonder in his eyes. An emotion too exquisite to describe in mere words.

'No, it isn't sex I'm wanting, actually. I'm a bit tired myself. But let's put a pin in the spanking for when we get to France, shall we? And make a date with a certain rustic table in the garden of a certain villa, eh?'

John waggled his sandy eyebrows at her. 'Done deal, my love. Your fantasy is my command. As always.'

Tomorrow, they'd fly to the south of France, in a private hire jet, for their honeymoon, returning to the lovely villa they'd stayed at before. John had bought the place from his friend without telling her, as a surprise wedding present, but this was one pre-emptive strike with which she certainly wasn't going to take issue.

'What, even a pair of leather trousers?'

'Maybe one of these days…just for you.' John reached up to stroke her face. 'But seriously, if you don't want me to make love to you or smack your gorgeous bottom, why did you wake me?' He smiled at her.

And that was it. The main reason she'd woken him.

She had to see the smile.

This was the smile that had bewitched her, the smile that had won her all those months ago, down in the Lawns Bar. It was a smile not just on the lips, but in the eyes, the face, and in the whole being of her wonderful, wonderful man.

Lizzie's heart swelled with happiness. She was so lucky, so loved by John. She knew now that she'd see this beautiful smile every day for the rest of her life, and always reflect it right back with a smile of her own. Lit with her love.

Dipping down, she laid her lips against his. And the wonder-smile became a long and loving kiss.